To my children, Margarita and Anthony

Other Books by Joyce Gatta

In Hugger Mugger (2020, 2023)
In the Shadows, a Sequel (2023)

Life is a dance. Your first steps are awkward and timid, like a child's, full of joy and fear; sometimes forward, sometimes back. You bump and stumble, cutting a path, changing direction, changing partners, pressing or yielding, until you are spent. Then the song fades away, the beat stops, and it is over.

—Joyce Gatta

PROLOGUE

It was time. The baby was insisting on being born, and Catherine Navarro had no choice but to deliver it. She had screamed and screamed for them to stop her pain, but to no avail.

The anesthetist covered her mouth with a breathing mask and began to release the pain blocker. Her eyes stayed open, and her flailing continued.

"Up the dose," her doctor ordered.

The anesthetist had an audible intake of breath.

Her doctor glared at him. "Just do it. I'll take the responsibility."

When the infant girl made her debut to the waiting audience, she was slapped on her bottom but let out only a whimper. Her mother had cried enough for the two of them.

"You are the mother of a healthy baby girl," said the nurse, cuddling the infant in her arms.

Catherine didn't hear a word; she was out cold.

*****

When she woke up the next day, she looked around at the stark hospital room, its gray walls and white sheets, the bed with its metal sidebars, and the drab blinds closed to prevent any light in. *This is a hellhole. I've never been in a room so grotesque.* Her thoughts turned to her unwanted pregnancy, how unnatural it had felt during those long months. The nausea. The pain. The protruding belly made her feel she was no longer a woman, but some hybrid human being.

How much she had missed her regular haunts, where she had spent hours every day dissecting the latest fashions or elaborating about suspected affairs.

"It's finally over," she groaned. "I can't wait to be out of here and pick up where I left off. Now I can start drinking again."

When her husband came to see his infant daughter in the viewing area, he smiled at the miracle tucked in a pink blanket among other infants in tiny cribs.

Tears came to his eyes. An attendant asked him if he would like to hold her.

"May I?" he whispered.

Gently he rocked his daughter in his arms. "You have the same dark hair and dark eyes as your mother," he observed. "I think we should call you Catherine."

*****

On the same day, at about the same time on the other side of the country, a young woman lay bleeding as she lay in an ambulance, wailing its way to the nearest hospital, twenty-five miles farther down a two-lane road in Sonoma Valley, California. Even though she was in extreme pain, she muffled her cries, perhaps because she was in shock at what had happened that made her bleed, or perhaps because she knew she needed to put all her energy into pushing the fetus down the birth canal and into a world that was both kind and cruel.

She felt blood flowing down her abdomen and legs.

"Push, push!" the emergency technician urged.

A final push, and the baby was out. She heard the ET gasp. She raised her head enough to see blood trickling from the infant's head and its tiny arms and legs moving jerkily.

"Give her to me," Sophia Sbaglione demanded.

The ET hesitated. "The baby has a deep head wound. It's not going to survive."

"Give her to me, damn it," she sobbed. "I need to hold her."

She reached up and took the baby, gently lying her on her chest.

"My darling, you have a mother who loves you, who has wanted you so badly," she whispered in the baby's ear.

The baby's cries lessened as Sophia caressed her, stroking her back and kissing the wound on top of her head. The ET watched in fascination as mother and daughter bonded for the briefest of moments.

I haven't even given her a name, she thought.

Then they both fell into a state of unconsciousness.

When the ambulance arrived at the hospital, the baby was dead and the mother was rushed into surgery. The husband was nowhere to be found.

THE FIRST DANCE PARTNERS

SONOMA VALLEY, CALIFORNIA; SOPHIA BELLINI AND CARLO SBAGLIONE

They had met in a cave, surrounded by barrels of aging wine. Sophia, the daughter of the winery's owner, had stumbled—or maybe had been pushed—and she felt hands around her waist, very firm and hard, holding her much too close. She turned to see an attractive stranger ogling her.

Her first thought was to free herself from this molester. Seeing her expression, he dropped his hands, apologizing profusely. They introduced themselves.

"I'm Carlo Sbaglione, the new director of winemaking."

"I'm Sophia Bellini, the owner's daughter."

His leer suddenly turned into a sly smile, his mind processing how he might use this relationship to his advantage.

*****

Sophia Bellini was taller than most women. Her height was the first thing everyone noticed about her. At five-foot-eleven, she hovered over many of her high school classmates, both male and female. This genetic trait made her stand out at dances, like a long-necked swan in the middle of stunted ducks, and boys stayed clear of her, gravitating to girls who were shorter than they were. It satisfied their need to be controlling and macho.

So to give her confidence, her mother taught her how to walk without looking clumsy, how to carry herself with grace, and how to use her height to her advantage. If she was going to perform on life's stage, her mother declared, then she must relish her role.

Sophia considered herself attractive, and perhaps a bit captivating. Her heritage became a matter of curiosity to people. Anyone looking at her thought she might be Italian or Spanish, given her dark hair and eyes, full lips and bosom. But the more one looked, the more one thought she might be Indian or Middle Eastern. There was a slight curve to her eyes, a tan glow to her skin, an upturn in her smile.

Her international features and bearing made both men and women give her a second glance. When she was in college, a few fellow students, teaching assistants, and even an occasional professor attempted to seduce her. She did not succumb. She had her own desires. She was determined to become a highly educated woman, independent and successful.

Her parents never had the opportunity to attend college, and as their oldest child, she wanted to make them proud.

Stanford University was hard, but she didn't mind spending long hours in the library or on her computer, doing research, analyzing data, or writing papers. Her disciplined mind naturally gravitated toward law. One of her professors told her that much of the practice of law involved understanding human nature, knowing how to read clients, opposing attorneys, and judges. There were ways to tell if people were lying to you or were dismissive only because of your sex or were uncomfortable with your self-confidence, and once you recognized their behavior, you had the advantage over them—if you were clever enough to outsmart them. For that reason, she chose to minor in behavioral psychology. If she were to become a prominent attorney, she wanted to have every advantage.

Her immigrant Italian father grew grapes to produce wine, and her immigrant Italian mother painted scenes of the neighboring hills and valleys in Sonoma, California. They sold both the wine and the watercolors in the salesroom adjacent to the wine cellars. Their talent and hard work made it possible for them to open a restaurant next to the winery, featuring their favorite foods from the old country.

Her younger brother, after graduating from California Polytechnic State University with a major in viniculture, took over many of the duties of the day-to-day running of the vineyard and winery, leaving her father and mother to run the restaurant. The family business gained a reputation for fine wines, delicious food, and a festive atmosphere.

Upon graduating from Stanford Law School, Sophia was offered a position to teach legal ethics there. She accepted immediately, knowing that any résumé that included such a prestigious college post would open doors to higher-paying jobs.

To engage her students in the ethics of law, she asked them to pretend that they were members of the jury and consider not only the facts but the demeanor of the defendant—his eyes, his lips, his posture, even his hands. "If you suspect that a witness is lying, you must ferret out the truth, expose his lies, bring justice to the innocent, and let the guilty pay."

After three years, she became a full professor and author of a popular text called *Rules for Lawyers to Follow*. Her situation was satisfying but incomplete at the same time. She had no intention to teach law forever; she longed to be in an actual courtroom, to cross-examine witnesses, to steer the judge and jury to her way of thinking, to reveal the truth.

One day, when she came home for a visit, her father asked her if she was interested in working in the family business. He missed her. In truth, she missed her family and the relaxed atmosphere of the rural surroundings. As much as she loved teaching and being surrounded by cultured people, there was a pretension among many of the intellectuals that she could not stomach.

It was time to move on. She told her father that she would stay a year as a sales manager and then look for a career in law.

The nagging thought of approaching thirty and still unmarried was also weighing on her.

In her early twenties, when she had become of marriageable age, she had imagined being in a satisfying union with a man—loving, respectful, and comfortable in each other's presence. She had taken her time to find someone who had similar qualities like her father.

*****

When she met Carlo, hired while she was away at Stanford, the physical attraction was immediate. They were both in their late twenties and had sown their wild oats, although, in Sophia's case, her upbringing kept her from going all the way. She thought Carlo was going to be the closest match to what she wanted in a husband.

If it feels right, then it must be.

She rethought her decision to stay only one year.

I can raise my children in the same environment in which I grew up while working in the family business. I will have a chance to use my talent in other ways.

She decided to wed Carlo Sbaglione.

Carlo was, in a way, like her, a person of mystery. He said he came from a hill town in southern Italy and learned about how to grow grapes on his father's land. When she tried to pin him down to exactly what town, he said that it was so small it wasn't even on a map.

"But much of southern Italy is too hot to grow grapes and the soil is poor," she argued.

"Well, I did it. Are you going to doubt me?"

He said he became successful enough to sell his vineyard and to come to America and try his luck in Sonoma Valley, trying to sneak his vine cuttings past the airport security.

"How did you expect to do that?" she asked. "Customs agents are always on the lookout for agricultural products being smuggled in."

"I had wrapped and tapped the vines around my legs, but they were discovered when the agent patted me down," he replied. "They took the cuttings and I had to pay a fine."

When she asked about his family, he grew tense.

"I grew up with just a father, and when he died, the land became mine."

"How did your parents die?" she wanted to know.

"It's too difficult to talk about. Stop asking me questions. You sound like a cop."

"How do you know what a cop sounds like?" she wondered. "Have you been in trouble with the law?"

He only grinned at her, a foolish look that said *how stupid you are* or perhaps *how smart you are.*

It was easier to talk with him about her father's business and their future together. Wine was the one thing that they had in common but a commodity that only he was obsessed with.

"A great wine is better than gold," he told her. "It increases in value the older and scarcer it gets."

Her parents wondered if she was rushing things.

"I know what I want," she told them.

"But do you know Carlo well enough to be sure he truly is what you want?" her father asked.

"How can anyone be absolutely sure of anything?" she protested, dismissing her parents' concerns as being overprotective of her.

The English translation of *sbaglione* means "big mistake," and she found it amusing to see the reactions from those who asked what his surname meant. Carlo did not find it at all funny.

"It's my family name, my heritage. Who knows why my ancestors were called that?"

"Perhaps when we get married, you can take my last name?" she offered, joking.

"Are you crazy, Sophia? That would be like cutting off my right arm."

I can't tease him, she thought.

"Then I will keep my maiden name and my right arm," she countered. "Many women do today."

"No. Impossible! I don't want my wife with any other name but mine," he said angrily, his crooked smile bordering on sinister.

My name is part of my identity. I want to keep it. Should I indulge his ego and cave? Is this what married couples are supposed to do? There is no middle ground. Either I keep my last name or take his.

She wondered if this disagreement was worth battling over. She decided it was not.

He takes everything so seriously. Sometimes I wonder why I am attracted to him. It's not just for his looks. There is more to him than that. He is ambitious, a risk-taker, and a charmer. He did not go to university, but he has a natural intelligence about viticulture. My father hired him because he knows a lot about varieties of grapes and wines and knows how to market them. And, she admitted to herself, *I am twenty-eight years old with two college degrees, but I feel incomplete as a woman. I want children, and I can't have children without a husband. At least, I've learned that much.*

Within a year after they met, they were married.

Sophia Bellini and Carlo Sbaglione should have been compatible. They were both Italian-born, with a common religious background and an interest in wine and cooking. Although her education was in the practice of law, Sophia became director of sales for Bellini Winery, and she loved her job. Work at the winery brought her into daily contact with laborers and businessmen, as well as tourists from all over America.

The setting was beautiful, the people were engaging, and the atmosphere was expansive. She felt at peace with the world.

A year went by, and arguments with Carlo began over the right time to have children. They could never agree. He said simply that he was not ready to be a father. She said that she was more than ready to be a mother and wanted children while she was in her prime.

Sophia wondered why her husband was so adamant against having children. He refused to explain his feelings, so she was left to imagine the worst.

He hates kids!

When it became obvious that they were in opposite corners on childbearing, any pretense of mutual affection was dropped. No more stroking each other's cheek or pushing back a stray curl on the other's head. No more kidding about who had cooked the better meal, since they always had taken turns to prepare a delicious dinner. No more flirting with the other about having sex.

When it occurred, Carlo initiated it as a challenge, as if to say, "Don't you dare deny me my rights as your husband."

Once, just once, Carlo moved across the room and grabbed her arm forcefully. Sophia flung herself away, trying to break free. When she finally shook him off, she said simply, "If you ever hurt me again, I'll leave you."

She wanted to run to her parents and take shelter in their arms, but she was too embarrassed. Growing up in a small town, isolated from much of the world, she had few friends to confide in and worried that if she confessed to anyone about her difficulties, she would appear weak.

Finally Sophia decided to act. She desperately wanted a child, and Carlo had the necessary sperm. Divorce to her was a sign of failure, especially after only a year of marriage. She felt it was giving up too easily.

Perhaps a pregnancy just needed to happen. She made the unilateral decision to stop using birth control and waited. She became pregnant within weeks but kept it a secret.

Now she put renewed energy into saving their marriage. She cooked Carlo's favorite foods, she flirted with him before going to bed, and she sympathized with his complaints about the staff at the winery. She tried to make it easy for Carlo to accept fatherhood.

He did not change. He started to call her demanding and haughty.

"Just because your family owns the winery doesn't mean that you own me!" he shouted. "I was the one who suggested that your father grow grapes, like the Brunello in Italy. Your father doesn't appreciate my abilities."

"You were instrumental in getting him to try to grow Brunello-like grapes here, but it took years of studying the chemical analysis of the soil and perfecting the climate conditions to produce a wine worthy of the name. You had nothing to do with the process of getting the vines to flourish. Dad promoted you to be in charge of winemaking, which is one of the highest-paid positions in the company. It should be enough."

"*Basta?*" he said, using the Italian word. "We could be rich if he takes my advice. Your father doesn't listen to me anymore, now that I have made him successful. You need to speak up for me instead of always taking your father's side. I've told him he should go public and sell stock. That's the way to make lots of money."

"You know money is not important for my papa. He is proud of the company's reputation as a good winery, vineyard, and restaurant. He wants to keep the business in the family."

"I'm part of your family now. When we married, he should have made me his business partner."

Sophia's eyes widened. "Is that why you married me? In the hopes of becoming a partner in the family business?"

He looked away and did not answer.

It is true, she thought. *I am just a means to an end for him. How did I not see that?*

She swallowed, pushing down the ugly taste in her mouth. Her shoulders sagged.

He used me to further his own ambitions. I have a failing marriage, and I am pregnant. I can't deal with both a divorce and a pregnancy right now.

She still hadn't told him about the baby.

It can't hurt to wait a while before I tell him, she decided. So she put it off, hoping that something would happen to make her problems go away.

*****

Months later, after the baby's birth and death, after her husband had fled from the house, the town, and the country, and after Sophia obtained a divorce, she felt she had to leave California and begin again in a place where she could hide, where no one knew her past.

She escaped to the other side of the country, to Manhattan, to a prestigious job with National Services Insurance Company as head of their sales department. To everyone in her new office, she was Sophia Sbaglione, single, Stanford Law graduate with a small apartment on the lower West Side of Manhattan. That was as much as she let on about her private life. She needed time to heal her wounds, both physical and emotional.

The day she left California, her father said simply, "Next time, marry a man who makes you smile."

EASTPORT, CONNECTICUT

ROBERT NAVARRO AND CATHERINE CHADWICK

They had met at a dance, a wedding dance in which everyone formed a conga line, and Robert was behind Catherine, his hands on her waist. Catherine wondered who it was that held her body so gently yet firmly. When she turned and saw him smile warmly, she decided to introduce herself to this attractive stranger.

"Hello, I am Catherine Chadwick. To whom do I have the pleasure of meeting?" she asked when the dance had ended, never giving him more than a flicker of a smile.

"I am Robert Navarro, assistant district attorney in this county," he replied.

A young high-placed lawyer, good-looking and well-mannered, she thought. *I need some diversion, and he looks eager to please me. I'll bet I can make him jump through any hoops I hold up.*

*****

Robert Navarro tried not to stand out in a crowd. Although he was tall, good-looking, and friendly, he deliberately chose not to be the center of attention. His father had impressed upon him the importance of proper behavior, that what one says and does matters more in the long run than succumbing to the need to be the court jester.

As soon as he was old enough, his father took him to meet the movers and shakers in the small Eastport community: Men of wealth—merchants and bankers; and men of power—police chiefs and judges. Robert studied their behaviors, absorbing and subconsciously mastering their manners and dress. His father's most important advice was about his future occupation. "Whatever your future holds, weigh your decisions carefully. Look before you leap."

He was the only child of a loving couple who took pains not to spoil him too much. His parents were well-off, but their affluence came not only from inherited wealth but from hard work, honesty, and integrity. They were determined to teach their son those values. Robert's ancestors had found success in banking and investments. They had made money, new Spanish money. Not as respectable as old Yankee money, but money is money.

The men in his family were quiet about their possessions, reserved in their behavior, understated in their dress, and unblemished in their reputations. As *foreigners* in a mostly Yankee town, they tried hard to fit in. Robert's grandfather and father were admitted to the exclusive yacht club. His grandmother and mother, unqualified to join the DAR, became members of the women's auxiliary of various service clubs. As a family, they attended Catholic Mass but never brought up religion or any subject that made them appear different or strange or foreign.

During his boyhood, Robert found it hard to be accepted as an equal. As an only child, he had naturally sought out companions and tried to attach himself to kids at school, almost all of whom had Anglo-Saxon heritage, Yankee traits, and privileged upbringings. The other boys were elitists from birth. They paraded their pedigree proudly in the outfits they wore—tan slacks with a navy blue sports jacket—and in their conversations: "Who let him in?" or "Summer in the Catskills is getting sooo boring" or "Mummy wants to sail to Europe on the Queen Mary, but Daddy thinks that is too bourgeois."

Even though Robert rejected their attitudes, he still hung around with them, staying in the background, withholding judgment. Luckily, one of the most influential in the pack took a liking to him. In exchange for Robert's help with school assignments, Samuel came to his defense whenever his hell-bent buddies were looking for someone to torture.

But it was a friendship with a catch. Samuel demanded loyalty as part of the bargain for befriending him—unwavering loyalty, no matter what. If Robert alienated Samuel, they would all turn on him, and then he would have no friends.

When Robert was twenty, his father was killed in a car accident. Matthew Navarro had been delivering Christmas presents to his neighbors on Christmas Eve. He was backing out of a driveway when a car, going fifty-five miles an hour in a thirty-mile-an-hour zone on the wrong side of the road, smashed into the driver's side of his vehicle. He never even knew what hit him.

The drunk driver was the son of one of the richest and most influential men in town. Who caused the accident was obvious, except that it wasn't—not to the police chief. Robert's mother took the driver to court, but the investigation by the police concluded that Matthew Navarro had been negligent. The defendant's lawyers, of which there were several, managed to get the jury to agree by twisting the truth and drawing sympathy for the young perpetrator.

It was then that Robert decided to become a lawyer himself. He wanted justice, if not for his family, then for others.

After graduating from Yale Law School, he found employment in the local district attorney's office. It was a good experience. All types of criminal activities were tried in court: from petty theft to grand larceny, from child abuse to murder.

When he began to make a name for himself, he thought it was time to settle down and start a family. Although in his late twenties, Robert had limited experience with sex. He was not a womanizer. His good name was his passport to success, and any blemish on it, like a revengeful lover or an illegitimate child, could destroy his dignity and worth. Robert looked around and chose someone who was respectable and well-mannered and beautiful. He did not think beyond that.

*****

Robert Navarro decided to ask Catherine Chadwick to marry him. She was the daughter of a man whose family's history could be traced back to Elijah Chadwick, one of the founders of the town. Her Yankee blood coursed through her veins, like dark crystals running through white marble. If you tried to remove the dark crystal, you destroyed the marble.

Catherine dressed conservatively, had proper manners, exhibited a quiet (some said bland) personality, and kept her observations about *others* to herself (until *others* were out of hearing range). She came from wealth but never admitted to feeling entitled. She also never admitted that she was a snob or a grouch or a bitch. That's what others said of her, even some of her closest friends.

One thing everyone agreed on: Catherine was gorgeous. Her blemish-free white skin stood out against her long dark hair, but what attracted men to her were her flirtatious dark eyes, like black pearls embedded in white orbs.

Because her family came from old money, they could afford to send their only child to a private girl's boarding school, then off to a secondary school academy, and finally a coed college where many girls studied drama to improve their theatrical strut, French to polish their aura of mystery, and art to distinguish between a fake and a genuine Picasso, all of which were needed to land them a rich husband.

She seldom smiled (it ruined her makeup) and never, ever laughed at someone else's jokes (it only encouraged them). She understood that the only reason she was invited to social events was because of her looks and her money, and there was no way she would devalue either of those precious assets.

Catherine accepted his marriage proposal, partly because two of her closest friends had just tied the knot, making her feel like the perpetual bridesmaid at weddings, and partly because she was bored. She thought marrying an outsider would astonish her friends and give her an exotic air. Friends would marvel at her audacity, while foes would be jealous of the attention she received. *He's good-looking, rich, and well-mannered. I will train him to be like other men in my crowd,* she thought. *He will become as Yankee as George Bush.*

Robert's marriage to Catherine was considered to be a fusion of two cultures. "He looks different from us, but is still very fair skinned and light haired for a Spaniard, and he does have proper manners and some money," they allowed.

"She will legitimatize him," others surmised. "He will be beholden to her for making him as respectable as she is," was the common opinion.

Their marriage got off to a good start: a European honeymoon, paid for by her family, and the down payment on a house along the historic Millionaire's Mile, paid for by his mother. His father-in-law arranged an interview for him with National Services Insurance Company in Manhattan.

Because of Mr. Chadwick's influence, along with his own family's financial connections and his outstanding accomplishments at Yale Law, Robert was hired as vice president. To begin near the very top in a national insurance company was heady, but he remained reserved and respectful to his colleagues and staff.

It took a while for Catherine to become pregnant. She didn't like sex, but she put up with it because it was just another duty she was expected to perform, like thanking a hostess for the delicious scones when inwardly her stomach was in distress, or pretending to listen attentively to an eligible bachelor give a monologue on liquidity in the stock market while she plotted her escape.

With Robert absent so much of the time, working long hours in New York City, she continued to live her life as if she were single. The social calendar for the year was written in blue blood ink: concerts, plays, flower shows, social teas—all important events at which to be conspicuous in front of some and to conspire against others. It was all a game to her: secrets to share, tales to tell, reputations to ruin.

From the terrace at her new home in Eastport, Catherine sipped her morning mimosa, then savored her afternoon wine at a waterside café, and later drained her evening cocktail in the salon of a dowager, day after day, in an unending round of pleasantries and put-downs, until one day she realized she was pregnant. Three months pregnant! Her doctor strongly advised her to stop drinking all alcoholic beverages for the next six months. She reacted with horror, as if she were being publicly punished for committing a sin, like what her Puritan ancestors had to endure at the pillory. How could she survive? Everyone drank, all day long. The temptation was all around her.

She blamed Robert, saying that it was his fault because he got her pregnant, so to punish him for his sexual desires and to keep the booze at bay, she checked herself into a health spa for the remainder of her pregnancy. She thought her life could not get any worse. Until she was in labor.

The waves of pain felt like knives slicing through her abdomen, twisting ever so slowly to prolong the agony. She screamed at the doctor, the nurse, anyone who was in the delivery room.

"Why can't you stop my pain?"

They gave her so much anesthesia that when the baby finally made its way out of the birth canal, Catherine fell into a deep sleep, more dead than alive.

*****

When she woke up the next day, the memories of her torture came rushing back.

"Why would any woman have more than one child and go through that excruciating pain twice? Never again," she vowed.

The trauma she experienced during the delivery left her alienated from Robert. He was the one who caused her pregnancy, and from the baby, it was the one who caused her pain. She refused to breastfeed, calling it barbaric.

The infant had colic, hardly ever slept, and was constantly hungry. During the first three months of the baby's life, she seldom held *it*, as she referred to her daughter, handing her off to Robert or a maid to feed and rock.

When it was time to baptize the baby girl, she told Robert she didn't care what name he gave it, as long as it wasn't Catherine. He chose the Spanish version, Caterina, hoping his wife would come around to accepting her own flesh and blood.

After the ceremony, Catherine told Robert that she did not want and could not ever have sex with him again.

"Are you saying you want us to be married but sleep apart for the rest of our lives?"

"Yes, that is exactly what I am saying. It's what my parents did after they had me."

"Catherine, that may have been agreeable to them. I do not consider that arrangement acceptable."

"That's because you are not a Yankee. Get yourself a mistress. I don't care. That's what my father did."

"What kind of marriage is that?"

"I should have known better than to marry outside my class. If you expect to get anywhere in this town, you have to conform to our ways. And I do not feel the slightest attachment to that...that creature. It howls constantly for milk. We need to hire a nanny to raise it."

Robert was appalled. "How can you pass off your obligations of a parent onto someone else?" he demanded to know.

"How can I have any peace with it underfoot?" she retorted. "I was raised by a governess, and there is nothing wrong with me! As soon as the child is old enough, it's off to the boarding school that I attended and where I was taught proper manners and how to secure a rich husband. The child will learn to do the same."

Robert had some misgivings about their marriage from their first weeks as man and wife, but he had pushed them aside, hoping things would improve. Now he knew that his marriage was doomed.

"I cannot accept your demands," he said with more relief than sadness.

Within a few days, she drove away in her Porsche and left Eastport, Connecticut, for Newport, Rhode Island, washing her hands of her husband and daughter for good. Robert immediately filed for divorce on the grounds of desertion.

The shock to his system was intense, as though he were experiencing postpartum depression. It was not in his nature to belittle her reputation in front of others or to pass the blame for his failed marriage onto her. Instead he withdrew from Eastport society and became a seldom-seen figure around town. The home that his mother enabled him to purchase was in his name only, and he quickly sold it and moved back to the house on the family estate.

His mother lived with him until Caterina started nursery school. Then she moved into the small guest house close by. Living among the townspeople with a small child and no wife was awkward and embarrassing, so he spent long days in Manhattan, partly to escape the shame he felt. At work, he pretended to be married. He never talked to his colleagues about his family or his private life, guarding his feelings under a cloak of secrecy. It was easier just to play the role of husband, even if he never felt comfortable doing it. For years, he built a thick wall around his heart, protecting it from further pain.

His mother said simply, "Next time, marry a woman who knows how to smile."

THE SECOND DANCE PARTNERS

Everyone around the long conference table was tired and more than a little annoyed, but for different reasons. The meeting of the top management of National Services had started well after five o'clock, and now it was nearly seven. Sophia Sbaglione, now a vice president, believed she had presented a well-thought-out plan on how the company could better handle claims and, in the long run, bring in more business.

Her background in sales proved that she knew the efficacy of what she was proposing, but her presentation did not sit well with the other executives because, in effect, she wanted to make it easier to file an insurance claim, rather than have claims drag on and on until the claimants gave up.

"We will gain a reputation for handling claims with speed and efficiency. That will bring in new clients."

Her eyes wandered around the room. All five of the other vice presidents looked like carbon copies of each other, wearing gray suits, white shirts, and subdued ties. *They act in lockstep,* she thought. *Not one of them is daring enough to challenge the norm.*

Even though she had produced convincing evidence of the worth of the long-range effect of such a policy, they balked. *They tried to play me before. This time, I am going to play them.*

During her first year with the company, Sophia had devised a clever plan to reward sales staff with bonuses rather than raises, arguing that getting more money immediately, rather than incrementally, was a greater incentive to sell more policies. After they dismissed that plan as unworkable, within weeks, it was presented as the conception of one of the vice presidents. It was her plan, with a few minor changes.

Her outrage almost got her fired on the spot, but the firm did not want to lose her creativity, so they gave her a promotion from director of sales to vice president, becoming the first female to reach that uppermost strata.

When the naysayers finished their criticisms of her current proposal, she knew she had lost her battle. *Fine,* she thought, *this isn't the only career I am qualified for.* Gathering up the pages of her report, she accepted her defeat, knowing that she had no future there.

It was then that Robert Navarro came to her defense. He began by noting the company's advertising was not bringing in many new clients and by reminding the board that her idea had the potential of changing the company's tarnished image. He challenged the people at the table, all making multimillion-dollar salaries, to divulge the real reason why they were rejecting her plan.

"Is it that initially, the company's profits and, therefore, your bonuses, will be less?"

Dead silence ensued.

Sophia rose from her seat, tucking a stray hair behind her ear, and straightening her navy blue dress. She began to stuff her papers inside her briefcase, saying, "Since it is your collective judgment that my plan is not acceptable, I know what I must do," and started to leave.

"Leave the plan here for us to study," offered one senior vice president.

She smiled. "So you can present it as your own? No, thank you."

The company president shouted to her as she headed for the door. "If you leave now, you're fired."

She turned around, raising her eyebrows and said quietly, "Really? I don't give a damn. I am resigning and taking my idea with me."

As soon as the door closed behind her, she stopped to lean against the wall in the corridor. *This is not how I envisioned my career in this company would end. Now I have to find another job and I will have no references to take with me.*

The absurdity of their stance rattled her. *They cannot accept that a woman dare think outside of their comfortable code of commandments.* Back at her office, she started to clean out her desk, smiling as she recalled the shock on their faces when she told them she was quitting. *They all ganged up on me. All except for Robert Navarro. His comments were surprising and touched me deeply.*

When they had first met years ago, she had liked being in his presence. When he spoke, his voice was soft, like the crinkles around his hazel eyes. There was nothing loud or flashy about either his wardrobe or his demeanor. He always came to work with a positive attitude. His humor was often wry, self-deprecating. His staff knew when they were in his presence, no matter how badly they goofed up, they were safe from open criticism. He spoke easily about issues at work but kept his private life private.

Sometimes she wondered what it would be like to date him, but she never even flirted with him. She knew only that, according to his personnel files, he was married and had a kid. That meant he was off-limits—to her, anyway.

She had almost finished clearing out her desk when he appeared at the door, startling her.

"Is the meeting over so soon?" she asked, her voice edged with the emotion that she was still feeling.

"No. I left early." He hesitated, looking at her with a wry expression. "I did suspect that things would turn out this way for you," he said softly. "Some of the other veeps felt you were disrespectful toward them."

"Because I put long-range planning over profits? They can't see beyond their bank accounts." She smiled at him, thinking of how he had argued in favor of her proposal. "Actually, I am glad I'm out of here. Too much backstabbing for my taste."

He was surprised by how composed she was. "I agree. I've quit as well," he said.

She looked up, stunned. "But why? Surely your job is not in peril over the comments you made."

"No." He paused, uncertain how much he wanted to reveal about his reasons for departure but feeling a new freedom from his self-imposed rules of behavior. "In my case, I informed the CEO months ago that I was leaving because I need to spend more time with my family. I've gone into a law partnership with some friends in Eastport, Connecticut. The law office is only a mile away from my house. For the last seven years, I have had to travel over an hour to get home, and with these late meetings, my child is often asleep by then."

Sophia felt surprised that Robert was talking about his private life. He had never once mentioned his family in the nearly six years they had worked together. They had gotten along well from the start, enjoying a feeling that can best be described as *simpatica*, which, in English, means more than agreeable, like being on the same wavelength. It was a trust that came from an acknowledgment of the other's abilities and way of thinking, but that relationship never had extended beyond the office.

"Oh, I'm glad that you did not quit because of me."

They left her office together and walked to the elevators.

"Thank you for speaking up for me in there. It's nice to know that at least one executive sees a female colleague as something other than a threat."

"You did not need my support," he countered. "I've never seen you lose an argument. You held your ground, and they were furious because they could not control you. They probably won't give you severance pay or a good recommendation since you've quit. It may be a while before you find a similar position. Will you be all right?" he asked.

She was touched by his question. She lowered her head, hoping he did not see her smile. "Yes, not a problem."

Once in the elevator, she pressed the button for the lobby.

"Aren't you going to the parking garage?"

"No, I didn't take my car today. I'll get a taxi."

He stared at her, a bit bewildered. "You do realize that you are in downtown Manhattan on a rainy Friday night. You'll be soaked before you find a cab. Let me drive you home. It's the least I can do."

She smiled at him, thinking how lucky his wife must be to have such a thoughtful husband. She hesitated. No one in the office knew where she really lived. *This is my final day at work as well as his. What difference will it make if he finds out my address?*

"Okay. You can drive me home, but it is in the wrong direction from Eastport."

"Oh, I won't be going straight to Eastport tonight. I'm tired, it's raining, and the traffic will be bumper to bumper leaving the city. I'll stay at a hotel that is right on my route."

The elevator doors opened into the garage, and Robert led the way to his car, a sporty Lexus RX.

"You do know," she said, laughing, as he opened the passenger door for her, "that police stop more red cars than any other color?"

He grinned. "It's called matador red, not that bright, and yes, I do know that, so I obey all traffic laws."

She glanced in the back and noticed an overnight bag but no child seat.

"How old is your child?"

"She is six going on sixteen. That's one of the reasons I need to keep better watch on her."

A six-year-old daughter. That thought upset her.

"Well, your wife must help out with parenting."

He did not respond but stared straight ahead. They were now exiting the garage and Robert began to turn right.

"You should take a left here."

"Don't you have an apartment on the lower West Side?"

"Yes, but I rent it out. I live on the upper West Side. I'll give you directions."

"You are a woman of mystery," he said, his interest aroused.

She did not want to repeat her statement about his wife, but she hoped he would say more. They drove on in silence. After several minutes, he said, "You asked about my wife. She is, has been, my

22

ex-wife for some time. She left me within months after our daughter was born."

She stared at him. The shock on her face was obvious. *He is a bad husband!*

"You are probably wondering why she left me." He paused and took a deep breath. "She decided that she wasn't cut out to be a mother—or a wife."

That's strange, she thought. *What is wrong with him as a husband?*

"So you have sole custody?"

He nodded.

"How often does she see your daughter?"

"Never. The last communication I received was from Newport, to acknowledge our divorce. I claimed desertion. I've made myself believe that it is for the best, but it's hard for Cat to grow up without a mother. Cat is what Caterina likes to be called."

"Oh, I like it too." She tried to imagine a six-year-old girl who wanted to be called Cat. "What is Cat like?"

"Tall for her age, dark-haired. Closer to your color, like her mother's. Curious about everything, like a cat." He paused. "A reader from about age three, something of a bully—no, maybe that is too strong. She answers a question with a question. She argues with me about everything, has the mind of a lawyer. Determined to get her way, for sure. And getting harder to control each day."

"She sounds like a challenge."

"That is a kind way to put it. She exhausts me."

"She needs to have her abilities and her energy redirected, like when you turn a flowerpot so the flowers will bloom faster and fuller. Oh, take this next left and go into the underground garage."

"Wouldn't it be easier if I left you off at the front entrance?"

"No because you are staying at my apartment tonight. I have a guest bedroom and I will cook you dinner. I'm starving. Aren't you?"

She turned to the back seat and grabbed his overnight bag as he pulled into the space beside her car. Before he could come around to open her door, she had left, with his bag in one hand and the box with her personal effects in the other, leaving him sitting alone in the car.

As she headed for the elevator that would take them up to her apartment, Sophia felt a euphoria that surprised her. She had trained herself not to act on impulse, yet here she was, asking—no, telling—a colleague who was a stranger to her outside of the workplace to sleep in her apartment. With her release from being a company employee, she felt free from her rules for behavior in the office. *We are both single adults and no longer have ties to National Services.*

They were not the only ones in the elevator that rose up into the Manhattan sky that night. Two other passengers rushed in before the doors closed. Robert had not noticed what button Sophia had pressed. Three floors were lit up—8, 14, and PH. He dismissed the penthouse as a possibility until the others had exited and the two of them were now speeding upward to the last stop.

Sophia took out a remote as the elevator stopped. The doors opened right into her apartment. Robert felt as though he had just stepped into the sky.

They were in the large foyer, and in every direction were stunning architecturally designed features, from vaulted ceilings meeting at sharp angles to Palladian windows looking out onto the city skyscraper. In front of them was the open door to a small, cozy study. The kitchen and dining room were to the left, and beyond the dining area was an enormous living room, and behind its windows glistened an enclosed lap pool beside a terrace.

While he was trying to take it all in, he realized Sophia was talking to him.

"You can put your bag in the last bedroom on the left down that hall. Perhaps you'd like to change before dinner. I am going to do the same and then make us a steak and salad."

She tossed her handbag on a table and placed the boxed items on the floor and disappeared into the kitchen. A large golden retriever with white markings around its neck came bounding out of nowhere and went up to Robert for a sniff and a pat.

"That is Bruno, my roommate," she called out to him. "I have had him since he was a pup. Wherever I go, he goes."

Robert gave the dog a friendly pat while it licked his hand.

As he walked down the hall, past several closed doors, past walls decorated with stunning watercolors of wildlife and landscapes, he thought of how little he really knew about his colleague, Sophia Sbaglione. *She has a penthouse on the upper West Side of Manhattan. I am in for an interesting evening.*

The feeling of anticipation made him smile. He washed up in the teak and ebony bathroom and changed into dark slacks and a light blue cotton pullover that he retrieved from his bag. Then, slipping on a pair of Dockers, he emerged to find Sophia, in casual clothes, at the kitchen counter, opening up a bottle of red wine.

"I want you to try this," she said. "It's a variation of the Brunello di Montalcino grown in Italy, but this is produced in California."

Her eyes ran over Robert's changed appearance.

"You look more approachable in casual clothes." She laughed, admiring Robert's smart look.

"A person should dress for the occasion," he replied. "Your outfit is a far cry from the subdued colors you wear at the office. And you seem, hmm, more relaxed in your kitchen."

"Red is too bold for our office, and I am very comfortable in a kitchen. Perhaps now we do not have to impress anybody but each other."

"I am impressed. Please forgive me for asking earlier if you were going to be all right. I had no idea you lived like this."

She ignored the apology and the compliment. "How do you like the wine?"

He swirled his glass, sniffed, and took a sip. "It's exceedingly smooth with a boldness I like." He picked up the bottle and looked at the label. "Bellini Vineyards. I've heard of them. They produced the first wine worthy to be called a Brunello in the United States."

"The only wine worthy of that name," she corrected him.

"Do you have some connection to this winery?" he asked.

Just then, her cell phone rang, and she began speaking into it in rapid-fire Italian. Not wanting to listen in, he walked around the large dining table and peered at the photographs on the walls. When she closed the phone, he said, "Your Italian is very good."

"I was born in Italy and came to the United States when I was eight."

"Ah, so no trace of an accent."

He turned back to gaze at the photos. One picture made him stop. It showed Sophia with her arm around a man, along with an older couple and another man who resembled her. The caption underneath read *The Bellini Family in Front of the Wine Taster's Award for Best Red Wine in America.*

"To answer your previous question, my family owns the Bellini winery. Sit down and eat. I hope you like your steak medium rare. That is the way it's cooked in Italy and in the Bellini kitchen."

He sat across from her, the dishes placed opposite one another at one end of the rectangular dining table.

"Yes, the steak is just the way I like it. Who is the man beside you in that picture?"

"My ex-husband, Carlo. I divorced him six years ago," she said dismissively.

"I never knew you were married. And you kept his name."

She said nothing.

Robert probed a little further. "Do you have children?" he asked.

She pressed her lips together. "No children," she whispered, and then louder, "and I kept his name to hide my identity. When you have a famous name, people make assumptions about you."

"Yes, I understand how that could be," he said thoughtfully, chewing on a piece of steak. "And they make assumptions if you are single as well. I thought that because you did not date or flirt with anyone in the office that you might be a lesbian."

She laughed. "Yes, I am sure that was the gossip going around after I pinned John against the wall and threatened to break his arm if he touched my behind again."

"I remember that scene. Some women in the office told me afterward that they were so thankful that you put him in his place and that you had the muscle and nerve to do it. But I've noticed that you don't flirt with any of the men."

Hmm, she thought. *He keeps an eye on me.*

"I will never date men with whom I work." She stopped to take a sip of wine. He waited, hoping that she would say more.

"It's a no-win. If it works out, the women will call me names, and if it doesn't, the men will. This way they can make up any story they want about me, but everyone will know it is a lie."

Sophia was saying more about her personal feelings than she had intended, but it was easy to talk with him.

"So you are protecting yourself from being hurt," Robert concluded.

Sophia thought about that. "Perhaps from being further hurt. The man I was married to worked for my father's company. In hindsight, I should never have become involved with him." She closed her eyes, remembering the pain, the anguish, and the deep hole it sent her spiraling down into.

"I want to learn from my mistakes," she said ruefully.

Robert tilted his head. "Don't we all?"

He liked the fact that she could look at herself critically, a trait always absent in Catherine.

Once the dinner was over, she put the dishes and utensils in the dishwasher while he removed the napkins, straightened the chairs, and petted Bruno, his long fingers stroking her dog along its back. Sophia watched from behind the counter and tried to suppress a feeling of jealousy.

"Do you have a dog?" she asked, noticing how comfortable he was with her pet.

"No, just a cat, a kitten, really. Two cats, if you count my daughter."

He looked up, grinning, and she felt his hazel eyes warming her skin. She smiled at his wry humor, something Carlo never had.

They moved into the living room, sitting close to one another, and continued to talk long into the night, sipping wine, letting their guard down, opening up about their childhood and college experiences. He mentioned his father's tragic death.

"That's why I became a lawyer, to get justice, although I did not expect to find it working for an insurance company. That was my father-in-law's idea. I went along with it to please him."

"Now you will be interacting with your neighbors in your hometown instead of powerful executives in a corporation," Sophia said. "That will bring you a great deal of satisfaction."

"Yes, exactly. It is what I wanted all along. Money is not everything."

He was pleased that she got why he was giving up a hefty salary for a more modest income.

Sophia nodded. "When I was at the winery," she explained, "I earned a lower salary than if I had been in legal practice, but I came to work every day, loving what I was doing. I got pleasure from talking to the pickers and the bottlers and the restaurant staff. Everyone who worked there was proud of their part in making a fine wine or serving a fine meal. I hope I can find a job that is as satisfying. Money is necessary, but it does not give value to one's life."

"Yes," said Robert, "I totally agree."

If at work they had enjoyed a meeting of their minds, now they were enjoying a meeting of their hearts. It was as if all the questions that they had ever wanted to ask each other were now permitted.

At some point, she glanced at the clock. Almost midnight. Not wanting to say good night quite yet, she suggested they go out on the terrace.

"I know it's late, but from there, the view of the city at night is spectacular."

They walked over to the door by the pool and stepped outside in the still misty air, and the partially obscured buildings of Manhattan came into view.

"It looks like the rain has stopped," she said.

In spite of it being midsummer, there was a breeze high up that made Sophia's long dark hair whip around her face, making her smooth it back behind her ears. Her dog ran the length of the terrace and back in great excitement.

"Too bad it is still cloudy," she remarked. "On a clear night, I feel I can almost touch the stars."

"Right now, there is a satellite orbiting the Earth," Robert said. "I can see it from my terrace in Eastport."

"Where is Eastport from here?" she asked.

"Let me orient myself. There, to the northeast. Just after Eastport, there is a lighthouse, warning of dangerous reefs."

"Show me."

He took her hand and raised it to a spot where the sky met the land. They were standing very close, his chest pressed into her back. The scent of his cologne stirred some longing in her.

"Yes," she said softly. "I see."

He turned to face her and raised her hand to his lips and kissed it. "Thank you for a lovely evening. This is a night I will remember for a long time," he said softly.

She looked into his eyes, so proper at work yet so intimate here on her terrace.

"Do you only kiss a woman on her hand?" she asked.

She was surprised by her boldness. *It must be the liquor,* she thought. They had finished off one bottle of wine and had chased that down with a glass of cognac.

His eyes opened wide. "No." A pause. "Sometimes I kiss a woman on her cheek."

He leaned in to her cheek, but she suddenly turned her face so that it was their lips that touched. She had only intended to kiss him lightly, to just give him a quick peck, but she found she could not back away. His lips stayed pressed to hers, feeling soft and smooth and warm. His hands were on her waist, moving lightly, softly stroking her sides.

She raised her hands to his shoulders, not knowing where else to put them. His muscles under his jersey were firm, rippling slightly as he moved his fingers toward her back. Never had she felt so tender a touch.

Their lips stayed pressed together, as if locked in place. Even though there was a definite chill in the air, that high up, a surge of warmth went through her. Finally it was Bruno's bark that brought them back to the present.

This time, when Sophia drew back and looked into Robert's eyes, she saw desire. *I can't,* she thought. *It's too soon.*

"It's late." She moved back, turning on her heels with all the determination she could muster and headed inside. "You promised your daughter that you would be home early tomorrow morning. I'm sorry to have kept you up."

Sophia led the way, moving quickly, as though she was afraid that her willpower would crumble. Robert and Bruno followed close behind.

"I am sure you will find everything that you need. Good night. Come, Bruno."

She fled down the hall with Bruno looking back in sadness at having to leave his new friend.

He stared after her, watching her quickly disappear behind the door to her bedroom. He went into the guest bedroom, wondering what had just happened. *She turned her head so that our lips met. Her kiss was reciprocal and passionate. Was she just teasing me?* He refused to believe it was fake.

He tossed and turned during the night, having been aroused by the kiss but upset that it ended so abruptly, without any real explanation.

*****

The next morning, his wristwatch came alive at five, telling him it was time to get up. He showered, dressed quickly in the same casual clothes from the night before, and went out to the kitchen and studied the coffee machine. *I may wake her up if I grind coffee.*

He remembered seeing a coffee shop just before they arrived at the building. Bruno was walking around the kitchen nervously, and Robert decided that he would take the dog along with him. Its leash and the remote were on the table by the elevators. Off they went.

When they emerged from the building, the rain was long gone, and the air smelled fresh from last night's cleansing. He saw the coffee shop a block away and headed toward it, certain he would be back before Sophia awoke.

In her bedroom, Sophia opened her eyes and stared at the closed drapes with the sunlight filtering in around the edges. The clock by her bed read five twenty. Normally, on a Saturday, she would have turned over and slept for at least another half hour, but she had a guest in her house.

Rising from her bed, she stretched her arms over her head and repeatedly bent herself in half, making her fingers touch the floor several times. Waking did not come easily this morning because she, too, had not slept well. All night long, she had repeated visions of the kiss and her slamming the door shut on advancing their relationship further.

I can't remember feeling desire that strong. It took all of my will-power to break away from him. I should have given him some explanation. He did nothing wrong. I was the one who asked to be kissed when I turned my head to meet his lips.

She showered and threw on a green silk robe. When she walked into the hall, she was surprised that Bruno was not loping toward her to beg for a walk or food.

In the kitchen, she softly called his name. No response. She walked around the apartment to check to see if a door had been left open or if he had escaped out to the terrace or was in the pool. Nothing. Then she glanced at the table by the elevator. No leash and no remote!

She had just picked up her iPhone to dial Robert's number when the elevator door opened and the two males walked out, both seemingly pleased with themselves.

"Where did you go with my dog?" she accused, standing before them with her hands on her hips.

Robert ignored her tone. "Just down the street to the coffee shop. Here is yours. Cappuccino. No sugar. I believe that is what you like to drink in the morning. Bruno did his duty and is ready for breakfast, as am I."

"You...you might have told me," she persisted. "I didn't know what to think."

"Now really, Sophia, what do you take me for? A dognapper?" he joked.

That made her smile, and she relaxed.

"No, of course not. I-I guess I was surprised that you would go off with him without first telling me."

"I did not want to wake you," he explained. "Forgive me if I worried you."

She moved into the kitchen. "Most mornings, I make myself a frittata. Will that do?"

"It sounds delicious. Let me help you."

"You may set the dishes and cutlery on the café table. We can eat in here."

She moved about the kitchen, cracking eggs and adding spinach and cheese.

"I'm not used to sharing my dog with anyone. He means a lot to me."

"Bruno, it looks like you are going to be my competition."

Bruno barked in dismay.

They ate in silence at the small round table, their body postures complementing each other, he with his long legs angled toward her and she with her long legs stretched out near his. It was an intimate composition, but neither one of them drew their legs back to a more modest posture. To a trained eye, the scene spoke of familiarity and longing.

Bruno interrupted the stillness, noisily wolfing down his food.

"Did you sleep well?" she asked, expecting a polite reply.

"No," he answered quietly.

"Oh, what was wrong?" She held her breath.

"What was wrong was your abrupt departure." He spoke so softly that Sophia bent forward to hear. "It was obvious that we both liked the kiss, so why did you turn and run?"

Her face reddened. She pulled her body back as far as it would go, without her chair tilting over.

"Robert, I do not do one-night stands, and I felt—I felt that that's where we were heading."

She was slightly annoyed at his remark. *Did he expect me to sleep with him?*

So she wanted more as well. He leaned in across the small breakfast table so that there was no place for his words to escape.

"I don't do one-night stands either," he said firmly.

That surprised her. *Most men don't have such high standards.*

She opened her mouth and then quickly shut it again. *I have to give him some further explanation. What can I say?*

"Look, outside of work, we hardly know each other." She wiggled her legs, trying to find release from her nervousness. "I know nothing about your personal life. You have never talked about your wife and your daughter until last night."

"My ex-wife, if you please. And I knew nothing about you being married or your family's business or"—he stopped to look down at Bruno—"your devotion to your dog. But I know, from the six years that we worked together, a lot about you. I believe you have high moral standards, you treat everyone you meet with respect, from the CEO to the janitor, you know how to analyze a problem, how to think on your feet, when to speak out and when to keep quiet." He stopped and raised his eyebrows. "Shall I continue?"

She had to smile. "Please do."

"You are very good at making disparate personalities work well together."

"I should hope so. I studied behavioral psychology at Stanford."

"And you seem to have a sixth sense about knowing what people need and to say just the right words to calm people down or lift them up. It's a rare gift."

"It doesn't always work, believe me. A case in point is my divorce."

"I am sure it is harder when strong emotional attachments are involved. But in the daily grind at the office, you are—were—a force to be admired."

"All that got me in the end was being entangled in greed, ego, and power. And misogyny. Quitting is against every belief I was taught." She sighed. "First my divorce and now this job. My track record isn't impressive. Maybe you will write a recommendation for me."

They both laughed at her suggestion.

"I would like to get to know you better socially," he said softly. "Perhaps you will have dinner with me or lunch."

Inwardly she smiled. She resisted accepting his offer immediately, regretting the long holiday she had planned.

"On Monday, I am going on a monthlong trip out west, first to California to see my family and then to New Mexico to visit my college roommate."

"I can wait until you get back."

"Then I'll be looking for a job." She paused. "Something where I have more control of my decisions and income, something other than corporate America. And you will be in Eastport, working at your law firm."

"Sophia, I am sure we can both find time during the week to meet. Let's see, twenty-four hours in a day times seven days. There has to be some downtime to check each other out."

She laughed. "Yes, yes, of course. I didn't mean that we can never see each other again. I just meant that it will be harder."

"But not impossible, Sophia?"

His voice was hopeful.

"Definitely possible, Robert."

Her smile emphasized the point.

"That's settled. I'd better be off."

They rose, he picked up his bag, gave Bruno a farewell pat, and then stopped to look at Sophia. He wanted to lean in and kiss her. She was staring at him, wondering what he was thinking. *A goodbye kiss?*

If she kissed him again, she knew it would not stop there.

Robert sighed and headed for the elevator.

A sudden thought occurred to her. "Robert, you said that you were just starting up your law firm." She was walking with him toward the elevator. "Are you in need of lawyers?"

He looked at her quizzically. "Well, right now we could use someone who can afford to take pro bono cases as well as paid ones. Surprisingly, there are a lot of people with low wages living around Eastport who need legal services."

"I may be interested. I'd like to check out your office and meet your colleagues."

Robert beamed. "Sure. I'd love it. When you get back, give me a call."

"How about today, this morning? I have the whole day off. I can pack for my trip tomorrow."

"Seriously?" He didn't wait for her to answer. The elevator door had opened. "I'll text you directions to the office, and do plan to come to my house for lunch afterward."

He stepped inside. The elevator door started to close.

"And bring a change of clothes. Come sailing with us in the after—"

The rest of his words were swallowed up in the shaft.

EASTPORT, AUGUST 1

Sophia stared at the closed doors of the elevator and smiled with the same satisfaction that she had when she knew she had given a brilliant lecture, when she had kept her audience of law students spellbound and wanting more.

He had invited her not just to his office, but to his home to meet his daughter. An hour or so to get there, meet with his colleagues, lunch, and then sail around the bay. *I will be home for dinner. It will give me an opportunity to get to know him better. If I find anything problematic, I will make my excuses, get in my car, and leave.*

"Bruno, we are going on an adventure today."

It was not even seven o'clock. She had plenty of time to dress and stuff a few clothes in a bag. She looked through the array of apparel in her closets. *Something casual but still classy,* she thought. She chose a white cotton shirt with navy blue capri pants and slip-on flat shoes with rubber soles for the morning and afternoon activities. After the sail, she planned to change into a simple rose silk jumpsuit that complemented her hair and skin tones.

The lingering scent of cologne greeted her when she entered the bedroom where he had slept. She breathed deeply. The air around her felt lighter, friendlier than just a day ago. For the first time in six long years, she felt joy.

• •

As Robert drove home on Route 95, heading toward Eastport, his head was filled with images of Sophia—in her kitchen, humming to herself as she cooked, sitting close to him in her living room as they shared memories about their past, and kissing him on her terrace. It was all so good. Soon she would meet Cat and his mother. He hoped that they liked her as much as he did.

• •

Sophia had never been to Eastport, but with GPS, it was an easy drive. She made one stop, picking up a package that was waiting for her at the checkout counter of a store she seldom frequented. A few minutes before her arrival at the law offices, she texted Robert with her location.

The building had little to recommend it as a law office—just a plain gray cement one-story building with small windows high up close to the roof. *It couldn't be much uglier,* she thought.

He was outside waiting for her, a welcoming smile on his face. As he walked toward her car, his sandy hair caught the rays of the sun. *There is no denying I find him handsome.*

They greeted each other in broad daylight with a tension that surprised both of them. They exchanged mundane comments.

"How was your ride?"

"Have you been waiting long?"

What were they now? Former colleagues? Close friends? Expectant lovers?

"Is it okay to bring Bruno inside?" she asked nervously. "I don't like him sitting in a hot car." It was already promising to be a summer scorcher.

"Of course," he said. "Two of my partners are already here, Sam Wyman and Arthur Blake. We were students at Yale. Marion Stephens is the other lawyer, and she is bringing a new client, a woman who often gets beaten up by her husband, but she has no bank account in her own name, so it's a pro bono case."

"So she wants a divorce?"

"Yes, but Marion said the woman is terrified that her husband will find her. We are looking for a family shelter that will take her in, but so far, no luck. There are so few around here, and they fill up quickly. Right now, she's staying with Marion."

"That is a lot to ask of a lawyer."

"Lara didn't ask. Marion offered."

"Any children?"

"No, thank God."

They were now in the reception area of the law offices of Wyman, Blake, and Navarro. A wave of refreshing cool air washed over them. Because it was a Saturday, the firm's secretary was not there.

"They are in the meeting room at the end of the hall," Robert explained, pointing the way.

As they walked along the corridor, Robert described the layout: the lawyers' offices, supply room, printing and faxing area. They stepped briefly inside his office near the end of the hall because he wanted to get a file. While she waited, she noticed that there were no family pictures on his desk, nothing personal at all. *Maybe he hasn't had a chance to settle in to make his office his own,* she thought.

He walked over to her as she stood by the door, smiling at him. It gave him a feeling of comfort. He stopped in front of her, smiling back. He wanted to kiss her but thought better of it. *It would be inappropriate in my law office.* Instead he reached past her to open the door wide. They walked out into the corridor and then entered a large room with high narrow windows and a conference table with piles of books and folders spread out.

At the far end were Sam and Arthur, poring over some papers. Sophia quickly checked out the two attorneys. They were opposites in looks and style. Sam was of medium height and pudgy, with a beer belly. His face had a reddish tinge, usually a sign of an alcoholic. He wore a shirt opened at the neck and baggy tan pants. His casual attire surprised her.

Arthur was tall, reedy, and impeccably dressed in a light gray business suit and striped tie. Strong cheekbones, thin lips, and pale skin. He had a concerned look in his eyes, as if Sophia were not what he expected.

"Well," Sam remarked, "you are back with a lovely woman at your side. I understand you are looking for employment here," checking Sophia out. "I'm sure Robert told you we only hire women who have beauty first, brains second."

Nobody laughed at his comment; in fact, Arthur looked pained. *He obviously does not share Sam's opinion,* Sophia surmised.

Robert introduced Sophia. Sam Wyman rose to greet her, his shirt and pants rumpled, looking like a man who cared less about his stodgy appearance and more about his power to control. His blond hair was combed from ear to ear, in a pitiful attempt to cover up hair loss was Sophia's first impression.

He put out his hand, while his narrow blue eyes gave Sophia a once-over, resting on her bust, making her feel uncomfortable. Then he sat down. Arthur was more polite, looking her in the eye and waiting for her to be seated.

The conversation began with pleasantries and soon moved on to their new client and her safety. Ideas were tossed around: A motel in town, a friend or family member. To Sophia, the answer was obvious.

"If her husband is so threatening, those would be the first places he would look for her. You all have long ties to this community. Don't you know anyone who has an empty guesthouse on his property, an estate where entry is permitted only by opening a gate? Surely there is one rich person in this town who has sympathy for an abused wife and will offer to put her up for a while."

"What a great idea," Arthur said. "I know a dowager who may do it. She is the president of a club that holds raffles for all sorts of causes. I'll give her a call."

"Don't be so sure," Sam interjected. "Those old biddies are not that generous." He was annoyed that Arthur was backing Sophia's idea. "It'll be a waste of time."

Just then, Marion popped her head in.

"Hi, everyone. I have Lara in my office. I don't want to bring her in here just yet. Too intimidating."

Robert made the introduction. Marion looked approvingly at Sophia and shook her hand.

"It's always a pleasure to meet a female colleague. There are too few of us around."

She radiated professionalism and confidence. Her short brown hair was sprinkled with gray lines, but other than that, it was hard to tell her age. She was fit, attractive, and candid. Sophia liked her immediately.

"May I be allowed to meet your client?" Sophia asked her. "Although I am not a member of your firm, I would like to interview her with you present to give you an idea of my qualifications."

"That is not ethical," Sam replied quickly, even though her question was directed at Marion.

Sophia turned to stare at Sam, assessing his comments. *Obviously he feels that he is running the show. This is definitely not an equal partnership.*

She pressed her case. "Marion can explain that I am a visiting lawyer and ask her permission. If she agrees then?"

"If she clearly understands that anything she says to you will be held in confidence," Sam stressed, sounding as if he were an angry parent.

"Of course!" Her words came out emphatically, as if there could be no other possible interpretation of her request. "Thank you." She smiled sweetly and turned on her heels, wanting to get away from him quickly.

"There is something else," Sam added. "In this office, we pride ourselves on our professionalism. You are not dressed like a lawyer should be."

"Neither are you," she snapped back, whipping her head around, giving his attire a second look. His big ears and his beady eyes reminded her of a jackal. She imagined him stalking his prey like a greedy carnivore, and that thought made her smile, even though he was definitely getting on her nerves.

Sam glared at her, unaccustomed to a woman speaking back to him. She kept her smile. Then out of her deep pocketbook, she produced a stylish scarf and tied it around her neck. She dug deeper and retrieved a thin navy blue cotton jacket that matched her capri pants.

In a few moments, her look changed from casual to classy. She stood silently, waiting for his approval.

"That's better," Sam muttered.

Sophia strode out of the conference room with Bruno, following Marion to her small office down the hall.

As they walked, Marion turned to Sophia and said, "You've got balls. He gets under my nerves, too, so I just try to stay clear of him."

"No one else challenges him?"

"Occasionally Robert will disagree, but Sam always shoots him down."

Back in the meeting room, Arthur turned to Robert with a puzzled look.

"She certainly has confidence in herself. Where did you find her?"

"She and I worked together at National Services for six years. You can trust her integrity and professionalism. She is top-notch."

"And she left the company because—"

"The other execs wanted to use her ideas without giving her credit. They did it once before to her, and she swore that it wouldn't happen again."

Sam butted in, "You do know a small law firm is far different from a corporation."

"Are you saying that I am not qualified to work here?"

"I know you. You're a Yalie. Where did she go to school?"

"Stanford."

His eyebrows went up. "Really? Okay, so she's smart. I'll give you that, but dealing face-to-face with small-town clients is very different from impressing corporate big shots. As far as I'm concerned, she's on probation."

He had already decided that if Sophia joined the firm, he was going to make her life as difficult as possible.

When Marion brought Sophia into her office, the new client was sitting with her head down and her arms around her body, as if she were held together with Scotch tape. Lara was pretty, of average height, with a small bone structure.

Marion said, "Lara, I'd like you to meet Sophia. I don't remember—"

Sophia stepped forward. "Hi. I'm Sophia Sbaglione, a visiting lawyer. Would you mind if I talked to you about your difficulties? I will keep what you say in strict confidence."

Lara found Sophia's soft tone and earnest look comforting. She nodded. Sophia pulled up a chair across from her and leaned forward.

"Tell me about you and your husband's relationship. When did it change, and how did you try to cope?"

Lara began hesitantly, with Sophia affirming each piece of information she offered. Soon her words were bursting from her lips as if a spigot had been opened. Tears followed, and she wiped them away, apologizing for crying. Marion had been taking notes nonstop.

Sophia gave Lara a warm smile.

"You may be feeling overwhelmed by what you are going through, but I can assure you many of us women have had similar difficulties in marriage, and when there is violent behavior and your life is threatened, the only way out is divorce. You made the right decision to come here. This firm will do whatever it takes to find you a safe place to stay and guide you through the legal proceedings."

"Thank you, Miss Sba—?"

"Call me Sophia. As you know, I am currently not a member of this firm, but if you need someone to talk to, call me any time." She reached into her pocketbook and pulled out a small purse, unzipped it, and found her business card, now outdated. "I will write my iPhone number on the back. If we do not meet again in person, at least we can stay in touch by phone. I must go now. Come, Bruno."

Marion went out with her into the hall.

"That was a very generous offer. Do you do this often? Tell a stranger to call you any time?"

"Marion," Sophia whispered so Lara did not overhear, "it's not much of a sacrifice to take a phone call. Lifting up her spirits can make a significant difference just now, when her confidence is so low. She may or may not call me, but just her knowing that I care enough to make the offer may give her some comfort."

Marion nodded. "Right. Well, you certainly are expert in handling clients. You asked all the right questions and a few I never thought of."

"Good luck. My, it's already eleven-thirty. Robert promised to bring me to his house for lunch."

"You must rate very highly. He's never made any of us that offer."

"Really?"

She walked down the hall, thinking, *What is he hiding from his colleagues?*

Before Sophia had a chance to open the door to the conference room, Robert came out.

"Ready to meet my family?" he asked, a touch of anxiety slipping out.

She smiled broadly, hoping to relax his tension—and hers.

"I'm looking forward to it."

As they walked back down the hall, Robert gave her his assessment of her visit.

"Arthur likes you and I know Marion does too. Sam doesn't like to be criticized, as I'm sure you have gathered, but he deserved to be scolded for his comment about your clothes."

"And I like Arthur and Marion," she said softly. "And you," she added, not wanting to leave him out.

ROBERT'S HOUSE

Sophia's nerves were causing her heart to race during the short ride to Robert's home. He had told her that his mother was going to be joining them for lunch. *I now have two family members to meet and impress.* He seemed jittery when they left the law offices. *Does he think that I won't like his daughter? And why has he not invited his colleagues to his home? Does he not like to be social with them? I hope I have not made a mistake by moving this relationship along so quickly.*

She followed closely behind his car since he still had not given her his address but had simply said, "You can't get lost. It's just up the street." The houses that lined the route were large, elegant structures, many with wrought-iron gates and high hedges that were intended to block the views from passersby. All the homes on the left were on the waterfront. *Is this where he lives?* she wondered.

After about a mile, Robert turned left into a long, curved driveway that led up to a large, sprawling house spread out against the backdrop of a blue ocean. From its red-tiled roof and breezy blue stucco exterior to the landscaping that cradled plants, flowering bushes, and garden animals around its base, it looked like a scene out of a *Shangri-La* movie. Far off to the right was nestled a charming cottage mirroring the colors and outside decor of its neighbor, with a neatly mowed huge expanse of green lawn in between.

Well, this is much more than I expected. Taking Bruno's leash, she stepped out of her car.

"This is lovely, Robert."

He smiled and escorted her to the front door. They walked into a large foyer with a red-tiled floor and arched openings that led into various rooms and corridors. The low ceiling in the hall had a pleasing white textured finish, giving the space an informal look.

Farther down the corridor, Sophia saw mahogany beams spanning the ceiling of a different area.

A young girl skidded around a corner and stopped. She was dressed in a pink jersey and shorts, holding a small kitten and looking at Sophia with curious eyes.

"Sophia, this is my daughter, Cat."

Sophia's face froze. Something deep within her stirred. A memory, ripped and bloodied, that had been shoved into the back corner of her subconsciousness. *She looks nothing like Robert. In fact, she could be my daughter.*

"Hello, Cat," she managed to say.

Bruno gave a short woof when he saw the kitten, which made it cling tightly to Cat's jersey.

"Well, I'll leave you ladies to get acquainted while I go make lunch."

Robert headed down a hall toward a large living area.

Sophia saw Cat's keen eyes were studying her carefully from head to toe, like a detective looking for clues in a murder case.

She knelt on the floor and said, "I'd like to meet your kitten. What is its name?"

Cat came a little closer, still checking Sophia out. "Guess!" she said.

Sophia smiled, understanding what Robert meant when he said his daughter did not answer a question directly. "Hmm. She has white and gray fur, like how clouds look. Fluffy?"

"No. I'll give you one clue. It's a nickname like mine."

"Oh, well then, it must be Kit for kitten."

"Yes!" said Cat, pleased that this lady had guessed correctly from just one clue. "What is your dog's name? Brownie?"

Sophia's eyes lit up. "Almost. It's Bruno, the Italian word for brown. I don't think Bruno has ever seen a cat before. I wonder." She patted Bruno and whispered something in his ear. He lay down on the floor next to her, keeping watch on Kit.

"I don't think Kit likes dogs," said Cat. "She hunches up when she sees them."

"She's not hunched up now. Let me try something." She put her hand by Bruno's mouth, and he immediately licked it. Then she reached over and had the cat sniff her hand with the dog's scent on it. The cat licked Sophia's hand, and Sophia brought her hand back to Bruno's nose. "Smell is a very important scent in animals. Now that they know the other's scent, they may become friends after a while."

"Does your dog bite?" Cat wanted to know.

"No," Sophia said with a twinkle in her eyes. "I don't think he finds people very tasty."

Cat giggled at her comment, and Sophia smiled.

Robert came back to find all of them sitting on the floor. "What's this? A campfire meeting?"

"Don't be silly, Daddy. We are doing an experiment to see if Kit and Bruno will like each other."

"Oh, of course. I can see that now. Here is Grandma. Mom, I would like you to meet Sophia. Sophia, my mother, Margaret."

Margaret had walked into the house using a key, which she was slipping into her pocket. She was a tall, spry-looking woman with hazel eyes and hair that was changing from sandy to gray around her temples.

"Hello, Margaret." Sophia had gotten up from the floor and reached out to shake her hand. "Cat and I were getting acquainted."

"Hello, Sophia. I didn't catch your last name."

Her manner was cordial but guarded.

"Sbaglione. It's a mouthful for most people to get their tongues around."

Margaret gave Sophia the same critical eye as her granddaughter had.

Robert chewed his lip, noticing his mother assessing Sophia.

"Lunch is almost ready. Here is a glass of white wine, Sophia. It goes well with the lobster."

Sophia took the wine glass, understanding intuitively that he was putting her on stage for his mother to critique. She followed the family into a large terraced area that overlooked the bay below, stopping to take in the panorama of flowers, ocean, and sky. Sunlight made the water dazzle, mesmerizing the eye with its colors and movement.

The outdoor space was covered with a canopy of vines and surrounded by a railing sheltering potted plants. It smelled like a flower garden. A long table had been set for four at one end, one setting having a bowl instead of a dish.

Cat took the seat with the bowl in front of her. "What's your favorite food? I like mac n' cheese." She was still checking out Sophia.

"Oh, I guess it depends on the occasion. When I was your age, I ate a lot of spaghetti." She turned to Margaret. "I was born in Italy and came to the States when I was eight."

"Speak Italian," Cat demanded.

"*Questa casa è molto bella così come le persone in essa,*" Sophia quickly replied.

Robert was placing the dishes of stuffed lobster tail, coleslaw, and watermelon salad on the table.

"What does that mean?" Cat asked.

"I said that this house is very beautiful as are the people in it."

"Well, we have to agree with that assessment, and that includes our guest." He raised his glass. "A toast to Sophia Sbaglione who impressed my colleagues earlier today with her insightful comments."

"Are you also a lawyer, Sophia?" asked Margaret, after sipping her wine. There was a concerned look in her eye.

"Yes, I am."

"And she is considering joining the law firm, seeing if we measure up to her standards."

They devoured the meal with just small chitchat in between bites. The canopy of vines made the terrace feel cool and secluded, filling the air with a scent of gardenias.

It was so pleasant that Sophia didn't want the lunch to end; she would have been happy to spend the rest of the afternoon there.

When coffee was served, Margaret resumed her questioning. "Now why would you want to relocate to this area?" she asked.

I am being cross-examined.

Sophia took a deep breath. "Margaret, it took me a while to realize that much of the corporate world is run by greedy and unethical people. At least from my experience with National Services."

"And you did not realize this before? You must have been living under a rock," she said lightly.

Sophia smiled. "I do sound naïve, don't I? Before coming to Manhattan and National Services, I did live under a rock, so to speak. I worked for my father at the family winery where casks of wine are stored under rocks, in caves."

Cat cut in, "You lived in a cave?"

Sophia laughed lightly. "No, I did not live in a cave, but I visited the caves almost daily. The winery is pretty remote, and it is a family business, which means we lived by a different set of values, better values than most of corporate America."

"Oh, I see," Margaret replied. "And why did you leave such an idyllic place?"

Sophia paused. *I cannot relate my gory tale on such a beautiful day in front of a child.*

"It's a long, unpleasant story. I...I will tell you in private if you insist, but I warn you, it is very painful for me." She looked at Cat and then back at Margaret.

Margaret backed off. "Oh dear. I have been prying into your personal life. Forgive me."

Robert, who was listening to this intently, said, "Well, it's time for a sailboat ride. Cat, help me bring some supplies down to the boat. I'll let you ladies relax a bit."

After the two had left, Sophia decided it was her turn to ask questions. "Margaret, how do you spend your time?"

Margaret suspected why Sophia was there. *If she is interested in Robert, at least she knows how to engage me in conversation.*

"When my husband died, I enjoyed traveling with friends, but after Robert's wife left, that has been hard. Since I live next door, and I'm the only family Robert has, I have had to be babysitter, chauffeur, and back-up parent as well as grandmother. You know about Catherine's desertion, I presume?"

"Yes, Robert told me last night."

"He doesn't much talk about it. It was a blow to his ego as well as a shock. Her departure was so sudden, and then having to raise Cat without a mother." She paused. "It seems we all have our difficulties." She looked at Sophia, hoping for more information.

"My story is sad as well. I could not stay at the winery because it was there that I went through a terrible ordeal, after which my husband left me suddenly, but for me, it was a blessing." She stopped.

Margaret said, "Oh?"

A long silence ensued. *She wants to hear more. What choice do I have?*

Getting up, Sophia stood with her arms folded, looking out at the bay and related her tale as quickly and as unemotionally as she could. When she had finished, she turned back and saw Margaret wiping tears from her eyes.

"Now you see why I had to get away from such bad memories. It has taken me this long to tell my story dispassionately, but it still hurts inside."

Margaret got up and put her hand on Sophia's arm. "Of course, and it will hurt for a long time. You know, when I first saw you, kneeling on the floor, dirtying your slacks, I wondered why you would do that. Now I understand your wanting to connect with Cat. She and you are both *needy*."

"Why is Sophia needy, Mom?" Robert had come in quietly.

Quickly, Margaret deflected his question. "They are both so smart that they need to have their cleverness confirmed by others." She turned to Sophia. "Enjoy the sail, and I hope to see you here again soon." Then she hurried off before Robert had a chance to question her more.

Robert watched his mother disappear and then looked at Sophia. "What was that all about?"

"I'll tell you later. Are we ready to sail, Captain?"

"Well, you obviously have impressed my mother. I think Bruno should stay here, where it's cool, don't you?"

"I suppose so," she said with some reluctance. "He's never been in a boat, so it's better we don't chance it. Let me give him something to nibble on before we leave."

Robert and Sophia walked down a long, steep stairway to a dock where a thirty-foot sailboat named *Kit Cat* was tied up. Cat was already sitting by the helm, sporting a thin life jacket.

"I want to go fast like the wind!" she shouted.

Robert took the wheel, wearing his captain's hat, with Cat beside him and Sophia beside Cat. They sailed out of Eastport Harbor into Long Island Sound, with an afternoon breeze ruffling the water. The August sun was relentless in its intensity. Sophia took a crushable sun hat out of her bag and put it on her head, tightening the string under her chin.

Small boats motored by and their occupants waved a friendly hello. Farther out they saw large container ships and yachts.

Robert pointed to the left. "There is the lighthouse that I mentioned when we were on your terrace. There are several more up and down the coast."

"Are they all automatic?" Sophia asked.

"Yes. Most large boats use electronic navigational aids rather than depend on a lighthouse, but on a small boat like this, they are helpful in warning about reefs and sandbars. Do you sail?"

"Since I was six. Have you taught Cat yet?"

"No." He turned to see if she was being serious.

"My father taught me. Let's teach her. Cat, come sit on my lap and take the helm, and I will give you your first lesson in sailing."

"Really? Wow."

Robert moved closer to Sophia and watched as Cat moved the wheel with Sophia's guidance. He put his arm around his guest, delighted at how the afternoon was progressing.

"Look, I am making the boat move, Daddy!" cried Cat.

At times the boat tipped, and a spray of salt water covered them. It felt refreshing on such a hot afternoon. Robert passed them bottles of water and sun lotion, knowing the effects of the summer sun.

After several minutes, Sophia took back the wheel. "You did great," Sophia beamed.

"I'm tired," said Cat.

Between the sun and the sailing lesson, her energy was gone. She snuggled up in Sophia's arms while Robert took over the controls. Sophia bent down, instinctively kissing the top of Cat's head. She noticed it was hot.

"I think Cat has become overheated. We should head in soon." She took her large hat off and put it against Cat's head and body to shield her.

"You feel so soft," Cat murmured, her hand resting on Sophia's chest. She began to move her hand around, and it slipped under Sophia's shirt.

"What's this?" she asked, exposing Sophia's nipple.

"That is a nipple which a baby sucks on to get milk," Sophia whispered, her hands not free to cover herself up. Robert's attention was on the sail.

"Oh," was all Cat said. Then she closed her eyes and fell asleep.

Sophia's hands were full, holding Cat and her hat. She shifted her position, leaning against Robert so that her shirt moved, once more covering her breast. Sophia pressed her head back against the cushion, enjoying the warmth of the sun and holding a child who felt so comfortable in her arms.

Robert turned to look at Sophia, whose shoulder was pressed next to his. Her eyes were closed and her lips formed a smile as his daughter slept in her arms. At that moment, he was so happy his eyes misted over. He had been hesitant about bringing a woman home to meet his family, wanting to wait for the right one, and now he was struck by how well Sophia had gotten on with his mother and now Cat. *This day is turning out to be better than I thought possible.*

For the rest of the ride, he said little, thinking and hoping of how the day might end.

When they returned to the dock, Sophia handed Cat to Robert, who carried her up to the house. Once they were on the cool terrace, Cat awoke but was groggy.

"I think it's time for a shower and a change of clothes," Sophia said. "Oh, I just remembered something. I brought you a present,

Cat." She went to her car and came back with a package. "Why don't we girls go in your room and open it there?"

"I have to anchor the boat out by the buoy and take a shower as well. See you in a little while." Robert headed back to the dock.

In her bedroom, Cat ripped the paper off her gift and opened the box. In it was a pink cotton jumpsuit with white polka dots.

"I love it!" Cat shouted. "Can I put it on now?"

"You need to cool off. Have you ever taken a shower?"

"No. Just baths. Can I take one with you?" Cat asked.

Sophia paused, startled by the child's request.

"I guess that will be all right," she said, unable to think of a way to say no politely.

While they were showering, Sophia helped Cat wash her hair. Then they dried themselves and put on their jumpsuits, one rose-colored silk and the other soft pink. They both had hair that was long enough to twist into a braid to keep the wet hair off their backs. *We look so much alike,* Sophia thought. *It's uncanny.*

"We're almost the same," said Cat.

"Yes. Let's go show the rest of the world."

They came out to the terrace where Robert was sitting, sipping a Scotch.

"Wow," was all he kept saying.

"I guess you like Cat's new outfit." Sophia and Cat were enjoying his reaction.

"I-I love both your outfits." He pulled his eyes away from Sophia and turned to Cat. "Are you sure you are my daughter? Did Sophia switch my Cat for a teenager?"

"Nope. I'm still Cat." She turned all around, happy to have her father's attention.

"Cat, why don't you go to Grandma's house and show her your outfit?"

Cat ran out the door, and immediately, Robert came to where Sophia was standing.

"You look lovely. I hope you will stay the night. Otherwise, I will think that my family did not measure up to your expectations."

"Play fair. I came to see your law partners and meet your family. It has been such a pleasant day—the lunch and the sail were wonderful. I must get back so I can pack for my trip."

"Must you? We have had so little time alone." He came closer and kissed her lips, surprising her.

The fact that they were in his home with his daughter around made his action uncomfortable. She raised her arms to push him back and heard Cat say, "Grandma isn't home. Why are you kissing?" It startled them both.

Robert stayed silent. Sophia blushed and said quickly, "I was just thanking your father for the lunch." Her tone was curt. *Damn it! Why did he do that without asking me?*

"Well, you don't have to kiss him!"

"No? How should I thank him?"

"Just say, 'Thank you for the lunch. It was very good.'"

Sophia turned to Robert and, with a flat voice, repeated Cat's words.

He asked, "Would you care for something to drink?"

"Just water. I am driving home soon. I think Cat needs to wear a hat when she is out in the boat. Her head was hot. She got overheated, and it made her drowsy."

"Yes," Robert agreed. "I never thought of that."

"I should feed Bruno and then be on my way."

"Do you have to leave today?" He sounded close to begging. "You will be gone for a whole month."

"Sophia, you won't be back here for a month? Why?" Cat wanted to know.

"I am going to visit my mother and father who live in California. It's been such fun today, Cat. I hope to see you again."

She gazed at Robert, bronzed by the sun, sporting white slacks and black jersey. She imagined a future romantic relationship with him was indeed possible.

"I will let you know when I return and we can plan something."

"Let's have a bite to eat, and we can discuss your departure later. There's plenty of time. Come in the kitchen, Sophia, and we'll prepare a simple meal together."

Sophia stared in disbelief as Robert turned to leave. *Didn't he hear what I just said?*

He stopped and said to Cat, "Why don't you go play with your dolls, Cat? Sophia and I want to talk."

"I don't like dolls, and I want to listen."

"Cat!" Robert's voice sounded more pleading than angry.

"I will leave if Sophia will tell me a bedtime story tonight."

"See! What did I tell you? She wants to negotiate with me all the time."

"You were right when you said she has the mind of a lawyer," Sophia observed, while thinking of how she could get out of staying for supper without disappointing Cat.

"I'd like to stay, but I really need to leave soon." *I am not going to spend the night here.*

Then Cat wrapped her arms around Sophia's waist and, gazing wistfully into her eyes, whispered, "Please."

Sophia became unglued. When she looked at Cat, she saw her own daughter standing there, asking her to stay. Her eyes filled up. *How can I say no to her?*

"Okay, Cat. I will tell you a bedtime story right after supper and leave then."

Cat jumped up and down. "Yippee! I'm hungry. When is supper?"

Robert was delighted. He went into the kitchen, with Sophia and Cat following close behind.

Suddenly everyone was famished, including Bruno. Robert grilled hamburgers and hot dogs, while Sophia took out the leftovers from lunch. Then they sat down to eat, watching the changing colors on the water as the sun continued its descent to the horizon. Cat said she was not tired, so they played card games until it became too dark to see. Cat especially liked *Concentration*, winning every game.

"Bedtime, my Cat. I see your eyes starting to close," Robert said.

"Come with me, Sophia. I will show you what I built with my Legos before you tell me a story."

Robert stared after them. *That is the first time Cat ever went to bed willingly!* He called his mother to say good night and to tell her what had transpired.

"I have some advice for you, Robert. Don't let Sophia get away."

"You really like her that much?"

"Don't you?" Margaret asked her son. "I think she is what you have been looking for. You have been single a long time, and both you and Cat need her for different reasons. And"—she paused—"she needs both of you."

"Why does Sophia need Cat?" He wanted to know.

"Sophia will tell you in her own good time. Good night." She hung up.

A while later, Sophia came out to the terrace where Robert was sitting, watching the news. He immediately shut it off when he saw her wiping tears from her eyes.

"What's wrong?"

"I'd like a sip of your Scotch, please."

She took the glass with two hands and spilled some before the glass reached her lips. She took a big gulp and sighed heavily. Her close-fitting rose silk jumpsuit accentuated her breasts and hips.

He stared at her, ashamed of feeling lust for her while knowing she was upset.

"Sophia, tell me what happened." His voice had a touch of panic.

She took another long sip before she spoke. "I told Cat a bedtime story, one that my mother used to tell me, of a princess who lived in a far-off land. I saw that she was totally mesmerized by it, as I had been at her age. When I finished and bent over to kiss her good night"—Sophia wiped away more tears and continued—"Cat whispered in my ear, 'I wish you were my mother.'"

She sat down on the sofa beside Robert, and he put an arm around her.

"Robert, I was taken aback. I've known her for less than a day." She stared into space. "It's my fault. I should have realized how *needy* she was, growing up with no mother. What have I done? I never expected my behavior would create so strong a...a bond."

He pulled her close, and she let him, needing a shoulder to comfort her at that moment.

"What did you say to her?" His mind was processing this, mixing his daughter's feelings with his and seeing how well they blended.

"She was so earnest. I couldn't brush it off. I said, 'Wouldn't that be wonderful?'" She whispered the words, panicked at their suggestion.

"Hmm, I agree with Cat," he whispered. "You will be an excellent mother to her."

She stared at Robert. "Wh-what are you saying?"

"What I am saying," he murmured, "is that Cat loves you and so do I. Why not make us both happy?"

He's asking me to marry him!

"Robert, you can't be serious!"

This is so unlike him. At work, he never made hasty decisions.

"We've never even dated. We've never been intimate."

"No, but we can fix that now. Stay here tonight and give me your answer tomorrow morning."

He wrapped his arms around her and kissed her softly on the lips. She felt her body relax into his.

"I believe, Counselor, that my argument is far stronger than yours." He pressed his lips to hers once more, a long and passionate kiss. "I rest my case."

The sweet smell of flowers wafted through the night air. Sounds of lapping water and rope creaking against buoys filtered up to the terrace. It was so soothing. She felt her body go limp. The day had been exhausting—Sam's unpleasantness, his mother's grilling, and then sun fatigue.

His hand was moving slowly over her body. She barely had enough energy to say, "I didn't bring a nightgown."

"You won't need one." His eyes were crinkled in mirth, amused by her protests. "Any other objections, Counselor?"

"Was this your plan when you invited me to your house?" she murmured.

"Not a plan. More like an intense longing for you, ever since we kissed last night on your terrace, and I saw desire in your eyes."

It's true. I had felt desire. All her reasons for leaving suddenly seemed foolish. *If I want to know him better, sleeping with him will certainly help. I can't get pregnant.* She took his fingers that were on her midsection and moved them to the top button on her jumpsuit, helping him undo it, and then down to the next and the next, slowly revealing her naked body. When they reached the bottom button, she put his fingers still lower and closed her eyes.

They stayed on the terrace a long while, neither of them wanting to interrupt the mood they were in. When the sea air became chilly, they rose from the sofa, gathered up their clothes, and made their way to his bedroom.

*****

In the early morning, Robert opened his eyes and saw Sophia next to him in bed, still naked, lying with her back toward him. He moved his fingers gently across the curves of her shoulders and then to her hip. She awoke and turned toward him, letting him see her in the day's thin light.

"Good morning. Did you sleep well?" he asked, mimicking her words to him from the morning before.

She stared at him, half wishing she was home in her own bed and half wishing that this was her bed. His hair was uncombed and his cheeks and chin slightly grizzled, but his smile was unchanged. She smoothed her hair back, imagining what she must look like.

He grinned at her gesture. "Don't worry. You still look ravishing."

"Or like I've been ravished." There was merriment in her eyes. "I did not sleep all that well because I was…busy with other pressing matters. You know how to weaken a woman's defenses."

"That is because our very first kiss told me everything I needed to know." He paused. "Let me restate my proposal that I made last night. You are smart and can run circles around me with your legal knowledge. You are caring and will make Cat an excellent mother. You are passionate and will wear me out as a lover and, most importantly"—he stopped dramatically and deadpanned—"you can cook."

Sophia's lips opened in a smile. "You are impossible. Mad."

57

He continued, "The court can come to only one decision, Your Honor. Sophia must marry me."

Sophia couldn't help but be amused by his summation. "That is quite an argument. Perhaps I should ask the court for a recess to consider your request."

"Agreed. We'll call it an engagement period. That will do while you decide on a permanent resolution to this matter."

Good heavens! Did we just become engaged?

His hand moved over her, stroking her breasts and belly.

"How did you get the scar on your abdomen?" he asked. He put his finger on the jagged pink mark.

"Please don't touch it!" she demanded, visibly upset. She moved his hand away. "You can touch me anywhere but there."

"What happened, Sophia?" Her tone surprised him.

"Not now. Someday I might tell you." *I need to change the subject.* "There is something, though, I wanted to ask you. Marion said that you have never invited your colleagues over for lunch. Is that true?"

"Yes, it's true."

"Why not?" she wondered.

"Because the one time I had them here for drinks after work, they didn't want to leave. They stayed past midnight and were arguing about some case so loudly that Cat woke up crying. Sam had gotten so drunk that Arthur and I had to carry him out to his car and drive him home."

"I see. I thought that you might be trying to hide something, like a dark secret," she joked, trying to make light about her concern.

He smiled. "I have no secrets, other than the desire to kill any man who flirts with you."

"Is that supposed to be reassuring?" She laughed but wondered if he was the possessive type, like Carlo. "I want you to know that I am not in the habit of sleeping with a man on a whim. I let my guard down last night. I drank too much."

She tried to blame it on the Scotch, but deep down, she knew it wasn't the liquor. She had wanted him.

"I hope you are not sorry. For me, it was the best sex I ever had. Catherine never actively participated."

"She didn't like sex? With you?" Sophia's face registered shock. "How long were you married to her?"

"A little over a year."

"What a waste," she said. "The woman must have been an iceberg."

She paused. *Should I be honest with him about Carlo? Well, he was honest about his ex.* "Sex with Carlo was like being in a wrestling match. Last night was like…like sky rockets in flight." A pink blush crept over her cheeks. "You have to know how much I enjoyed it."

Her honesty made him grin. "It certainly appeared that way. In one month, I hope to see you in this exact spot. You have an open invitation."

"I told you I don't do one-night stands, so I will accept your invitation."

"Wonderful. I will hold you to your promise, and I'll give you the house key."

Her eyes widened. *He is that sure about me after just one night? Am I that sure about him?* She needed to find out.

She threw a long naked leg over his body. "Remind me again what I am going to miss during the next four long weeks."

*****

At breakfast, Robert wore navy blue pajama bottoms. Sophia wore its matching top. They were sipping coffee on the terrace, barely awake, when Cat appeared and told them what she had seen when she walked by the cat's bed.

"Daddy, Kit was sleeping on Bruno's belly!"

Both Robert and Sophia became alert.

"No! For real, Cat?" he asked his ever-vigilant daughter.

"Yes, I saw them sleeping together!"

Sophia called Bruno over to her side. She looked him in the eye and asked, "Did you sleep with Kit last night?"

Bruno looked away.

"Hmm. There must be magic dust in this house."

That made Robert chuckle. Cat looked from her father to Sophia, confused.

"Magic dust?" Then she noticed something that made her father and his guest turn red. "What are those pink marks on your necks?" She tried to look at her own neck. "Do I have them too? Some bedbugs bit us," said Sophia, not comfortable having to lie. "But not you, Cat. They only like older people."

Cat smiled at her, believing her every word.

Before Sophia left, she promised Cat that she would return to visit in about a month.

"What day? I want to put it on my calendar."

Sophia gaped at Robert. *She uses a calendar?* she mouthed.

Robert shrugged.

"Cat, I can't be sure. Maybe the last Friday of the month, but it could be that Saturday or Sunday."

"Promise?" she asked, refusing to let Sophia leave without making a commitment.

Sophia stared at this six-year-old girl demanding a promise from her. Her heartstrings were stretched to the breaking point.

"Yes, Cat. I promise."

MANHATTAN AND OUT
WEST, AUGUST

Wow! That was an adventure, she thought as she drove into the borough of Manhattan. *I am in this relationship a lot deeper than I thought I'd be. I didn't expect to enjoy being with them as much as I did. Cat is smart and inquisitive, although I can understand why Robert gets exasperated with her aggressiveness, but that can be channeled properly. His mother softened toward me after asking me some very pointed questions. Was I right to tell her my story so soon after meeting her? His family is lovely. His colleagues are pleasant, except for Sam. Robert's house is so comfortable and is beautifully situated with a view of the bay, and he gave me the house key. He wants our relationship to end in marriage. He made that clear.*

Her mind went back over the emotions she had felt during the last twenty-four hours and the possible implications. Robert had so many of the qualities she wanted in a husband: Devotion and commitment to his daughter and mother, caring and thoughtful, as well as lighthearted and witty. If this relationship continued, she needed to think about what it would mean to give up her independence and be married once again, with a six-year-old child from someone else's womb, with God-knows-what needs. That thought made her pulse speed up.

She sighed. This vacation was coming at just the right time. She glanced at Bruno.

"We have a lot to think about, you and me. You found a girl-friend and me a family. One thing is for sure, I will take my time before committing to marriage. I want my next one to be my last."

Her voice of reason was barely winning out over her emotions. In less than a day, she had come to feel a yearning to be part of his family, to have someone to love and to be loved. *I miss them already.*

When she got back to her apartment, its sharp-angled white walls and expansive, high ceilings appeared cold and stark compared to the warm mahogany beams and curved arches in Robert's home. She tried to concentrate on packing for her trip, but her mind kept wandering back to the night before, in bed with a lover who was gentle and adoring. *I never felt so compatible with Carlo, even during the early days of our marriage. I wonder if there is any way I can shorten my trip out west.*

• •

At the San Francisco airport, her parents greeted her and filled her in on family happenings, the winery, and the restaurant. She had not seen them for several months, not since she had made a quick trip there on Mother's Day weekend.

"How are the grapes doing this year?" Sophia asked.

"The weather has been cooperating, and the crop is ready to be harvested. It seems our remote winery has been found," her father boasted. "Day-trippers are coming from all over the area. Joe is working with an architect to design an inn to be built next to the restaurant that will accommodate guests from farther away, although besides drinking wine and eating Italian food, there's not much else to do."

"Hmm. Some activity that the families can enjoy outdoors. What about building a miniature golf course next to the inn?" Sophia suggested.

"That is a great idea. It would be fun for kids as well as grown-ups, and it wouldn't cost that much to build. That, along with the hiking trails and the inn's swimming pool, should keep the visitors entertained."

"So what is new in your life? Besides your being unemployed," her mother asked. "Any beaus coming around?"

Sophia knew this line of questioning was coming. She didn't want to lie, so she tried to keep her answers somewhat vague.

"Saturday, I was in Eastport, Connecticut, visiting a former colleague's new law firm. He invited me to lunch at his home, and we went for a sail afterward."

"Oh," said her father, who loved sailing, "what type of sailboat?"

"A Pearson 30. Very sleek and trim. It brought back memories of our sails off Santa Margherita."

Her father chuckled. "Such carefree days back then in Italy."

"Just the two of you in the boat?" her mother inquired.

Sophia took a deep breath. She had to answer truthfully.

"No, he brought along his daughter. He's divorced and has custody, so there were three of us."

"Why would he have custody? Is his wife unfit?"

"His ex-wife left him shortly after the baby was born. She decided she was not meant to be a mother."

"Oh, the poor little girl. When was that?"

Silence.

Her mother turned back to look at Sophia, who was staring out of the rear window. "Sophia?"

"Six years ago." It came out in a whisper. The rest of the car ride was in silence.

Maria and Giorgio Bellini lived in a well-appointed home near the family vineyard. It was spacious and aesthetically pleasing, having secluded spaces in which to read or converse in private. Sophia had always loved its warmth and charm, decorated with pastoral landscape watercolors and antique wine bottle collections. Her parents were always busy with some activity, either work or hobbies. They kept abreast of their children's lives and doted on their grandchildren.

Sophia found herself talking about Robert during casual conversations with her father and mother.

"His demeanor is so calm and steady, unlike Carlo's."

"When we talk, we have so much to say to each other, not just because we are both lawyers, but because we enjoy the same things—cooking, sailing, hiking, pets."

"He and Bruno bonded instantly."

"He has an easy laugh."

"I feel as though I know Robert better after only one day together than I knew Carlo after being with him a whole year."

Her father and mother sat back and listened contentedly, pleased that she had found a reason to smile again.

*****

Weeks later, near the end of her visit, she found herself alone, deep in thought, on the terrace of the family home that faced east toward the Rocky Mountains. She had been to her gynecologist the day before to find out why she had not gotten her monthly period, only spots of blood on her panties. The doctor had examined her and performed several tests to be sure, the results of which she had just learned during a phone call minutes ago.

Her mother came out and sat across from her in an opposing lounge chair.

"Something is on your mind. What's wrong?" Maria Bellini asked, showing concern for her only daughter.

Sunlight made Sophia's dark hair shimmer, and her tanned skin glow. She appeared to be the picture of health. Sophia turned her head away.

"I know you, my dear." Maria stared at her firstborn, who had accomplished so much in her professional career but who had suffered so much in her private life. "You are in the throes of a decision, aren't you?"

"It's worse than you can imagine, Mom," Sophia confided. "I just learned that I am pregnant!"

"Oh, dear," her mother gasped. "I thought that was impossible."

"Apparently one chance in a thousand is still possible." She closed her eyes. "How could I have been so stupid? Robert asked me if he needed a condom, and I said, 'No, I can't get pregnant.'"

"How far along are you?"

"We were together just that one night, the Saturday before I arrived here. Then I missed my period, which never happens. I went to my gynecologist, thinking it was easily explainable, maybe the stress I have been under at work. She was just as surprised but wanted to be sure."

Never had Maria imagined that her cautious, disciplined thirty-seven-year-old daughter had been careless.

"Have you told Robert?"

"God, no! Not yet. I just found out. We've only worked together. We've never dated. I've always liked him, but until that weekend, I've only been with him professionally, never socially, not even at office parties or picnics, which neither of us ever attended."

"What did the gynecologist say exactly?"

"She believes that my chances of getting pregnant are still one in a thousand. She thinks this is the exception."

"So you may never get pregnant again."

"Exactly." Sophia looked at her mother in anguish. "I can't abort it. I just can't. I have always wanted a child—at least one—and this is it, if it lives." She shuddered, having finally said out loud her worst fear.

"Don't even go there. Of course, it will live." She was surprised that Sophia was comparing her current pregnancy to her earlier one. *She has always been confident and forward-thinking. The baby's death is still haunting her,* Maria thought.

"Robert may think I tricked him into getting me pregnant. This might change the whole dynamic of our relationship," she groaned, pulling at strands of her dark hair, as if wanting to punish herself.

"You must tell him." Maria's voice was soft but firm. "He has a right to know that he will be fathering a child."

"Yes. I will tell him, but it will be my decision alone as to whether this fetus lives. The doctor said there is a higher risk that it may have some abnormalities, given my age. My remaining eggs are older, and unlike aged wine, they do not improve. If the fetus is normal, I am going to have it, even if I have to raise it by myself."

"Whatever decision you make, we will support you, and if Robert loves you, he will want to marry you. Do you feel you know him well enough to marry him?"

She hadn't told her mother that he had already proposed. It was still unreal to her.

"I don't know. Not really. I do feel very comfortable with him. When we talk, we each listen to what the other says. And he never seems to get rattled. He said that he hardly dated anyone in the six years that he has been without a wife. He was wary of making another mistake after his wife left him. That says a lot about the kind of man he is." She closed her eyes. "I still can't believe I got pregnant from being with him just one night."

"Sophia, were you in bed with him the entire night?"

She nodded.

"Then it is not that surprising. Will you call and tell him?"

"No, this is too important to say over the phone. I will wait until I get back to New York. I'll have to tell him the details of how my first pregnancy ended in order to explain why I thought I couldn't get pregnant. I'm dreading it."

"Yes, that will be difficult," said her mother, thinking again of Sophia's trauma and subsequent depression. She continued, "But with this pregnancy, either he says he is in love with you and will marry you, or he doesn't believe the child is his. That can be proven, of course, but you wouldn't want to enter into a marriage based on a paternity test. You'll be leaving for New Mexico tomorrow and then back to New York. We may not see you again until…the birth of your child." She leaned over to hold her daughter's hand. "Take your time and think things through. Perhaps you need to see more of Robert before you decide what to do."

Sophia put her head down, thinking of their lovemaking, and how easily they had shared their personal histories the night before, in her penthouse.

"When he stayed over in my apartment, we talked well into the night about ourselves. We laughed and commiserated over our successes and failures. It was so relaxing and satisfying to have a man listen to me and confirm how I felt. We understood each other on a deeper level than I had thought possible. But to marry him so soon? And with Robert will come a child of six, another on the way, a mother-in-law next door, and a law office that will be our common workplace. It will be a lot to manage."

"Tell me more about his daughter," her mother asked. She wondered if Sophia was emotionally ready to raise another woman's child.

Sophia's eyes lit up. "You'd love her. She's cute, clever, spirited, and outspoken. And she is enthusiastic about sailing. I handed her the wheel and told her the basics of how the wind in the sail makes the boat move. She was sitting on my lap and afterward, and she scrunched in my arms and slept. It felt so…natural." She shook her head, trying to push away bad memories. "Oh, she saw my nipple and wanted to know what it was."

"She has a lot to learn about the female body and about life, and you'd have to teach her. You don't have a blank slate to start with either. She must hurt inside to see other mothers walk their children to and from school. I wonder how she gets on with other kids."

"I have no idea. She'll be going into second grade. Classes will have already begun when I see her again."

*****

The next day, Sophia flew to Santa Fe, New Mexico, and had a joyous reunion with her college roommate, Dolores. A Latina by birth and an artist by nature, she had made her mark on the art world from her little corner of the Southwest. Dolores loved life—dancing, entertaining, feasting. If she went anywhere by herself, within minutes, the space she was in filled up with admiring strangers. Sophia expected a whirlwind few days of activity.

Dolores greeted her like a sister, smothering her in kisses and going on about the latest trends in art, new Latin dances, and her lover, Ricardo.

When things settled down after a delicious meal of black bean soup, bison steak with grilled corn salsa and rice, Dolores noticed that her friend had not touched her wine.

"Why aren't you drinking?" she asked. "You're not pregnant," she joked.

"Actually, I am," Sophia responded.

"No! Tell me the tale," she begged.

When Sophia finished, Dolores said simply, "You realize that this is meant to be."

"If it is meant to be, why don't I feel better? I don't know Robert well at all."

"Don't be silly. You cannot see the trees for the forest—or is it the other way round? You say that you hardly know this Robert, but you do know him. Working side by side for six years? Nobody can hide their true personality for that long. Robert Navarro? He's Spanish, no?"

"His ancestors. Yes."

"There are two types of Spanish men, the conservative, proper type who do everything by the book, and the flashy, fun-loving type. Your Robert is not for me—too reserved and steady, but for you, he is perfect. And this girl, this Cat, she is what you lost and have found again. You see that, don't you?"

Sophia stared at her.

"Tell me, when you are with Cat, how do you feel? Happy or sad, eh?"

"Happy," Sophia admitted.

"See. God has put them in your lap. Don't throw away what is there, waiting for you to love them back."

"I am sure that Cat is going to test me when I ask her to do something, just as she tests Robert."

"He's a man. What does he know about raising a girl? You are clever. You have studied human behavior. Already you have passed the first test. She wants you to be her mother. All the rest will come easy compared to that!"

Dolores had a way of making hard decisions seem simple. She could cut through the fog and come out the other side in a bright light.

Am I too emotionally involved to be able to stand back and separate fact from fluff, to get to the crux of the matter? She tried to look at her situation analytically. *I have always been attracted to Robert. Fact. Spending the day and night with him was very pleasurable. Fact. His mother may be a meddler. Not likely. His associate Sam doesn't much like me. Fact! And very likely to hurt my success at the law firm. I will have a daughter who accepts me as her mother. Hmm. That is yet to be tested.*

MANHATTAN, AUGUST 27 TO 29

With Dolores's approval lifting up her spirits, Sophia flew home to Manhattan, landing at the airport on Thursday evening. As soon as she walked into her penthouse, she opened her iPhone and punched in Robert's number. They had decided that, because of the time difference and their schedules, they would not call each other during her absence but only communicate by texting. Sophia said that she needed time to step back and reflect on their sudden intimacy.

Robert concurred: "We can go slowly, if that's what you want."

Now when she heard Robert's voice on the other end of the line, her heart warmed.

"I just got back. How are you and Cat?"

"Miserable. Just waiting for you. When can you get here?"

"I want to meet you for lunch tomorrow, maybe halfway."

He was immediately suspicious. "You sound tense. Are you leaving me for another man?" he asked, only half joking.

"No," she said lightly. "It's nothing like that, but I do want to tell you a few things about myself, face-to-face." She was trying to keep her voice calm while a flood of anxiety washed over her.

"Like what? Sophia, give me a hint."

"For one thing, about the scar on my abdomen and something else that you need to know. *No more questions.*"

There was silence at the other end.

"Please, Robert," she whispered.

"Just one more. Do you love me?"

She paused. They had been together socially for one day and physically for one night. *How can he ask me that so soon?*

"I love everything about you in the short time we have really gotten to know each other." No response. "Robert, the truth is I have missed you and Cat, and I do want to see you again—as a friend and as a lover—if that's what you are worried about. But I need to tell you something that may affect our relationship."

"Okay. Where and when?"

*****

They met at a restaurant midway between their two homes, in hot, humid, wet weather.

Robert arrived ahead of Sophia and was waiting for her in the foyer. Sophia had chosen to wear a gray pantsuit with a white top, subdued colors that matched her mood. Robert stood alone, his navy blue jersey accentuating his tanned skin and sandy hair. Sophia noticed women staring at him. She felt a pang of jealousy. As she drew near to him, he held out his arms, and they embraced, kissing in front of a large group of waiting patrons.

"You look ravishing," he teased. He held her close, as if he were afraid she was going to disappear. It felt so good to have her back.

She clung to him, basking in the strength of his arms. Neither had thought of making reservations, and for some reason, the restaurant was crowded.

Sophia bit her lip. "Could we talk in your car?" she whispered in his ear. "I'd rather say what's on my mind in private."

When they had settled into his Lexus, she looked at him anxiously and began.

"First I want to tell you about the scar on my abdomen. This is not going to be easy for me. Please wait until I finish before you speak."

"Okay," he agreed, feeling her discomfort.

"I got married to Carlo within a year of my meeting him. I thought we had a lot in common, coming from similar backgrounds. Things went well until I began to press him to have children. We had agreed that I would take the pill until we were both ready. A year went by, and Carlo said it was still not the right time. He gave no good reason. We were both financially comfortable and were getting along well, or so I thought.

"I was twenty-nine and I did not want to wait any longer, so I went off the pill without telling him, figuring that he would accept my decision, eventually. Well, I got pregnant right away. Then I was afraid to tell him, knowing that he might pressure me to get an abortion.

"After three months, I was starting to show a little, and I decided I had to tell him. He went crazy, screaming at me to abort. I said it was too late. He began having very hurtful sex with me, as if he wanted to destroy the fetus in my womb. Finally he gave up and started drinking heavily. We slept apart.

"Months went by, and nothing changed, except that I heard he was seeing other women. When I began to have labor pains, I went into my bedroom and locked the door and waited until they were a few minutes apart. I called for an ambulance because I didn't trust Carlo to drive me to the hospital. A short time later, I came out of my room into the kitchen and saw him, bleary-eyed with a glass of Scotch in his hand. I told him an ambulance was coming."

Confusing thoughts were going through Robert's head. *She was pregnant! She told me she had no children. Where is her child? How could she fall for this guy?*

She looked out the window at the rain still beating down, as if hell was pouring out its wrath upon the earth with water rather than fire. The humidity in the car was making her perspire, her gray pant-suit sticking to her, adding to her unease. *Now comes the hardest part.*

Sophia braced herself. Her arms were tight around her body. She told it in gasps and sobs, trying to suppress the memory of her pain. Then her voice became calmer.

"Carlo ran out, and in walked the ETs. On the way to the hospital, I delivered a beautiful girl, who was perfect—except, except for the deep gash in her head."

She heard Robert moan, but she dared not look at him. She needed to finish. She took a deep breath and said the next words in a rush.

"I demanded that they give me the baby, and I held her on my chest and talked to her until her heart stopped."

The tension in her body lessened. The worst was over.

Robert wrapped his arms around her. "Oh, Sophia." He was crying too.

A calmness came over her, and she spoke matter-of-factly. "If she had lived, she would be six years old now," wiping tears away.

He thought back to his mother's words about her needing Cat.

"Sophia, what you experienced was pure hell."

She turned to face him and put her finger to his lips. "I'm not through. I have something else to tell you that may make you angry with me."

She took yet another deep breath, thinking this may destroy any future hope of a relationship.

"During my recovery, my doctor told me that, due to the damage to my female organs and birth canal, there was only one chance in a thousand that I could ever be pregnant again. *One chance in a thousand!* So when I told you that I could not get pregnant, I believed it.

"Robert, I just learned that I am pregnant with our child, and however you feel about it, I intend to keep it. I will raise it on my own if I have to, and I will not hold you responsible for its support." She put her head down. "I did not try to deceive you, honestly."

"Are you finished?" His voice was shaking.

"Yes." She held her breath.

He held her tight and whispered, "How could you possibly think that I do not want a child by you? I am thrilled, and Cat will be over the moon. This means we must get married right away." He took a small box out of his pocket and gave it to her. "I had already planned to give you this when you returned. It is my grandmother's engagement ring, but I think it will double as a wedding ring."

She opened the box and stared at a large round diamond with rubies encircling it.

"It's stunning."

"The rubies are for love and the diamond for strength, the two things I want to give you in our marriage." He took it out of the box and placed it on her ring finger. "Sophia Bellini Sbaglione, will you marry me—today?"

"What! Marriage is not something to enter into hastily. I'm not ready. I need time."

He rushed on as if he had not heard a word she said. "I am sure I can arrange it. I am well-connected in the Manhattan courts. It will be a civil marriage. If you want to have a church wedding, we can do that later. We'll get married today, and you can move in with me afterward."

"Robert, this is crazy. I can't marry you today, never mind move in with you on such short notice."

"Of course, you can. Think of how Cat will react when I tell her that you are her mother—well, stepmother."

"I need to think all of this through. About marrying you and what I will do with my apartment. I need time to sort this all out."

"So go back to your apartment and settle the details. Bring whatever you can fit in your car. How much time do you need? A day or two?"

"Mamma mia! You are like Cat, persistent in getting your way."

He laughed. "It will be better if we are married before you move in with us. Otherwise, Cat will have lots of questions. I can wait a few more days before you are back with me, permanently."

"You are really serious about this, aren't you?" She stared at him, amazed that he was so confident about their relationship after so short a duration.

"Yes. I felt certain when we kissed on your terrace. I have never felt so positive about anything. You know, my mother gave me some advice after my first marriage failed. She said, 'Next time, marry a woman who knows how to smile.' Do you know you smile a lot when you talk to Cat and my mother and anyone you meet, even Sam? It's like your calling card. It makes you beautiful on the inside as well as the out."

Sophia sighed. *What a lovely thing to say. What should I do? Marry him on the spur of the moment? There must be another way.*

"Robert, what if we just date a while and get to know each other better?"

"If you weren't pregnant, I would agree, but I want our child to be born with a mother and a father who live together. Don't you?"

Sophia could only nod.

"And Cat needs a mother, and she wants you."

Sophia's eyes glazed over. *He is pulling on the heartstring that really matters to me—giving Cat a mother.*

Robert saw her deliberating. "Look, you have known me for six years. We are not exactly strangers. We always enjoyed working together, right?"

Sophia agreed. "But Robert, this is much more serious than a workplace relationship."

"What I am trying to say is how we feel about each other deep down. We clicked from the first day we met. The only way that two people really get to know each other is by living together. Marry me today, and let's get to know each other as man and wife."

She looked down at the ring on her finger. *He was going to propose before he knew I was pregnant.*

"Well, you make an excellent case for us marrying now." She paused. *I made the mistake of not asking him to use protection. I have to accept that and live with the consequences. What did my father say? "Next time marry a man who makes you smile." He does make me smile.*

There was still one nagging thought. "Robert, Carlo lied to me and cheated on me. If you ever did either one of those things, I—"

"Stop!" His voice became tender. "It took me six years to find you, and I'd be crazy to lose you by doing either of those things." His hand was stroking her cheek. "I promise to be a man you will always be proud to say is your husband."

Her remaining doubts dissolved away.

"All right, I will marry you today," she whispered, not believing the words coming out of her mouth.

His smile was huge. "That's settled. Now I need to make a few calls. I will get a judge to waive the twenty-four-hour waiting period after we get the marriage license so we can marry this afternoon. Not a problem."

*****

They married at a courthouse with two witnesses—a bailiff and a stenographer who knew Robert. It was over and done, without any fanfare. They kissed goodbye, rather quickly since Robert had to pick up Cat from school. Sophia headed back to her apartment to pack, while Robert drove back to Eastport to prepare for Sophia's arrival.

On the way home, Sophia called her mother.

"Hi, Mom, I have some news. Robert and I were married this afternoon. He already had an engagement ring in his pocket."

"He was ready to propose to you before learning of the pregnancy? Congratulations! How do you feel?"

"Mostly numb. Anxious. This has all come about so suddenly, and I feel so unprepared. There is much I need to do before I can move into Robert's house."

"Do you know what you will do with your apartment?"

"Not really. I do not want to sell it, not yet anyway. I may rent it to a friend I know. He is an entrepreneur and loves to impress clients when they come to town by arranging for swank accommodations, so it would be a sporadic rental but still something to help cover the costs. And I will have it at times for my own use."

"That sounds perfect. Take care of yourself. You need to find an obstetrician if you do not have one yet."

"I'm working on that. I made a few exploratory visits to websites and plan to call a female ob-gyn on Monday."

"Keep in touch, dear. Let me know what Cat says when she first sees you—as her mother!"

"I will. Love you. Ciao."

*****

Sophia arrived back at her apartment, where Bruno was waiting with the dog walker who had agreed to keep him while she was away.

It took Bruno five minutes to lie down after licking and wagging and barking in greeting. Sophia felt unusually tired and decided to put all the necessary calls off until Saturday morning.

After a simple supper, she snuggled up under the duvet cover on her bed, thinking she would take a nap. *I am alone on my wedding night,* was the last thought she had before falling fast asleep with her clothes on.

She awoke at 2:30 a.m. It was too early to contact anyone, so she took a shower and sat down with a cup of coffee, instead of cappuccino, which was now strangely unappealing, and made lists of everything she needed to do.

*****

Robert had arrived in Eastport just in time to pick up Cat from school, which had started the day before. She immediately asked about Sophia.

"Is she at our house?" Cat wanted to know.

"No, not yet, but she will come tomorrow or Sunday for sure."

"Why can't she come today?" Cat asked.

"Well, she has things to do in her apartment. Listen, I have something to tell you that I know you will like. Sophia and I got married today."

There was no reaction from the back seat. He was turning into their driveway and could not see her face.

Finally, she said, "What does that mean? Is she going to live with us?"

"Yes."

"So where is she?"

This is not going the way I expected, he thought.

"She will be here as soon as she can settle things with her apartment."

"Can we go to see her in her apartment?"

"You'd just be in the way. She has to pack and—"

"I can help her pack."

"Cat, she wouldn't want you there because she is so busy. Sophia and I—your mother and I—got married this afternoon without expecting to. It wasn't planned, so now there are lots of things for her to do."

He got out of the car and opened her door. She climbed out and stomped into the house.

What did I say that upset her? he wondered.

Then he called his mother.

"I took your advice. I did not let Sophia get away. We were married this afternoon."

"What!"

His mother's shock came right through the phone. He moved the phone away from his ear, bracing himself for what her reaction was going to be to his next words.

He continued, "We had to get married, for Cat's sake."

"Robert, you are not making any sense. I remember what I said, but I did not mean a hurried wedding. What was the rush?"

"Sophia is pregnant." There was silence on the other end. "Mom, she thought she couldn't get pregnant again. She had damage to her birth canal from the birth of her first child. She was told it was a one-in-a-thousand possibility." He paused. Still silence on the other end. "The baby is due at the beginning of May."

Margaret considered that news. A horrible thought flashed through her mind. *Was the baby really his?* But she dared not mention it.

"My God, I never thought that you would act so rashly. What happens now?"

"She is settling things at her penthouse in Manhattan and will move here this weekend. I told Cat about our marriage but nothing about the baby. We want to wait until Sophia starts to show."

"How does Sophia feel about this pregnancy?" His mother was trying to make sense of it all.

"She is determined to have the baby, no matter what, even if she has to raise it by herself. Her doctor thinks this is a one-time event, that she'll never be pregnant again."

His mother sighed with relief. *That shines a new light on her pregnancy.*

"I suppose that you have both acted honorably, given the circumstances. It's going to be an adjustment for everyone. Don't expect things to go smoothly at first. Cat has never had a mother, and Sophia has never had a child or one that lived very long. Be prepared for difficulties, Robert. Make it work. And I will help in any way I can."

*****

When Sophia talked to her friend Charles about renting her apartment, he asked if she had checked with the building association to see if that was legal.

"No, but I'm sure it is. Other owners in the building have done it."

"Maybe for a definite term, but we are talking about occasional occupancy. Neither of us wants to break the rules, especially you, being a lawyer. Also, my lawyer will want to draw up a contract with you."

"Of course. You're right. I haven't had time to think things through. I am busy packing because I want to leave here by tomorrow night at the latest. Can we postpone it until later next week?"

"Let me check my schedule." He paused. "I have guests coming in from Geneva on Tuesday. Will it be available to them then?"

Sophia groaned inside, not wanting to pass up this opportunity. "Yes, I am sure that Tuesday will be okay."

"Maybe I can have Tom put together a loose agreement, and we'll work out the details later. How's that?"

"By tomorrow afternoon?" she pleaded.

"Tomorrow is Sunday. He may not want to work then. Let's say by Monday at noon. I'm late for a meeting. Talk to you soon." He hung up.

Sophia's iPhone immediately lit up. It was Robert.

"Hi, Soph. Any regrets?"

She shivered at the word *Soph*. No one ever called her anything but Sophia, her given name.

"Only with the rush for me to leave here. How is Cat? Did you tell her?"

"Yes, yesterday. I tried to call you last night, but there was no answer."

"I was dog-tired. I fell asleep with the phone on silent mode and woke up very early this morning. What did she say?"

"To put it kindly, she was very disappointed that you were not here."

"Damn it. She's not going to like what I tell her now. Put her on."

"Hello, Sophia."

Sophia's heart froze. *I am still Sophia. Of course, what did I expect?*

"Hello, Cat. I missed you."

"Daddy said that you didn't want me to come there to help you pack because I'd be in the way."

Jesus, Robert!

"Well, you won't know what I need to take. I have lots to do before I move into your house."

"When are you coming?"

"I'm not sure," she hedged.

"Today or tomorrow? Which day? You promised me."

"Cat, I will try to get there by tomorrow night, but it may have to be Monday."

"Will you walk me to school on Monday? I called my friends and told them I have a mother now, but some kids didn't believe me."

"I will try to be there in time to walk you to school, but I am not sure I can come that early."

"Please. It's important."

"Cat, I will try." The phone went dead.

"I am going to kill Robert!" Sophia shouted when she closed the phone.

Bruno barked.

"That's right, Bruno, and you are my witness." Bruno pressed his nose against the sofa cushion and studied her.

Sophia texted Robert, "*Please say you did not tell Cat that she would be in the way here!*"

Robert texted back, "*Well, she would, right?*"

Sophia: "*Damn it. You cannot say it to her without her feeling unwanted.*"

Robert: "*I want you! So when do you make your appearance?*"

Sophia: "*To be honest, Monday sometime. I need to pack and put some things in storage. Loving you is not getting easier.*"

Sophia tracked down Tom, and he agreed to write up a preliminary agreement and text it to her by Sunday night.

Beautiful, she thought. *I'm good.*

AUGUST 30 AND 31, SUNDAY TO MONDAY, MANHATTAN AND EASTPORT

The weekend sped by as Sophia changed her mailing address, notified the building association, switched her entry passcode (the dog walker knew it), and contacted the maid to give the unit a thorough cleaning on Monday. She had never rented the unit before. It had been her home for six years, and now she needed to inventory certain expensive items as well as lock up some of her possessions that were to remain there for the time being.

On Sunday night, as promised, Tom texted the initial agreement, which she signed and forwarded to the building association, hoping that they would rush it through for approval. She made food for Bruno to eat for the next several days and packed it in a cooler. She hated store-bought dog food, and the recipe given to her by the vet was easy to prepare.

"Oh, the vet! I will have to have Bruno's records sent to the vet that Robert uses for Kit." More emails to write. And so went the rest of the night. It was after twelve by the time she undressed and fell into bed.

In the morning, her alarm went off at 5:30. Thinking she had plenty of time to shower, dress, and eat breakfast before driving to Eastport in time to walk Cat to school, she moved at her normal pace. About 6:15, her phone rang. It was Robert.

"Are you on your way?"

"No. I was planning to leave by 6:45."

"You'll be cutting it close."

"Why? The traffic is coming into the city at this hour, and I'll be leaving."

"Yes, but at some crossroads, the red lights on your side stay on a long time to allow cross traffic coming into the city to get through. I should have told you earlier."

"Yes, you should have. So I'm already behind schedule!"

She hung up the phone and doubled her pace. She left at 6:35, hoping to be at Robert's by eight and walk or drive Cat to school. There were delays because of a car accident. Her car pulled into his driveway at 8:10. Robert texted that he had dropped Cat off at school and went straight to the law office, and from there, he was heading to court. He was expected to be gone all day.

She let herself in with the house key Robert had given her. Sophia was angry at herself, at Robert, and even a little at Cat. *I am sure that eventually this will not be a big deal, but it is a terrible way to begin motherhood.*

She made numerous trips from her car to the house, carrying clothes, toiletries, family albums, lawbooks, all the items that defined her life. Robert's house felt so cozy compared to her penthouse, and she immediately felt at home there. She went from room to room, acquainting herself with the layout.

The terrace was especially beautiful, with wildflowers covering the slope all the way down to the shore. Columbines, sunflowers, asters, and milkweed bloomed in clusters, gracing the landscape with their colors and shapes. Her eyes stopped at the sofa where she and Robert had been intimate, greedily satisfying themselves for several hours after years of being alone. The thought of them together inflamed her desire once more. *I'll be with him tonight.*

She was heading for a comfortable lounge chair that was too cozy to pass up, hoping to relax a bit before lunch, when her iPhone rang. It was Robert. *Now what?* she thought.

"Soph, I just got a call from the school. Cat has been involved in some sort of incident at recess, and she is in the principal's office. They asked me to come there because she is being uncooperative.

Can you go and sort it out? I know this is a lot to ask, but I'd rather not have to send my mother. She has a doctor's appointment now."

"I don't think I have a choice."

"Thanks. Gotta go. The judge just entered the courtroom."

*****

After googling its location, Sophia decided to walk the mile and a quarter to the school to give herself a chance to think about how she would deal with Cat. *It must be pretty serious if they are keeping a six-year-old in the principal's office.* She took Bruno along. He had not had his daily walk. When she arrived at the school, she tied his leash to a railing by the building entrance, where there was shade.

Then she walked into the principal's outer office and introduced herself.

"I am Robert Navarro's wife, Sophia. I am here to see my—my daughter Caterina." *I refuse to say stepdaughter.*

The secretary looked at her, surprised.

"Yes, of course. Mrs. Benson is expecting you. Go right in." And she reached for her iPhone.

Sophia paused momentarily before opening the door. She glanced back at the secretary, who was already engrossed in passing along the news of Sophia's arrival. *This is it,* Sophia thought. *My second test.*

Cat was sitting in a chair, arms crossed, with a long pout on her face. Her dark eyes stared down at her feet, her body rigid. Mrs. Benson was busy at her desk, writing.

"Hi, Cat," she said softly.

Cat glared at her, not responding. Tears spilled out, and she quickly wiped them away with her sleeve.

"Mrs. Benson, I am Sophia, Caterina's mother."

Mrs. Benson stood up and shook her hand.

"Well, I am pleased to meet you. We were unaware that Mr. Navarro had remarried. Please take a seat."

"We were just married this weekend," she said, sitting next to Cat, who was now staring straight ahead.

"Congratulations."

Mrs. Benson picked up the phone and pressed a button.

"Hold all calls," she said into the phone. Then she turned to Sophia. "Caterina told her friends that, and some of them didn't believe her. She got into a fight with a boy in the playground. I have asked her to apologize since it is clear that she started the fight, but she refuses. I will not allow her to return to class until she does."

Her tone was pleasant but firm. As she spoke, Sophia studied her. She wore a pale gray suit, a bright blue blouse, small pearl earrings, and a wedding ring. Her short hair was brushed back in soft waves, covering her ears. To Sophia, she looked and sounded professional.

"I see." Sophia leaned toward her daughter, whose hands were balled up. "Please tell me what happened, Cat."

Cat scowled at her. "I didn't start it. Billy started it. He called me a liar when I told him I had a mother." She pulled her blue cotton jumper down so that it covered her knees. *Her dress is too small for her,* Sophia observed. *She has outgrown it.*

"And then what happened?" Sophia asked, her mind back to the current problem.

"I punched him in the face." Her words burst out, and more tears welled up.

Sophia leaned back and considered that.

"I can understand why you were angry," she said quietly. "You knew what you said was true, but hitting a person is wrong."

"He was wrong too. I wasn't lying." Cat pushed back.

"Hitting him will not change how he thinks, Cat. He has not seen proof that you have a mother."

"You promised to come back by Sunday, so it's your fault. I hate you!"

The principal began to admonish her. "Caterina, that—"

But Sophia waved her off. She looked at Cat, a girl whose mother had left her at infancy, a girl who did nothing to deserve her present situation. *It was stupid of me to make that promise to her. It is my own fault.*

85

"Hmm. That is too bad," she said sadly, "because I love you, Cat, no matter what you do or say. I will always love you." She paused and then added, "And I will never leave you."

The words stayed in the air, hovering, refusing to disappear.

Cat stared down at the floor. Her young heart was torn between love and hate, desperately wanting a mother—*this* mother—and feeling shamed by her absence earlier.

"You promised," she whimpered. Her lower lip trembled.

Sophia thought of all the reasons she could give as to why she was late: Closing up her apartment, sorting out the legalities of renting, discontinuing services, traffic lights, accidents—all beyond her control and none of which a six-year-old would understand or accept.

"Yes, I did, and I am sorry. I was wrong to make you that promise. I hope you can forgive me."

The silence was broken only by the ticking of the clock. Mrs. Benson had stopped breathing. Cat sniffled.

Sophia reached out to touch Cat's hand.

"I am ready to be your mother if you will have me."

Cat raised her head a little. Tears streamed down her cheeks. "Okay," the word came out in a sob. She buried her face in Sophia's chest.

Sophia wrapped her arms around her and then wiped away her tears with her hand. Mrs. Benson held up a box of Kleenex.

"Does anyone else need a tissue?"

When all three occupants in the office had composed themselves, Sophia said, "There is still the matter of an apology. Mrs. Benson, I believe Cat is ready to apologize. I want to be present so Billy can see for himself how wrong he was. Is that okay?"

"Yes, that will certainly clear the air. Caterina, are you ready?"

Cat nodded.

When the trio walked into Cat's classroom, it became quiet instantly. Sophia studied the rows of students, mostly seven-year-olds, full of energy and mischief and curiosity. *How taxing it must be to keep them engaged for the entire school day,* she thought.

Mrs. Benson said, "Class, this is Caterina's mother."

Since Sophia had not used the word *stepmother*, neither did she. The children's eyes opened wide at the tall attractive woman smiling at them.

"It is nice to meet you. I was delayed and therefore was not able to walk Cat to school today, but I will be doing so from now on."

Cat was beaming, enjoying the kids' reactions, including Betty Wyman, Sam's daughter.

Mrs. Benson introduced Sophia to Cat's teacher, Miss Creighton.

"You have a superwoman's job teaching so many lively children," Sophia told her. "I admire you."

Miss Creighton, fresh out of college, said, "The children and I are learning together."

Mrs. Benson turned to Cat. "Caterina, I believe you have something to say to Billy."

"Billy, I apologize for punching you in the face," Cat said. She looked truly sorry.

Billy fidgeted. All the kids were waiting for him to say something. A slight red mark on his cheek was visible. Finally, he mumbled, "It's okay."

"Well, I must leave now. Our dog is waiting outside. Cat, I'll see you when school is over." She bent down and kissed her on the cheek.

When she and Mrs. Benson were alone in the corridor, the principal said, "I have a question to ask you. Are you a psychologist?"

Sophia smiled. "No, I am a lawyer."

"Well, your handling of that situation was masterful. I think you could teach some of my staff a thing or two."

*****

On her walk home, Sophia texted Dolores, relating what had just taken place: "*You said the rest of the tests were going to be easy!*"

Dolores texted back: "*Eh, what do I know about six-year-olds? You passed the second test, so stop complaining.*"

Then she called her mother.

"Practically the first words out of Cat's mouth were, 'I hate you.'" She went on to describe the rest of the meeting.

"Sophia, you did marvelously. What a gift you have for saying exactly the right words. I'll bet you could use a strong drink."

"Yes, but given my condition—"

"Oh dear, how did I forget that? Make yourself a cup of tea and put your feet up. The rest of the day will go smoother."

Sophia gave Bruno a treat before she made herself a salad and tea. "I will have to do some food shopping tomorrow, Bruno. There is room for improvement in this refrigerator."

The liquor bar that held various wines and spirits stared back at her while she ate. *It is tempting, but nothing is going to harm this fetus if I can help it.* She lay on the lounge chair and closed her eyes and woke up an hour later. She glanced at her phone. No calls. *Great! School lets out in an hour.*

The second walk she and Bruno made to the school went more quickly, and they arrived ahead of the dismissal. She decided to introduce herself to the other waiting parents, mostly mothers.

"So Caterina really does have a mother," remarked Thea Wyman, Sam's wife, sounding disappointed. "How strange that Robert never mentioned that he was getting remarried. After our lovely Catherine left him so quickly, we all thought he was not the marrying kind."

Sophia's back went up. She stared at this woman whose words felt like a slap. Thea's voice was shrill, like it was coming out of a loudspeaker. *She has a face like a bird, with a sharp nose and small mouth, no chest, and a small bump on her stomach.* Thea wore a blue, green, and golden brown silk outfit like a peacock. Her platinum blond coiffure and her designer heels screamed wealth and status. *Apparently her blue blood has even bubbled up into her eyeballs.*

Sophia decided to play with her, to let slip some innuendos that she knew this type of woman lived for. She smiled mysteriously. "Actually, Robert and I have been casual friends for over six years but only recently fell in love."

"Really? How unusual." Thea's thin lips curled into a smirk. "You're going to need a firm hand to control Caterina. She has the reputation of being a spitfire. Punching a boy! Really!"

Sophia's bile rose higher. *She already knows about this morning's incident! The tweeting must have started as soon as recess was over, probably by the school secretary.*

"My daughter doesn't lash out unless she is provoked," she said in Cat's defense.

Their conversation was overheard by a grandmother nearby. "I don't remember Margaret Navarro saying anything about a wedding. I'm surprised she never mentioned it. Poor Catherine. It was never really clear to any of us what made her run off, as if she just had to get away from something," offered the older woman with silvery blue hair, wearing jeans and pearls.

Yes, her own daughter! And who picks up a child dressed in pearls?

"It is a second marriage for both of us, so we kept it small," she replied.

Shouldn't the dismissal bell have rung by now? She glanced at her watch. Five more minutes.

Before anyone had a chance to ask how small, she said, "My dog doesn't like to sit for very long. I need to walk him around a bit. Nice meeting you."

She had covered the length of the school building and was heading back to where the women were still waiting, watching, and whispering, when the school bell rang and kids burst out of the main door. Bruno was startled and started to bark.

"It's alright, Bruno. Look for Cat. She will be here any minute."

Some mothers were waving and calling their kids over. Sophia decided not to. *She'll see me. I am taller than the others.*

She and Bruno waited, searching the stampeding herd for Cat. Bruno saw her first and barked. And then she emerged from the cluster of kids, walking toward them like a proper young lady.

A boy shouted to her, "Who are you gonna punch tomorrow, Cat?"

She ignored him and kept walking. "Hi, Mummy!"

This time the greeting was unexpected. A visible shiver went through Sophia's body. *I really do have a daughter.* She put her arm around Cat, and together they walked home, with Bruno leading the way, by now familiar with the route.

As they proceeded along Ocean Drive, Sophia asked, "Did Daddy help you to get dressed this morning?"

"Yes, he picked this jumper for me to wear."

"It seems too small for you."

"I told Daddy I needed some bigger dresses, but he said it looked okay. He doesn't know anything about what clothes I need."

"Well, I do. From now on, I am going to help you pick a school outfit each morning, and on Saturday, let's go clothes shopping and buy you some new things."

"Will you let me choose what I want?" she asked excitedly. "Daddy and Grandma bring home clothes for me so I don't get to pick."

"Yes, but I will be there to give you advice."

Cat leaned her head against Sophia's body and smiled.

In Cat's bedroom, where Sophia was helping Cat change out of her school outfit, they had a discussion about consequences. Cat had brought it up first.

"Is Daddy going to punish me?" she asked.

"I don't know. I have not spoken to him since this morning."

It suddenly occurred to her that disciplining Cat might get controversial. Who was to do it? One or both of them? And if they disagreed, what then?

"The good thing is that you apologized. I am sure he'll take that into consideration. One thing I do know is that you must tell him exactly what happened."

"Why?"

"Because he is your father and has a right to know. Please put your dirty clothes in the hamper. Today has been tiring, and I refuse to make supper. Let's order something and have it delivered. What would you like?"

"Pizza."

"Fine. I'll order a pizza and a salad. And for dessert?"

"Chocolate chip cookies!"

"I should have guessed. Okay, but next time, I want you to choose different things."

"Why?"

"Because I want you to taste other foods." Her voice became mysterious. "You may decide you like something else better, like octopus or snails."

"Yuck!"

Sophia smiled. "I bet someday when I cook octopus, you will ask for more."

"You cook octopus?"

"I grew up on seafood. My family lived near the sea in Italy, and we had fish often."

"Tell me a story about your family."

"Okay, as soon as I order the food."

*****

When Robert arrived home about five, there was no one to greet him at the door. He walked into his bedroom and found them stretched out on the bed with photo albums about.

Sophia looked up at him and smiled. "I am showing Cat photos of my family."

"What a lovely sight," he responded.

She got up off the bed and kissed him.

"How was your day in court?"

"Good. The jury members have been chosen. The trial starts tomorrow with opening statements. And how was your day?"

"Busy. Are you hungry?"

"Famished. I made reservations at Dario's Restaurant for six p.m. I thought we'd celebrate."

"Cancel them. Supper is on the table."

His eyes lit up. "I didn't expect you to cook after all the moving you had to do today."

"I didn't. I ordered out and had Cat pick the menu for tonight."

He frowned. She gave him a peck.

"Pizza, salad, and cookies. It could be worse. Come and eat."

They moved into the dining room, took their seats, and immediately attacked the pizza.

Sophia caught Robert's eye and winked. "We need to fill you in on the day's happenings, and then we'll have an early night."

"What's an early night?" asked Cat.

Sophia smiled. "It means that after supper, you are going to do the homework that Mrs. Benson assigned you, take a bath, get into your pajamas, and go to sleep."

"And what are you and Daddy going to do?"

"We have work to do as well. The briefcase that your father carries has papers that he has to study for trial. I still have to do some unpacking and emails to send. Oh, God! I forgot to call the ob-gyn doctor."

"What's that?" asked Cat.

Robert interrupted, "You don't have to answer all her questions, Sophia."

Sophia gave him a withering look that said, "*Don't tell me what to say.*"

"But I do! I am trying to build a relationship with my daughter. It is going to take time, and I will decide how I go about it." She stared at Robert, daring him to contradict her.

Robert shrugged. "Fine."

She turned to Cat. "I have to see a doctor who checks a woman's body to be sure everything is working properly. When you are a grown woman, you will need to be checked as well. It doesn't hurt, so it's not a big deal. Now, before dessert, Cat is going to explain about the incident at school."

"I forgot about that. What happened?"

Cat had rehearsed the story. "I told Billy that I had a mother, and he called me a liar. That made me angry, so I punched him in the face."

"Cat!" Robert scolded.

Sophia said, "Finish the story. Why were you in the principal's office?"

"Because I wouldn't apologize, but Mummy told me that punching him won't make him believe me, so I apologized. Mrs. Benson told me to write down what I learned about hitting kids. That's my homework."

"Good," said Robert. "The punishment fits the crime."

"What crime?" asked Cat.

"It's just an expression," Sophia answered. "And now for dessert." She produced a platter of monster-size cookies.

Robert's iPhone jingled. "Yes, Mom. Come over now. We are having dessert."

Margaret stayed only a short time, wanting to congratulate them on their marriage. Since Cat was listening, she did not bring up the pregnancy.

When Margaret got up to leave, Sophia walked her to the door and mentioned that she had told a few parents at Cat's school about their marriage.

"I said it was a small wedding and rushed away before they could ask for details. One of the mothers was Thea Wyman."

"In that case, Facebook must have crashed from the posts, not only about your wedding but about the scuffle Cat had."

"That news did travel at warp speed. Thea mentioned it to me at dismissal."

"I'm not surprised. It's the curse of living in a small town. Well, you certainly had a baptism of fire today. Tomorrow will be better."

"Thank you for your support, Margaret." Sophia's face flushed. "I did not envision Robert and my relationship to move along this quickly. I should have taken precautions when Robert and I were together." She sighed. "I thought I was unable to bear children, but I was wrong." She paused. "Robert and I have a lot to learn about each other, as well as my getting to know Cat."

"I am happy for you both, although it was a shock when Robert told me that he had married. You did the right thing. I will try not to be underfoot, unless or until you need me."

*****

That night, as they got into bed, Robert said, "Cat was very upset when I dropped her off at school. I thought she would be angry with you today."

"She was. When I first saw her, she said she hated me." And Sophia filled him in on the details of their encounter.

"You are a clever woman."

"Not clever enough. I slept alone on my wedding night!"

"Funny thing. So did I."

"We have a lot of catching up to do. I hope you are not too tired," she whispered.

"Tomorrow morning I may be, but tonight I intend to ravish you."

"Again?" She smiled. "You better keep your word."

SEPTEMBER

LAW OFFICES OF WYMAN, BLAKE AND NAVARRO

The next day, Sophia pulled up in front of the cement block law office building about eleven o'clock. She had awoken at six, in time to shower, dress, and walk Cat to school, accompanied by Bruno. There were still some matters that she needed to attend to before heading to work. At the top of her list was calling the obstetrician to make an appointment. Next was the building association. They had hesitated to grant her permission to rent sporadically, but they finally agreed to it on a trial basis. She called Charles and left a message on his iPhone with the good news. Then she went to the supermarket for fruits and vegetables and returned home to put them away and to plan that night's dinner. Finally she drove to her new workplace.

The lawyers were scattered about—Marion on her phone, Arthur with a client, and Robert back in court. When she walked by Sam's open office door, he looked up from shuffling papers and called out to her, "Banker's hours! Actually, even bankers don't arrive at work this late."

She kept walking.

"Hey, I want to talk to you," he yelled, coming out into the corridor, looking more professional with a suit and tie on, although his tie was pulled away from the collar and the top button of his shirt undone.

She stopped and turned. "Yes?" she replied sweetly. "What is it?"

"Don't think because you're married to a partner that you get special privileges."

His voice was unnecessarily loud. She raised her eyebrows and said quietly, "Only people who don't like me would think that."

He bristled at her nerve and moved closer to her, with his fists clenched. She stood her ground. His eyes bore into her, and he pointed a finger at her chest.

"And right now, the only cases we can give you are pro bono ones. Sorry." His grin put a punctuation mark on his words. "The low man on the totem pole takes the garbage."

At that, she seethed. "Is that what you think of some of your clients? Throwaway people who do not deserve respect?"

Sam laughed. "C'mon. Cut the *shit*. We all know why you married Robert. You got fired from your job, needed money, and you saw him as a rich guy you could twist around your finger."

"Really? How clever you are to have thought of that." Her voice was modulated and honeyed, as though she were talking to a child. "Does Robert know that you put two and two together and got five?"

"Huh?" he asked. His tight-fitting suit resembled a straitjacket, making him look like an escaped inmate.

"In plain English, you are wrong." She kept her smile, thinking of the nickname she had given him earlier, *the Jackal.*

"It's obvious to everyone but Robert what you are. A leech! I'll give your marriage six months, tops."

"In the interests of full disclosure, I am independently wealthy." She put one hand on her hip as if to say, "*You know nothing about me.*"

"Like hell you are, lady. I checked. You own a two-bedroom apartment on the lower West Side of Manhattan, right?"

True," Sophia said, beginning to enjoy this exchange.

"That's not exactly wealthy," thinking he had caught her in a lie.

"No, you are right for once. But that is not my only asset." She used the word *asset* deliberately, waiting to see how he would interpret it.

Sam looked her over, like she was a secondhand car, checking for telltale signs of wear and tear. Sophia felt her skin crawl. She half expected him to squeeze her boobs to see if they deflated.

What did Robert ever find likable about him? she thought.

"I've seen better-looking women. You'll divorce him as soon as you get tired of having someone else's kid to raise. Stepmothers don't have a good track record. Robert should have made you sign an iron-clad prenup."

"Actually, it's the other way around," she countered, airily. "I should have asked him to sign one."

She continued down the hall. Sam stared after her, thinking, *If that is an act, it's a damn good one.*

When she entered Robert's office, she looked through his files. There were cases on four clients but no pro bono ones.

I will check with Marion on the status of Lara's divorce. If she does not want to keep that case, I'll offer to take it.

Her iPhone lit up. Robert.

"Where are you?" he asked.

"I am sitting at your desk," she answered.

"I am heading there now. The judge had to recess until tomorrow because one of the jurors took ill. How about lunch?"

"Sure, but I haven't been here very long. I doubt that Sam would approve."

"We don't need Sam's permission. I'll see you in ten minutes."

*****

After lunch, they drove back to the office. A conference among the five lawyers in the firm was scheduled for two o'clock. Sophia had a chance to ask Marion about Lara.

"She's doing a lot better now that she is living in the guest house on Bunny Lawrence's estate," Marion explained. "Bunny was thrilled to be able to help her after learning of her situation."

"Who has the case?"

"I do, but if you're interested in taking it over, be my guest. It's pro bono, as you know."

"Yes, I am very interested."

"Good. Lara was pleased when I told her that you had joined the firm. The three partners decide on the assignment of cases, but I am sure there won't be a problem."

All five of the attorneys were meeting for the first time. Sam led the discussions, reviewing individual cases and assigning new ones. Marion brought up Lara's divorce case.

"If there is no objection, I am handing it off to Sophia. They have already met, and—"

"No," said Sam, "I want that case."

Everyone else around the table looked, stunned.

"Why?" asked Robert. "You already have your hands full with another divorce case, a disputed will, and several property entanglements."

Arthur agreed. "It's pro bono, Sam. You've never wanted those cases."

"I want it. Period. Let's take a vote."

Robert shook his head. It made no sense.

Sam raised his hand. Arthur followed suit. The vote was two to one, with Robert voting no.

Sophia excused herself to go to Cat's school to pick her up, disgusted by what she heard.

Arthur voted yes, even though he disagreed. He is nothing but a boot-polisher. She left the building in a rage.

*****

That night, in their bedroom, Sophia asked Robert about Sam's personal life.

"He's married with a daughter, a second child on the way."

"What about at Yale? What kind of student was he?"

"Smart but never studied much. Took the easiest courses and spent most of his time dating coeds. I don't know how he passed his exams. The rest of us were up late, comparing notes, quizzing each other while he slept. Something of a goof-off. Why do you ask?"

"Something is not right. Why should he want a pro bono case when he told me earlier today that those were garbage cases, given to the newest members of the firm? I know he doesn't like me, but still, it doesn't make sense to deny me that case."

"I'm sure he likes you, Sophia. He likes all women. That's his problem."

"So he's taking the case, why? Because he likes Lara? God help her. She's in a delicate state as it is. I hope he is sensitive to that."

"Of course, he is. He's a professional."

"Really? Then why wouldn't he say why he wanted her case?"

Robert had wondered that as well. He just shrugged. His casual attitude irritated her.

"Sam is a narcissist who lacks empathy and feels superior to others. A battered wife is in need of emotional support, and Lara is not going to get it from a lawyer who carries his family's wealth and status like a passport which allows him unrestricted permission to say and do whatever he wants."

She understood what it was like to be threatened and demeaned by a husband.

"You are judging Sam unfairly," he replied, not wanting to accept her analysis. "He can be testy at times, but he will be respectful of her situation."

"You are letting your friendship with him override evidence to the contrary."

They left it at that.

*****

The weather was turning colder. Sophia had taken only warm-weather clothes with her when she left her Manhattan apartment. She suggested to Robert that they spend the weekend in Manhattan and gather up the rest of her wardrobe.

"It will be fun to show Cat the city, and Bruno will be on familiar turf."

Cat had never been to the Big Apple. Her questions in the car were endless.

"Why are the buildings so tall? How do they get up to the top? Where do kids play?"

When Cat got into the elevator, it started to ascend rapidly up the shaft, and she wrapped her arms around Sophia's waist.

"My stomach feels funny."

"It will be okay. You will get used to it," Sophia said.

Bruno wagged his tail in great excitement. When the doors opened into the penthouse, Bruno bounded out, but Cat was afraid to step into the room.

"Come, Cat," Sophia said, taking her hand. "I want you to see where I lived for six years."

They checked out the kitchen first. The refrigerator held only a few items, so they had brought already prepared food for the day's lunch and the next day's breakfast. That evening, they planned to take Cat out to a nearby restaurant and have her experience a meal in an elegant setting.

Beyond the kitchen were the dining room and living room and then the terrace and enclosed pool. When they walked out onto the high deck, it was windy, and Cat clung to Sophia, feeling both awe and terror.

"Tonight when the stars come out," Sophia assured her, "we will bundle you up and sit here and watch how the city looks and sounds when it is dark."

"Can we swim in the pool?"

"Yes, later. Now let's go back inside, and this time you can help me pack."

For Sophia, the apartment brought back memories of lonely nights in which she grappled with the events ending her first marriage and fun-filled weekends, holding small dinner parties with some of the other building occupants, or joining them on visits to the Met, the Guggenheim, off-Broadway shows, and Carnegie Hall concerts.

It was a reflective period during which she contemplated things she had done wrong and right and what was important to her going forward.

Now Robert and Cat were the ones who made her happy. She was surprised at how quickly she had pushed aside her former life.

Later that afternoon, after her SUV was filled to its limit with clothes and some of her mother's artwork, they all went into the pool for a swim—even Bruno. Cat wore a flotation belt rather than a vest so she had more maneuverability. Robert and Sophia swam laps, while Cat splashed around with Bruno. The heated pool had a plexiglass roof, so when they floated on their backs, they had a view of the sky overhead.

"This is heavenly, Sophia. Did you use the pool often?" Robert asked.

"Almost every night. I was tempted to ask if you wanted to swim the night you came here, but I guessed you did not have a bathing suit," she said, swimming close to him, her long hair tucked under a rubber cap.

"Actually, I did," Robert said. He pulled himself up to sit on the edge of the pool, wiping water off his face with a towel. "I always keep one in my bag in case I want to use a hotel pool."

His sandy hair had darkened from being wet, and his long, muscular arms and legs showed off his fitness. She moved away, floating on her back, staring at him.

"What are you thinking?" he asked.

"Of what Dolores said to me when I first told her about us, that it was meant to be."

"She must be some smart lady. I'd love to meet her."

"I'll invite her to come at Thanksgiving if she can get away." *Delores said conservative men are not her type. Thank God because she loves to flirt.*

They dressed up for dinner. Sophia had chosen a long dark red skirt and a matching top, with a colorful paisley shawl, while Robert wore a wool tweed suit in navy blue with a red floral silk tie that Cat had picked out during a mother–daughter shopping trip. Sophia admired the tie and told Cat, "You have expensive tastes but also a good eye for fashion." Cat drank in her mother's comments as if she had been starving for praise.

Cat's new rose-colored dress with matching coat was one she had picked out herself. After they were seated in the restaurant's ornate dining room, Cat watched her parents place their napkins on their laps and study their menus. She did the same, although her menu was just one page long.

When the waiter came and asked them what they wanted to drink, Robert ordered champagne. Then the waiter turned to Cat and asked, "And for you, Miss?"

"I would like a Shirley Temple, please."

Robert smiled. "Do you know what a Shirley Temple is, Cat?"

"No, but the picture of it matches my dress."

"Good choice," said the waiter.

Sophia ordered shrimp stuffed with crabmeat for her entrée. Robert had the filet mignon. Cat was torn between the mac 'n' cheese or the pasta and meatballs.

"I doubt that the pasta and meatballs will be as good as the Bellini recipe," Sophia advised.

"All the children rave about our mac 'n' cheese," offered the waiter. "You can't go wrong with that."

The mac 'n' cheese filled her up. She said she wasn't hungry for dessert, but then she saw the waiter putting a torch to something at the next table.

"What is he doing?" she whispered.

"He is caramelizing the sugar on the top of a custard," Sophia said.

"Will I like it?" Cat asked.

"I think so, but you won't know until you try it."

The waiter came over to the table and asked if anyone was interested in dessert. Cat hesitated, curious as to how the torch worked.

"I dare you," Sophia smiled.

Cat looked at her mother, challenging her to try something new. She could not back down.

"Okay," said Cat.

"My daughter will have the crème brûlée."

"Ah," said the waiter, "a very sophisticated dessert for the young lady. A good choice."

Cat watched in fascination when the waiter pulled out a torch lighter and lit the sugar granules on the top and was amazed as they changed to a bronze color. She picked up her spoon and took the tiniest amount of the dessert and put it to her lips. Her eyes lit up.

"Yum. It's really good."

"I thought you would like it. I am proud of you for taking that risk. It is the only way that you will test yourself and experience what the world has to offer."

Cat knew her mother was telling her much more than trying a new dish. She stored it in her mind for future use.

*****

Later that night, they all snuggled together, covered in blankets on a cushioned lounge chair in the middle of the terrace, and breathed in the cool night air. Neon lights blinked on and off. The sound of an ambulance's siren cut through the darkness, and car horns squawked like angry birds. The lights and sounds were hypnotic.

Cat soon fell asleep, and Robert carried her to bed. Then they were ready for bed themselves, this time together in Sophia's bedroom.

*****

The next morning, they rose to a whole different panorama. Sunday in the big city was relatively quiet. The night owls in the Manhattan apartments were still in their nests. Only the occasional police car or taxi or ambulance was seen speeding down below.

Up in the penthouse, the occupants were enjoying a rare holiday. Cat and Bruno sat next to each other at the table, one on a chair and the other on the floor. Sophia made French toast and hot chocolate for Cat. She and Robert enjoyed bacon and eggs with avocado toast.

"Mummy, did you like living here all by yourself?" Cat asked, while Sophia was clearing the table.

"Yes, most of the time. I had Bruno for company, and neighbors downstairs came up occasionally."

"I like our house better. This house makes me feel lonely," said Cat.

Sophia knew what Cat meant. There was no place to sit and cuddle up by a fire. The tall ceilings and large expanse of white walls made its occupants feel small and insignificant.

"Sometimes people need to be alone with themselves," she answered, knowing that was not exactly what Cat was referring to.

"Why?"

Sophia anticipated that question. How could she explain to her daughter what the trauma she had experienced years before had done to her, how it had made her want to retreat into a stark setting of concrete and glass and steel that was impersonal, nonintrusive?

"It's normal to want to be by yourself occasionally, to have quiet time. When you go to your room and play with your Legos or to read a book, you are alone."

"Yes, but I wish I had someone to do it with."

Sophia smothered her response of, "*You will.*"

Robert said, "Maybe you will have a sister or brother someday."

Cat turned to Sophia. "I wish I had a brother, like you had. You told me it was fun to play with him when you were little."

She winked at her daughter. "You wished I was your mother, and that wish came true. Maybe this one will too."

"Where do babies come from?" Cat wanted to know.

Sophia paused. "Babies grow inside a woman's abdomen." She moved on quickly. "We are going to stop at FAO Schwarz on our way back home."

"What's that?"

"A toy store!" All further questions about babies were forgotten.

*****

"That was quick thinking on your part," Robert complained later, "but did we have to buy her an expensive toy?"

"I am fairly certain you were a six-year-old once."

"My parents never spoiled me with expensive toys."

"Never once? An only child? Let's see what your mother has to say about that."

EASTPORT

As fall began to settle in, the school curriculum became more challenging for Cat. Besides reading, writing, math, science, and geography, the second-graders were introduced to the basics of geometry and Spanish. Cat was doing really well—thriving, actually. Her teacher sent home a midterm report, noting Cat's high verbal ability, reasoning, and math skills.

Margaret made long-delayed plans to travel abroad with friends in early November and to return just before Thanksgiving. It was a river cruise, beginning in the Paris suburbs and ending near Nice, a trip that she had put off for six years. She hoped that a vacation abroad would be an annual event, now that she was no longer needed to play mother. And she had a travel partner, Andrew, a longtime friend of the family and, like her, widowed.

At the weekly meetings of the lawyers, there had been no updates on Lara's case. Sam kept his comments vague when it was brought up, although he went into detail about another divorce case. He said next to nothing about the property rights cases, divulging only how complex they were.

"What is so complex about the property rights cases?" Sophia asked, not wanting Sam to skirt over them without some explanation.

"You are ignorant about this town and its complicated building codes and survey maps. It shows when you ask stupid questions on matters that you are not involved in," he said sharply.

Sophia was familiar by now with Sam's blunt criticisms of her abilities, but she wouldn't let it go.

"So enlighten me! I may have a property rights case sometime, and it would be useful for me to know."

"Not in this law firm you won't. You don't have the background to be assigned those cases."

Sophia stared at him. *It just isn't my lack of knowledge of codes and surveys he's afraid of. Something else is going on.* She gave Robert a sidelong glance. He had his head down and remained silent. *Maybe he won't speak up in my defense because Sam will accuse him of playing favorites. I don't know how long I can last in this stifling environment, being assigned cases a first-year law student could handle.*

But to Sophia's surprise, she was given a challenging matter to resolve. A request for a mediator came up on the agenda. A dispute between the teachers' union and the school committee needed to be resolved, and rather than hire a professional mediator, one of the union leaders had suggested asking Sophia to do it.

She jumped at the opportunity. Although she had never mediated a dispute involving educators, she was sure she had the necessary skills, and nobody else in the firm was interested because it very likely meant long hours around a table with hostile opponents. For once, Sam had no objection. He thought the skills required were way out of Sophia's skill set and that she would either fail or quit. Either way, it would damage her reputation.

Sophia was warmly welcomed by the union and the school committee. Her reputation as a competent attorney and as a liaison between teachers and parents was well-known.

First she familiarized herself with the teachers' contract. The issue was about overtime pay. The teachers wanted compensation for time spent at afternoon and nighttime events, doing everything from selling tickets at the school's sporting events to chaperoning dances to directing school plays. Although teachers were not assigned to take part in such activities, pressure was put on them to *volunteer*, to show their support for their students outside the classroom.

Second she reviewed the school budget to understand the monetary constraints they were under. Then she examined teacher contracts in school districts of similar size.

During the first negotiating session, the school committee balked at having to pay teachers anything extra, saying it was part of their job.

"If they are not assigned these tasks, how can they be part of their job?" she countered. "The teachers volunteer so that these activities can take place, right? If they did not volunteer, what would happen? Either the events would not take place, or you would have to hire people to supervise them. Do other civil employees work overtime for nothing?" Sophia argued. "The police and firemen don't, and neither do the public works employees. Teachers should not be treated any differently."

The school committee reluctantly agreed but wanted to give them only a small stipend for any amount of time they spent after regular school hours. Sophia argued that they should be paid by the hour and more than the minimum wage, since they were professional caretakers of children, but since the teachers did not have to prepare anything ahead of time, their extra pay should not be on the same scale as they received in the classroom.

It took some intense negotiating, but finally both parties agreed on an overtime wage. The stalemate was over after only two sessions of talks. The teachers' union was thrilled at the resolution of this long-standing issue, while the school committee members felt that Sophia had cleverly backed them into a corner, weakening their stance with numerous examples of overtime pay in other communities in the state. She had done her homework.

With this success, she felt she was now a lawyer with some standing in the community. She breathed in her victory; it was food for her soul. However, Sam Wyman minimized her accomplishment, saying, "You were just lucky that the issue was so simple. Any two-bit lawyer could have gotten them to agree."

*****

In mid-October, while Sophia was still not "showing," she and Robert held a small dinner party at their house, inviting a few friends that Robert had known from high school, along with Dolores, who was exhibiting her artwork at a Manhattan gallery, and of course, their law office colleagues. Sophia had insisted on inviting the office secretary, Eileen, a genteel woman from a wealthy family, who, because of some unfortunate choices, found herself raising a daughter on her own. Her family had disowned her for marrying a man they disapproved of, and his sudden death from cancer forced her to go to work. Sam had hired her, thinking that because she needed the job so badly, she was indebted to him, and any secrets that she learned about him would be kept to herself.

"Quite a motley crew," Robert had said of their guests. "I hope they mix well."

"All the women have proper manners. Let's see how the men behave."

He looked at her curiously. She still had not told him about Sam's comments to her on her first day at work.

The dinner began at seven with cocktails and shrimp appetizers. It was a mild night, with a clear sky. The view from the terrace never failed to impress visitors. It was one of the reasons that Robert didn't like to have people over, complaining that once they came, they didn't want to leave.

When the outside temperature cooled, the guests came into the great room, which was forty feet in length with a massive stone fireplace at one end and the dining room/kitchen area at the other. The guests found a seat on one of the cushioned chairs or sofas and made themselves comfortable, while Sophia and Dolores kept watch over the food in different stages of preparation.

"I am so happy that you drove here from Manhattan to meet my new family," Sophia said to her college roommate, handing her a platter of homemade ravioli to put on the dining table. "We don't see each other often enough."

"You planned this party for me, no? You knew I could not refuse an invitation to meet your husband and daughter. I have never seen you so happy."

"I am happy. Besides having a caring man and a beautiful girl, I have a lovely home."

"What about your job? How is that going?" Dolores asked.

"I've locked horns with one of the partners," she said quietly. "He runs the show like a ringmaster, making the rest of us jump when he raises his whip. But I can't quit this soon. My employment record is already dismal." She handed her friend a dessert platter to put on a side table.

The evening meal was an Italian food lover's delight. Ravioli with sauce made from the best tomatoes was a hit, even for those who had sworn off pasta, but couldn't resist taking just one, or maybe two, so as not to offend the hostess. Then came veal marsala and chicken piccata, roasted vegetables, salad, and finally, some simple desserts—biscotti and gelato, followed by espresso coffee.

Sophia had learned her culinary skills in her family's kitchen. Both her parents cooked, especially for their big Sunday meal when friends seemed to show up regularly, saying that they were just passing by when everyone knew they had timed their visit at precisely the moment when dinner was to be served. Then the wine flowed, laughter followed, and everyone went to bed with a full belly. Sophia hoped to recreate those happy times here in Eastport, among a new set of family and friends.

It was nearly nine when the guests left the table and retired back to the living room, where Robert had the fireplace going to take the chill out of the autumn air. Cat was getting sleepy, but she begged Robert and Sophia to stay up a while longer.

"We never have a party. Please, pretty please, Mummy."

Reluctantly, Sophia agreed, and Cat sat on her lap on a loveseat with Robert beside them.

Marion smiled at her host. "My, what a lovely threesome you make."

"Thank you," replied Robert. "I'm lucky." He had his arm around Sophia, and Cat was now stretched out in front of them with her head on Sophia's chest.

"You sure are," said Sam gruffly. "Not every woman would take on a kid who was practically an orphan when you were working in Manhattan."

"That's not fair, Sam. I spent every weekend with her and some nights when I managed to leave the office early."

"Yeah, sure, whatever you say." Then Sam asked, "Cat, who do you love more, your stepmother or your father?"

Sophia's face froze at hearing his question.

"I am her mother," Sophia corrected him, "and your question is intended to be hurtful."

"I-I love them both," was Cat's answer. "Mummy, I don't like him," she whispered.

Sophia leaned down and murmured, "You have good judgment."

Cat smiled. She wasn't sure what that meant, only that it was good.

Sam's comments had spread unease among the other guests, but he didn't care. He enjoyed being the center of attention, pleased at how quickly he had angered both Robert and Sophia.

"While we are talking about Cat," Sam persisted, "too bad she has to grow up as an only child. You know what they say about them, don't you?"

The other guests just glared at him, not wanting to egg him on by responding.

"They are spoiled brats, for one thing," he said.

Robert leapt to defend his parenting. "We haven't spoiled Cat."

"Then why is she here, listening to adult conversation? She should be in bed."

Although Sophia agreed with Robert, she smelled trouble.

"Cat, I think it is time for bed. This discussion is not for delicate ears."

"Wait," said Sam, basking in Sophia's discomfort, "I'm not finished. An only child usually has trouble socializing. Now we all know that's true about Cat. It's all over town that Cat punched a kid in school."

He glanced at the faces of the other guests. No one showed surprise.

That comment made Robert flush. *There is no reason to remind everyone of that incident.* He glared at his childhood friend, wondering why Sam brought it up in front of his guests.

"Sam, leave my daughter's behavior out of the conversation. That's nobody's business but mine."

Even though he had spoken the words quietly, the anger inside him was smoldering. Robert felt tempted to get up and show Sam to the door.

"Hold on. I'm not saying anything everyone here doesn't already know," Sam said, trying to defend himself.

"Then why bring it up?" Robert said sharply, his grimace showing his anger.

"I'm trying to prove a point. Your daughter does and says what she wants. She's spoiled."

Robert had heard enough. "Are you finished? Isn't it time that you went home to your wife and kid?"

"Or your girlfriend," someone said.

Heads turned to where the voice came from: Marion.

"I can fire you for a crack like that," Sam bellowed, already on his third scotch.

"No, you can't or won't because I can prove that you're looking elsewhere for *satisfaction.* A friend of mine saw you fondling a young lady as you two were leaving a restaurant in Norwalk. In fact, she sent me a photo. I can pass my phone around if you like. And what's worse, I have texts from Lara saying that you started hitting on her at the first attorney-client meeting you had. She didn't know what to think or do. This week, she finally got up the courage to contact me because you made it clear to her that she would get what she wanted when you got what you wanted. She asked me if that kind of thing was expected from pro bono clients."

Sam flushed bright red.

"Jesus, Sam!" Arthur yelled, jumping up out of his seat. It startled everyone because he had always supported his friend and colleague. "That could ruin the firm's reputation!"

"What about Lara's?" Sophia protested. "She is the injured party here." The look she gave Robert said, *"I told you so."*

"Okay, okay," Robert stood up and began to usher Sam and Arthur into another room. "We'll work this out. Please put Cat to bed."

Sophia left with Cat, only for Cat's sake.

"Mummy, why am I the only one to have an early night?" Cat whimpered.

"Because you are six years old and need more sleep than adults do."

"What does good judgment mean?" she asked as they walked into her bedroom.

"It means you are correct in how you see things. Now into bed, my little one. Enough questions for today."

Dolores came in to say good night.

"My little chica, I must see you again. Maybe your parents will have a wedding reception, eh? I will show you how to dance and make the *niños* fall in love with you."

"I know what *niños* are—boys. We are studying Spanish in my class."

"Wonderful, *mi ciela*. The next time I visit you, we will speak about boys only in Spanish." She kissed Cat on both cheeks.

"Please, Dolores, don't make her boy-crazy at six years old. I am enjoying this age," Sophia complained.

"She needs to know how to flirt," Dolores insisted. "It takes practice."

When they returned to the living room, Sam and Arthur were gone.

The evening was spoiled because of the confrontation. The other guests said they wanted a rain check because of what had ensued—an abrupt end to what had been an enjoyable party.

Eileen, in particular, thanked Sophia for including her and whispered that if she ever needed *dirt* on Sam, she knew much more. "I know who he dates because he keeps a black book with their names, photos, and numbers."

"Thank you, but it would be unethical, and you might be fired if Sam found out. We will have you over again, hopefully without the drama."

When the dishes were put in the dishwasher and the remaining food put away, Robert and Sophia said good night to Dolores, who was staying overnight in the guest room, and then they got ready for bed. Sam's behavior had unnerved them both, but they had remained tight-lipped.

Sophia closed the bedstead light and curled up, her back toward Robert. He lay beside her, undecided whether to speak then or wait until morning. Finally he said, "Arthur and I told Sam he must turn Lara's case over to you, and he agreed."

"Wonderful," said Sophia, her voice dripping with sarcasm. "I get to represent a woman who has been beaten by her husband and now hit on by her lawyer, while Sam gets away scot-free."

"What else can Arthur and I do? Sam is a partner."

She turned around in bed to face her husband. "Do you really think that this is over, that he won't try something again on a client who can better defend herself and sue the law firm? You know, I don't want to work in your law firm if that slimeball stays."

"He promised us he—"

"Bullshit!" she said, louder than she meant to. She lowered her voice to an angry whisper. "You know nothing about psychology. You are enabling him because he received no punishment for his behavior."

"Look, Sam is my best friend from childhood. He stuck up for me when other kids made fun of my last name and my religion. I want to give him a break. Maybe it was a moment of weakness."

"Robert, he doesn't respect women. That is who he is. Period!"

"That is your opinion."

"Okay. Maybe I'm wrong. Please tell me what you like about him."

Robert searched his brain. *Loyalty is the only reason I put up with his behavior.* He said nothing.

Sophia pressed her case. "You need to tell the bastard he must leave for the good of the law firm."

"I can't."

"You mean you won't."

Robert tried to imagine the scene—Sam screaming and cursing at him, threatening to ruin him as an attorney. It made him cringe.

"Sophia," he begged, "it is not something I can or will do."

"Then you must suffer with the consequences of your decision. This will not end well for Sam or for you."

EASTPORT, OCTOBER

The next morning, a Saturday, Sophia and Dolores sat on the chilly terrace in their robes, sipping coffee, and discussed the previous night's fireworks. The water in the bay was calm. Sophia was not.

"Sam is an embarrassment to the firm," Sophia grumbled. "The sight of him makes me cringe."

"He's a piece of shit," Dolores agreed. "He has a pregnant wife and a daughter, and yet he's on the prowl for young women to sleep with. *Merde*! I am glad I am not married."

"Not all men are like that. Carlo was selfish and demanding. But Robert, no. He is more laid-back. However, he is intimidated by Sam's personality. Sam yells when he is threatened, and Robert never yells. He cannot stand up to yelling, and so Sam gets to run the law firm as he wants, and I will never get the cases I want. He hates me for challenging him, and he will convince Arthur to side with him on any issue. I have no future there. I need to start my own law firm.

"I have not been in this town long, but I do have a following. I attended a parent–teacher meeting, and Cat's teacher introduced me to the gathering. When they found out my background, they asked me to speak at their next meeting about the rights of teachers and parents. I updated them about the laws that require school systems to provide special services for needy children, who have physical, emotional, and cognitive issues. I gave them websites that listed the names of advocates who specialized in those areas. When I finished, there was applause, and several came over to personally thank me.

Now the teacher's union has asked me to give a talk on education, psychology, and the law."

"Will you do it?"

"I will have to prepare very thoroughly, but yes, I will. I want to discuss how to deal with difficult situations in the classroom so as to diffuse confrontations."

"You are thirty-seven years old and creating a whole new career for yourself. I admire you."

"I feel empowered by my acceptance in this community, especially with educators." She liked being in control and now, finally, she felt she had the power to make choices that would strengthen her career. "I still have to make peace with Robert. We had words over Sam's behavior. It's put a rift in our relationship."

*****

That night, Robert and Sophia declared a truce in their battle over the disposition of Sam, who was put on the back burner where he stayed for weeks. *Avoidance is never a permanent solution*, Sophia thought. *I learned that lesson when I was avoiding Carlo. Sooner or later, we will have to confront Sam's behavior because it is not going to change.*

She refused to go back into the law office building. Sophia met her pro bono clients elsewhere—in their homes or at quiet restaurants or even in her car. Lara was visibly relieved to have Sophia as her attorney. In a matter of days, a court date was penciled on the calendar, corroborating witnesses were interviewed regarding her husband's violent nature, and distribution of assets was discussed.

"You have done so much in so short a time," Lara told Sophia. "Sam told me these things can take months whenever I asked him how things were progressing."

Sophia had to be careful not to badmouth another attorney. It was unethical. "Every lawyer has his own way of handling a case. My way is to get you a satisfactory divorce settlement as quickly as possible."

"When Sam said he was too busy to work on my case, I hoped it was you who took it. I can't thank you enough for everything you've done."

Sophia was always uncomfortable when she received praise. She changed the subject. "Do you know what you want to do after the divorce?"

"No, not really. I used to be a secretary before I met my husband, but I haven't worked in a while. He insisted I stay at home."

"That was his way to make you dependent on his income," she observed. "Would you like to be a secretary again?" Sophia asked.

"Sure. That's what I went to school for, but I'm pretty rusty. I doubt anyone would want to hire me."

"Do you have your own computer?"

"Yes, of course."

"When you have a chance, go online and type in 'skills needed for legal secretaries.' Become familiar with the legal terms and practice the skills that are needed. I will see if I can find a position for you when you are through with the training."

"Really? That would be great." Her eyes danced with delight at the opportunity.

"You have some spare time now, so use it wisely."

*****

At home one evening, at the end of October, Sophia finally brought up Sam.

"The main reason why I will never go back to the law office is because Sam does not behave professionally, to either his clients or to his colleagues." Then she told him what Sam had said to her on her first day at work. She replayed the scene in the office corridor, including Sam speaking loud enough for Arthur's client to hear.

"He really said that you married me for my money?"

"He did. Arthur and Marion must have heard him. He hoped that you had made me sign a prenuptial agreement."

"Jeez! He's really changed."

"No, I do not think he has changed at all. When you were both students in college, you described yourself as a scholar and Sam as a libertine. You told me so yourself." She put her hands around Robert's neck, looked him in the eye, and said matter-of-factly, "He is not an asset to the firm. His behavior will do him in eventually, but I cannot wait until that happens, and I cannot practice law without an office. When I start to get paying clients, I am not going to interview them next to a pizza oven. In two months, I am either going to return to your offices and sit where Sam sits or I will open my own office. Your choice."

"Two months? That is not enough time, Soph."

Sophia was about to say that she did not like to be called by a nickname. She pushed the words back down her throat. "Those are my terms, and they are not negotiable."

"You'll be taking a risk, opening up a one-lawyer law office."

"I'm not afraid." She stared at him, thinking it was what he should have done instead of attaching himself to Sam. *He took the easy way, hitching himself to a well-connected figure in the community, who used his family name to get clients and family money to win cases. How can I get him to see that?* "Why do you think Sam gets upset when I ask him questions about his cases? He is a shyster who is hiding some wrongdoing."

"You're just guessing. You have no proof."

Sophia threw up her hands and started to walk away.

"Soph, are we still good? I mean, you're not thinking of leaving me over this, right?"

He sounded so nervous that she had to smile. She came back and wrapped her arms around his neck and kissed him as she had done in his bedroom months ago.

"That is how I feel about you as a husband," she whispered softly. "Does that answer your question?"

"Mmm, it does."

"And," she smiled, "I will take you on as a partner, if you are interested." She stroked his temples and nuzzled her nose against his. "Think about it," she breathed. "Bellini & Navarro Law Offices."

118

Robert frowned. "Not Navarro & Bellini or Navarro & Navarro?"

"That is negotiable." She kissed him, indicating with her tongue she wanted more.

He put his hands on her behind and squeezed. "Soph, I am happy and proud that you are my wife. My mother was right. You are just what Cat and I need."

"Your mother said that?" She smiled again. It felt good to have Margaret on her side.

"And she said you needed both of us."

"She is right. Cat satisfies my need to nurture. She is like a little bud that I must feed and water until it blossoms full-grown into a flower. As for you, I need you as a friend and as a lover, more than you know."

As they headed for their bedroom, Sophia sighed. *If he only could be the macho man in the law office that he is in bed.*

EASTPORT, LATE NOVEMBER

"Mummy, where is Dolores going to sit?" Cat was putting the glasses next to the plates. "I want to be next to her."

It was Thanksgiving Day, and the small family, including Margaret—who had recently returned from her vacation in southern France and was glowing with happiness—were busy with the holiday dinner preparations.

"Why? So she can call you her little *ciela* and talk to you about *niños*?" Sophia teased as she mixed the softened potatoes, butter, and cream in a blender.

"Yes. She makes me laugh when she rolls her eyes and moves her hands all around. Why isn't she married?"

"Hmm. You'll have to ask her. No, maybe you better not," Sophia said, remembering how Dolores enjoyed playing the field. "You may embarrass her and me," she muttered under her breath. She heaped the potato mixture into a large bowl.

"Why? Don't boys like her?"

"I am sure they do, Cat. I guess she was having a hard time choosing the right one."

As usual, everyone was assigned a task. Robert was in charge of the turkey and gravy, Sophia the side dishes, Margaret the pies, and Cat the table setting. There were eight seats. Besides Dolores, they had invited Marion and her husband, as well as Margaret's close friend and travel companion, Andrew.

At one o'clock, the guests started to arrive—Dolores from the airport and the others from around town. When everyone was seated, Robert asked Cat to say grace.

"Thank you, God, for this food, especially the pies and ice cream"—she stopped to giggle—"and for my father and mother and Grandma and our friends. Amen."

"Do you mind being the only child at the table?" asked Marion's husband, Phil, as the dishes were being passed around.

"Hmm, no, but soon I am going to have a brother, so I won't be the only child," she said.

"Oh," said Phil, his blue eyes showing surprise. He looked at his wife, embarrassed. "Did you tell me this and I forgot?"

"No. I didn't know you were expecting, Sophia." Marion looked doubtful, although Sophia had put on a little weight around her middle. "Is it true?"

"We are expecting a child in May, and its sex is yet to be determined," Sophia emphasized.

"Well, I want a brother, so that's what it will be," Cat insisted.

Robert pursed his lips. "So if it's a female kitten, we'll send it back."

"Daddy, Mummy can't have a kitten. And besides, we already have one."

"Two, to be precise. Kit and Cat," Sophia noted, "and Cat, you do not get to choose the sex."

Marion asked, "Have you picked out names yet?"

"Only if it's a boy," she answered.

Dolores chimed in, "If it's a girl, I want Dolores. Sophia owes me a big favor."

Robert asked, "What favor did you do for Sophia?"

"I convinced her to marry you. Right, my friend?" She looked to Sophia to confirm.

"Yes, you did. When I visited you last August, you told me it was meant to be."

"The name Dolores goes to the top of the list," Robert said. "We can call her Dolly."

"No, no, no." The expressive Latina waved her finger back and forth. "It's *Dolores* or *notheeng*!"

"And if it's a boy?" Marion asked.

"Anything but Sam," Sophia begged.

Margaret had to explain to her friend Andrew who Sam was. Everyone else knew.

"If it is a boy, we had decided to name him Matthew, after my father," Robert said in a quiet voice.

"Mateo is a good name," said Dolores. "And you can't make it into a nickname."

"You already have!" said Sophia.

"Eh, Matthew, Mateo. What's the difference? You call him Matthew. I call him Mateo. A good Spanish name, eh, Roberto?"

Cat giggled. "Daddy, can I call you Roberto?"

Robert raised his eyebrows in mock horror. "Only if I can call you Caterina."

Cat made a face.

"Perhaps someday you might want to be known as Caterina."

"It's too long," Cat protested.

"You may grow into it."

"Daddy, did you ever have a nickname?"

"No, never."

Marion and Dolores both said that they never had a nickname either. Others around the table discussed what they had been called as children. Margaret was Madge, which she had hated, Andrew was Drew, and Philip said nobody ever called him Philip, only Phil.

Marion smiled at her husband and quoted Shakespeare. "A rose by any other name would smell as sweet." She gave him a peck on his cheek. "What about you, Sophia? Did you have a nickname?"

"No. Not until I married Robert." She forced a smile. "He sometimes calls me Soph, but not often."

"Oh," said Marion, sensing her discomfort. "That's not much of a nickname."

"I like my given name. Our name is what we carry with us our entire lives, and if we like it, we should be called that. If people have a name they don't like, they usually are stuck with it, or they'll choose a nickname for themselves."

"Like I did," Cat said.

Robert made a mental note to always call her Sophia.

"I see everyone has finished eating. Let's move into the living room and find comfortable chairs. We'll have dessert there."

As pleasant as the day was, with no one creating a scene, there was an underlying tension between the host and hostess. The deadline that Sophia had given Robert was now only a month away. Sophia had put her penthouse up for sale. If she found a buyer at her asking price, she could sell or not, depending on whether Sam stayed or left.

Robert had finally talked to Arthur, the other partner, about the two of them putting pressure on Sam to leave, but as expected, Arthur remained loyal to his friend and colleague.

"Robert, it was just one time. Isn't he allowed a second chance?"

"You are forgetting that he insulted Sophia at the office and embarrassed me and my daughter in my own home, Arthur. It's not just one time for me."

"You have known Sam all your life. You know what he's like. Get over it." Arthur sounded hostile. "Don't let your wife tell you what to do."

Robert brooded over that.

Was she going to make all the decisions in the family and keep giving me ultimatums whenever an issue came up? How would it look for me to be at one law firm and her at another, one which she runs or finds a partner to join her?

Marion and Sophia have become very close since the Lara incident. If Marion leaves to go with Sophia, the firm would be left with only men. Not good.

The more he thought about staying on as a partner with Sam and Arthur, the more he wanted to leave. Arthur will always side with Sam on any vote taken among the partners, and that will leave me as the third man out. It was a gloomy thought.

On the other hand, if he and Sophia partnered together, along with Marion, he felt sure the cases would be handled differently. The three of them were compatible, making it easier to decide who gets what cases without any of them being "the boss." He imagined it more as a collaborative, as opposed to what his law firm had evolved into—a dictatorship.

And Sophia had become "known." In the short time since she had moved to Eastport, word had spread of her marriage to Robert Navarro, a native son; about her guest appearances before parents and teachers; and about her role as mediator between teachers and the school committee.

Mrs. Benson, the principal, was one carrier of praise; Cat's teacher was another. Sophia's talk in front of the teachers' union had been impressive. She used slides and examples from actual lawsuits and had the attendees practice various classroom scenarios among themselves. Her clarity, legal knowledge, and patience in answering their questions were refreshing.

The law firm of Wyman, Blake, & Navarro began to get calls from residents who specifically asked for Sophia. That didn't sit well with Sam, who tried to talk them into retaining one of the men, saying that they were more experienced. He saw Sophia as a threat, not only to his law firm but to his reputation.

She is trying to destroy me, but I will find a way to ruin her before I let that happen.

EASTPORT, DECEMBER

Cat's seventh birthday was December second, and it was the first birthday party that she was having at her house with her friends. She had such a hard time deciding who to invite that Sophia said, "Why don't you just invite all nineteen in your class? That way, no one will be offended."

"Even Billy?" Cat asked.

"Sure. Why not? He accepted your apology."

Cat spent hours making up the menu and planning games and packaging the favors in gift bags. With only a few suggestions from Mom—Cat decided *Mummy* was now too childish—she had her friends licking their fingers over the desserts, shrieking with laughter during musical chairs and, as they left, clutching bags filled with favors: Glitter pens, chocolate silver dollars, and tiny kaleidoscopes.

Because the Christmas holidays held bad memories for both Robert and his mother, his father having died on Christmas Eve, the festivities were muted. Santa gave Cat a pink bicycle with training wheels, which she wanted removed after the second day of riding around inside the house.

"When the warmer weather comes, you can ride your bike in the driveway and on the walks within the property," Robert told her. When summer came, they planned to have her cycle in the state parks while they walked or jogged along.

At the end of December, Sophia notified the firm that she was quitting. The only case she had left that was still in litigation was Lara's divorce, and the other attorneys had no interest in taking it over. She began to look for an office near the center of town because she had found a buyer for her penthouse. Before she passed papers, she wanted to have a small party in the Manhattan apartment and say a final goodbye to her lofty residence. On New Year's Eve, Margaret and Andrew, along with Dolores, came to celebrate the coming new year in luxury.

There were four bedrooms, just enough for her family and the guests.

Margaret gasped when the elevator doors opened. "Oh my, this is quite a layout, and the views are spectacular."

"Yes," Sophia agreed, "but our present home is more suitable to raise a family, and its views are just as spectacular, although very different."

"Were you happy living here?" she wanted to know as they paused to look at the view of Central Park.

"It is what I needed at the time, a place to hide from the world and to let go of the trauma that I experienced."

"What does *trauma* mean?" Cat asked.

For the first time, Sophia ignored her question. She continued, "I had Bruno to keep me company." At the mention of his name, Bruno's ears perked up, and he came to sit on the floor next to Sophia. She began to rub his back. "I poured my heart out, talking to him." She smiled. "He probably could write a book about my life—and *rebirth*."

"What's *rebirth* mean?" Cat wanted to know, her mind always filled with questions.

Sophia studied her dark-haired, dark-eyed daughter. "Cat, when you are a lot older, I will answer all your questions about the time before I came to live with you and Daddy. Please wait until then."

Cat felt her mother's sadness. "Okay."

"Thanks, my darling," Sophia whispered.

*****

That evening, Robert had a quiet conversation with Andrew, who, like Margaret's husband, had been an investment banker.

Robert mentioned that Sophia was planning to open up her own law office.

"She is convinced that she can be successful, but she's new in town. Nobody likes to change attorneys who have been part of the fabric of the town for years. I think she'll be butting her head up against an entrenched Yankee clique of lawyers."

"I happen to think that your wife will do fine."

"Really?" Robert was surprised. He knew Andrew was a conservative type of guy like himself. He surmised that Andrew would think Sophia was stepping on the toes of long-standing law firms. "You think that she will be accepted and have success as a newcomer and a woman?"

"Yes. She is well-liked and respected. I also think you should partner with her. The two of you will make a formidable team—you with your impeccable reputation and your family's ties to Eastport, and Sophia, marrying you and raising your motherless daughter and getting involved with the schools. Those things get noticed. What's more, the composition of the town is changing. More minorities are moving in, some with money. They will need a lawyer at some time and will choose Navarro over a Yankee name any day." Andrew's words gave Robert the extra push he needed.

Right after the holidays, he walked into Sam's office and told him that he would be leaving the firm to join his wife. Sam's narrow eyes froze in their sockets.

"No," he said sharply, "you can't. You signed a contract. The three of us have to stay at least one full year, which isn't over until the middle of May. Your wife put you up to this, right? And a husband-wife law firm isn't going to fly in this town. She'll bankrupt you and then dump you."

Robert chose not to tell Sam about Sophia's money. He was tired of Sam's negative comments every time Sophia's name came up. Now he was stuck there until May, just when the baby was due. Sophia took the news better than he had thought she would.

"Okay, so you have to stay another five months, but I cannot wait that long," she said as they climbed into bed. "I plan to make an offer on a house near the center of town and—"

"Wait, Sophia, hold on. You are going to buy a building?" Robert thought of his father's admonition to make important decisions only after testing the waters. "Why not just rent space for now?"

"If I thought there was a chance of my practice not taking off, I would rent. But this decision is not going to end in failure. I know I can do this—we can do this. And renting means spending money to convert a space into law offices that don't belong to me. It also makes sense taxwise. If I roll over the profits from the penthouse into another investment, I will pay less in taxes. I want to buy a large, elegant-looking house in a prominent location that doesn't have the feel of a plain concrete building. Our offices are going to be warm and colorful, with plush armchairs to make people feel comfortable, important. I spoke to Marion about joining our firm, not as a part-ner—she can't afford it—and she was thrilled. And I am using my maiden name from now on. It's easier to remember, and I want to have my own identity."

She saw the hurt look in his eyes.

"Imagine if tradition expected that you had to change your name after marriage. You would feel like a piece of you was being cut out and forgotten. Our children will have your last name, as they should. Together we will be a husband and wife legal team, and when you join the firm in May, I will have to stay at home to nurse the baby, so you and Marion will be in charge. The timing is perfect." She paused and smiled. "Can I trust you alone with Marion?"

He grinned at her tease. "She is attractive."

"And I won't be, right after the birth, with extra weight on me. I will have to think of some way to keep you from philandering." Her dark eyes flirted, moving slowly over his face and chest.

"I am here now," he whispered.

"Then I must use my time well." She kicked the covers off her legs and held out her arms.

EASTPORT, JANUARY–FEBRUARY

It took longer than Sophia had hoped to buy the Victorian house and begin to convert it into law offices. The house was in a business district, so its use as a law office was permitted under the zoning codes, but it did not meet the building codes. A handicap ramp had to be built by the main entrance, the old pantry was made into a wheelchair-accessible bathroom, and the whole house needed a sprinkler system. She also had the contractor put in a security system. The entire interior of the first floor was repainted to give it a fresh new look. The winter months delayed any outside work that needed to be done.

In the meantime, Sophia had picked up several small cases: writing a will, being present at a house closing, settling a dispute out of court over back pay. She worked out of her home office and met her now-paying clients wherever it was most convenient—sometimes at their house, sometimes in a quiet section of the library. She explained her lack of an office was temporary and made herself available at night and on weekends to make up for the inconvenience.

In mid-January, she got a call from a woman looking for an attorney. She had just fired her own attorney and wanted to hire her. The case was a civil dispute over land titles. Nancy Harris claimed to have proper ownership of the land where her neighbor's new house had encroached two feet onto her property. She wanted the protruding section removed and the required setback adhered to. She had the survey map and deed to prove her case. The affected parties had a court date set for April 1.

Nancy had recently learned that the neighbor, Will Cummings, and her own attorney, David Smith, had been buddies in college, and a friend of hers saw and heard them talking about the case in a restaurant. Nancy was outraged.

"Isn't that unethical?" she asked Sophia.

Reluctantly, Sophia acknowledged that it was. She knew Nancy's lawyer never should have taken the case because of a conflict of interest.

"We can ask the court to postpone the trial. It will give me a chance to catch up on all the facts of the case."

"Attorney Bellini, I gave you the facts. The land survey goes back to the early 1900s. Will Cummings built on my property, knowing he didn't own it. It's open and shut."

"All the same, Mrs. Harris, I will need to review your attorney's background information before we can proceed, as well as the history of the two properties to see if there was an easement or squatter's rights or some mitigating factor that could complicate matters."

"But this case has been dragging on for years, and now I know why. Please try to keep that date. With you, I will have already paid two lawyers, a surveyor, and the filing fees."

"I will do my best."

When Sophia closed her phone, she thought it sounded like a straightforward case. Boundary disputes were usually pretty clear. There were surveyor's maps that showed the borders of a house lot. She knew that Sam was handling some property entanglements.

There is no way that I will call him for advice. An ugly thought came to her that Sam was involved, but she dismissed it. *I'm overreacting.*

The first order of business was to call Nancy Harris's former lawyer and ask for his files. His secretary said that she would mail them. Sophia waited several days and became suspicious when they didn't arrive. She showed up at Smith's office and again asked for his files. His secretary became flustered and said she couldn't find them.

"Because they are nonexistent, aren't they? Tell Attorney Smith that I plan to file a complaint with the bar association."

"Oh, please don't. He already has two complaints on his record. A third one, and he may be disbarred. I'd lose my job."

"In that case, Attorney Smith better send me something on the case. He's had it for several years. I will give him four days before I act."

On the fourth day, she received a thin folder with notes that looked scratched out hastily with a pen. Also included was the name of the attorney hired by the defendant: Sam Wyman.

Sophia stared at the name and groaned. *Shit. Sam is involved. This is going to be a lot tougher than I thought.*

Sam had close associations with town hall officials, the police, and even judges. He was popular in town. He gave to various local causes, shook hands with townspeople at every event, drank with the locals at the service organization gatherings, and was present at high school athletic games. Wherever there was a crowd, Sam showed up—mostly alone, without his family.

Sophia didn't enjoy making "appearances" just to become known. That wasn't her style. She wanted people to hire her as their lawyer because of her professionalism. Robert felt the same. Be sociable but reserved. They looked forward to doing things as a family, enjoying their leisure time without others looking on, making judgments.

Sophia considered the situation she now found herself in. *It will be the first time going head-to-head with my former colleague, and I have to be prepared for double-dealing. Robert said as much. Sam has an advantage of being a hometown boy, but he cannot win a case based solely on his popularity. Whoever prevails will make headlines. It better be me. I need to familiarize myself with all the laws and regulations involving land titles.*

She immediately went to the town hall to look for Eastport's survey maps and to familiarize herself with the zoning and building codes. She left there with her briefcase crammed with material that she needed to study.

*****

In late February, Cat's school vacation made it possible for them to fly to California to see the Bellini family. Sophia's parents had planned a wedding reception of sorts, given that she and Robert had been too busy to do it themselves.

Giorgio and Maria Bellini were both dignified-looking people in their late sixties, with white hair, straight silhouettes, and pleasant demeanors. They had been born in northern Italy, not too far from Milan, which was famous for its designer fashions and sophistication. Although not born into wealth, they exhibited cultured tastes—from the tailored clothes they wore to the grace and charm with which they greeted friends and family.

"Come in, come in," said Giorgio, opening the door of their Italianate-styled home. He wrapped his arms around his daughter, shook hands heartily with Robert, and bent down to give Cat a buss on both her cheeks. "Now my family is altogether, and we can celebrate a wedding and a baby that is coming soon."

Cat loved her grandfather from the moment she saw him. His neatly trimmed, snowy white mustache and beard, and his rosy cheeks made him look like Santa Claus without the belly. His lovable disposition sealed her opinion of him.

"What do I call you?" she asked, eager to have him as a grandfather.

"Nonno. Will that do?" he asked. "That's what my other grandchildren call me."

"Nonno, Nonno," said Cat, practicing it on her lips.

"And you I call *mia gatta*, my Cat."

Nonno already had a following. His two other grandchildren adored him and shadowed him everywhere. Sophia's brother, Guiseppe, or Joe as he was called, was two years younger than she but already had a son, Joey, who was eight, and a daughter, Cristina, who was five.

His wife, Grace, was a lovely, intelligent woman, whom Joe had met in college while he was on a study abroad program in France, but she always felt like an outsider—being neither Italian nor knowledgeable about grapes. Sophia made it a point to sit next to her in the stylishly furnished Bellini living room.

She asked, "How is your new house coming along?"

"We move in around mid-March," Grace said. "Its location is close to the kids' school. It will be farther for Joe to drive to work, but I won't have to make the ten-mile round trip twice a day to school and back."

"Yes, and their school friends will be living close by. How exciting for you all."

"Was it a big adjustment for your stepdaughter to have a mother?" Grace asked, pushing her dark hair away from her eyes.

Sophia hesitated. She never referred to Cat as her stepdaughter but did not want to embarrass Grace by saying that.

"What a stupid question," Grace blurted out. "I am sure it was difficult."

"My daughter and I did get off to somewhat of a rocky start, but things are much better. I hope that you and Joe and the kids will visit us sometime this summer. We want to have a wedding reception with Robert's mother and friends present. It will be a bit unusual with our daughter and a baby there as well, but such is life."

"I have never been east, so it will be a treat for me. I'm sure Joe will enjoy having a vacation too. The only time we went away was to visit my family in France."

During the reception, which included all the workers at the winery, Maria Bellini spoke of her daughter's path—first as a young adventurous child in Italy, then as a shy, bookish girl in Sonoma Valley, to a graduate from Stanford Law.

"She has done so much in her life already, despite hardships, and we are all so proud of her. Her enthusiasm and compassion are what attract people to her."

Her brother, Joe, told of Sophia's daring deeds, how they got lost in the hills when they spotted a coyote and fled, not paying attention to where they were going, when they uncorked a wine barrel to taste its contents and had trouble getting the stopper back in, and when they ate so many unripe grapes they got bellyaches.

"She got us into a lot of trouble," he said, "but, of course, I was an angel, being the only son."

Giorgio shook his head. "You went along for the adventure, so you were guilty by association."

*****

The week was over much too soon. Sophia repeated the invitation for the entire Bellini family to visit them in Eastport.

"We have room to put you all up, and we will spend the days sailing around Long Island Sound."

Giorgio looked as if he had just been granted his dearest wish. "*Non veda l'ora!* I am delighted, and I have some Brunello de Sonoma wine left in our reserve supply from a few years back. It was our best year yet. I will have some cases shipped to you in time for the celebration."

Sophia thought about the wine bottles with the Bellini label on them at her wedding reception. A plan began to form in her mind. *Sam will see who I am and what I am capable of.*

EASTPORT, EARLY MARCH

And soon it was back to school for Cat, back to the office for Robert, and back to wherever Sophia found a vacant table and chairs. The renovations of the Victorian home were coming along. The contractor thought May first was a realistic date for the grand opening, which was right around the time of the baby's due date.

During her research into Nancy's border dispute, Sophia learned that the neighbor's house had received a building permit from the town, based on a town surveyor's map of that district in 2010. No one had bothered to check to see how and why it changed from the previous 1907 survey. *Why did the town's building inspector require a new survey in 2010?* she wondered. She looked up the inspector's name and number to get the answer and, to her surprise, up popped Benjamin Wyman. *Another Wyman. I am beginning to understand what I am up against.*

The once cut-and-dried case now became as intricate as a spider's web. And the trial date was a month away. *What should I tell Nancy? That she can't beat city hall or, in this case, town hall? No, there has to be some way to get a favorable verdict without ruffling too many feathers.* She searched for the 1907 map that Nancy Harris told her about and finally located it on microfiche, buried in the archives of the town's historical society. It was not just a survey of Nancy's land, but it included the entire district. Getting out her iPhone, she took pictures of the entire map.

Then she got in her car and drove around the rezoned area, street by street, taking more pictures. It took her so long that when she arrived at school, Cat was one of the few children still there, waiting to be picked up.

"Hi, Cat. I am sorry that I am late," Sophia said as Cat climbed into the back seat.

"Hi, Mom, what took you so long?"

"I was putting together the pieces of a puzzle."

"Did you finish the puzzle?"

"Not exactly."

"I can help you because I am good at puzzles," Cat offered.

"Strangely enough, in this puzzle, the pieces do not fit together, but I found out the reason why. Let's think about dinner. What would you like?"

"Hmm. How about some Bellini ravioli and meatballs?"

"That is a delicious thought! I believe I have some in the freezer."

*****

During supper, Robert noticed that Sophia was in high spirits, teasing Cat about her interest in a certain boy whose name she kept mentioning, and humming as she produced freshly baked chocolate pistachio biscotti, Robert and Cat's favorite.

"This is a treat," said Robert. "Something is up. Did you get good news about the renovations?"

"No," said Sophia coyly.

"Did the doctor tell you we're having twins?"

"*Dio mio!* Absolutely not!"

"Well, are you going to tell me or do I have to keep guessing all night?"

"I can't tell you or shouldn't tell you. You will know in a few weeks."

Robert saw Cat paying close attention to their conversation.

"Cat, if you go and do your homework now, I promise that I will play *Connect Four* with you when you're finished."

"Do you think you can beat me?"

"I am going to try very hard."

"Okay," she said, and taking a biscotti in each hand, she disappeared down the hall.

Sophia waited for Robert to speak, knowing he wanted Cat out of hearing range.

"Sophia, I want to warn you that Sam does not like to lose in court." Robert sensed that she had found something to strengthen her case.

"Neither do I," she replied, seeing his discomfort. *Whose side is he on?* she wondered.

"But he has a great advantage over you. He knows everyone, is in bed with everyone. For good or bad, he makes sure that he and the firm stack the deck, so the odds of winning are high even before a trial starts."

"You mean he cheats by bribing people or threatening people? If that is the kind of lawyer you want to be associated with, then you should stay in your law firm, although it's obvious that you are not an equal partner. He runs the show. He takes the cases that he likes and gives you and Arthur the crumbs."

"That's not true."

"No? Then why does he have all the property rights cases? All of them! At my first meeting with the firm, when you mentioned that there were several property rights issues, I thought it strange to have so many for a town this size, and today I discovered why there are so many and why he wants to litigate all of those cases."

She noticed Robert's surprise.

"From your reaction, you are obviously not in on it, thank God. Sam is trying to hide a crime, and when I reveal it in court, it will ruin him as a lawyer."

Robert stared at her, stunned.

"If that is true," he said softly, "then if you expose him, you not only ruin his career but mine as well."

Sophia shook her head in disbelief.

"How so?" she asked, her voice registering shock.

"I am still a member of the law firm until May. There is a saying: *'A man is known by the company he keeps.'*"

She paced up and down the long living room, confused by how quickly her legal case had changed from a sure win to now having to protect her husband's career. She saw a weakness in her husband that sickened her. He did not have the confidence to go it alone as a lawyer in his hometown, so he hitched himself onto a scoundrel. He knew what Sam was like, and he did it anyway.

She stopped and stared at him. "So if I win, I ruin your reputation. If I lose, I ruin mine."

"Yours won't be ruined, Sophia. Every lawyer loses a case now and then."

"But not when I know what has been going on illegally and don't reveal it in court. It is something I cannot live with, and I don't think you can either. This lie cannot be hidden forever, and when it comes out, and it will, then what? We sail off in your boat, never to be seen again, or we disappear into the caves in the Sonoma hills?"

She suppressed the urge to tell him what she had found because now she wondered if she could trust him to keep the information secret. *Why can't he see the danger in hiding a crime? He's not stupid, only ridiculously loyal.*

He was sure that whatever evidence she had turned up was explosive. He had been suspicious of Sam's insisting that he alone had to try the land disputes, but he thought it was because they were sure wins that would enhance Sam's reputation.

This is bad. Sophia knows the law, and she doesn't bluff.

"Tell me what you found."

"Sorry," she pushed back. "It seems you are in bed with Sam. It's time you divorced him," she said bitterly.

Then something made her stop. She clutched her groin and moved to the nearest chair.

"What's wrong, Sophia?" He rushed over.

"I'm suddenly very tired," she lied. "I need to lie down."

"Here. Let me help you to the bedroom. Get some sleep. I promised Cat I'd play that game."

As she sat on their bed, she tried once more to get him to understand how serious the matter was.

"Robert, you are playing with fire, and if you stay loyal to Sam, the fire will consume you, along with your unethical friend."

He felt she was right but could not bring himself to say it out loud.

When Robert returned to their bedroom, he found Sophia in bed, fast asleep. He changed into his pajamas and sat for several minutes on the edge of the bed, thinking of Sophia's last words.

I am playing with fire! I wouldn't put it past Sam to do something unethical. I should have left the firm sooner, but now I'm caught up in a lawsuit between my wife and my law partner. What has she found out?

In the corner beside the dresser was her black briefcase. She had purposely bought one that was a different color from his so they wouldn't get them mixed up. He stared at it, thinking.

It was tempting to take a peek. He listened, wanting to make sure she was really asleep. Her breathing was slow and steady.

"Sophia," he said quietly.

No response.

He tiptoed over to the corner, unlatched the tab, and then paused.

I am about to sneak a look at another attorney's private papers.

He sighed heavily and pulled open the case. Inside there were loose pages, parts of a survey map, and a pad with notes scribbled on it, which he couldn't read.

Damn it, he thought. He knew she often wrote in her own shorthand when she was in a hurry or wanted to be secretive.

He quietly flipped through the pages of maps, noticing certain places with lots highlighted. One had the date printed in the corner, and he wondered why that old survey map was of any use to her when it had been replaced by a newer one.

Searching for some clue, his eyes fell on the street map where Nancy Harris and Will Cummings had adjoining properties. A different boundary, in red ink, had been drawn where the two lots met.

Only one of these boundaries can be correct.

There were several other properties highlighted in the same way that were also under litigation.

How could so many properties in the same district be under dispute? he wondered.

As he was quickly stuffing the sheaf of papers back in the brief-case, some slipped out. He stuck them on top of the pile, latched the case, and climbed into bed. Even though he was lying beside the woman he loved, he felt alone and ashamed.

*****

The next morning, Robert left early for the office, saying that he had left some papers there he needed to look at. He had given Sophia a quick peck on her cheek before rushing out. She stared after him, sensing that he wanted to escape.

Maybe he intends to ask Sam about the property cases. It's too late for Sam to make amends. I intend to reveal his deception on the first day of trial.

Sophia drove Cat to school and returned home, for she, too, had papers to examine. Using the living room floor as a table, she began to spread out the sections of the map that she had photographed in the town offices and then reproduced on her home printer.

Bruno and Kit watched her as she began to arrange the pages, one by one, in a straight line. She had only put a handful of photos next to each other when she realized that they were out of order.

This group of maps belongs in the middle of the district, not here. I know I put them in my briefcase that way.

She remembered putting her briefcase in the corner of the bed-room before she had climbed into bed. Now they were mussed up.

"Oh, fuck! Robert must have gone through them when I was asleep. That was why he rushed away. He was embarrassed."

She felt deceived, like he had cheated on her. *He has crossed the line, and I can never forgive him for that.*

With anger building inside her, she placed the entire group of small maps in the correct order so that now she had the entire survey map recreated in front of her. Then she took some tape and attached the pages so that they formed a whole map, a reproduction of the original map of 1907.

She took out a copy of the 2010 map that she had obtained from the assessor's office. She compared them for a while, made more notes on her legal pad, and finally folded each carefully, like a road map, and put them back in her briefcase.

There is no point in hiding them. He knows. What is he going to do with this information? We are now on opposite sides and only one of us can come out a winner.

Suddenly she felt a sorrow so intense that she had to sit down. *He promised me that he would never lie and that he would be a husband I was proud of. I can't trust him anymore, just like I couldn't trust Carlo. Was I wrong to marry him so quickly, not really knowing him well? Have I failed again? I so wanted this marriage to work. I have tried so hard with Cat, thinking she would be the obstacle, not Robert. Damn it!*

If this case ruins Robert's career, it may lead to a divorce. Who would get Cat? And my soon-to-be-born child?

She knew the sex of the fetus but had not told Robert. She was not sure why she was keeping it a secret. One thing was sure: She needed a child or children around her. Cat made her happy. *So much to teach her and so much to enjoy with her.* She could not picture a life without Cat. Or without Robert.

She did not want to change husbands. It was too hard to even contemplate. *It hasn't even been a year since we were married. I can't keep disposing of husbands like they have a shelf life.*

She stared at the briefcase and weighed her options.

It did not take long to decide what her moral code of ethics compelled her to do.

Sophia called her client, Nancy Harris.

"Mrs. Harris, I have found evidence that supports your claim that Will Cummings knowingly built on your land. However, this knowledge must be kept quiet until the trial. Strictly between us, Will Cummings may still win in the land court. Why? Because the judge may not permit the evidence to be included or disregard the evidence. What I am saying is that any negative ruling is grounds for appeal to the state court of appeals, and then not only will that court order the Cummings house to be modified or torn down, but you will be rewarded damages for your legal fees and, most likely, for your emotional pain and suffering. That is how I see this case progressing."

"I don't have the money to appeal," said Nancy Harris. "What can I do?"

"Do you have a mortgage on your house?"

"No, it was paid off long ago."

"Then you can borrow on the equity in your home. Let's wait until we get the land court verdict before you take any further steps."

"How sure are you about the final outcome, Ms. Bellini?"

"As sure as I am talking to you now."

She closed the phone, smiling in anticipation of what was to come.

EASTPORT, MID-MARCH

Sophia needed to call her doctor regarding the pain she had felt in her abdomen. She wasn't doing much housework anymore, so she knew it was not caused by overexertion. A maid was coming in once a week to change the bed linens, do laundry, and clean the floors, kitchen, and bathrooms. Sophia still cooked, mostly easy meals that required little time and preparation.

Although the doctor was not too alarmed, she did want to see her immediately.

"Everything appears okay," she said after giving her patient a thorough exam. "I want to deliver the baby by cesarean section. Not so much for the baby's sake but for yours. A fetus passing through your already damaged birth canal may cause ruptures and bleeding. And I do not want to wait until May first, which would be the full nine months. I think we need to do it by April 15 or sooner. Come in next week. I should have a better idea then."

The doctor saw the worried look in her eye.

"Everything is fine. Soon you will be the mother of a healthy baby boy."

Sophia gave her a forced smile. She actually had been worrying about making it through the trial.

*****

That afternoon, when Robert came home from work, he found Sophia sitting on the floor, with her back against a coffee table in the living room, pen in hand. The two land maps were on either side and her notepad on her lap. He realized that she was writing a brief for the upcoming trial. She did not look up at him or try to hide the maps.

A cold shudder passed through him. *She knows that I looked in her briefcase.* He wanted to pretend that everything was normal, but he couldn't. He stood there, looking like a traveler who had arrived at his destination but was still lost. *What can I say? I can't tell her I am sorry I looked in her briefcase because I'm not. I needed to know.*

The silence was broken by the March wind whistling outside the terrace doors. Then footsteps sounded in the hall, and Cat walked into the room, followed by Bruno, and then Kit.

"Hi, Daddy, how was your day?"

He had to smile. *Cat is mimicking her mother.*

"Hi, Cat. My day was…good. How was your day?"

"My teacher said I got the highest mark on a vocabulary quiz."

"That's my Cat."

He turned back to watch his attorney wife using their living room floor as her office.

"Sophia, if you need quiet, we can go in another room."

She wrote a little more and then looked up and glared at him with a stony face.

Putting down her pen, she closed her legal pad, carefully put all her papers back in her briefcase, and locked it with a key.

"I am through for today. I know how to proceed." She paused. "And you?"

She is asking me what I am going to do, knowing what I know.

"I have a loyalty to the firm that I must honor." His voice sounded weak.

"You do what your conscience tells you to do. You have to live with yourself."

Robert's heart sank. He knew that he had lost her over this.

"I have not had time to make supper," she said. "Let's eat out."

That night, they went to a Mexican restaurant where they ordered burritos, tacos, and quesadillas.

"Is this what Dolores eats?" Cat asked as she prepared to bite into a taco.

"I am sure that she has had everything on the menu, but she eats lots of other foods too."

"When will she come to visit us again?"

"Well, we are having a wedding"—she paused, the word *celebration* sticking in her throat—"a gathering of family and friends sometime this summer."

She dared not look at Robert, and he remained silent. There was so much she had to tell him, wanted to tell him—about the pain in her groin, about the birth procedure, the new delivery time, the child's sex. *He has a right to know these things*, she kept saying to herself, but her emotional hurt was so deep it made her heart ache.

*****

That night, when she lay beside him in bed, she tried to sort out her feelings. She did not hate him or fear him or dread sleeping next to him as she did with Carlo. She felt a sadness that he was not the man she had imagined him to be, wanted him to be—someone who walked the walk, whose actions reflected his honesty and integrity.

*****

A week later, at a French restaurant, they were quietly eating their meal, when Sophia asked, "Would you like a taste of my French onion soup, Cat?"

"Yes, please." She took a sip. "Mmm, that's good. When my baby brother is born, can he eat food or just have milk from your nipple?"

Sophia flushed. "At first, he will just have milk." *I must tell Robert of the baby's sex.*

She looked sideways at Robert.

"It is going to be a boy," she whispered, her voice flat.

"A boy! Cat was right. When did you find out?" he asked.

"A little while ago."

145

"Today?"

"No, much longer than that."

"What? And you didn't tell me?"

She raised her eyebrows. "We have not been talking much since—"

She didn't need to finish the sentence. He knew the rest of her unsaid words. Since he opened her briefcase, they had become more like liars than lovers, saying bland greetings and acknowledging small courtesies for Cat's sake. They had slept with their backs to each other from the day after he looked through her papers. Even though sex was now unadvisable, they had avoided all bodily contact.

"Why are you and Daddy whispering?"

"We have things to say to each other that are personal, Cat," answered Sophia lightly. "Shall we order dessert? There's ice cream on the menu."

"Anything else?" he whispered, his voice tinged with anger.

A waiter had come over, and Cat began to order her favorite ice cream.

"The doctor thinks a cesarean should be scheduled for April fifteenth at the latest."

"Why?"

"Because she doesn't want to take any chances. My birth canal was damaged before."

"Is that all?"

She hesitated. The waiter was standing in front of them.

"No dessert for me," she said.

Robert shook his head, and they had privacy once again.

"Well?" he demanded. His irritation at being left out of this information was clear. *It's my child as well as hers.*

"I am starting to have sharp pains. I had another one today, just before you came home."

"Sophia, you must take it easy for the next month." He said it not as a request but as an order.

"How can I? The start of the trial is two weeks away."

"What is more important to you?" he spat. "Arguing a case or having a baby?"

She turned to face him, and with a voice full of hurt, she spoke loud enough for others around them to hear, "How simple you make it! My choice is gut-wrenching! Do I resign from a case that I know I can win, and whose outcome is going to right some terrible wrongs? Or do I try the case and put in danger the life of our baby, whose very existence is a small miracle? Aren't you lucky? It's a choice you will never have to make!"

Her fury took all her energy from her. She closed her eyes and tried to calm down.

Robert felt the stares of the other patrons on them. His face turned red.

Sophia spoke to Cat, "As soon as you finish, we will leave. I need to get out of here."

"Why, Mom?" Cat asked timidly.

She didn't understand what her parents were talking about, only that it was making them upset.

"I can't breathe."

Robert had been faced with a tough decision as well. He knew what was at stake: His marriage, his reputation as a lawyer, Sam's legal career, and the very existence of the firm. Also he knew that the town surveyor, the building inspector, and even the judge in the case, depending on how he ruled, could face dismissal or worse.

Robert had gone to work early on the day after seeing the maps because he wanted to look through Sam's files before Sam arrived. He had opened Sam's office door and had gone directly to his file cabinet, pulling out the property dispute cases.

He found six. *Six! I thought that there were three.* He noticed that they were all in the same district. He made a note of their addresses and went next to the surveyor's office.

"I want to see the land surveys of these properties."

The clerk looked at the list, wondering why there was such a sudden interest in those six properties. Robert examined the survey maps from 2010. The earlier survey map was nowhere to be found. When he finally tracked it down, buried in the archives, he saw what Sophia had seen—changes made in the newer map without explanation.

It was beginning to dawn on him what deep trouble Sam could be in if this information came to light. He had left the town hall and had gone to a nearby café for a cup of coffee and to think.

Sam may win the case in the land court, but if Nancy takes it to the state appeals court, it will reverse the decision. Sam can't bribe all of those judges. Once that happens, the truth will come out, Sam is disbarred, and my association with the firm will hurt me.

He opened up his computer and reread the contract that he, Arthur, and Sam had signed on May fifteenth the previous year.

I could leave the firm sooner than that date for just cause, like a partner being disbarred, which would reflect on the entire firm, but that won't happen soon enough, if at all.

He saw only one remote possibility for everyone involved to come out unscathed. He went back to the computer and looked up some information. Then he knew for sure what he was going to do.

Fifteen minutes later, he walked into Sam's office. As usual, Sam was sitting at his desk with a drink of some kind in his hand. Robert guessed it was not water.

Without any greeting, he said simply, "The jig is up," and told him what he knew about the 2010 suspicious land survey. "You have to make this right. Otherwise Sophia can prove that survey is false and you'll be disbarred."

"I had nothing to do with it," Sam protested.

"Don't lie to me, Sam," Robert said calmly. "I checked the signature on the land survey of 2010. Your cousin Ben was the surveyor. You know what's going on. There are currently six cases of property disputes which you alone are litigating. Now why is that?"

Sam remained tight-lipped. That was all the confirmation Robert needed.

"Fix it. Settle out of court. Save your career and your reputation, or otherwise, you and your cousin and several others will be going to jail."

"You'd never let your wife screw me like that. You owe me."

"Whatever support or protection you offered me years ago, I have paid back. And you screwed yourself by being involved in wrongdoing. You should know better than to imagine I will go along with that scheme."

"I'll think about it," was all Sam promised him, but Sam knew he had no choice but to destroy the newer map.

It wasn't so much him losing his license to practice law that Sam had to worry about. He came from money. he could still support his family. It was his reputation in a town that his ancestor, Samuel Wyman, had founded. To have his name smeared by such a scandal would be a disgrace from which he could never recover. His face contorted as he thought of Sophia Bellini.

If I'm going to pay dearly, so is she. I am going to shame her in court and fix it so that she loses the Harris case. Then I'll find a way to destroy her and Robert. Nobody gets the better of me.

EASTPORT, MARCH 22

The back pain wouldn't go away. No matter how she stood or sat or lay down, Sophia felt uncomfortable. *Was it this bad during my first pregnancy?* she thought, trying to remember back seven years. *Maybe I am carrying this fetus differently than the other one.*

After seeing her doctor, Sophia did try to take it easy: Putting her feet up, taking Bruno on shorter walks, driving Cat to and from school, and carrying on her law practice over the phone. Her clients understood, one even giving her advice on relaxation methods. She tried to sit and concentrate on her clients' cases but found herself having to get up frequently to go to the toilet or to move around the room to ease her discomfort.

She and Robert were barely civil to each other. Instead Sophia found herself talking to Bruno as she used to do in her penthouse apartment. It wasn't exactly a one-way conversation, and Bruno's responses were comforting, if repetitive. Kit wasn't so much into intimacy. A pat on her head or a quick belly rub was enough to make her run off and hide for hours or sit on the windowsill and stare out at the birds.

That afternoon, Robert came home in high spirits. He picked up Cat and twirled her around, promising to finally beat her at Connect Four later on. Bruno got an extra pat, and even Kit stayed while he scratched her neck.

Sophia, whose back had been bothering her all day, sat in a recliner and watched in amazement. She hadn't seen Robert in such a mood in months.

"Shall I cook dinner?" he asked her, assuming that she was in no condition to eat out. "What do you feel like having?"

"I took some shrimp out to defrost. I thought we'd have shrimp scampi."

"Shrimp scampi it is, with linguine, a salad with walnuts and thinly sliced Parmesan cheese, and for dessert, cannoli!" And, from his briefcase, he produced a box of Sophia's favorite Italian dessert.

"I'll help you." She started to get up.

"No, you won't. Husband's orders. Cat and I can handle it."

"I guess you had a good day." She leaned back and closed her eyes. Ten days to trial. *How am I going to manage it?* The pain and her extra weight were all-consuming, robbing her of any positive energy.

"Actually, I believe you had a good day as well."

"How is that possible? Other than making a few calls and the usual routine with Cat and Bruno, I've been in this chair all day, resting."

"I will tell you after dinner, when our guest arrives."

"What guest?"

He disappeared down the hall.

"Robert!"

No response. She could hear him ask Cat to set the table. Soon Cat came into the kitchen and laid out placemats and napkins. Then she went to get the silverware.

She is becoming so responsible, thought Sophia. *She accepts our requests to do her share of whatever is needed.*

A few minutes later, Robert emerged in tan slacks and a long-sleeved navy blue jersey and immediately started preparations for dinner. She knew he wasn't going to tell her who was coming over; she would just have to wait.

She watched him from her chair, getting out the ingredients and the chopping board and knife, his movements deliberate and deft. He reminded her of her father in her family's kitchen, sharing the work, as if any Bellini ever called cooking *work*. This is how she had pictured her marriage with Robert: Two people enjoying the simple pleasures of life—family, food, friends.

She closed her eyes, and tears started to spill out onto her face. She tried to wipe them away, but they kept flowing, like a ruptured breach in a dike.

Why does life have to be so difficult? I married for love of a man, for a child that was denied me by Carlo. Everything was good. Then I take an open-and-shut case which turns out to be a nightmare, playing havoc with my marriage and possibly Robert's career.

"Mom, why are you crying?" Cat was standing beside the lounge chair, looking anxious.

"Come up here, my love. Sit beside me. There's room. I just need a hug."

Cat climbed up and hugged her tightly and said, "Don't cry, Mummy. I love you very much and I will never leave you."

Sophia smiled through her tears. *Where had she heard that before?*

"Cat, you make me so happy." She nestled her closer, and Cat put her hand on her mother's abdomen. She drew it back quickly.

"I felt something move."

"That is your brother Mateo kicking, wanting to come out."

"How does he come out?"

Before she could answer, Robert came over to say that dinner was almost ready. He looked at his wife's tearstained face. He was sure her tears were because of him.

I hope that she will forgive me when she learns what I tell her later.

"Daddy, feel Mom's tummy! Mateo is kicking in there."

Robert came around the other side of the chair, sat on its arm, and put his hand on Sophia's bulge.

"He has a good kick. Maybe he'll be a soccer player." He bent down and kissed the top of Sophia's head.

She looked up through her tears and said, "You'd like that."

"I'd like whatever my wife and children do that will make them happy."

"I'm hungry," Cat declared.

"Me too," Sophia said.

Dinner was delicious. Sophia and Robert were sipping espresso and munching on cannoli when Cat repeated her earlier question.

"How does the baby come out?"

Sophia wasn't about to make up a silly story that Cat wouldn't believe anyway. *Keep it simple,* she thought.

"My doctor is going to cut my abdomen and take Mateo out that way."

"Will it hurt?"

"No, I'll be asleep."

"Then what happens to your ab…domen?"

"Oh, she'll just stitch it up. It will leave a scar, that's all."

"Is that how you got the scar that's on your belly?"

Sophia stared at Cat. *How did she know?*

"You remembered that from when we took a shower together?" Cat nodded.

How do I explain the scar? A white lie?

"Yes, Cat, I had a baby years ago when I was married to another man. My daughter didn't live very long."

"Really?" Cat said sadly. "What happened to her?"

Sophia was not ready for this question.

"She was…she was—" Sophia looked away, not able to finish, trying to erase the image of her infant daughter's last breaths. Her lips trembled.

Robert spoke up. "The baby was sick. And afterward, Mom was very sad not to have a daughter, but then she met you, and she decided right then and there that you were the daughter that she always wanted."

"Really, Mom?"

"Yes," said Sophia, looking at Robert in awe. "Yes, that is exactly right."

The doorbell rang.

"That must be our guest." Robert went to open the door.

When Sophia saw Marion, she was suspicious. "What's going on?"

Robert was more polite. "Would you care for a cannoli? We were just licking our way across the platter."

"I am a sucker for cannoli," Marion confessed. She chose a ricotta-filled one and rolled her eyes after biting into it.

"Well, what's this all about?" Sophia demanded.

"So...you haven't...told her yet." The words were spoken as Marion munched. She brushed some powdered sugar off her navy blue pantsuit.

"No, I was waiting for you."

"Told me what?" Sophia pleaded.

"Ladies first. Marion?" Robert bowed slightly, giving her due deference.

Marion reluctantly put the cannoli down before she spoke.

"I told Sam I was resigning immediately because I was joining your law firm."

"I am sure he wasn't surprised by your wanting to leave. Now he's left with an all-male law firm. But why immediately? Our law offices won't be ready until May."

Robert raised his hand, ready to speak.

"Sam and I had a friendly chat."

Sophia snickered. "And?"

"All six property cases will be settled out of court."

Sophia was stunned. She looked from Robert to Marion in disbelief.

"What! How did you manage that?"

"Sam had no choice. I told him that if Nancy Harris's case went to court and she lost, you would appeal on the grounds that a false survey map was created in 2010, with his knowledge. So he's promised to remove that map from the records with no one being the wiser."

"*Damn it.* He gets away without being punished."

Sophia looked over at Cat, who had one antenna up.

"I shouldn't have said a swear, Cat. I'm sorry."

"That's okay, Mom. Boys say it all the time at recess when they're mad."

Sophia rolled her eyes.

"Sam will pay the costs incurred by settling out of court, so it's a huge financial punishment," Robert stressed. "He will be able to retain his law license, though, and his reputation."

"Too late to save that. But this will not be the end of it. He will want revenge."

Robert and Marion looked at each other, wondering how Sophia could be so sure.

Sophia smiled at their naïveté.

"I have studied behavioral psychology. He fits the classic model of a narcissist: Arrogant, selfish, manipulative. That type does not take losing lightly. Trust me, he will find a way to try to ruin my reputation and yours as well—and yours, too, Marion, since you revealed his cheating on Thea and are now crossing over to the enemy."

There was an uncomfortable silence.

Marion broke it by saying, "I hope for once that you are wrong. By the way, any news on the renovations? I've moved out of my office."

"To be honest, I have not had the energy to check on the progress. I'll pay them a visit tomorrow."

"No, you won't," Marion ordered. "Robert and I are taking over all your duties until the birth of Matthew or Mateo or whatever you'll call him. That's why I have resigned now. We'll share walking the dog and picking up Cat from school. And we will both take turns checking on the renovations. I no longer have an office to go to every day, so I have the time."

"What happens to the cases that you have been working on?"

"Sam says I can keep those clients. Too many questions if he took them away. He was furious, of course, but he knows I'm aware of his duplicity. It was nice to see him get the short end of the stick, for a change."

"Thank you, Marion, for helping me. It is going to be a pleasure working with you in our new offices." She did not mention Robert.

Marion said her goodbyes and left.

"Come, Cat, it's time for bed." Sophia had noticed how closely Cat was listening to their every comment and watching their interactions. *I need to discuss legal matters in private with Robert from now on. I do not want Cat passing along snippets of our conversations to her classmates or teachers.*

"Will you tell me a bedtime story?" Cat asked as they started to walk toward the bedrooms.

"Of course." She stopped. "Have you heard the one about the deer and the crow? The deer did not listen to the crow and became friends with a jackal, who trapped him in order to kill and eat him." She paused. "I believe it took place in this town."

"There's a jackal in this town?" asked Cat. "Have you seen it?"

"Many times," said Sophia. "He has a clever disguise, so he fools a lot of people."

Robert saw Sophia turn and give him a look that told him the parable was for his ears and that she was not happy with his news.

After Sophia had kissed Cat goodnight, she came into their bedroom. As soon as the door closed, Sophia gave Robert her opinion of what he had just done.

"You saved Sam. I hope you can save yourself."

"I did it for you, Sophia." His voice was pleading.

"No, not really. If it had been some other attorney, would you have gone to the mat for him? You did it to help Sam, but there is a limit to being a loyal friend. You enabled him to cover up a crime. Aiding and abetting, I believe it's called."

She began to undress. Robert was sitting on the edge of the bed. He watched her remove all her jewelry as she did every night. She took off her wedding ring to put it back in its case.

At least she still wears the ring I gave her. He sighed.

Then she removed her top, exposing her enlarged breasts, filled with milk.

She is so beautiful, even eight months pregnant. I love her so much.

Sophia turned to see him staring at her.

"Sophia, you are the best thing that has ever happened to me."

She didn't respond but slipped on her nightgown and got into bed beside him.

"My intention truly was to help you...as well as Sam," Robert said quietly, moving closer to her.

"You should not have looked in my briefcase or spoken to Sam about its contents," she answered just as quietly. "It is your behavior as an attorney that I cannot accept. It hurts me deeply."

"I know it must. I just wanted the lawsuits to end fairly so the injured parties did not suffer and you did not have to try the case so close to giving birth."

Sophia raised her voice. "You took the evidence of illegal activity that I had unearthed and had Sam bury it, without telling me or any legal authority. That is just plain wrong. I can't be that type of lawyer or work with someone who does that."

Robert remained calm. "I've never done that before, and I will never do it again. I promise."

She turned sideways to face him, her protruding belly filling up the space between them.

"You committed a serious breach of your oath as an attorney." She closed her eyes, feeling that the pain in her heart was now stronger than the pain in her back.

"I do not want another husband," she sighed. "I am happiest when I am with you and Cat. I am carrying your child." Her voice shook and became louder. "I have no other option but to stomach what you have done and go on." Now she was almost shouting. "But you cannot expect me to simply forgive and forget!"

He felt relieved that she was not going to leave him. She had not pardoned him, but he had hope that eventually, she might.

EASTPORT, MARCH

It began with a rumor. Cat had told her friends at school about her "Aunt Dolores," who was her mother's best friend and came to stay with them now and then. "They hug and kiss a lot," she said. From that innocent remark, carried home by Betty Wyman, came whispers of Sophia and Dolores in a relationship right under the nose of Robert.

"Latinos are known for being lovers," Betty's mother whispered to the biggest *blabbermouths* in town. "Maybe it's a threesome," the *mother-in-pearls* added. Thea Wyman took that thought and ran with it, all the way to Margaret, who sat beside her at the women's auxiliary luncheon.

Margaret said it was absurd.

"If anything, Dolores is man-crazy. From what Sophia has told me about her, she has three beaus dangling on her chain."

"Perhaps she says that to keep you in the dark. No women I know hug and kiss each other a lot."

Margaret stared at the wife of Sam Wyman. She was as thin as a pencil in spite of having given birth recently. *She must inhale rumors for breakfast, lunch, and dinner.*

"Sophia and Robert are very happy together. You do not see what I see. And you should not spread gossip. It may come back to bite you." Margaret had heard stories of Sam's womanizing but never repeated them.

Thea wanted to believe the rumors, however, and loved the attention she received when she told them, so she ignored Margaret

Navarro's warning. In fact, then and there, she tried to throw Marion Stephens in the mix, wondering out loud if those two female attorneys were together in bed as well as in business.

That was the last straw for Margaret.

"Is that all you can do? Start rumors?" she asked her fellow member of the women's auxiliary. "Get a life, Thea. I think you need to get out more. Accompany your husband on his travels about town. Be seen together as a couple. Otherwise people might say that you and Sam aren't getting along and make up stories about your own marriage."

Thea sat back in her chair, wrapping her arms around her thin body in an effort to appear strong.

"Sam and I have standing in Eastport. Our ancestors settled this town. Nothing that you or anyone else says against us will be believed. Sophia is an immigrant"—saying it like it was a despicable word—"and for that matter, so is Robert."

Margaret laughed.

"Well, if you go back far enough in history, so are you and Sam, unless, of course, you are Native Americans."

"Well, we practically are!" Thea replied, her shrill voice carrying above the chatter around them.

"No history book I've ever read suggested that the Puritans were indigenous people. And when your ancestors arrived here, it was the natives who helped them survive through the first winter. You should go find a member of the Pequot tribe and thank him or her for your very existence."

Thea turned to her, looking like she wanted to scratch her eyes out.

"I will do no such thing! We are superior to them in every way!"

"Only by having guns to drive them off their land or kill them," Margaret declared.

"Nonsense. They were *savages*. We had to protect ourselves."

"*Savages*," said Margaret. "That term is used throughout history to refer to people who are different. I studied American history when I was in college and have read that the Native Americans not only showed the Puritans where and how to hunt and farm but also told them what plants to use to cure their social diseases."

Thea's blue eyes turned a steely gray.

"Margaret, I am a member of the Daughters of the American Revolution, and their records say nothing about that. Now you're the one spreading lies!"

Margaret knew that the Puritan conquerors sugarcoated their own chronicles to sweeten the tale and that Thea ate it up. Any further comments she made to Thea would be shoved right back in her mouth.

The hearsay about Sophia and her friend didn't stop. It traveled along on the March winds, finding admittance into every tilted ear and suspicious mind, tainting the landscape of Eastport gray, like the dirty March snow that now covered the sides of the roadways.

Marion had heard the rumors as well and realized how prescient Sophia had been to predict Sam's revenge. There was nothing to do but wait until the rumors died out from contrary evidence. She decided not to tell Sophia.

*****

Nancy Harris, upon advice of counsel, refused to postpone or cancel the court date until a satisfactory settlement was signed, sealed, and delivered. Neither she nor Sophia trusted Sam Wyman with a handshake.

On March thirty-first, the day before the trial, Sophia heard from Sam late in the day. He offered to settle the suit for a paltry lump sum of cash. Sophia laughed lightly and said she would speak to her client. Nancy laughed even harder.

"What does he take me for, a fool?"

Sophia texted Sam, *"See you in court tomorrow."* She ignored the texts that Sam sent back. It was after office hours.

This haggling could go on all night, and I need my sleep.

Robert was angry that Sam had reneged on his part of the bargain, but he had to stay out of the negotiations now. It was Sophia's case, and she had to see it through to its conclusion.

*****

APRIL 1

Sophia, walking slowly to keep her back pain in check, showed up in court at the appointed hour. She and Nancy Harris sat outside the courtroom at nine o'clock, waiting for the case to be called. She had not opened any texts from Sam.

If he wants to play hardball, so can I.

Sam Wyman, looking smug, walked past them with his client.

What is he up to? Sophia thought. *Something funny is going on.*

Finally, at ten-twenty, the case was called, and Sophia and Nancy walked into the courtroom and took seats in the plaintiffs' area. They sat and waited as the judge peered at some papers on his bench. Sophia had taken a single pill to reduce her pain, and it was having no effect.

I must get through this.

A quick look over at Sam worried her. He looked pleased about something. The judge began to speak.

"I have just received confirmation that a settlement had been reached and therefore the case is dismissed."

Sophia shot up so quickly from her chair that it almost toppled over.

"Your Honor, my client has not agreed to a settlement."

Sam rose slowly, giving Sophia a pitiful stare.

"She certainly has, Your Honor, as you can see from the signed agreement in front of you. Perhaps Ms. Bellini does not recognize a settlement when she sees one."

Sophia shot back, "Your Honor, may I approach the bench to see the document in question?"

It was Sam's turn to object. "Your Honor, Ms. Bellini is just wasting the court's time. I have tried to contact Ms. Bellini for days, and she has not returned my calls or texts or emails. No professional attorney behaves that way. It's all been agreed to, and now she is trying to back out of the deal."

Sophia's head was exploding. It was all a lie, and he knew it, but she was there to protect her client's property, not herself from untruths. Sophia surmised that there was something on the agreement that Sam did not want her to see.

"Your Honor," Sophia replied, "I insist on seeing the document in question."

The judge hesitated, staring at Sam. Sophia saw a look pass between them.

This judge has been bought off.

She knew, however, what the lawbooks said regarding evidence, and she felt she had the upper hand. "Your Honor, under the procedures of fair trial and due process, I have the right to examine the document you hold in your hands. If you deny me that right, I will file for a mistrial."

And you know I will get it, she thought. Judges hate to have that on their record, especially when it's been determined that it was due to their own error.

The judge stared at the document, weighing his options.

"Very well, Attorney Bellini, you may approach the bench."

As she got up from her seat, she could hear Sam swearing under his breath. The judge handed her the document. At first glance, it did appear to be an agreement between her client and Will Cummings.

It can't be. Nancy would never sign anything without consulting me first.

Then she noticed the date.

"Is this date accurate?" she asked the judge.

The judge looked at Sam, who hesitated before saying, "Yes."

"Just to be clear, Mr. Wyman is saying that my client signed this document yesterday, on March 31."

Sam had not addressed her as Attorney Bellini, and she showed him the same disrespect. Again the judge looked at Sam, waiting for confirmation.

"Yes," Sam replied.

"In person?"

Sam's face sagged. He shuffled some papers and then said to the judge, "It was done electronically."

Sophia smiled and stood taller. "In that case, I want to see proof that my client was in communication by iPhone with Mr. Wyman's office yesterday."

"Your Honor, I cannot produce proof at this time."

"Why not?" Sophia interrupted. "It should be right there on your cell phone."

Sam cursed silently that his cell phone was on the table in front of him, in plain view.

"I erased it by mistake." Sam looked pale, his *boozy-looking* face notwithstanding.

"Your Honor," Sophia replied, her expression showing pity, "any ten-year-old knows how to retrieve a text that has mistakenly been deleted. Unless, of course, Mr. Wyman permanently deleted it, in which case, it was no mistake."

She sat down and gave Nancy Harris a reassuring smile. The judge waited while Sam fidgeted with his phone.

"Well, Attorney Wyman? How long are you going to make us wait?"

Without raising his head, Sam muttered, "I ask that you recess until Ms. Bellini and I can work this out."

"Fine. Find an empty room and complete the paperwork," said the judge, looking annoyed at Sam. "Case postponed until later today."

Sophia turned to her client, who was in a daze, trying to figure out what had just happened, and said, "We are good. I'll explain later."

Sam had been caught in a lie, hoping to trick Nancy Harris into believing that she had signed an agreement by mistake. He also made Sophia appear in court eight months pregnant and then questioned her competence and her legal knowledge.

I am going to make him regret it, she promised herself.

*****

Hours later, with the signed agreement in hand, Nancy Harris and Sophia walked out of the courtroom and into a reporter from the town's newspaper.

"I am thrilled at the outcome," Nancy told the press. "If anyone asks me if I know a good lawyer, I will suggest Sophia Bellini."

To Sophia, that was better than receiving the money from the fee she charged. The next day, the local gazette's headline read *Harris vs. Cummings Lawsuit Settled Out of Court* and went on to describe Nancy Harris's success regarding her boundary dispute.

Sophia was quoted as saying, "Justice prevailed." She made no mention of Robert's part in brokering the deal. Even if she wanted to, she couldn't, because now, according to the town's records, the 2010 survey map had never existed.

*****

"Any news from the building contractor?" she asked Robert the next evening.

"Only that he is still on schedule to complete the work by May first. He has put up the wrought-iron frame for the shingle. He asked me if the shingle is ready to be hung."

"It's ready, but I don't want it up until the day before we open."

He waited for her to tell him what the shingle would read, but she went on to another issue.

"We will need a legal secretary. After Lara's court appearance, I will offer her the job because she went to secretarial school and has passed an online course for legal secretary. And she understands how important it is to keep client information private. There are enough ugly rumors going around this town about us already."

Robert's eyes opened wide. "You know?"

She smiled.

"How? You practically haven't left the house for weeks."

"Have you never heard of Facebook? I don't frequent it ordinarily, but since I've been holed up here, I have had plenty of time to explore that and other sites. And I have been thinking and planning."

"What? Tell me," he begged.

"Not until I have put the finishing touches in place. By the way, we have to pick a date for our wedding reception. How about August first? It's our first anniversary as a couple. The baby will be four months old, God willing, and by then, I will have him on a bottle so I can return to work and a social life. It's not an ideal time to stop nursing, but many decisions aren't ideal."

I know, thought Robert. *Why can't she understand that my decision to solve the property lawsuits was not ideal but necessary?* He chose not to voice his thoughts. She was about to give birth to their son.

"We need to decide where to hold the reception," he said.

"We'll have it here, outside on the front lawn. It is large enough for fifty people."

"Are we inviting that many?" Robert looked worried.

"Yes, the more, the better. We will have a small orchestra, a dance floor, a catered buffet, and chairs and tables. I want it talked about all over town. It will be the event of the summer."

"So family and friends, then? As many as fifty?" He was still trying to imagine the guest list.

"Let's say family, friends, and *frenemies.* If you want to dispel rumors, invite the biggest gossipers in town." She smiled.

"Sam?" he asked, incredulous.

"Of course, he is at the top of my list of *frenemies.*"

"Are you sure you know what you're doing?"

"Oh yes, Robert. I will not allow Sam to ruin my reputation or yours or Marion's. He is going to be punished for his misdeeds in a most satisfying way."

Robert stared at his wife, his insides roiling in frustration. *Since our marriage, I have gone along with every decision she made that involved the two of us, and I was never asked to give my opinion. It's time I spoke up.*

"Sophia, let's just have a quiet reception for family and a few friends and forget about getting back at Sam. After all, he did lose the suit, and he paid a high price."

Sophia put her hands on her hips, her dark eyes showing no mercy.

"Have you forgotten that he broke his word when he promised to settle out of court, that he fully intended to deceive Nancy Harris into making her believe that she had somehow signed an agreement? Have you forgotten that he refused to assign me Lara's case, how he has belittled my legal skills at every turn? Why are you still defending him?"

"I just want the whole thing to be over. He can no longer hurt your career."

"It's not over for me. He needs to pay for his illegal and immoral behavior."

"Are you his judge?" he asked, realizing for the first time how badly Sophia wanted to see Sam suffer.

"More like his executioner," she answered.

EASTPORT, APRIL 7

Seven days before Lara's divorce trial was to begin, Sophia began to have spotting. It was midmorning, and she was alone in the house. She called her doctor, who said, "I want you to come to the hospital in Norwalk at once. Have someone drive you or call for an ambulance. I will be there waiting for you. And bring an overnight bag."

Sophia immediately called Margaret. "I need a ride to the hospital. It's urgent."

"The baby?"

"Oh, I'm sorry. Yes. There is some bleeding."

"I will be right over, by your front door."

Sophia retrieved her bag, already packed with a nightgown and a change of clothes. She gave Bruno a treat and checked to see that both the cat and dog water bowls were full.

I'll ask Margaret to eat with Cat and Robert tonight. I am sure Cat is going to have questions and Margaret will know how to answer them.

When she opened the front door, she saw her mother-in-law's car pulling up in front. Margaret got out and rushed over to help Sophia to the car, talking nonstop.

"Now don't be frightened. At eight months, the fetus is fully developed and can survive outside the womb. How are you feeling?"

"I'm fine. Actually my thoughts are on my client's case coming up in a week. Tell Robert he must let Marion know right away, so she can prepare to take my place. We do not want to delay the trial yet again."

"My goodness. You modern mothers are something else. You treat having a baby like cooking dinner, just one more thing to do."

Sophia laughed. "Not quite, but I do take my responsibilities seriously."

"And now you will have your own child to be responsible for and to love."

Sophia shook her head. "I already have my own child. I feel as though Cat is my own flesh and blood."

"Well, not really." Margaret was on the main road, passing slower-moving vehicles as she sped toward Norwalk Hospital.

"Really! I feel she is mine. She looks like me and has many of my traits. Did you realize that Cat and my daughter were born on the same day at about the same time?"

"Robert told me that, but it's just a coincidence."

"No, no. The day my daughter died, a part of me died too. But when I saw Cat for the first time, a spark went through me, as if my heart had been jolted awake. Every time I look at Cat, I see my own daughter staring back at me."

Her words had such a finality to them that Margaret did not protest any further.

Fifteen minutes later, they arrived at the hospital lobby to her waiting obstetrician.

"There is no point delaying any longer," her doctor said. "You are ready to deliver. We will prepare you for surgery."

Sophia thanked Margaret, hugging her warmly, and, refusing a wheelchair, strolled down the corridor with an attendant.

Margaret called Robert. "Sophia is in surgery. You will soon have a son."

"I am with a client but will leave here immediately. Sophia is alright?"

"She had a little bleeding, and the doctor decided to do the cesarean section now. Who picks up Cat today?"

"I'm supposed to. Can you do it?"

"Of course, and I'll take care of supper. Keep me informed and call Marion about Lara's case. Sophia said she will have to fill in."

"Right. And, Mom, if I haven't thanked you before, please know that I am so grateful for your help, not just today but during the last seven years. It's been a lot to ask."

"None of what happened with Catherine was your fault, except, I suppose, marrying her in the first place, but who could have foretold her desertion?"

Robert ended the call and explained the situation to his client, who left immediately. Then he gathered up some papers, put them in his briefcase, and rushed out of his office. He bumped into Sam in the hall—literally.

Sam, in trying to tarnish Robert's character, found that it was a lot harder than casting doubt on Sophia's. Robert came from Eastport and was part of a family who lived in the area for generations. His quiet demeanor had earned him respect, not only by the members of the sailing club and court officials but by the town's merchants and civic leaders. He gave no offense and took no false credit.

Also unsettling to Sam was that the makeup of the town's residents was changing. What had been a largely white Protestant community where every important office was run by people with long ties to Eastport was slowly evolving into a more diverse population. More minorities, including tradesmen, had bought homes in the town, and a few even had the nerve to run for town selectman or a position on the school board. Those folks were not just living in Eastport but looking to make their presence felt.

It was a worry to Sam, but his more immediate concern was Robert Navarro.

Perhaps I can start a rumor that he is cheating on his wife while she cheats on him with her girlfriend. Her pregnancy gives him motive, and her need to stay home to rest gives him opportunity.

He needed to find a likely candidate. No one came to mind, until just recently.

"Hey, slow down. I was coming to see you. There is something I want to discuss."

"Not now, Sam. I'm in a hurry."

"I heard a rumor that you and Eileen are lovers. Now it's none of my business, but—"

Robert had been tense for months, waiting for things to return to normal between him and Sophia, but they could not find common ground about Sam. Now Sam's words ignited a fuse to the emotions that he had held in check, causing him to explode.

Robert slammed his longtime friend and law partner up against the wall.

"Look, you bastard, I've had enough of your goddamn rumors! The only person I'm shacking up with is my wife, which is something you should do to stop rumors about your own philandering!"

He shook himself off Sam and started to walk away, then stopped and turned around. Sam cowered. He had never heard Robert even raise his voice, never mind become physical.

"I'm on my way to the hospital to witness the birth of my son," he shouted into the air, "and just in case there is a hard-of-hearing person within two hundred feet, I'm taking a paternity leave! That means I won't be back here—ever!"

From the entire suite of offices, there wasn't a sound. Robert's client had left. Only Eileen had heard Sam's insinuations and Robert's shouting and had come out of the reception area to watch.

Sam straightened his tie and smoothed out his suit jacket. He saw Eileen standing in the doorway with her hands folded across her chest, a disgusted look on her face.

I played that poorly, he thought.

All his words were lies. He knew it, and she knew it. He also knew that there was no policy on paternity leave in their agreement, but it would be foolish to challenge his partner's absence. It would be also embarrassing since he, too, had recently fathered a child, another girl.

"Good riddance to him," he muttered.

But he knew it was far from over. He had made plans to take Sophia down, to ruin her career and her marriage.

*****

As he drove to the hospital, Robert smiled at the idea of a paternity leave. He hadn't thought of it before. *I can help Sophia with*

Mateo, spend time with Cat, maybe give her sailing lessons, and set up the new law offices.

When he arrived at the hospital, he was asked to wait in the visitors' area. A cesarean section required surgery, and he was not allowed to observe. He called Sophia's family in California, then Marion, and then Dolores.

She volunteered to fly there immediately.

"No rush. I've left the law firm, so I'll be home, and my mother is here, not to mention Cat. You are welcome to come anytime, of course, but Sophia will have lots of help."

"She may need emotional support. Postpartum depression is a real thing. My sister had it bad. I will come next week when things have settled down. And call me back when you've counted his fingers and his toes."

Robert chuckled. Dolores had a way of simplifying every event to its very essence—in this case, the baby's digits.

He wondered if she knew of the rumors about her and Sophia. *If people actually had met Dolores before these rumors started...*

He sighed. *There aren't many Latinos in Eastport, that's the problem. Hugs and kisses are a way of greeting for them. Heartfelt. They show their feelings, rather than keep their emotions stuffed in their shirts, like so many Yankees in the town.*

"Mr. Navarro?"

"Yes!" he started. "Yes," he repeated, fully alert.

An attractive young woman was standing in front of him, her white hospital jacket bearing a tag that read *Emily Harris, Registered Nurse.*

"You don't know me, but I am the daughter of Nancy Harris."

Robert's brain was not connecting the dots.

"Your wife, Attorney Sophia Bellini, handled my mother's case?"

"Oh, yes. Sorry. I was miles away." He stood up to shake her hand.

"I work in surgery and heard your wife is in there now, about to have her second child, and I wanted—"

"Her first, actually. I mean, I have another child by my first marriage."

"You mean Cat is not Sophia's daughter by birth? I have seen them together. They look so much alike."

"Yes, well, it just happened that way."

"How fortunate, in one sense. I just wanted to say best of luck with the birth. My mother talks about your wife in glowing terms. I will tell her that I met Attorney Bellini's husband."

She smiled and walked away.

Robert watched her go. *I am the one who got Sam to settle Nancy Harris's case without going to trial. Sophia got the credit. And she is still angry with me for letting Sam off the hook.*

He didn't begrudge Sophia for her victory (it was well-earned because she found the discrepancy between the two surveys); however, he felt she was punishing him for something that was not his fault.

I had no hand in creating a false survey, and yet she blames me for finding a way to resolve the problem.

*****

Hours later, Robert walked into Sophia's hospital room and saw his wife holding Mateo in her arms. He bent down and gave his wife a peck on her cheek. She unwrapped the thin blanket so that the baby's arms and legs were exposed.

Robert examined his son.

"He looks perfect. How are you feeling?"

"A bit groggy from the anesthesia. And sore where the stitches are."

She smiled at him, feeling proud that she, by some miracle, was able to give him a son.

"Cat has a playmate."

"Let's hope she doesn't try to boss him around," he said. *She copies what she sees.*

"You will have to teach him how to be a man and give back as good as he gets."

He wondered if he should do the same with her.

"I will start the day you come home. I am on paternity leave."

"What? You never told me you had—"

"Self-imposed. I'm afraid I got rather emotional with Sam, when he brought up still another rumor, this one about me and Eileen."

"No!"

"I am sure she heard Sam make the accusation. That was enough for me to paste him to the wall and tell him I'm staying home to be with my son." He looked down at Mateo, who was sleeping. "Thanks, son, for coming at just the right time."

"He has your hair color," Sophia whispered, gently touching the fine light-brown hairs on the baby's head.

"What about his eyes?" Robert asked.

"I haven't seen his eyes yet. When he wakes up, I'll check them out." She leaned back on the pillows and closed her own eyes, obviously tired. She opened them in a flash, her mind ever active.

"Eileen can't stay there, working for that slimeball. I will have to bring her on board as well."

"If you are going to hire all the battlefield casualties from Sam's attacks, there won't be enough room in our new offices to interview clients," he said. *Another decision that she is making without consulting me.*

"I'll find room," she countered.

He knew that this was not a good time to debate the issue. He checked his watch.

"Cat will be home now. I'll FaceTime my mother and we will show them Matthew."

"Speaking of Cat, I have been thinking that I would like to adopt her legally. If anything happened to you, I would not automatically have the right to claim Cat as my daughter, so it makes sense for me to adopt her. Your ex-wife has to consent to it first. Do you think she would stop me from doing it out of spite?"

Robert was surprised. *I am not even forty, and she is worried about something happening to me.* He smothered his feelings.

"Catherine has no interest in being a mother. I doubt she would protest. Do the wheels in your head ever stop spinning?"

EASTPORT, APRIL 10

"He doesn't do anything," Cat complained. "He just sleeps." She was leaning into the recliner where Sophia sat with Matthew in her arms and watched him make faces with his eyes shut tight.

"Give him time, Cat," laughed Margaret from the kitchen, where she and Robert were preparing dinner. "In a few months, he will be grabbing and dropping everything in sight, then crawling and standing and, at some point, running faster than you."

"Really?" Cat asked her mother. "My baby brother will run that fast?"

Sophia took one arm away from the baby and put it around Cat. "Yes. Grandma is right. He will be a tall boy, given his long legs. You will be tall, but he may end up being your big brother."

"Hmm. Why are boys taller than girls?"

"Many boys grow to be taller than girls because of their genetic makeup, which is a term you will come across in high school or college. Also many boys get to be physically stronger than girls because they are built differently. They have more upper body strength, but that's where their advantage ends. Girls can be just as smart or, in some cases, much smarter than boys."

"Yes, I know. When Miss Creighton asks us to subtract numbers in our head and raise our hand when we know the answer, lots of girls can do it before the boys."

"I hope you don't tease the boys about that."

"No, I just smile."

She is learning, thought Sophia. *A smile can be more satisfying than a smirk.*

"Did you know that Dolores is coming next week? She is going to stay for a while to keep me company."

"I want her to keep me company too. She said she would teach me how to dance. And I want to get my ears pierced like she has."

"Someday when you are older, you can have your ears pierced, but not now. Dolores can teach you some simple dance steps so you can dance at the wedding reception. While she is here, maybe you and Dolores and Dad can go out shopping for some new summer clothes. You have outgrown most of last year's."

"Do you think that wise, Sophia?" Robert questioned, half listening to their conversation from the kitchen. "More grist for the *rumor mill.*"

"A threesome out in public? I'd like to hear what they can make of that."

"I'm sure Sam will think of something *diabolical.*"

"What does *diabolical* mean?" Cat asked.

"Wicked," answered Sophia.

"Like the wicked stepmother in Cinderella?"

"Exactly," Sophia said. *I'm surprised Sam hasn't already thought of that slur.*

*****

He had thought of it, out of desperation. Sam knew that nothing Sophia said or did in public indicated that she was mean to Cat, but he thought he could twist her words and actions to put doubt in people's minds.

He told his friends that Sophia kept her stepdaughter up late, allowed her to listen to adult conversation, and forced her to eat foods that no child needed to taste. Even though she had her own car, she made the girl walk more than a mile home from school.

He purposely misrepresented what his daughter had told him about Cat's birthday party. According to his account, kids were shrieking so loudly that the neighbors complained to the police, and

Robert used his position in the community to stop the cops from pressing charges for disturbing the peace.

Sam also knew that all small towns have one thing in common: People sticking their noses in other people's business. *All I need is for a few to imagine and believe that an ambitious woman, who is opening up her own law office, and using her husband's money and name to reach her goal. She can't enjoy being saddled down with a seven-year-old. I should know. I have one. History is filled with such grasping, ruthless, scheming women. I thought Robert was smarter than to fall for that bitch.*

EASTPORT, MID-APRIL
TO MID-MAY

Lara's divorce trial lasted two days. Marion presented evidence of both physical and mental abuse. The judge asked if Lara was aware that she could press criminal charges. She declined to do so. Instead she was asking for a generous financial settlement. Her husband did not want to go to jail and agreed. She was awarded 70 percent of the value of the assets as well as alimony and an order that James would not come within two hundred feet of wherever she lived.

That evening, Lara and Marion, along with her husband Phil, came to the Navarro residence to celebrate. They toasted with champagne and a seafood paella.

"You should not have gone through all the trouble to make this dish for me," Lara said.

"It wasn't that hard," Sophia protested. "A whole dinner in one big bowl."

Lara commented to Robert on his two children, "Your son looks like you, and your daughter looks like Sophia. You each have a carbon copy of yourself."

Robert was about to correct her when Sophia interrupted, "I first met my daughter when she was six, but somehow my DNA is in her blood."

Lara looked confused. "You're not really mother and daughter?" she gasped.

Sophia smiled. "More than if I had birthed her," she replied.

Lara looked from Cat to Sophia, not understanding.

Marion took Lara aside. "Their similar looks are just a coincidence."

"What happened to Cat's real mother?" she whispered.

"Gone within months of giving birth. Leaving with the exhaust from her car's tailpipe polluting the air. Never to return."

"My goodness. Cat is indeed fortunate."

"And Sophia as well. Their relationship reminds me of a Gordian knot. Inseparable. Almost from the very first day they met."

"Another coincidence!"

"Yes and no. When Sophia met her, Cat was a demanding child, who needed direction and nurturing. Sophia worked hard to gain her love and trust. It took a lot of patience. Any other mother would have tired of Cat's endless questions. Sophia enjoys explaining things to her. She wants to encourage her daughter to dream big. Did you know Sophia taught at Stanford Law for a while, right after graduating from there? She must have been a brilliant student. Aren't we lucky that we will be working with her every day?"

"We?" asked Lara.

Marion's eyes widened. "Oh dear, I thought Sophia had already asked you. I've let the *cat out of the bag.*"

The week after Sophia had given birth, Dolores called to say that she had to cancel her planned visit. The brother of her steady boyfriend had died suddenly, and she decided that she needed to accompany Ricardo to Argentina for the funeral. Cat was more disappointed than anyone else. Her dance lessons were postponed.

The next few weeks were busy. Everyone connected to the law firm, except Sophia, reported to work at the Main Street building every day, setting up filing cabinets and office equipment, testing out machines, and decorating the space to make it welcoming.

Sophia had given Robert a list of items to get from a storage locker that held the contents of her former penthouse. She wanted them placed in the reception area and in the offices, displaying beauty and warmth to the eye of onlookers. He took some of her mother's paintings depicting the Sonoma hills, photographs of the Bellini vineyards, as well as a Japanese statue that she had bought in San Francisco's

Japantown and a blue-and-white Chinese garden vase that a Stanford professor had sold to her when he needed to downsize. Margaret and Lara decided on the placement of the pieces, while Robert and Marion unpacked the lawbooks, supplies, and letterhead stationery.

There were four offices on the first floor. Since Sophia was not there, Robert and Marion picked the offices they liked. Robert chose the large office in a prominent spot next to the reception area while Marion picked the smaller room next to it. The two remaining offices were across the hall. The one facing Robert's was smaller than the one in back, so he decided that Sophia would enjoy the larger back office better.

Robert hoped to find a male lawyer to fill the vacant room, but he was in no hurry. He knew the three of them were a good team and would work well together.

On April 30, the Navarros and the Stephens family celebrated privately at the new law offices. Lara Trumbull met them there. Everyone, including Margaret and Andrew, toasted to the grand opening of the law firm. It had taken nearly four months from the purchase of the home to its completed renovations, inside and out. Fortunately, the contractor had been able to switch his workmen from painting outside when weather conditions prevented it to painting inside and kept the work on schedule.

The shingle out front read:

Navarro and Bellini Law Offices

Robert Navarro, Esq.   Sophia Bellini, Esq.   Marion Stephens, Esq.

Sophia had decided to give Robert top billing, since he was a town native and she was a newcomer. Even though she had put up the money to buy and renovate the building, she felt her husband's name was well-known and deserved to be first. Robert was pleased with the shingle, but for him, it was a hollow victory. He was a native of Eastport, and it was expected that his name should be first.

When the family and friends entered the offices, they stepped on plush Oriental rugs and sat in rose-colored cushioned chairs in the entrance hall. An antique mahogany desk and chair for the receptionist/secretary gave the space charm. On the wall behind the desk was a row of mahogany bookcases with cubbyholes for files and forms. All the modern equipment—printer, fax, and shredder—was hidden behind a partition.

Past the reception area was a hall with doors to the private offices of the attorneys. The extra office was used for conferences. In the back was a lavatory and a small kitchen. The second and third floors were still being converted into three apartments, to be rented out when completed. There was also a large basement with windows and an attached two-car garage in back, which remained empty for the present time.

The townspeople drove slowly by the old Victorian, noting its fresh blue siding with white trim and red door. The overgrown bushes and tall trees hiding the house had been cut back or cut down to reveal the asymmetrical architecture of a Queen Anne–styled building with its pitched roof and turret. Everyone agreed that the Navarros had resurrected the neglected home and restored it to its former elegance.

*****

The next day, the law firm was opened for business. Lara sat at her desk in the reception area and typed up legal papers while waiting for the phone to ring. She was working for all three lawyers, although Sophia's workload was much lighter than the others. During the first few hours, it was quiet. Then, all of a sudden, the phone began to ring constantly. Townies who had put off making wills or updating them called for an appointment. A woman who had tripped, fallen, and broken her hip on a wet floor in a supermarket asked if she had a claim. A man whose wife had a setback after being given the wrong pills in a rehabilitation clinic wanted to know if he could sue the owners of the facility.

"Good morning, Navarro and Bellini law offices. How may I help you?" Those words were to be repeated many times over the following days and weeks.

Lara had eagerly accepted the position as legal secretary for the three lawyers, but she had a lot to learn, even after passing a course online, and her mistakes cost the firm. Sometimes she omitted a paragraph from a will, causing a delay in the client signing it, or she did not have the correct figures on a settlement statement, causing a delay in a house sale.

Marion was more patient with her than Robert, who was used to perfection. "She'll learn quickly," Marion said.

Within a few weeks, Lara was unable to keep up with the work-load. She needed help. Sophia asked Eileen if she was interested in joining Lara in the reception room as their senior legal secretary. She immediately gave her two-week notice to Sam, who predicted that Sophia would not succeed, and soon Eileen would be without work.

"Attorney Wyman, as usual, you misread the situation. It is you that will have no clients."

CONNECTICUT, JUNE TO JULY

Cat's school let out in mid-June, and the family began to take hikes together on the days when there was a light workload. It gave them a chance to be alone as a family, enjoying the outdoors and having the privacy Sophia wanted to nurse Mateo. They found that some of the state parks did not permit pets, and they were not willing to leave Bruno at home. Bennett's Pond State Park had several trails and did allow dogs, and it was only thirty minutes away. That became their favorite place to hike and enjoy nature.

Sometimes Cat brought her bike and rode ahead of them, sometimes so far that they lost sight of her.

"Cat, you must stay where we can see you," Sophia demanded.

"Why? I won't go in the woods."

"Cat, just obey us without an argument," Robert sighed. "We have to know where you are."

"If you let me have my own phone, you can call me, and then you'll know," she answered back.

"Stop pushing us," said Sophia. "We've already told you that you have to be in the double digits before you can have a phone."

"But I can't wait three years. All my friends will have them by then."

"If you keep arguing with us, we'll think that you are not ready to have a phone when you're ten and we'll have to postpone getting you one until you're thirteen."

Cat stopped pushing.

All during their walks, Bruno tugged on the leash, curious about the strange smells coming from the thick foliage along the path. One day, while they walked along a deserted part of the trail, Robert decided to let Bruno run free, even though that was forbidden. He had always come whenever Sophia or Robert had called to him, whether they were inside their home or when Bruno was allowed to roam on their property.

He took off Bruno's leash, and immediately Bruno ran ahead to sniff and examine the forest floor. Everything was fine until Bruno spotted a rabbit. His instincts took over, and he chased it into the woods.

"Bruno, come back!" Sophia called.

Robert yelled his name even louder. They heard some thrashing, and then nothing.

"Let's stay here until he returns," Sophia said.

They waited a while, calling his name every so often.

Hikers passed them and learned of the missing dog.

"Don't worry. Dogs have a strong sense of smell. He'll come back," they said.

When Bruno did not return after an hour, Sophia was in a panic.

Cat said, "Mummy, we cannot go home without him."

Robert knew he was responsible. He suggested that he drive Sophia and the children home and then return to that spot.

"Sophia, he will eventually get tired and come back here. He's a pretty big dog. He'll be okay in the woods."

Robert said what he hoped was true. But he knew that coyotes and foxes traveled in packs, and a golden retriever wouldn't stand a chance if Bruno encountered them.

"No, let me drive home, drop off the children at your mother's, and come back with signs that we can tack on trees along the path. You stay here with his leash in case he returns."

He helped her put Mateo in his infant car seat, and he hooked up Cat's bike to the rear of the car. He started to walk back toward the trail when Sophia called to him. He came to the car and bent his head in the window.

"Take care you do not get lost," she whispered, kissing him with emotion. "I don't want to lose you too."

He watched as she drove away, bemused by her concern for him. *I thought she would be upset with me, but it's just the opposite.*

He stopped at the entrance gate to notify the park authorities of his missing dog. They, in turn, notified the surrounding towns. Police radio buffs (a.k.a. busybodies) were therefore alerted as well. At Sam Wyman's home, the news was heard and a plan put into motion.

When Sophia returned to the park almost two hours later, she found Robert waiting for her with Bruno on his leash.

"Where did you find him?" she asked, hugging her dog and checking him for ticks.

"It was the strangest thing," he said. "I walked up the trail for a few miles and came back to find a young couple holding him. They said a man had tried to put Bruno in his car, but Bruno resisted so much that they were suspicious and went to see what was going on. At that point, the man jumped in his car and fled."

"Did they describe the man?" Sophia asked.

Robert hesitated. "Yes, a heavyset guy with blue eyes and straight blond hair combed across the top."

She looked at her husband, her face registering shock.

"Sam?" Sophia gasped. "But why?"

Robert looked pained. "I've never known Sam to be violent. He's yelled at and threatened people, enough to get them to do his bidding. This is something new."

When they had settled themselves in the car, Robert sat behind the wheel, staring at Sophia. "He must really hate you."

"He hates anyone who stands up to him, and that includes you and Marion as well as me."

They decided that if it was Sam, they could never prove it.

*****

The waters in Long Island Sound drew them out of their house and onto their boat, like a receding tide draws out any loose pebble from the beach. When they went sailing, they left Mateo at home with Margaret. Sophia was uneasy about bringing him on a boat while he was still an infant. Between the hot sun and his naps, he would have to remain with her in the boat's cabin for much of the time, so what was the point?

Their sailing trips were shorter, hugging the Connecticut coast up and down the Sound. Cat sat beside the helm when either of them was working the wheel and the sails, getting further lessons in how to control the speed and direction of the boat. Often, when Robert anchored in a cove, he fished on one side of the boat while Sophia and Cat swam on the other. Then they made themselves presentable to eat lunch at a dockside restaurant.

A week after the attempted dognapping, while they were heading for their favorite cove, secluded from the boat traffic and seaside homes, Robert noticed a boat trailing several hundred yards behind them. It was a cigarette boat known for its speed and maneuverability on the water. He disliked being around them because the captains liked to show off by gunning their engines as they came up to a sailboat, causing waves, forcing the sailor to tack and adjust his sails.

Robert tacked, aiming toward the shore, hoping the other boat would stay far out. It followed behind, closing in, and sped over to the left, into the sailboat's new path.

Robert yelled to Sophia, "We have a hotdogger on our port. Probably a teenage son of the boat owner. Hang on."

Robert tacked again, this time to the right. The speedboat followed suit.

"What the hell!" yelled Robert, clearly irritated. "He's still on our tail. Call the Coast Guard. I'm not playing dodge 'em with this kid."

Sophia put the call through and explained the situation and described the speedboat. The official suggested they put into a pier and wait him out.

"It will take us a while to get a Coast Guard vessel to your area. See if you can get the name and registration number."

Sophia took a photo of the boat as it came head-on, but it did not turn enough for her to see anything that revealed its identity or the operator. She had an idea.

"Robert, turn and try to chase it. The boat will either have to turn around to escape or we may get close enough to get a photo of the operator."

He tacked so that the sailboat's path was now angled toward the speedboat. Sophia turned on the video mode and filmed the other boat's movement as it turned tail.

"Got it!" she screamed. "It's the *Sally W.*"

"Mom, that's Sally Wyman's new boat. Her daddy named it for her."

"Are you sure, Cat?"

"Yes, she told me so herself."

Sophia and Robert looked at each other, first in disbelief, then with concern. As they headed home, their outing ruined, they wondered why Sam Wyman would act so childish. Had he been drinking? Or was it something more sinister?

On July Fourth, the family, including Margaret, sat out on their terrace to watch a fireworks display on the town dock, which was visible from their terrace. They had invited Eileen and her daughter, Jenny, who was ten years old and, like Cat, inquisitive, to join them. Jenny and Cat bonded immediately. The girls had no other siblings to play with, Jenny being an only child and Mateo being still so young. Both loved reading fantasy stories and creating things out of whatever they found.

The girls got bored waiting for dusk before the fireworks started and went off to play in Cat's bedroom.

Nobody paid any attention to them. In fact, Sophia was relieved because she didn't want Cat to hear so much adult conversation. She served drinks and snacks while they waited. Robert discussed the known facts about Eastport's early history and its first settlers.

"As the story goes," he said, knowing the beginnings of the town better than anyone else, "three men left Norwalk in a drunken state and made it as far as what is now our town center and declared that the area was a perfect place for a new town. So Samuel Wyman,

Elijah Chadwick, and Thomas Pratt cleared the forest and set up camp. They were *persona non grata* in Norwalk, so they couldn't return there without being locked up. That is the proud beginning of our town," said Robert. "How far we have come or maybe not."

"Why couldn't the men return to Norwalk?" Eileen wanted to know.

"They were caught stealing fish from other people's nets."

"So these are the men we honor every year on Founders' Day?" Sophia said. "So many ugly stories are buried with the pioneers in the town cemetery, and so many impressive stories are never recorded. We never read of the women who married these men and what they had to endure—the stillbirths, the deaths from smallpox or fever, or famine."

"It's a wonder so many of the pioneers survived at all," Eileen declared.

"You can thank the local native tribes for helping them," Margaret responded. "I had an interesting conversation with Thea Wyman about immigrants. When she called Robert and Sophia immigrants, I turned to her and said, 'So were you once!' She denied it. She said she was practically a Native American!"

Everyone was still laughing about that when Jenny and Cat paraded in, both dressed from head to foot in red, white, and blue. Cat looked like something Betsy Ross might have worn. She sported Sophia's red blouse with rolled-up sleeves and her blue shorts that came down to mid-calf, and on her feet were her mother's blue wedge shoes. She had wrapped a white scarf around her head.

Jenny wore Sophia's red jumpsuit, much too big for her. Around her waist was a white belt and about her neck, a blue-and-red scarf. She was trying to stand up straight in a pair of white high heels. There was a tear in the jumpsuit fabric near the bottom, probably made when Jenny stepped on the fabric in the high heels.

Sophia was not amused—not because they had on her clothes, but that Cat had rummaged through her closets and drawers without permission. She eyed Cat critically, thinking about what to do, while the others were quietly making comments about how patriotic they looked.

Just then, a boom was heard, and seconds later, a burst of red lights filled the night sky.

Sophia said, "Jenny, you may stay and watch. I need to have a talk with my daughter." She took Cat firmly by the hand and began to leave.

Cat protested, pulling back. "I want to watch the fireworks."

"Right now, you are coming with me."

From the tone of her voice, Cat knew her mother was upset. She tried to escape her grasp, but she couldn't.

When they reached their parents' bedroom, Cat started to cry, and with good reason. The scene before them made her mother gasp. Not only were closet doors and drawers opened, but clothes had been pulled off their hangers, lingerie was hanging out of drawers, and belts and shoes were piled in a heap on the floor. It looked like someone had broken into their home and ransacked the place.

Sophia turned to look at Cat.

"Have I taught you nothing?" she said sadly. "I am so disappointed in you."

She sat on the edge of her bed, running her hands through her hair, trying to decide what to do.

Cat stood with tears running down her face, looking sullen. She heard the fireworks blasting in the air as they exploded.

"I want to see the fireworks," she whined.

"And I want you to take off my clothes and put everything back the way it was," Sophia said firmly. "Only then will I allow you to go back on the terrace."

As Cat began to remove her outfit, Sophia asked, "Cat, why did you go into my closets and drawers and take things without asking me first?"

"It was Jenny's idea to dress up in red, white, and blue, but I didn't have those colors, and you did."

"Don't you dare blame Jenny for this mess! Why didn't you come and ask me for permission to go through my things?" she asked again.

Cat shrugged. She stared at her mother, angry because she was missing the fireworks.

"You alone are responsible for what you do. We will stay here until the room is in satisfactory condition. Only then will I allow you to go and watch the fireworks."

"What about Jenny?"

"Jenny is not my daughter, and this is not her home. You were the one who showed her where my clothes are, so you are to blame."

It took a while for Cat to put every article back where it belonged and folded or hung up correctly. When Sophia and Cat returned to the terrace, they were just in time for the fireworks finale. Jenny had removed Sophia's clothes and heels, and they were in a neat pile on a table.

Eileen had Jenny apologize to Sophia. Then Eileen mentioned the rip in the hem.

"I can take it to a tailor who might be able to make an invisible repair. Please allow me to do that. I feel badly enough that Jenny went through your closets. I would have been upset if the situation was reversed."

"I will let you do that if it makes you feel better, but please know that I do not hold you responsible, and this won't affect our friendship."

Sophia said nothing more about the incident, but Cat continued to pout all evening. When Sophia went into her bedroom to say good night, Cat said, "Jenny's mother didn't punish her, and it was her idea."

"Cat, are you telling me that whatever Jenny suggests, you must do?"

"No, but she is older than me."

"Is everyone older than you smarter than you?"

"No."

"Whose idea was it to rummage through my clothes?"

Cat looked down, not answering.

"You alone are responsible. I know you understand because you are smart."

"I didn't mean to be diabolical," Cat said. "Just patriotic."

Sophia sighed, knowing Cat was using words she had learned to impress her.

"If you had come to me and said that you and Jenny wanted to dress up like patriots, I would have picked out some things for you both to wear."

"Did I look like a patriot?" Cat wondered, hoping her punishment was worth the trouble she had gotten into.

Sophia had to smile. "Yes," she said, kissing her good night. "You would have made Martha Washington proud."

When Robert and Sophia were getting into bed, Robert turned to her and asked, "Weren't you a little rough with Cat? No real harm was done."

"No real harm was done this time, but she has to learn that her impulsive behavior has consequences. Suppose I laughed it off, and the next time, she went through my briefcase, or your closet, or your briefcase. She was punished by missing part of the fireworks, and she will remember that she needs to ask permission to look through other people's personal property."

"But still, Sophia, in front of guests, you took her away. She was embarrassed to be led off like that. Couldn't you have waited until after?"

"After what? After the fireworks had ended and the guests had gone home? Then what would her punishment be? Robert, you are only looking at the moment and not the long-term impact. She rummaged through my closet and drawers without bothering to ask me. She is acting impulsively. It's better that she learn the danger that comes with that now, early on."

"Have you ever gotten into trouble by acting impulsively?" he wanted to know, not convinced that Sophia had acted wisely.

Her mind went back in time.

"Yes. Once when I was a little girl, I stole some lira that were on my parents' bureau and bought fistfuls of chocolate candy. My mother found out when she saw some chocolate pieces still in my hand. She said nothing about it, and I thought I had escaped punishment. That night, after supper, she put three cannoli on the table—one for my father, one for Joe, and one for herself.

"'Where's my cannoli?' I asked.

"'You had your dessert earlier.'

"'But I want cannoli,' I said.

"'And I want the lira you took,' my mother replied.

"I never did it again."

She paused.

"When I married Carlo, I didn't listen to my parents who cautioned me that I didn't know him well enough. He came to this country with no family and no friends. No one who could vouch for his character. I saw what I wanted to see, a man who was self-educated like my father and who wanted to succeed. I was blinded by wanting a family." She thought for a moment. "Then there was the time that I invited you to sleep in my apartment, but I convinced myself that you would not be a dangerous guest." She laughed. "In one sense, you were dangerous. Once I found out you were divorced, I figured you were worth the risk." She leaned her body closer to his, feeling his warmth. "What about you?"

"I once stole a candy bar from a counter in a store when the clerk wasn't looking. It bothered me for years afterward. My parents never found out, but I kept thinking of how ashamed my parents would have been if I had been caught. And I married Catherine without really knowing her well. I thought that because she was respectable and educated and beautiful, that everything else would work out because I was ready to have a wife and family. That decision had terrible consequences."

They lay side by side in the bed, staring at the ceiling.

"Do you still think that I was rough with Cat?" Sophia asked, second-guessing her reaction to Cat's raid of her closets and drawers. She felt she needed his approval.

"No. You were right. If Mateo went through my wardrobe and came dressed in my clothes and ripped my pants, I would have been upset."

"So you understand how I feel. In behavioral psychology, that is called having emotional empathy."

"Well, I would call it having an epiphany."

She smiled, thinking of how perfect that term was. *He understands my actions.* Her body nestled even closer to his. *We are of one mind on this.*

EASTPORT, JULY

Three weeks before the wedding celebration, the invitations were mailed to fifty family members, friends, and frenemies.

ROBERT NAVARRO AND SOPHIA BELLINI

REQUEST YOUR PRESENCE AT THE CELEBRATION
OF THEIR MARRIAGE AND CHILDREN

CATERINA

AND

MATTHEW

AT SIX IN THE EVENING ON SUNDAY, AUGUST FIRST
AT THEIR HOME AT 271 OCEAN DRIVE, EASTPORT A
BUFFET DINNER ON THE LAWN WILL BE FOLLOWED BY
DANCING TO THE MUSIC OF THE LATINA ORCHESTRA

COCKTAIL ATTIRE

NO GIFTS, PLEASE

Months earlier, Sophia had booked the caterers, orchestra, stage, and lighting crew, and rented tables and chairs from a local service club. The only thing she couldn't book was the weather. If it rained, she would stuff all the guests in their living room and dining room, set up the caterers in the kitchen, and place the orchestra on the terrace, rolling down the shades to protect them and their instruments.

She prayed for good weather so that the guests could eat and dance outside. Keeping track of so many people in her home would be a nightmare. *I can't put outside locks on all the bedroom doors.* She began to wonder if it had been such a good idea to have the reception on their property.

She soon realized that she had something much more nightmarish to worry about. Carlo had been spotted driving through the Sonoma town, only a few miles from the winery. Grace had texted her that one of their trusted workers swore it was her former husband. Sophia hadn't thought about him for quite a while, the belief being that he had gone back to Italy.

That's what the police told me. He would be a fool to come back to the States, knowing that there was still a warrant for his arrest. He had always been a risk-taker, but what could he possibly want at the winery?

The plans for the reception took up most of her time just now, so she dismissed the sighting as a case of mistaken identity.

A few days later, she took Cat to a downtown Manhattan store that sold dresses for everyone in a wedding party. Even though Cat was not going to be a flower girl—that role was never in her plans—she did want to buy something special for her daughter to wear.

They found a pink dress with lace around the collar and midriff, just enough style to make her look adorable. After purchasing it, mother and daughter headed for a nearby shoe shop. Cat fell in love with a pair of white Mary Jane shoes with a double buckle.

"If you want, I could attach little pink bows to them," Sophia said, picking up the shoes to examine them. "Would you like that?"

She looked up because Cat hadn't answered her. Her daughter was staring at something behind Sophia.

Sophia turned to see what had caught her daughter's attention and saw nothing, no one. "What is it, Cat? What were you looking at?"

"Mom, there was a man staring at me, smiling. He went over that way," pointing to the exit.

Sophia became alarmed. She wanted to rush to the exit to see for herself, but she dared not leave Cat alone, still in her stocking feet. *He's probably just a harmless, lonely old man,* she thought.

"Let's buy these and go home. We've done enough shopping for today."

On the train ride back to Eastport, Sophia asked Cat to describe the man she saw in the store.

"He was tall and thin, and he had dark brown hair."

So he wasn't old at all!

"What else do you remember about him? His eyes? His nose? Were his lips thin or thick?"

"Hmm. His eyes were dark. I don't remember his nose, but his lips were thick," said Cat. "And he had a crooked smile."

Worry lines creased Sophia's forehead. *She is describing Carlo.*

She looked around quickly, checking out each male passenger in view.

"Cat," she whispered, not wanting to alarm her or let anyone in the seats around them overhear their conversation, "if you see this man again, do not go near him."

"I don't talk to strangers because you told me not to."

"But especially this man you described."

"Who is he?" Cat asked.

"I'm not sure. He could be someone I once knew." She put her head down, thinking.

Taking out her iPhone, she pulled up her photos library and scrolled down until she saw what she was looking for.

"Did the man you saw in the store look like him?" She pointed to the photo of her family at the wine taster's award ceremony.

"That's Nonno and Nana and Uncle Joe and you," Cat said. "What about that man beside me? Him!"

"It looks like him, but the man I saw had whiskers on his face."

Sophia sat back and tried to remain calm. *If it is Carlo, I won't let him escape again.*

When the train pulled into the station, they got out and headed for Sophia's car in the parking lot.

"There is something I must do before we go home." She drove to the center of town and she parked in front of the police station.

Later, at home, with only Robert and Margaret around to hear, she told them of Cat's observations.

"I asked the police to pull up the warrant for his arrest. The picture on it was the one I had given to them at the time. I told them that he has whiskers now. Under no circumstances must Cat be left by herself outside."

Robert shook his head. "What would he want with Cat? It makes no sense for him to come back here."

He stopped because Sophia had put her hands to her face and moaned.

"Robert, unless he thinks that Cat is his daughter! That's why he was looking at her instead of at me."

"He doesn't know his daughter died?"

"How could he? I delivered the baby in the ambulance, and when I arrived at the hospital, the doctors brought me into surgery to stitch me up. It was hours before I was awake and coherent enough to tell the police what happened. By then, Carlo had boarded a plane for Italy. Once there, he disappeared, and they couldn't trace him."

"So he thinks his daughter lived!" Margaret said, astonished.

Robert was still baffled. "At least he must know that there must be a charge of assault against him."

"He has tracked me down for some reason. I am using my maiden name, so it must have been easy. If I had used your last name, it would have been harder for him to find me."

"Good God, Sophia. Don't blame yourself for this. He would have found you no matter what name you used, *Bellini, Sbaglione,* or *Navarro*. Everyone leaves a paper trail. Are you absolutely sure it was him?"

"Yes. Cat had almost perfect recall of his face. She'd make a good witness."

A few days later, Sophia came to her law office to meet with a client to sign some papers. It was to be a quick visit because she was still breastfeeding Mateo. Cat had asked to come along, and Sophia thought it would be okay. Margaret stayed at their home, babysitting Mateo because Robert was in court.

The client was already sitting in the reception area when they walked through the entrance. Sophia greeted him and led him to her office, while Cat went over to Lara's desk to watch what she was doing.

Five minutes later, Sophia's intercom buzzed. She ignored it, wanting to complete the paperwork without interruption. Then the security alarm went off, which was tied in to police headquarters.

Sophia sighed. *Cat must have set it off accidentally,* she thought. She excused herself and went out to see what mischief her daughter had gotten into.

The reception area was at the end of the hall. Lara was at her desk, and Cat was standing right next to her, so close that there was no space between them. *Cat knows better than to bother Lara.* She was about to reprimand Cat when a figure came into view near them.

Sophia froze. All the pain and heartache that she had suffered seven years ago came rushing back. She tried to speak, but no words came out of her mouth. She was staring into the grizzled face of Carlo Sbaglione.

"Mummy, it's him!" Cat cried.

The man looked at Cat and then back at Sophia.

Carlo said, "So she lived after all. That's not what I heard around the winery. I thought they might be lying to make me go away."

His jersey and pants were wrinkled and dirty, like he had slept in them. The ragged look of his beard gave him the appearance of a tramp.

At the sound of his harsh voice, Sophia came alive.

"Get away from here, you bastard," she screamed. "Go away. Don't you dare touch her, or I'll kill you with my bare hands."

Carlo gave her a lopsided grin and reached out to grab Cat, but Cat was too quick for him. She ran behind Sophia's back, clinging to her slacks and started to cry. She had never heard her mother talk so angrily.

Sophia breathed a sigh of relief. *I am now between Carlo and Cat, and nothing bad is going to happen to her.*

"Don't cry, my darling." She put her arms behind her, feeling Cat's trembling body against her own shaking limbs. "I won't let him harm you. Call the police," she gasped to Lara, forgetting that the alarm had already been sent. "He's come to take my daughter."

"She's my daughter too," he argued, amazed that this little girl had no visible injury. He was enjoying the fright in Sophia's voice. "We could divide her in half, like King Solomon once suggested, or we could make a deal. You keep her but pay me handsomely."

So it's money he's after. Of course it is. That was all he ever wanted.

The client had come out of Sophia's office after he heard screams.

"What's wrong?" he asked.

"Call the police!" she said again, speaking more calmly, feeling safer with another person in the room. So far, Carlo had not shown a weapon.

"This man is wanted by the police."

"For what? I just want to see my daughter." Carlo pointed to Cat. He grinned, feeling he had the upper hand now.

The client looked baffled, but Lara understood exactly.

"This girl is not his child," Lara said. "She is the daughter of Attorney Robert Navarro."

"Yes," Sophia affirmed, "and there is a warrant out for your arrest."

"You are lying. I spoke to an attorney in the other office where you used to be. He said she is my daughter. And besides, she is the right age, and I can see for myself how much she resembles you. Call the police!" Carlo declared. "How can they arrest me for something that never happened? My wife is not well. *Crazy!*" he said, turning to the onlookers and moving his hand in a circle by his head. "She started screaming when I never even touched her."

Who could he have spoken to at the old office? *He's delusional,* thought Sophia. *I must keep him here until the police arrive.*

197

"So you came back here to bribe me. What did you have in mind, Carlo?"

"How much is she worth to you?" Carlo jerked his head, looking at Cat. "At least a million dollars, no?"

There was a long pause. The seconds went by slowly as each of the onlookers processed his words: Lara in shock that such a smart woman like Attorney Bellini had once been married to such a craven man; the client, still uncertain about who this little girl was; Cat confused because this man called her his daughter, and frightened because her mother had screamed; Sophia planning what she would do next.

"She is priceless," Sophia whispered. "And I divorced you, so we are no longer man and wife."

"No matter," spat Carlo, his eyes crazed with anger. "She is my daughter, my blood, and I have rights as her father."

Just then, police sirens were heard screaming through the walls, getting louder and more insistent. Carlo squirmed and blanched.

"She has to be my daughter," he said, trying to laugh at the notion that she wasn't. He studied Sophia's face, now so defiant, so confident. "The other attorney assured me that she was mine."

"What other attorney? Who said that Cat was your daughter?"

Carlo grinned. "The attorney at the law office where you used to work. I don't know his name."

"Cat," Sophia asked loudly, the sound of her voice giving her strength, "how old were you when you first met me?"

"I was six years old," she said weakly, still behind her and curious as to why her mother was asking. "Remember?"

"Yes, I remember, Cat," her voice trembling slightly. "I remember kissing you that night and you saying you wished I was your mother." She stared at her former husband and offered him a slight smile. "You are wrong, Carlo. This girl has no blood of yours in her, thank God." The memory of her dying girl made her swallow hard. "You will pay for what you did."

A calmness came over her as they waited for the arrival of the police.

Carlo started to tug at something inside his pants pocket. *He's reaching for a weapon,* Sophia thought, suddenly alarmed. She braced herself, ready to intercept a bullet or a knife, whatever it was, in order to protect Cat.

Out came a red object. Sophia immediately recognized it, and she relaxed.

Then there were blue lights flashing outside. Doors slammed. Running steps. Several officers rushed into the reception room. Within seconds, it was over. Carlo was led away in handcuffs.

A policeman said that a detective would need to talk to her.

"Later," she whispered, "my young daughter is here now."

When the crisis was over, Sophia sat down in Lara's chair, with her head buried in her hands, shaking.

"It's alright, Mom," said Cat, coming over to hold her mother's arm. "Where are the police taking him? To jail?"

Sophia looked up and hugged Cat tightly. She tried to explain to Cat what happened.

"That man was my husband, Cat," she said between sobs. "He thought you were his daughter, the infant that died."

"Because she was sick, right?"

"Right," she said huskily. "He did a bad thing, and he will be in prison for a long while."

"What did he do?"

"He hurt someone, and that person died."

Sophia noticed her client standing there, looking at her with pity.

"I am sorry for this disturbance, Mr. Bowen. Let's go back in my office and complete the paperwork."

"I will come back another time."

"No. I am alright now. A great weight has been lifted from my mind."

*****

On the ride home, Sophia tried to take Cat's mind off the confrontation and arrest.

"Dolores will be here in two weeks, and she will teach you to dance the waltz."

"Did you marry a bad man?" Cat asked, still thinking about the scene at the office.

Sophia thought back to the first year of her marriage and the happy times they had.

"No, Cat. He was not bad when I married him, but he became angry and unhappy when he could not get what he wanted. Sometimes people are too greedy and they do bad things."

She tried once more to change the subject.

"Would you like to ride your bike on the driveway and walks? I will sit outside with Mateo and watch you."

"Yes!" Cat said excitedly. "I will show him how to ride a bike!"

Sophia smiled, pleased at her daughter's confidence.

"I am sure you will be a good instructor."

Hours later, after giving Mateo her breast, after having lunch and talking with a detective who had come to interview Sophia and inform her of what they had learned, Sophia sat with her mother-in-law outside as they watched Cat race around on her bike.

"He will be extradited to California, where he will be tried. I will have to go and testify at his trial."

"So he came back to extort money from you. How did he expect to get away with it?"

"He told the police he was desperate, thinking that I would not want the publicity. He intends to plead not guilty to the charges. The police told me that he left Italy because there was a warrant for his arrest there for stealing money from a winery where he worked. He was found to have a passport with a different name."

"He seems to have fallen apart after he fled from you."

Sophia gazed thoughtfully at Mateo, sitting on her lap, his eyes fixed on Cat as she flew by. She softly touched the top of his head, not realizing what she was doing, the last image of her infant daughter flickering across her mind.

"After one year of marriage, I really didn't know him at all," she murmured, "not like I know Robert. Carlo was dodgy when I asked him questions about his childhood and family. That should have been a flashing red light. I must admit that I wanted a husband so badly in order that I could have a child. I made myself believe that we were a good fit, that whatever was wanting in him was fleeting and would go away," she paused, "like dirt and grime after a soaking rain."

When Robert came through the door in late afternoon, after spending a whole day in court, Cat rushed over to tell him what happened.

He stared at Sophia.

"You were both so lucky." He kept looking from Sophia to Cat and back to Sophia, shaking his head in disbelief. Finally he asked, "Did he have a weapon in his pocket?"

Sophia gave a half laugh. "No, just a *cornetto,* a small horn, a good luck charm."

"He'll need more than that to clear himself. I will go with you when his trial begins. Besides being there to support you, I want to see this creature for myself."

Robert walked over to where Sophia was standing. He wrapped his arms around her body and gave her a deep, lingering kiss.

"What was that for?" she breathed, flustered that he was so amorous in front of Cat.

"For being here to tell the tale," he whispered.

*****

After dinner, as they were getting ready for bed, Sophia whispered, "Carlo said something that made no sense. He said an attorney at our former law firm told him that Cat was his daughter. He didn't know the attorney's name or identify him in any way. Who would have told him that?"

For several seconds, they stared at each other. Then they both said, "Sam," at the same time.

EASTPORT, JULY 24

It was on a hot day in July when Dolores arrived in high excitement.

"This wedding reception will be unlike any you have ever seen," she declared. "We have lots of work to do."

"All the preparations are made," Sophia protested after she hugged and kissed her.

"No, there is more to do with the dancing," Dolores insisted. "I have to teach Cat to waltz, and I need to practice the steps of the tango."

"By yourself?" Sophia asked.

"Of course!" Dolores said emphatically.

"You can do the tango in your sleep. It's been your favorite dance since college when you taught me how to do it in our dorm room."

"Yes, but it never hurts to practice, and Ricardo cannot get here until the twenty-ninth, three days before your reception."

"Who's Ricardo?" asked Cat, seeming to appear from nowhere.

"My best boyfriend and best lover," Dolores answered.

Sophia signaled for her to be quiet and tried to shoo Cat out.

"You don't have to answer all her questions," Sophia scolded Dolores, sounding like Robert.

"Stop protecting her from life," cried Dolores. "She is seven, the age when reason kicks in, no? My little one, Ricardo is the master of the tango, and if we are to do it in front of an *angry crowd*, it must be flawless."

"They won't be angry," Sophia corrected, "just hostile. Some of them anyway." She thought about her preparations. "By the time our guests leave, they will all be delighted—"

She paused. Her plans for revenge, so certain up until a few days ago, were in limbo.

"All except one or two, perhaps."

Dolores gave her a thumbs-up. Sophia had let her in on her tactics for revenge weeks ago but not her reevaluation now. She was still debating with herself if it was fair to Thea if she shamed Sam on the stage.

"Cat, come with me on the terrace, and I will teach you to dance the waltz," Dolores announced.

"What about the tango?" said Cat, following her out. "I want to dance like you."

"You do not learn how to dance by doing the tango. You have to practice with simpler steps first. Now take my hand and put your other hand on my hip, and I will lead you."

*****

The reception was only eight days away. Everything was in order, planned down to the last detail. Giorgio insisted on giving a speech after the buffet was over, describing their family background and beliefs. Dolores wanted to speak as well. Sophia wasn't sure exactly what either of them would say, but she trusted their judgment.

Then she and Robert would begin dancing with a waltz, which was traditional at a wedding reception. The highlight of the evening was the tango with Dolores and Ricardo exhibiting their pirouettes and fluidity of motion.

Their performance would dispel any lingering thoughts about her relationship with Dolores. In order to get her revenge, she decided on a different tactic, one that required perfect timing.

The next day, the twenty-fifth, Sophia went to a realtor's office for a house closing. The process was interrupted when the buyer whom she was representing had missing paperwork, so the closing was postponed until the next morning.

Damn it! she thought. *My family is arriving tomorrow afternoon, and I still have to get ready for that.*

She blamed herself for not stressing to her client the importance of having all the documents at the meeting. She was in a foul mood when the meeting ended abruptly.

"This is such a busy week for me, and now I have to come back here tomorrow," she groused.

Grabbing her briefcase and her pocketbook, she drove straight home, expecting to spend some extra time with her best friend. When she walked into the house, she was surprised to find no one around. She went into Cat's bedroom and found her playing with Legos.

"Where is Dolores?" she asked.

"She and Daddy went down to the dock."

"When did they go there?"

"A little while ago. They told me to stay here and, if Mateo woke up, to call them."

What could they be doing on the dock? Checking the boat? She wondered. Robert had already gone over it from prow to stern to make sure it was seaworthy, for when the entire family sailed around Long Island Sound.

When she walked into Mateo's room, he was in his crib. He had just woken up, and when he saw Sophia, he started to cry, wanting to be picked up. It only added to her irritation.

How can they leave a child in the care of an infant?

She lifted him out of the crib, and his diaper felt heavy. Instead of changing him immediately, she carried him to the terrace, which had a partial view of the dock. Cat followed, describing what she and Dolores had done that day.

Sophia's thoughts were elsewhere, and she said, "Oh, that's nice." They couldn't have gone out on the boat and left Cat alone with Mateo. The hedges and plants that hugged the slope were in full bloom.

Sophia bent over the railing to get a better view, with Mateo squirming in her arms. The boat was still there, at anchor, but there was no sign of them. Then she saw a flash of color, and Dolores and Robert came into view, their arms around one another. The sight of them so close together was like an electric shock going through her body. Her grip on Mateo weakened, and he began to slip away from her.

"Mom, he's falling!" Cat screamed.

Sophia looked down to see Cat holding Mateo's arm, his whole body dangling over the side of the railing. Sophia grabbed at his other arm, and together they pulled him up. She wrapped him in her arms, hugging him tightly, then checked him all over to make sure he wasn't injured. Robert and Dolores had heard Cat scream and were rushing up the staircase.

Sophia's chest was heaving. As soon as she caught her breath, she turned on her husband.

"Well, you two looked like you were having a good time down there," she gasped.

"What happened?" Robert asked, ignoring her comment.

"You were supposed to be watching Mateo!" she shouted, not caring how angry she appeared.

"Sophia," Robert said quietly, "he was sleeping. Cat was in the next room in case he woke up."

"My friend, did something bad happen?" Dolores asked, coming up behind him, looking hot and sweaty.

Sophia shot her a look filled with daggers.

"He almost fell over the railing!" And then she began again on Robert. "What kind of a father are you to leave your seven-year-old daughter in charge of an infant?"

"I have already explained. He was asleep. Why were you so close to the railing with him in your arms?" asked Robert in a quiet voice. "You know how he likes to squirm."

"So I'm to blame!" she screamed. "You and Dolores were on the dock doing *God knows what*, and I come home to find Mateo left alone."

Robert and Dolores stared at her. She looked as though she had gone berserk.

"Maybe you should lie down," Robert advised. "You have been working too hard. I'll take care of Mateo."

He reached for him, but Sophia pushed him away.

"Go back to whatever it was you were doing. I can take care of my son."

She turned and stalked inside with Mateo crying on her shoulder. Her anger was intense, but it was justified, she thought.

I do all the work while they play.

"I have never seen her so upset," Robert said, mystified.

Dolores shook her head as she and Robert entered the living room.

"It's postpartum depression. My sister had it after giving birth. It can last up to six months."

"Six months! What can I do?"

"Either wait it out or see if she will take drugs to calm herself, but she first has to accept that she has it."

"Sophia never even takes an aspirin unless she is in extreme pain, and it's unlikely she will accept a diagnosis from either me or you."

Sophia took the baby into his bedroom, laid him on the changing table, removed his wet diaper, and cleaned him. He immediately quieted down and tried to turn over before she had a chance to put a clean diaper on. She reached for him and noticed the red marks on his arm where she had grabbed him.

The sight of them made her tear up, and she had trouble fastening the new diaper because she couldn't see what she was doing.

"Stay still, Mateo," she whispered as she pulled the tabs in place.

Her hands twitched when she picked him up and sat with him in a rocking chair. She began to move back and forth with all her might. Mateo was wide awake now, but Sophia didn't want to leave the bedroom and face her husband and friend. His cheek was next to hers.

I saw it with my own eyes, she fumed.

Her thoughts turned back to Mateo.

My muscles went weak, and I dropped him. If Cat hadn't been there, he would have fallen down the steep hillside.

Dinner was on the table when Sophia finally emerged with the baby. She started to put him in a baby jumper seat so she was free to eat, but Dolores came by and snatched him up.

"I will hold him. I like little men as well as the big ones."

Everyone laughed, except Sophia, who barely managed a smile.

Margaret had joined them, and Robert and Dolores acted like nothing had happened. There was talk about Cat's new clothes—a matching jersey and shorts—and teasing banter about the food. Sophia wasn't listening. Her mind was on the betrayal by her best friend. It hurt her more than she believed it could.

Of all the people for Robert to have an affair with, he had to choose her. Now they are acting so blasé.

Dolores interrupted her thoughts. "You have said nothing about Cat's pierced ears. Aren't the tiny pink studs so pretty?"

For the first time that day, Sophia looked closely at her daughter. Cat had wrapped her hair behind her ears so that the earrings were now in full view. Margaret noticed them also.

"Oh my!" she exclaimed, and then stayed silent.

Sophia's mouth dropped open. "Who gave you permission to get your ears pierced?" she asked.

"You did," said Cat, uneasily. "I asked you before, and you said someday."

"Someday when you are older, not when you are only seven years old. Did you do this?" she said, turning to Dolores.

"Sophia, she told me that you had agreed to it. I thought you were too busy to take her."

"What's the problem, Sophia?" asked Robert. "I was there when it was done. Cat was very brave about it."

"Since when is getting a daughter's ears pierced the business of a father?" she demanded. "You have never shown an interest in going shopping with her for clothes or school supplies or even taking her to doctor's appointments since we've been married. You should have asked my opinion before you did it."

"Sophia, why are you so angry? Dolores says that in Latin countries, the mothers have their infant girls' ears pierced. It's just tiny studs."

Sophia's eyes were blazing. "I am her mother. I know what's best for her." She turned to Cat. "How many other girls in your class have had their ears pierced?"

"None," Cat said guiltily, knowing that she had misled Dolores about what Sophia had said.

Sophia looked at Robert, triumphant. "You once told me that when you were growing up in this town, how important it was for you to fit in. Do you think Cat is going to fit in by having her ears pierced like little Latinas?"

Robert shrugged. "But they are so tiny."

Margaret spoke up. "Robert, Sophia is right. The studs will only cast her in a negative light."

Sophia appreciated her mother-in-law's understanding and support. She turned back to Cat, trying to modulate her voice so it sounded like a casual conversation.

"Cat, did you deliberately lie to Dolores, knowing that I said for you to wait until you're older?"

Cat gave her mother an angry look. "Yes, but when I told you this afternoon that I got them pierced, you said, 'That's nice.'"

She remembered Cat talking to her, but she hadn't been listening because her thoughts were elsewhere.

"Cat, I must not have heard you clearly. You are not to wear studs until I decide it is the right time. When you misrepresent what I say to you in order to get your ears pierced, you are being disobedient. And what you did is not acceptable. Come here."

Cat came over to where her mother was sitting. Sophia removed the studs from Cat's ears.

"You will not wear these until I tell you. Keep them in a drawer in your room until then."

"You broke your promise to me," Cat pouted, her dark eyes looking pained.

"What promise?"

"You said that you would love me no matter what I say or do, and now it's not true."

"Cat," Sophia said softly, putting her arm around her, "I still love you as much as ever. Loving you and teaching you how to obey are not mutually...one does not negate—" She stopped and sighed. "Cat," she started again, "as your mother, I have the responsibility to teach you what is best for you. I can correct you and punish you and still love you. In fact, it's because I love you that I need to teach you to respect my wishes."

Cat stared at her. "Daddy and Dolores said it was okay."

"Yes, they did, and sometimes fathers and friends don't understand the situation as well as a mother does." She hesitated. "And Cat, there is something else you should know. I love you so much that I have asked the court's permission to legally adopt you as my daughter, and I am waiting to hear if your birth mother will agree to give up all claim to you."

"What does that mean?" asked Cat.

"It means that I want you as my daughter legally, that you will not be my daughter just because I married your father. It means that I will have all the rights and responsibilities to care for you as if I had given birth to you, and that is what I want—to care for you and teach you how to be the best person possible."

"You're not mad at me anymore?"

"I'm upset because you did not obey me. It is not the same as being mad." She fixed a stray hair on Cat's head. "Please go in your bedroom, and put those lovely studs away for now."

When Cat had left, Sophia whispered angrily to Dolores. "You are putting ideas in her head that at seven years old, she needs to look like a teenager, not a young girl. Please keep your ideas to yourself from now on."

Dolores flinched. Sophia had never spoken to her like that.

"I am sorry, my friend. I did not think it was such a big deal." Dolores glanced over at Robert, who just shrugged. A long, uncomfortable silence ensued.

To break the tension, Margaret said, "I think it's wonderful that you want to adopt Cat. It never occurred to me until now that if anything happened to Robert, you would not automatically have claim to Cat."

"I didn't intend to tell Cat so soon. We still have to wait for Catherine's permission. It's been a while since I petitioned the court. I thought I would have heard from her by now. Do you think she will allow it?"

"She never wanted Cat, so I believe she will be grateful." She paused, thinking. "Yes," Margaret said with more certainty. "She moves at a snail's pace, but she will say yes."

Sophia made an excuse to go into the bedroom to give Mateo his bottle, something she could have easily done in front of the others since she had recently stopped breastfeeding.

I know what is best for Cat, and sometimes Robert doesn't have a clue. This is the first time Cat has deliberately disobeyed me. I better prepare myself because it's bound to happen again.

She looked at Mateo in her arms, taking his bottle, wide-eyed and innocent.

How close he came to falling down the slope. He needed me to protect him, and I almost failed in my duty.

She snuggled her son in her arms, all the while thinking of how she could have handled things better. Certain images kept popping up in her brain, no matter how much she tried to push them down.

Robert and Dolores. My husband and my best friend—together. He promised me that he would never cheat or lie, and now he has done both. He is no better than Carlo. So is this what happens in marriage?

It wasn't like Sophia to feel sorry for herself, but she felt like she was being punished for her motherhood.

Brooding is not going to fix anything, she told herself, and yet she remained in Mateo's room, her spirit crushed.

Later, after Mateo was asleep for the night, she came out of his room and realized that the house had gone silent. She checked Cat's room and saw that she, too, was asleep. There was no place to go but into her bedroom.

Robert was sitting up in bed with an earbud, listening to something. He took it out and watched her as she moved around the room, opening up a drawer and taking out her nightgown.

"What's wrong, Sophia?" he asked softly. "Are you still angry with me about leaving Mateo and with letting Cat have her ears pierced?"

She didn't answer. What could she say? *I saw you with your body against my best friend.* It sounded so weak, so petty. One frame in a reel. *What conclusion can I draw other than they went to the dock to be alone?* And Cat misled Robert, so it wasn't entirely his fault that he agreed to the studs.

"I'm tired." She changed quickly and closed the light by her side of the bed.

"You need your rest. Your family arrives tomorrow, and we'll be busy every day they are here. Good night."

She certainly was not in the mood for sex, but his remarks made her fume. They were dismissive.

Of course, he doesn't want sex tonight. He had it with Dolores earlier.

She tried to think of some way to bring up the scene that she had witnessed on the dock, the flash of him and her best friend, with their faces so close, without actually accusing him of infidelity. After several minutes, she gave up. She knew her voice would betray her feelings as soon as she spoke.

EASTPORT, JULY 26–27

The next day, Monday, the twenty-sixth, Sophia went back to the realtor's office for the closing, giving Robert instructions on what still had to be done in the guest rooms and bathrooms. Her family arrived in the early afternoon, all six of them coming from the airport together. She put on a brave face and greeted them warmly. Her parents were to stay with Margaret in her cottage, along with Dolores, while the others filled up the bedrooms in the main house. Cat and Cristina were to share a bed, Joey was put in Mateo's room on a cot, while the crib was moved into Sophia and Robert's room for the duration of the visit, and Joe and Grace had the fourth bedroom.

The entourage spent hours claiming their luggage, getting situated in their sleeping quarters, and walking the property, checking out the views. Dinner was on the long terrace. Extra chairs and tables reached from end to end so that all twelve of them fit.

Entertaining a crowd was no problem for the Bellinis, who were used to feeding friends and strays in their California home. Tasks were assigned to everyone. Mateo was in charge of entertaining them with his babbles and mimics, while the rest of the family moved around the kitchen and dining room, manning the stove, getting silverware and plates, ingredients and bowls, drinks and glasses.

In the heat of summer, everyone desired something light, so clams and mussels, corn on the cob, and coleslaw satisfied the adults. The kids ate hot dogs and potato wedges. Sophia insisted on using real dishes, not paper ones. It meant more work cleaning up, but with everyone pitching in, the load was lighter.

The following day, the twenty-seventh, in perfect weather conditions, they went out for a sail around Long Island Sound. The thirty-foot boat had a cabin with two sleeping berths, an ice box, hot and cold water, a two-burner stove, and a head. Everyone put on a life jacket, except Mateo, because there wasn't one small enough. They intended to stay out for hours, so Roberto had included seasickness patches and pills in the first aid kit.

A few miles out, Grace began to feel nauseated. The patch helped, but she was not enjoying the ride. Robert, who was at the helm, was having a hard time moving around a flotilla of sailboats, and that, along with a small chop, made the ride unsettling.

Sophia kept an eye on Cat, who, she insisted, had to wear a straw hat. It was hard for the children to stay in one spot, especially when someone shouted about a fish surfacing on the opposite side of the boat or a lighthouse that was visible from the prow.

Grace decided to go to the cabin to lie down, and Sophia followed her, clutching Mateo in her arms.

"Here, let me put a cool towel on your face. That may help."

Grace thanked her and lay on the seat cushions, groaning.

"I'm so sorry to ruin your day," she said.

"Don't worry. I am not missing much. I have been out sailing many times. It would have been better if you took the pills ahead of time, but you had no way of knowing you'd be sick. Close your eyes and just focus on your breathing."

Mateo had fallen asleep as he usually did in the early afternoon. Bits of conversation filtered in through the open portholes. Sophia was half asleep herself when she heard Dolores's voice whisper, "Does she know what we were doing?"

And Robert's voice answered back, "No. I don't think she suspects."

Her eyes and ears were alert for any more words, but none came.

How could Robert be so close to the porthole when he is at the helm? Am I dreaming?

She wanted to leave the cabin and go on deck, but what if she saw them together? Make a scene in front of her whole family? No, she had to remain inside until Mateo woke up. No one had come

213

into the cabin to check on them. She closed her eyes and rested. She needed to relax, to let go of her tension.

What is happening to my marriage? After only a year? It's about the same length of time when Carlo and I became estranged. What am I doing wrong?

The sound of footsteps awakened her. It was Margaret.

"I came to see how you are doing." She took a seat on the berth across from her daughter-in-law, taking in her tired eyes and sad expression. She looked at Sophia with concern. "When Grace came up on the deck alone, your mother thought you might be ill."

"No, I'm okay."

"Just okay?" It bothered her that her daughter-in-law appeared so sad. She thought of how Sophia had transformed Cat from a sulky, hostile girl to a happy, agreeable child practically overnight. She realized that she had never mentioned this to Sophia. "Cat is a much sweeter girl because of your efforts."

Sophia gave her a slight smile, too tense to make a proper reply.

"You must be so busy with work and two kids. I don't want to be the meddling mother-in-law, but if you need me to come and help you, just ask."

Sophia bit her lip. She could always count on Margaret for support.

"I'm okay," she repeated huskily.

"Your mother is concerned as well, but she doesn't want to leave your father."

Sophia immediately became alarmed. "Why? Has anything happened?"

"No. He's having a grand old time at the helm, but Maria is afraid he might run aground, not knowing these waters."

"My dad is sailing the boat?"

"Yes, and Robert encouraged him and went up to the front deck to sit. I'm sure Giorgio is a very capable sailor, but he admits to being a bit rusty. Robert has more faith in your father than he should have."

Fuck. I did hear them talking.

"Sophia, since we are alone, I want to say that I know what Robert did, and I hope you can forgive him. I told him how disappointed I was in him. That's not how my husband and I raised him."

"He told you?" She could not believe that Robert discussed his cheating on her with his mother.

"Just this morning. He said it's been weighing on his conscience. He had hoped over time you will judge him less harshly. He knows how hard it must be for you to forgive something like that."

Sophia reddened. *Is infidelity something all women must expect and accept and forgive?*

"Margaret, if it had been your husband, could you forgive him?"

"You ask hard questions, don't you?" She considered her answer. "I would have to—for the sake of my family."

"Women are still the ones who have to bend. Nothing much has changed, really."

"There are women who don't play by the rules as well. Sophia, Robert loves you very much, and he is afraid you may decide to leave him over this. I hope you can find it in your heart to forgive his behavior."

Sophia studied her mother-in-law.

She is giving me advice so her son will not be hurt, but what about my pain?

Margaret saw her hesitate. "He said he did it for you."

"For me?" There was a frown on her face.

"Yes, if Sam settled the case out of court, you would be spared having to go to trial."

Sophia's jaw dropped. *She's not talking about his infidelity!*

Just then, Mateo moved. She looked down to see him wide awake, his hazel eyes smiling at her, the exact same twinkle that Robert had used to win her heart. She smiled, picking him up to kiss his cheek. Then she turned to Margaret.

"I love Robert. I want him as a husband and a friend, but if he had come and asked me if I'd approve of his covering up a crime, I would have said no."

215

"We all know the kind of man Sam is and how much he deserves to be punished, but there are his young children to consider," Margaret replied.

Sophia leaned back and closed her eyes, trying to imagine having a father in prison.

If my daughter had lived, her father would be behind bars. Her airtight argument for getting revenge on Sam now had sprung a giant leak.

In midafternoon, the sailboat returned to the dock, and the passengers and crew wearily climbed the steps back up to the house. Everyone was spent. A half day out on the water in the July sun had drained even the most intrepid seagoers. The men made themselves drinks and went to sit on the terrace, while the women headed for the showers and a change of clothes. The youngsters went into Cat's room to play.

Sophia needed to give Mateo a bath. Afterward, she brought him out to where the men were sitting and handed him off to Robert.

"I want to shower. He belongs with the men."

It was the closest thing to a tease that she had said to her husband in a while.

"You are one of us," he said to his son. "We will teach you what it means to be a man."

"And a sailor, Robert," added her father. "He did well on his first boat ride, no?" he asked Sophia.

"He slept through most of it. The sound of Robert's voice just outside the porthole didn't wake him."

She looked at Robert, her eyebrows raised. Then she turned and walked into the house.

He watched her as she strode away and wondered what she had heard.

*****

That evening, it was Robert who was subdued, while Sophia was in high spirits. She chatted with the mothers about raising children while continuing to work, leaving Dolores with little to contribute to the conversation. Sophia expected her to go and join the men, but she remained with the women and listened quietly, most unlike her.

It was late when all the guests had retired to their quarters, and Robert and Sophia were getting ready for bed. He avoided her glance and slipped under the covers without saying good night.

"It was a good day, I think," Sophia began. "Everyone except Grace enjoyed the boat ride."

"Yes," he agreed, "the sail went very well."

"How did my father do at the helm? I was in the cabin most of the time and couldn't watch."

"He did very well." Robert turned toward her, probing her eyes in the darkness. "Do you want to talk about anything else?" he asked.

"No, I-I was hoping that you would ravish me tonight." She was not going to let Dolores have her way with him so easily.

He was stunned for several seconds. Then he was on top of her, running his fingers slowly over her body, and she let out a deep sigh.

EASTPORT, JULY 28

In the morning, Sophia woke and saw that Robert had already risen. She left their bedroom and went into the kitchen, started the coffee machine, and then went back into the bedroom and found Mateo awake and reaching for the mobile that was hanging over his crib. She changed him and brought him with her into the kitchen to give him his bottle.

Robert had just returned from taking Bruno for a walk and was filling up the dog bowl.

"Here. Let me feed him," he said. "You must be tired."

"A little tired," she admitted.

"I haven't seen you that passionate in a while," he whispered as she bent over to put Mateo on his lap.

Is that what drove him into Dolores's arms? she wondered.

Grace came in, along with the three children.

"What's for breakfast?" asked Cat. "I'm hungry."

"You are always hungry." Sophia smiled.

"Not always," Cat corrected her. "I'm not hungry when I'm sleeping."

"That's when you are dreaming of food. I am going to make pancakes with blueberries. How does that sound?"

"Yummy!" the three kids said in unison.

"I'll help you," Grace offered, still in her bathrobe but with her dark hair combed and gathered behind her ears. "Joe never gets to sleep late in the morning, so he's taking advantage of this vacation to stay in bed."

She watched Robert holding Mateo in his arms, burping his son, with a look of contentment on his face.

"We are so lucky to have married men who share caring for their infants," she whispered to Sophia. "I know mothers whose husbands wouldn't so much as reach for a baby bottle to hand to their wives, never mind feed and burp their babies."

Sophia thought about that. She tried to reconcile in her mind the image of Robert and Dolores on the dock, and the image of him now lovingly holding his son, as well as his pleasure during their lovemaking last night. It didn't make sense.

*****

The entire party stuck close to home that day, either playing bocce on the grass or driving around the area to see the sights, especially the lighthouses. Bruno chased or was chased by the kids all afternoon and finally fled to a quiet corner in the house to get some rest. Kit was nowhere to be found.

That night, Dolores came to sit by Sophia in the living room. They had not talked much one-on-one since her arrival days ago.

"I am here to listen if you need to talk," Dolores said.

"I've been neglecting you. I'm sorry. I've never had to care for an infant before, and it's a lot of work."

"I understand. Ask me to do whatever needs to be done. I know how to change a diaper and burp a baby."

"I can handle that or Robert can, when he is around," she couldn't help adding.

"Some Latin men feel it's beneath their dignity to do those things. You chose well this time. He is so handsome and pleasant and thoughtful."

Sophia decided to confront Dolores, hoping to make her understand the anguish she was feeling. She spoke slowly, choosing her words carefully.

"I need him, Dolores, more than I ever thought I could need a man." She wiped a tear away. "We have had some troubles lately, a serious disagreement over a legal case, and someone spreading vicious rumors around town about his and my infidelity. I have been miserable, trying to deal with suspicions and innuendos."

"Robert is a good man, a good father. He makes you happy in all the right ways, no? You know that. I know that. Everybody knows that. No matter what happens, he will always be with you in the end."

Somehow Sophia did not find Dolores's words comforting.

"What time tomorrow will Ricardo get here?" she asked.

"Not until one o'clock. I miss him. We have become very close lately. You know, when his older brother died suddenly, it hit Ricardo hard. It made him realize just how little time we may have on Earth. I flew with him to Buenos Aires to attend the funeral and to meet his family. They are lovely, so caring. His mother told me that I was good for him. When we got back home, I suggested we do a show together at his gallery—my paintings and his statues that have similar themes. We will pair them up, mine on canvas, his in wood and ceramics. I hope it may help to shake off his depression."

"That is so clever. I'm sure it will be a success."

"He is still sad, but I told him he had to come here because I cannot be at your wedding reception and not dance," she declared. "And I wanted him to meet my best friend at one of the most joyous moments in your life. Your happiness speaks well of marriage."

Sophia said nothing. She was thankful that once Ricardo was there, she no longer had to concern herself with Robert being with Dolores.

EASTPORT, JULY 29

Ricardo arrived from the airport in a flashy yellow convertible with a red interior. He looked like a movie idol. Everything about him—his enormous smile, his sophisticated clothes, and his Latin accent—attracted attention. The children were fascinated, the men were envious, and the women were charmed. He kissed the hands of every female and pounded the back of every male. His personality was big. One could not help but like him. In Sophia's mind, he was a mirror image of Dolores—generous in praise and also sincere and attentive in conversations. If he was depressed, he hid it well, Sophia thought.

"What a beautiful home you have," he told Robert. "It's designed to enhance rather than disrupt the water views. How do you get visitors to leave?"

"That has been and continues to be a problem," Robert admitted.

"If I owned this property, I would have a sign out front: *Paying guests only.* And," he said, producing a wrapped package, "I have brought you and your wife my payment for your hospitality."

"But we said no gifts," Robert protested.

"Then consider my sculpture on permanent loan here." He took off the wrapping to reveal a representation of a seated man and woman with their bodies entwined around each other.

The black ceramic figures were naked, but their closeness only made their pose suggestive, not erotic. The faces were almost touching, as if about to kiss. It was about a foot and a half high and fascinating to look at from all angles.

Sophia studied the piece. "This belongs in a museum. It deserves a spot all by itself." She went to a pedestal table in a corner of the living room, removed the vase with flowers, and asked Robert to carry the table to a more central place in the room, between two chairs. She carefully centered the statue on it.

"There," she said, "doesn't it look made for that spot?"

Everyone agreed.

"Thank you, Ricardo, for bringing us such an elegant gift." She kissed him on both cheeks.

Robert watched, slightly annoyed. The rest of the afternoon and evening, Ricardo held center stage, describing his work with different materials, and nodding as Maria and Dolores talked about all that goes into making a painting satisfying to the viewer. He and Sophia's father spoke passionately of wine and the role it played in bringing out the flavors of different foods. Robert moved around the room, checking to see if everyone had food and drink, and that no one was left out of the discussions.

Sophia had taken charge of Mateo that evening. She fed him and got him ready for bed. *It was Robert's family home, so he should play host tonight.* With Sophia busy with Mateo, Dolores took it upon herself to play hostess. She enjoyed pleasing people and being the center of attention as much as Ricardo did.

Around eight o'clock, Sophia emerged from Mateo's room, leaving him sleeping, and joined the party. She looked around for Robert but did not see him. Neither did she see Dolores. Ricardo beckoned her over.

"Are you looking for your husband?" he asked.

"Yes," she said.

"He's on the boat, checking to see if everything is, how do you say it? Shipshape for tomorrow's sail."

"Oh, at this late hour? And where is Dolores?"

"She went with him. Come and sit next to me. I have not had a chance to chat with you. Dolores described to me how you looked, but her words do not do justice to your beauty. I think women who have recently given birth are the most beautiful creatures in the world."

"Ricardo, I am not a young, gullible teenage girl. That line won't get you very far."

"No, no. I am being truthful. You have an inner beauty that cannot be created with lipstick and rouge. Roberto is a lucky man."

"Speaking of Robert, I need to find him to tell him he needs to return to his guests." She got up to leave.

Ricardo put his hand on her arm. "I do not think that would be wise."

Immediately she became suspicious. "Why ever not?"

He hesitated. He looked like a man who was reluctant to tell her the truth. "A man does not like to feel as if his wife needs to tell him how to act. Roberto knows his role as a host. He will return when he is ready."

She studied him, trying to read between the lines.

"Let him be," he said.

What is going on? Her mind couldn't accept what he was imply-ing. *How can he be so comfortable knowing that Dolores and Robert are by themselves? Are affairs approved forms of behavior today? Am I just supposed to turn a blind eye to their lovemaking?* Her thoughts were going wild.

Her legal mind went over the evidence. Twice now, he and Dolores had gone to the dock by themselves. He could have asked someone else to help him prepare the boat if that was what he really needed to do. The only conclusion she could arrive at was obvious, given the facts.

"Stay with me," Ricardo pleaded. "I hope I am not bad company."

Two can play this game, she decided.

"Your company is most welcome." She sat down again. "What are you drinking?" she asked.

"Scotch. Would you like some?"

"Yes. It is just what I need."

*****

223

An hour later, when dusk had fallen, Robert and Dolores returned to find Sophia and Ricardo on a sofa with their bodies next to each other, having an intimate chat.

"Hello," Robert said loudly. "Where is Mateo and all the children?"

She ignored his question, taking note of their sweaty faces. It was a warm summer night, but there was always a cooling breeze by the water. No one else was perspiring, she thought.

"Is everything shipshape?" she asked.

"What?"

"Weren't you checkin' out the boat in preparation for tomorra's sail?" She slurred her words slightly.

He stared at Ricardo, his blood heating up. "Yes, everything looks good."

Ricardo spoke up, "The rest of the group went off to their rooms a while ago in preparation for an early morning departure."

Robert noticed the Scotch glass in her hand, empty.

"Oh, so you've been here all by yourselves?"

"Yes, Ricardo and I are becoming well-acquainted, wouldn't you agree, my dear?" she said, looking at him with admiration.

"I think you are inebriated, Sophia," Robert said, his voice rising.

"I wouldn't call it by such a—hic—sophisticated name. Let's just say I'm drunk."

"I think it's time for you to go to bed."

"Ricardo said the same thing." She turned to Dolores. "You wouldn't mind if we went to bed, would you?"

"Who is 'we'?" Dolores asked, not believing what she was hearing.

"Does it matter? We are all good friends."

Robert had had enough. He took Sophia by the arm and guided her toward their bedroom.

"Good night," Robert said firmly, turning to glare at Ricardo. "You and Dolores are staying in the cottage next door."

Once in their room, Sophia climbed into bed with her clothes on.

"I am suddenly so tired," she murmured.

"Sophia, you have never acted like this. What is going on?" He tried to shake her awake, but her eyes stayed closed.

When he shut the light off, he heard her sigh. "It felt so good."

He was afraid to ask her what she meant by that.

*****

Sometime later, Sophia was in the middle of a dream when she heard a noise. *It must be Mateo.* She got up to find out what was wrong. The crib was near the door. She moved silently across the room, with just the soft moonlight to help guide her. When she looked in the crib, she saw Mateo was fast asleep.

She stood there, wondering what had woken her up. Maybe it was Cat, she thought. She opened the bedroom door and went out into the hall. There was no sound coming from Cat's room. Some force was tugging at her, drawing her away from her bedroom and her sleeping husband.

Now, fully awake, she walked in the other direction, and peered left into the kitchen and right into the living room. No one. The terrace door was partly open.

Robert usually took care that the house was locked at night. Maybe he forgot. She walked out onto the terrace and took a deep breath. The air was still heavy with the day's heat. The only sound was the lapping of the waves against the dock down below. She was enjoying the night's stillness, the moonlight shimmering on the water, when a strange sensation came over her. She felt someone was close by.

She turned to see a dark figure emerge from the shadows. She was startled, then recovered and said, "What are you doing here?"

"Waiting, hoping you'd come to me."

"I just came out for a breath of air," she turned away, suddenly realizing that she was wearing a thin nightgown.

"Let us breathe the air together." He came closer to her, so close that she smelled liquor.

"You must be drunk," she whispered.

"Yes, drunk with love for you." He leaned in and kissed her, more than a peck, more than a buss. It was as intimate a kiss as she had ever received from a man.

"I can't," she complained. "I'm married."

"Your husband cheats. Why can't you?"

"Because that is not who I am," she replied.

"So when you were flirting with me earlier, was that all an act?"

"Yes," she admitted, "I was doing it as a way to get even with Robert."

"Then you are deceitful. You knew you were playing with my emotions, and you did it anyway." His hands were stroking her, and she was getting aroused.

Should I let him? she wondered. *If Robert wants sex outside of marriage, where does that leave me?*

He began lifting up her nightgown so quickly that she had no time to protest. She started to groan, but then someone else had come and was calling her name and shaking her. She tried to push the hand away, but she couldn't. Her feelings were beginning to fade. She opened her eyes.

*****

"Sophia, are you all right?"

She turned to see Robert staring at her. She looked around, still half asleep. "Where am I?"

"You're beside me in bed. Where else would you be? You must have been having a bad dream. Look, you're all sweaty."

She looked down to see that she was in the same outfit that she had on earlier. It was stuck to her, wrinkled and damp. She sat up, remembering what her thoughts had been only moments ago, not sure how much was real.

"Well, what were you dreaming about? You sounded as though you were in pain."

"I have some bad memories that I can't shake," she mumbled.

Strictly speaking, it was not a lie, but neither was it truthful. It was too early to get up and too late to bother getting undressed. She lay back down. Her eyes were closed, but her mind was racing.

How would Freud interpret my dream? Is desiring a man the same as enjoying him? Am I no better than my husband for having thought about it?

She tossed and turned until the early sunrise mercifully got her up and out of bed.

AT SEA, JULY 30

July thirtieth and another day of sailing. This time, Grace took the seasickness pills ahead of time. In the early morning, the entire party headed across the sound, toward Long Island. They had made reservations to eat at a dockside restaurant in Port Jefferson. The water was calm, and it being somewhat cloudy, there were fewer pleasure boats making the crossing. Everyone on the boat was relaxed, more prepared for the sun and motion of the boat. Robert stayed at the helm.

The restaurant was crowded, but the Bellini party of twelve were given choice seats on the deck, under a sailcloth shade. Everyone loved seafood, so ordering was easy. Nonno enjoyed a seafood platter, while others had lobster rolls or fried clams. Mateo sat in an infant seat placed in a highchair or was passed around so that Sophia had a chance to eat with her hands free.

During dessert, Cat asked Ricardo if she could go for a ride in his convertible later on.

"I've never been in a convertible," Cat explained.

"Of course. I will take you when we get back."

"No, you won't," Robert said. "I forbid it."

Everyone turned to stare at Robert.

"I can assure you that I am a safe driver," Ricardo said, offended by his firm refusal.

"It's too dangerous."

"It's not dangerous," Cat argued. "Ricardo takes Dolores for rides, and Uncle Joe said that Cristina and Joey can go."

"Cat, this is not for you to decide." He spoke angrily, so unlike him. The adults felt that there was more to his refusal than his fear of an accident.

"Mom, will you let me go in the convertible? Please."

No one at their table moved, their eyes on Sophia. In the entire restaurant, there was hardly any noise to be heard. It was as if the table conversations had been put on pause. Sophia realized that Cat had put her in an impossible position; she either had to side with her daughter, who was challenging her father's judgment, or side with Robert, who was acting like a jealous husband. She knew what she had to say, as illogical as it sounded.

"Cat, your father is right. It might be dangerous for you to ride in the back seat of a convertible, even though you'll be wearing your seatbelt and Ricardo is a good driver."

"Why?" Cat didn't understand. Others were wondering as well.

"Well, a big wind might come by and lift you up out of the car and take you to the land of *Oz*." She put her head down, trying to stay serious while some around the table were chuckling.

"Mom, that was just a fairy tale, and fairy tales are not true. You told me so yourself."

"That is the only situation I can think of where it might be dangerous, Cat."

Cat turned back to her father. "Daddy, please let me go. Aunt Dolores will be with us."

Even though Sophia had supported his ruling, in a way, Robert felt embarrassed. He now had to climb out of the hole he dug for himself.

"Well, okay, maybe just around the block," he mumbled.

"Thank you, Daddy!"

On the sail back to Eastport, Maria offered to stay in the cabin while Mateo took his nap. Sophia decided there was something she must do out in the open so she could observe Robert's expression. Her study of behavioral psychology gave her confidence that she could tell when a person was lying or feeling a sense of shame. She moved to where her husband was sitting at the controls and asked, "May I sail for a while?"

He got up to leave, but she whispered, "I'd like you to stay next to me." He sat back down, looking upset.

She waited until she was in firm control of the boat before she breathed, "Do you still love me?"

He looked down at his hands, and then off to the horizon, away from his wife.

"I think the more proper question is 'Do you still love me?'" he snapped.

"I do, but I must admit it has been hard to accept some of your behaviors," she whispered, her face reflecting her hurt and jealousy.

"And it's been hard for me to accept some of yours." He turned to stare at her, his eyes flashing in anger at the memory of last night.

"Then we are even. Can we call a truce?" she suggested.

He was silent for a while, thinking of how she loved being in control of situations, no matter if they were personal or professional. *I still love her as much as ever.*

"A truce," he agreed. "But tell me, were you really drunk last night? If you were, you made a speedy recovery this morning."

She ignored answering him but asked a question of her own. "Were you really checking the boat last night?" She stared at him to see if he showed any signs of shame, but she saw none. "What were you really doing on the dock with—" She stopped because her father was standing up and waving his hands frantically.

"Sophia, you've got a motorboat coming up behind you on your left. It's moving much too fast!"

She whipped her head around and saw a large boat aimed right at them, maybe a hundred and fifty feet away. She immediately tacked, and the sailboat's movement created a spray, wetting everyone on deck. Her father hugged the rail to avoid falling down. The kids started screaming, not just because they were wet but because they, too, saw the boat heading for them.

"It's getting closer!" her father shouted. He waved an arm to attract the attention of the person at the controls. Now everyone could see the panic on the face of the operator.

"He can't turn the wheel!" Robert shouted.

"Cut your engine!" Giorgio yelled, and almost immediately, the motorboat slowed down, passing within five feet of them.

The man at the wheel called over to them, "A line must have snapped!"

"I'll call the Coast Guard to come and help you!" Robert shouted back, and he took out his iPhone, punched in numbers, and looked around to see where they were positioned on the sound.

Maria had come out of the cabin with Mateo to see what had happened.

"Thanks, Dad," Sophia said, her voice trembling. "I'm glad you were alert."

He came to sit beside her.

"Sophia," he said, gently putting his arm around her, "when you are out in the middle of a bay, in command of a sailboat, you cannot take your eyes off your surroundings."

She let Robert take back the helm and rested her head against her father's shoulder, trying to quiet her thumping heart.

When they got back home and were settled in the cool living room, some sipping chilled lemonade and some a frosty beer, Sophia raised her voice and said, "I want to apologize to everyone for the danger I put you in earlier. I was not paying attention to where other boats were on the water, and I know better than to be distracted, especially when it involves the lives of the people I love."

Grace spoke up, "To handle a boat that size takes skill and courage. I could never do it."

"Don't blame yourself," her mother said. "You are an excellent sailor."

Robert came to her defense as well, marveling at how Sophia took the blame for something that wasn't her fault.

"The problem wasn't with Sophia's knowledge of sailing but with another boatsman's lack of preparation. That fellow should have checked his lines before he went out. There is usually evidence of wear, like fraying, that can be easily seen with the naked eye."

"What's a naked eye?" asked Cat.

Everyone laughed, having heard her endless questions since they arrived.

"It basically means without the aid of a magnifying glass," Robert responded wearily.

The tension between him and Sophia had sapped his energy. Giorgio spoke in Cat's defense.

"My granddaughter has a very inquisitive mind, and we must encourage her to ask the questions."

Sophia's heart swelled to hear him say "*my granddaughter.*" He was as proud of her as if she were his own flesh and blood.

Her brother, who was sitting beside her, leaned in and whispered, "So what were you and Robert discussing so intently during the sail? I was watching you. By the look on your faces, I thought the boat had sprung a leak and you were deciding whether to stay on board or jump ship."

"Actually, that is exactly what we were talking about," said Sophia, giving her brother a wink. "We put some chewing gum on the leak and saved the day."

"Since we are talking in metaphors, I'll interpret that as very good news."

"Joey," she said, calling him by his childhood nickname, "sometimes you are much smarter than I give you credit for."

*****

Later in the afternoon, while Sophia was changing Mateo in her bedroom, Giorgio took Cat aside.

"My Cat, do you like having a brother?"

"Yes, but I can't play with him yet. He's too little," she explained.

"He will get big quickly. And what do you enjoy most about having a mother?"

"Hmm. I like how Mom answers my questions and explains things to me and how she reads me bedtime stories and kisses me good night, and when we go shopping, she lets me pick out things I like!"

Giorgio smiled. "That must make you very happy to have such a nice mom."

"Yes," she paused, "but she's not always nice to my daddy. She yells at him a lot."

"Oh, why does she yell at him?" Giorgio asked.

Cat listed all the times her mother had yelled at her father, in great detail.

"It must upset you when you hear her yelling at your daddy."

Cat nodded.

"My Cat, have you ever told your mother this?"

"No."

"I think you should tell her exactly how you feel when she yells at him. Do it tonight, before you go to bed. Promise?"

"Okay. I promise."

That night, when Sophia was giving Cat her bath, she noticed her daughter was staring at her.

"What's the matter?"

"Nothing."

"It has to be something. You look upset."

Cat didn't respond.

"Did you enjoy the ride in Ricardo's convertible?"

"Yes."

A one-word answer. That's not like her. Something's the matter. Maybe I haven't been paying enough attention to her, she thought.

"You were really sweaty from being out in the boat. Close your eyes, and I'll rinse the soap out of your hair. There. That's good."

She helped Cat out of the tub, knelt on the floor and put a bath towel around her daughter's body, hugged her, and said, "You are becoming such a lovely young lady. I am so proud of you."

Cat did not smile at her mother's compliment.

"Mom, why do you yell at Daddy so much? Don't you like him anymore?"

"What?" Sophia moved back from her daughter to stare at her, feeling like she had just been slapped.

"Today you made him move over so you could sail the boat. He was angry with you."

"Daddy wasn't angry," Sophia said, becoming flustered. "We were just talking."

"He was so. I can tell when he's mad. He doesn't like it when you yell at him so much."

"I don't yell at him, Cat."

The overhead light beamed down on her, making her feel exposed, vulnerable. The warm air in the bathroom was smothering. She wiped the perspiration off her face.

"Yes, you do," Cat insisted, sounding and looking like a judge with a robe wrapped around her. "You yelled at him on the terrace when Mateo almost fell."

"That was just one time," Sophia said nervously. She was beginning to feel like her daughter had her on a witness stand and was cross-examining her for a criminal offense. Her heart started racing.

"Uh-uh. You yelled at him when I got my ears pierced, and you yelled at him in the French restaurant. Remember? Everyone was looking at you."

Sophia leaned back against the wall, grabbing at the damp tiles to steady herself, and stared at her daughter. *Jesus! Am I yelling at him in front of Cat and in public?*

"I feel sad when you yell at him. And Daddy never yells at you."

Sophia's eyes flashed pain. By the look on her face, one would have thought Cat had stabbed her in the heart. *No, he doesn't yell at me. He can't stand up to yelling,* she reminded herself. *Wow. I am getting a putdown from my seven-year-old daughter.*

She sat on the bathroom floor, feeling completely limp, totally shamed, and watched as Cat put on her pajamas. The thought of how often she had lost her self-control made her blood run cold. She wanted to escape.

"Oh, Cat. I'm sorry. I didn't realize—I will try not to yell at him anymore."

"Okay. Promise?"

Sophia smiled. "I promise." She got up off the floor, wondering how she could have been so blind. *I didn't know what effect my behavior was having on her. I can't be the cause of Cat's unhappiness. I have to do better. This is one promise I must keep.*

EASTPORT, JULY 31

On the thirty-first of July, the day before the big event, the men went fishing. They motored out to the channel and then headed up the coast, leaving the compound before seven, to get to the best spots when the fish were most hungry. Giorgio took control of the helm, while the younger men baited their hooks, checked their fishing lines, and took seats near the stern. Robert was the most experienced fisherman, so the others watched and listened to his directions.

"We need to drop anchor away from the channel traffic. There is a cove farther north where I've had pretty good luck."

"What kinds of fish can we expect to catch?" asked Joe.

"Flounder and mackerel mainly. A bass if we're lucky."

Robert and Ricardo had been frosty to each other since the luncheon and their confrontation about Cat riding in the convertible. Now, in such close quarters, there was no escape. Robert decided to break the ice. He did not like to keep a grudge; after all, it was obvious that Sophia was only acting chummy with Ricardo because he had been with Dolores.

"What do you do to relax, Ricardo, when you are not in your studio?"

Ricardo welcomed the small talk. Staying angry or upset was not in his nature, either.

"Sometimes I play a little soccer with my friends. Dolores and I like to go dancing. We both enjoy entertaining, so we often have people at my apartment or hers. We love the camaraderie. It's what we look forward to at the end of the day. I play the guitar and sing while she prepares the food. I just obey Dolores's orders when it comes to cooking. She has a real flair for it. And you?"

"I spend my days at the law office or in court. In the evening, Sophia and I share the preparation for dinner. I learned to cook after my first wife left, and I refused to ask my mother to make dinner for me every night. On weekends, we go hiking or sailing and fishing— fun things to do outside as a family."

They had arrived at the designated spot, and Giorgio shut the engine and came to watch them. He took a seat beside Ricardo.

"How come you're still a bachelor, Ricardo?" he inquired, smiling in a teasing fashion. "Dolores is a lovely woman."

"Yes, we have been together for a while."

"So you are good friends?"

"Si. Actually, she is more like a partner than a friend."

"A lover, too? *E perfecto.* Sometimes you get one or the other, but when you can have both in the same woman, what more do you need, eh, Ricardo? And you are getting older. No one likes to be alone in their old age."

"Si. Si. I have been doing a lot of thinking since my brother died a few months ago. Dolores came with me to the funeral in Buenos Aires, and she met my family. They loved her. My sister said to me, 'How lucky that you have found a beautiful, talented woman who cares enough to help you through your grief. You should marry her.' It made me think of how I would feel if she left me for someone else. I cannot go on as if the world is staying still. I brought a ring with me. I am trying to decide when to propose."

"I will tell you the best moment," said Giorgio, and he whispered it in Ricardo's ear.

"My line is shaking, Robert!" Joe yelled.

"Reel her in!"

Robert leaned over the side of the boat with a net, and in flopped a flounder.

Later on, when they were heading in, after catching a few mackerel as well, Robert came over to give a bottle of water to his father-in-law at the controls.

Giorgio asked Robert to sit down next to him. "Have you found Sophia to be moody and weepy since giving birth?"

"She has been moody for some time," Robert answered.

"Tell me, when you are together, do you tease each other and make each other laugh?"

"We used to. I know we both enjoyed it, especially the teasing."

"Then this mood she is in is temporary. It happens a lot after the birth of a child. She'll get over it. For Maria, it was a difficult few months, right after Joe was born, because then she had two small children only two years apart." He read Robert's face. "Have patience with Sophia. I know she loves you very much. When she came to visit us last August, her face lit up whenever she spoke your name. She talked about all the ways you were a good man, how much she admired your love for your family, your temperament, your humor."

"I love her too," Robert declared. "But she is upset with me, and nothing I say changes her attitude. It's more than a mood, Giorgio. I did something unethical to spare her from having to go to court in April, during her eighth month of pregnancy. She had back pain and was uncomfortable sleeping. It was really making her miserable. I thought I was helping her by forcing my law partner to settle the case out of court to avoid a long trial, but she didn't see it that way."

"What did you do?"

"I told my law partner to destroy an illegal land survey rather than have it become public knowledge. He was to blame for its existence, and he paid a high financial price in order to correct things. By destroying it, Sophia's client was able to settle the day of the trial, but Sophia saw it as protecting my partner from criminal prosecution."

"So you kept your partner from going to jail?"

"Yes."

"And nobody found out what you did, except Sophia?"

"Just one other colleague, Marion, and she understands my actions."

"Hmm." Giorgio was silent for a while. "You know what I think? We were not born into this world to be perfect. You made the best decision under the circumstances—not the ideal decision, no— but better than letting your partner go to jail. Sophia was immersed in legal ethics while she was teaching at Stanford, and that ingrained in her a very high moral standard as far as following the law goes. I believe in time that Sophia will realize you found the middle ground, that you acted honorably." He clapped Robert on the back. "You are a good man. I am so happy that you and Sophia found each other."

"Thank you, Giorgio. I feel I can talk to you as if you were my own father."

"I am proud that you feel that way."

Seagulls flew overhead. One swooped down and grabbed a clam out of the mud by the shore. It flew up high over a large rock and dropped the clam. Its shell broke, and the gull landed next to the opened clam to eat its meal.

"Look," said Giorgio, "the seagulls are snacking on clams. It's making me hungry."

They opened a large cooler filled with sandwiches with mozzarella, prosciutto, tomato, arugula, and pesto, and containers of chopped watermelon, cantaloupe, pears, and pineapple, along with bottles of water, beer, and wine. The rest of the day, the crew spent relaxing and sharing stories from their childhood. Ricardo and Robert drank and laughed with the others in high spirits.

While the men were away, the women and children found activities to do around the house. Dolores and Maria entertained the kids with painting lessons. The two artists used very different techniques and materials. Dolores worked mostly in bold, brash oils, creating contrasts with shapes, colors, and sizes, more in the Picasso style. Her paintings were bought up for the striking effect they had hanging on a plain white wall in a modern home.

Maria painted what she saw around her, using watercolor techniques that required patience and precision, along with a sharp eye. Her realistic scenes of the Sonoma countryside were admired by visitors for their accurate rendering of the landscape and wildlife of the region.

Not surprisingly, Cristina and Joey showed a flair for watercolors, imitating their grandmother's technique. Cat's adoration for Dolores was apparent in her attempts to imitate her. She liked the freedom to make swirls and figures in different colors. Dolores encouraged her to take what she observed around her and make it bigger or a different color or draw it upside down.

"Take your brush and imagine something else. There is no right or wrong, just have fun."

At the end of their first lesson, the children each had a finished painting to hang in their bedroom.

While the children were occupied, Margaret, Grace, and Sophia made signs for the party, some with arrows to direct guests to the toilets, the trash bins, and even a first aid station. With fifty guests, anything might happen.

After the men returned from fishing, they sat on the terrace to relax and cool off. Maria took their haul of fish and cleaned and dressed each one. Her years of living by the sea showed as she expertly guillotined the fish and filleted the bodies. Grace and Margaret watched, fascinated at how easy she made it look. Sophia came out to serve the men drinks and snacks, knowing how tired they must be. She saw her father beckon to her.

"I want you to come with me for a walk. Is now a good time?"

"Yes, Dad," she said. "Mateo is still asleep."

She noticed that her father looked weary. *After being out on the boat most of the day, he wants to talk to me? Something is up*, she thought.

"Let's go across the lawn and sit under the shade tree," he suggested.

As they crossed the lawn, he began to speak to her, his voice sounding pained.

"You and Robert have a very nice home here. Are you happy, Sophia? Tell me the truth."

She looked away from her father and said nothing. The pause told him what he wanted to know, what he had already guessed.

Finally, she spoke. "I love my family very much."

"But?"

They had sat on chairs facing each other. She was forced to look at him, and that meant she could not get away with a lie.

"Robert did something unethical, and I have had trouble accepting it." Her voice was cold, as she thought of him sneaking a look in her briefcase while she was sleeping.

"Yes, I know. He told me about it this morning. Is that the only problem?"

Sophia was taken aback. "Are you dismissing his unethical behavior as a lawyer?" she asked, incredulous that her father was not more concerned about Robert's actions.

"No, I am not dismissing it," her father answered thoughtfully. "But if we look at it in the context of how he righted a wrong, I think he acted cleverly. He found a solution to a problem that he did not cause, and he helped both his friend and you." He stopped to look his daughter in the eye. "There are no perfect answers to complex problems, Sophia, just imperfect people trying to do their best to solve them."

She felt her world turning upside down. Nothing her father said was making sense.

During all her formative years, he had always given her sensible advice, sounding, at times, more like a wise philosopher than a humble grower of grapes. She had no reason to dismiss his advice today.

I know I am right. Robert committed a crime.

"But, Dad, he aided in a cover-up," she insisted. "He broke his oath as a lawyer."

"Be generous of spirit, Sophia. What your lawbooks discuss about ethics is not the real world, it is the ideal."

She stared at him, trying to take in his view of things. For the first time, she tried to consider Robert's behavior from another perspective.

Is my father right? she thought. *Have I been judging Robert too harshly?*

She watched as a bumblebee flew by and landed on a rose blossom, searching for nectar in its center. Then it hopped to another rose, not satisfied, looking for the ideal bloom, its noisy buzz showing its discontent. She stared at it and wondered.

Her father studied her. "But there is something else, isn't there?"

She had to look away, too embarrassed to tell him.

"I have never seen you look sad when you are sailing a boat, but yesterday, I could tell that you were miserable. What else is there that you are not telling me?"

She put her head down and whispered, "I think Robert is having an affair with Dolores."

Her father's jaw dropped, and he sat back in his chair.

"No, Sophia, I can't believe it. Why do you think that?"

She pursed her lips and took a deep breath.

"Twice they went down to the dock and stayed there for a long while, without any explanation except that he was checking the boat. Dolores knows nothing of boats. Why would he need to have her there, Dad? It doesn't make sense unless they wanted to be alone."

She put her head down, feeling shame that, after only a year together, she was not able to keep her husband interested in her.

"That's all?" he asked, stroking his snowy beard.

"Yes," she cried. "Isn't that enough?"

"Sophia, look at me."

She raised her head and forced herself to look into her father's tired eyes, lined with wrinkles.

He has so much to worry about, she thought.

She knew there had been very little rain in Sonoma Valley that summer, causing the vines to depend on irrigation or else wither and die before the grapes were ready to be picked.

Yet here he is, taking time to understand and help me with my problems.

"Are you and Robert still lovers?" he asked.

She was startled by his question, embarrassed to speak about such things to her own father. Finally, she nodded.

He shook his head.

"That is not how a man who is cheating on his wife behaves. While we were out fishing today, Robert told me how upset he was about your own behavior. He felt that you were still angry with him about protecting his law partner, and he didn't know what he could do to make you forgive him. I could feel his heart breaking. If he was cheating, why would he question your behavior?"

She sat back, amazed that Robert, who always contained his feelings, opened up to her father about their difficulties.

"If you are not more accepting and forgiving, you are going to lose him," Giorgio warned.

Sophia's heart stopped.

He thinks my marriage is in trouble! That Robert may leave me.

Despite the summer heat, she shivered. The ensuing silence was interrupted when Maria called from the house to say that dinner was ready. They rose to go inside, but her father stopped her.

"Sophia, stay here awhile and think about what I said. Resolve these problems, or you may not get another chance at happiness." He took her hand. "I know it's harder to step back and look at things when strong feelings are involved, but try."

"Thanks, Dad," she whispered. "You would have made a great psychologist."

He chuckled. "Perhaps. But I am happier with the grapes. They are easier to figure out than people."

She sat back down and considered the facts.

I was so sure of what I saw. They were together on the dock for a long while. Was that proof that they were having an affair? Would such evidence hold up in a court of law? No, she decided. *It would be thrown out as circumstantial.*

Sophia's eyes traveled across the lawn to their home, and she thought of her family inside.

I have so much to be thankful for, so many I love. There is no other place I would rather be. Am I about to throw it away because of a notion of what I think may have happened?

She rose and walked slowly back to the house. For the first time since she was married to Robert, she felt shaken in her ability to act appropriately toward her husband.

Both my father and my daughter have been critical about my behavior.

Maria had made a Ligurian specialty—pasta with walnut sauce, which, besides walnuts, included grated Parmesan cheese, pine nuts, and milk. It was a staple in Santa Margherita where they once lived.

That, along with the freshly caught grilled mackerel, salad, and gelato, was perfect on a warm summer's eve.

Over dinner, the discussion turned to their fondest memories growing up and, perhaps not surprisingly, much of it was about food.

Ricardo raved about his mother's paella, which she cooked on holidays. Dolores explained the secret for making tasty quesadillas, and Maria boasted about the tenderness of her octopus, first steamed and then marinated in green olives, celery, oil, and red wine vinegar.

"Mom," Cat said, stirring Sophia from her thoughts, "I want you to make octopus again. It really tasted good when you made it for me before."

"I will make some next week," said Sophia quietly, "after the wedding reception is over."

The kids wanted to hear about what it was like growing up in Italy. Joe shared stories of he and Sophia's escapades as young kids, some of which their parents were hearing for the first time.

"One day," Joe said in a mysterious voice, "Sophia and I walked down to the harbor and took a rowboat out into the bay. We could not have been more than five and seven, and we did not know how to swim and the two of us, together, could barely row the boat. At first the water was calm, so we just went around in circles until we got the hang of it. Then we headed out to sea, and the waves became stronger. Fortunately, a fishing boat captain who was heading into port saw us and towed us back in."

"Did you get into trouble?" Cat asked.

"My mother and father never found out—until now!"

Maria said, "My God, if I had known, the two of you would have been grounded until you turned twenty-one."

Giorgio disagreed. "Maybe just to eighteen, Maria. For good behavior."

Ricardo related his earliest memories of kicking a soccer ball around with his friends, sometimes all day long, and having to retrieve it from wherever it landed, in thorny bushes or on the other side of a tall fence.

"One time, the ball went into the ocean, and I was by far the best swimmer, so I was told to get it. Every time I swam close to it, it floated farther out. I knew I could not return without it, so I dived under the water and came up on the other side of the ball. Once I got hold of it, I tried to swim with the ball in one arm but couldn't. So do you know what I did?"

"You put it under your shirt?" Joey guessed.

"No, because I had taken off my shirt on the beach. I decided to let go of the ball and keep it in front of me as I swam in. It was hard because sometimes a big wave would come and push the ball far out in front of me in another direction. It took a long time, and when I finally made it to shore, my friends grabbed the ball and kept playing, but I went home, too exhausted to play anymore."

"What if you didn't bring it back?" Cat wanted to know.

"I would have been shamed and thrown off my team. That was the only ball we had. Nobody could afford to buy another."

"So you sacrificed yourself for the benefit of the greater good," Giorgio concluded, "so that your team could play on."

Ricardo looked surprised. "You make it sound noble. I just wanted to keep my friends."

Dolores told tales of growing up in a small town with lots of superstitions. One was that a cactus plant in a doorway or on a windowsill was supposed to ward off evil spirits.

"It was comforting to believe that, but of course, a plant is just that. It doesn't have superpowers."

Giorgio said, "Italians have many superstitions too. One is that a bent nail on a windowsill will protect them from harm. I suppose these fables make people feel they have some power over events in their lives. But we can control only ourselves and how we choose to act toward others."

Sophia wondered if her father's comments were directed at her. She had sat quietly during the conversations, contributing nothing, not even a smile.

Be generous of spirit. Those were the words he had said earlier. *I must remember that,* she thought.

After dinner, when everyone had helped clear the table and went in different directions to make final preparations for the busy day ahead, Sophia went into the living room and saw that it was empty. She asked the Alexa device to play a waltz. Then she searched for Robert and found him on the terrace with Joe and Giorgio, deep in conversation.

"May I have this waltz?" she whispered in his ear.

He was surprised and a little put out. *Does she think we need to practice dancing a waltz?*

He hesitated, not wanting to leave in the middle of a discussion.

"Please! I need to tell you something."

Her father waved his hand, indicating Robert should leave.

They moved into the living room and began to dance around the sofas and chairs. His steps were sure, easy to follow. She pressed her cheek against his.

"You are a very good dancer."

Surely this is not what she needs to tell me, he thought.

"Thank you. My mother taught me before my wedding. That is, my first wedding."

"You know," she murmured, "we have been together a whole year and have never once danced."

"When have we had the time?" he replied, taking her comments as an accusation. "We've both been rather busy. Especially you. Moving here, selling your apartment, buying a house, having a baby and moving into a new office."

"And planning a wedding reception," she added.

It had been her idea and she had decided on the location, the menu, and the guests—everything.

"Yes, it has been a busy year, without much relaxation."

Maybe dancing will help, Robert thought.

"I'll take you dancing anytime you like," he replied.

She was making small talk because she was trying to get up the courage to admit to him that she had held him to an impossible standard of behavior.

I just need to say it quickly.

"Robert, I have come to realize, just recently, that I was wrong to fault you for your actions involving Nancy Harris's case. You made a tough decision and acted in everyone's best interests."

Her words were coming out in such a rush that their meaning was confusing him. He stopped dancing to stare at her.

She continued nervously, "I once said that most decisions aren't ideal, but I didn't apply it to your situation. I judged you too harshly. I'm sorry I was so…so righteous."

She exhaled, finally having split her heart open to reveal a defect.

Her apology was so unexpected and so self-critical that he couldn't believe she was actually saying it. Seconds ticked by while his mind processed her words, so heartfelt that he had no doubt of their sincerity. At last, he whispered, "You have no idea how much that means to me."

He leaned in to kiss her.

She pushed him back. Sophia continued, "There is something else I want to say."

She stood facing him, forcing herself to look him in the eye. Her discomfort was apparent. He waited, wondering why she was so uneasy, fearing the worst.

"Cat told me that I yell at you a lot, and it made her sad." Her eyes misted up. She stopped, summoning up the courage to push aside her shame. "When I protested, she gave me one example after another, and she is right." Her voice cracked. She tried to relax her lips to force an apology out of her mouth. She whispered, "I have yelled at you a lot. Please forgive me."

She pressed her face against his. He felt the heat of her cheek, heard the tremor in her voice.

She is laying her soul bare, admitting to me a weakness that she was not aware of.

"It took our daughter to make you realize that." He marveled at Cat's ability to express her feelings in such a way as to make Sophia feel ashamed, not angry.

Sophia tried to burrow her face in his neck. "I am a much better judge of other people than I am of myself. I'll probably yell at you again, and when I do, please tell me to stop." She raised her head and looked at him expectantly.

His smile went from ear to ear. "I will," he said softly, and like a lover who had been deprived of gratification and was now eager to satisfy himself, he pressed his lips against hers.

She pulled away again. "One more thing."

Now what? he thought. *Is she going to confess to murder?*

She looked into his eyes, always so warm and welcoming. "You told me once that I was the best thing that has ever happened to you. I feel that way about you as well."

Gathering her in his arms, he found her lips open and waiting for a kiss. A feeling of euphoria came over him. His world had never felt so secure, with all the pieces in their proper place. He thanked whatever force had made her see herself and him for what they were—two people who had faults and disagreements but who enjoyed each other on many different levels.

"I have been thinking lately that you were lost to me," he whispered.

She murmured, "I was lost, preoccupied with trying to make you perfect."

"No need. I am as perfect as you are."

They both laughed.

He paused, and then he decided to take advantage of her conciliatory mood to bring up her need to control their workspace.

"Sophia, I know you are very capable and enjoy running things, but if we are law partners, I want to be included in the decision-making."

"Like what, for instance?" she said, regaining her self-control.

"Like who we hire at the office, for example."

She bristled. "You don't want Lara as our secretary? Or Eileen? What's wrong with them?"

He sighed. "Nothing. But you never consulted me."

"Oh." She had never considered discussing it with him first. "Anything else?"

He didn't feel like giving her a laundry list of her unilateral decisions about almost every aspect of their new offices.

"Let's just say from now on, when you want to do anything relating to our law firm, please consult with me." His words were soft but firm.

She wanted to object, to say that it was her money footing the bills, that she had a better eye for design than he had, that she was a better judge of whom to hire, but clearly, even if that were all true, she knew it was not what he wanted to hear her say.

I can't have it both ways, she thought. *We cannot be partners and yet have me make all the decisions.*

"Okay," she conceded, trying to make light of it. "I will have a sign made for my office desk that says, 'You Are Not the Boss' to remind me."

He laughed. "Perfect."

She thought for a moment and decided she needed to extract a promise from him.

"And when it comes to raising our children, will you consult with me before making any important decisions?"

Robert knew she was reminding him that he had allowed Cat to have her ears pierced without checking with her first. His eyes crinkled into a smile.

"Absolutely! When Mateo wants his ears pierced, we will discuss the matter and then tell him no."

They dissolved into laughter.

She put her arms around his neck and whispered in his ear, "You are such a tease!"

She asked the Alexa device to play another song. Sophia sang along.

"You are simply the best, better than all the rest."

Robert joined in. "Better than anyone, anyone I've ever met."

They let loose, dancing with wild abandon, weaving in and out among the furniture. Everyone came to watch them, singing along and swaying with the beat. Nonno stood next to Cat and winked at her.

She gave him a high-five in return.

THE NAVARRO RESIDENCE

In the morning, there was a buzz of activity out on the lawn. A crew was setting up the stage, placing overhead lights in the most strategic spots, testing the audio equipment, a laser projector, and timer. Other workers were arranging tables and chairs on the grass. Under a clear blue sky, the three young children sat on the steps to watch. Bruno was there, too, barking and straining at his leash to rush over to the men, who were invading his property.

"It's okay, Bruno," said Cat, who had put herself in charge of him. She whispered in his ear like she had seen her mother do, and immediately, Bruno quieted down.

When the workmen left, the children came in for lunch. They had just taken their seats by the counter when Sophia came running into the kitchen, screaming, and ran to Cat.

"She agreed! I can adopt you!" She picked her up off her stool and squeezed her. "Isn't it wonderful?"

Her cell phone was passed around for everyone to read the letter of permission written by Catherine Chadwick, who, having never remarried, reverted to her maiden name.

"A year ago, I met and loved you from the moment I saw you, and now you will be my daughter in the eyes of the law."

The adults shared Sophia's joy. The kids didn't fully understand what was going on but knew it was good news. Bruno gave a congratulatory bark. When Sophia was happy, so was he.

In the early afternoon, Dolores and Ricardo came out to practice the tango, wanting to be sure that there were no missteps on the small stage.

Later, around five-thirty, the members of the bridal party moved onto the green. Two pairs of eyes watched from the picture window in the great room, Kit at one end and Bruno at the other. They had the best view of the goings-on.

Robert wore white slacks, a smart navy blue blazer, white shirt, and red cravat, looking like a dashing yachtsman. He came to where Sophia was standing, resplendent in a warm white satin, ankle-length dress, with half sleeves and a V-necked bodice. Its skirt had a long slit running up one side. In her dark hair, she had put a red rose, a touch of fancy to an elegant look. He lifted her hands to his lips and kissed them.

"You look more beautiful every day," he whispered.

She looked him over and winked. "And you look and sound like a playboy." Her eyes shifted to the dance floor. "Look at the girls."

Cat and Cristina, wearing similar styled pink dresses, were on the dance floor, practicing dance steps that Dolores had taught them, looking like two fairy princesses.

Then Sophia saw Dolores heading toward them from the cottage across the lawn, in a red dress that flared below her waist, and ended at mid-calf, hemmed with a dramatic fringe. Pinned above the bun at the back of her head was a white carnation. Ricardo came behind her, all dressed in black, his dark, glossy hair combed back. They looked like they were born to dance the tango, she thought.

As the guests walked up the drive, Robert and Sophia stood near the edge of the green to welcome them and pointed the arrivals to the bar off to the left and the food next to it, and to the toilets, both inside and out. The dance stage and band were in the upper middle of the lawn, already playing soft background music.

Beyond the house, the water rippled across the sound in hypnotic waves, like sand slithering across a desert. The weather had cooperated. Fair skies. A light breeze. Nothing to detract from the festivities.

Bruno and Kit had not moved from their perches inside the house. Only the housekeeper walked from Mateo's crib to the living room and back, keeping an eye on the baby and directing guests to the inside toilets.

Robert and Sophia saw Sam and Thea at the same time. The mismatched couple walked up the driveway, their noses held high, sniffing the air. Their eyes jumped from one guest to the next, assessing their status, their clothes, their companions. Their gaze lingered at the banquet table, appraising the food.

Robert hadn't encountered Sam close up since their encounter in the hallway of their law offices. Robert greeted his former partner politely. His insides were roiling, with thoughts of Sam's behavior both in the law offices and outdoors on the water and in the state park gnawing at his calm demeanor.

Sophia, on the other hand, felt relieved. *The jackal and the peacock have arrived.* Her nemeses had actually come to the reception, feeling the need to strut about and be seen as important figures in the community, at the summer's most talked-about bash. Sophia did not look at Sam and simply smiled at Thea. There were no words to describe her happiness at their presence. She would get some revenge, after all. Nothing like she had originally planned, but still enough to keep Sam at bay.

The buffet included the mixture of foods from their two cultures: a tureen of chilled gazpacho, colossal shrimp stuffed with crabmeat, beef empanadas, risotto, a Caprese salad, Spanish almond tart, and chocolate amaro cake with passion fruit.

Their family and friends stood in lines on both sides of the long table and filled their bowls and plates. Once seated, servers went around carrying pots of coffee and cups of espresso. Some men and a few women had ambled over to the open bar containing several varieties of wine and beer, including bottles of Brunello de Sonoma.

"No Scotch?" asked Sam Wyman, looking over the bottles lined up behind the bartender.

"No, but we have a very fine red wine, made in California and shipped here especially for this occasion."

He glanced at what other guests were drinking—almost all had red wine.

"I'll try a glass," he said.

The bartender brought the bottle over and filled a glass. Sam took a sip.

"Wow. That is good. Let me see the bottle."

The label described the wine as having flavors of cherry, chocolate, and espresso. Then he saw the name of the winery—Bellini Vineyards. Sam was gobsmacked.

Sophia's family owns a winery? She wasn't kidding when she said she had other assets. He looked over to where she was sitting and froze. Her eyes were on him, her smile broad. He saw that she was enjoying his reaction. He turned away, trying to get his head around this revelation.

I was invited here so that I would find this out! His mind was racing. *Their law office building was bought with her money, not Robert's! I've made an enemy of someone who has the means to upstage me in my hometown.* A chill ran down his spine. *I am being played by a cunning woman.*

He turned back to see Sophia still staring at him. She lifted her own glass in his direction, as if to say, "*Touché.*" He did not return the gesture but slowly walked back to his seat, carrying the wine glass like it was a witch's brew, and hoped that there were no more surprises that evening.

Once the feast was over, the speeches started. Sophia got up to introduce each speaker to the audience.

As father of the bride, Giorgio Bellini spoke of his family's emigration from the old world to the new, from the Ligurian hills in northwest Italy to the Sonoma Valley in northwest California. His comportment and articulation were endearing to the Yankees in the crowd. If it wasn't for his slight Italian accent and his pleasing expression, he might have been mistaken for one of them—the God-fearing and upright descendants of the Puritan colony of Eastport.

"We started to grow grapes and to make wine. We created a family of workers, who lovingly watered and pruned the vines, and picked the grapes, then carried them to the wine presses and from there to the barrels in caves to age. For us, wine is more than a commodity. It is a work of art. Growing grapes to make wine requires love, commitment, and strength. You must learn to deal with the adversities that come your way. These three qualities—love, commitment, and strength—I taught to my children, and here, before you, is my daughter, who carries on my teaching, showing love and commitment to her husband and children, and strength to ride out any adversities she encounters here."

The town's gossipers looked at each other, wondering what he meant.

Next to speak was Dolores.

"My friends, I have known this beautiful woman since we were roommates at Stanford, she from a family of Italian immigrants and me from a family of Latinos. No shared history, but we did share a love of food, family, and a philosophy—to make our own little world a happier place. It may sound fanciful, but yes, we can create joy in people around us. I was a young college student who was overwhelmed by the workload and falling behind in my studies. Sophia brought me out of my sad mood, showed me how to manage the important things and to minimize all the rest.

"She went on to study law, while I was drawn to painting. She expressed herself through facts and logic, while I threw paints against a canvas and splashed colors around. Today I have an art studio in Santa Fe, New Mexico, while she has a law office here in Eastport, Connecticut. We are two women with careers as opposite as one can imagine. In very different ways, we both create truth and beauty, no? We are still close friends and will remain that way forever."

In her heart, Sophia agreed. *She has been my closest friend.*

Then, instead of handing Sophia the mic, Dolores gave it to Cat.

"What you are doing?" Sophia whispered in alarm.

"No worries, my friend. Cat rehearsed it with me."

Cat stood in the middle of the stage, wearing a fluffy pink dress with two pink bows in her dark hair. She looked around at all the people, mostly strangers, who were waiting expectantly.

"I am Caterina Navarro," she began in a soft voice, using her given name.

She was startled to hear her voice echo across the lawn. She looked back at Dolores, who nodded encouragingly, and then she continued.

"When I was born, I only had a father." There were murmurs from the crowd. "Well, I only knew my father. Then one day, this lady, Sophia, came to visit us, and I told her that night that I wished she was my mother, and my wish came true.

"Now I have a baby brother who doesn't do much, but he listens to me when I tell him of all the things we are going to do together when he gets bigger." The crowd smiled at this young girl's comments and confidence.

"And besides my grandma, I have a Nonno and a Nana and two cousins! I know my dad and mom love each other because they kiss." She stopped and sighed, and then rolled her eyes the way she had seen Dolores do. "A lot! I am really lucky."

There was applause and laughter as Cat took a bow.

Sophia took the mic from Cat. She bent over and kissed her daughter before she spoke.

"Cat never ceases to amaze me," she murmured.

Then she began to speak with an emotion in her voice that surprised even her.

"I met Robert seven years ago, when we worked together as executives in a Manhattan-based company. We were professionals, who both kept our private lives out of daily conversation. It wasn't until the day I quit my job that I learned he was divorced, and he learned that I, also, was divorced. Then I met Cat, the daughter I had always wanted, and today we have a son as well, whose conception was a one-in-a-thousand possibility, and I have a mother-in-law who is like my own mother. And I have a thriving law practice in a town where, less than a year ago, I knew only three people. To echo my daughter's words, I am really lucky."

Robert took the mic and squeezed Sophia's hand.

"We wanted to have this celebration to express our happiness in being blessed by such wonderful family and friends. I see some neighbors have come to join us."

Indeed, people were standing on the drive leading up to the green to watch and to listen. Robert waved for them to come closer.

"And now the speeches are over, let the dancing begin."

He signaled to the orchestra to play. He turned to Sophia, bowed, and asked, "May I have this dance?"

She was surprised when she heard the first notes of a tango, not a waltz. *The orchestra is playing the wrong music!* She panicked. *He doesn't know how to tango. He told me so himself.*

Robert was smiling at her. "We'll do fine," he whispered.

With a hand on the other's shoulder and arms straight out in proper position, they waited for the right note. Then their bodies began to move to the Latin music, a little tentative at first, not having ever practiced together.

Soon they were stepping, dipping, twirling. Their backs bending, their legs lunging, their heads turning sharply—simple moves, no exaggerated flourishes, just graceful and elegant. Two people whose sophistication and beauty were mesmerizing.

The orchestra had shattered the stillness of the summer night air as its mellow double bass, its sweet violin, its pounding drums, its thick bandoneon bellows, and its tinkling piano keyboard—all pulsating a rhythm that reached into the soul and made every face smile.

No one on the lawn had ever seen anything like it—two prominent members of their community performing on stage before the large audience of admirers and critics. The guests grew silent. Gawkers on the drive pushed forward for a better view.

The sun had set. Stars were twinkling in the heavens, shining down on the two dancers below. Sophia's long ivory-colored dress swirled with every step she made; the slit in her skirt made her long legs appear and disappear as she kicked and spun away, only to be pulled back. Every motion that Robert took was mirrored by Sophia; they moved like two kites floating across the sky in perfect formation, their tails dipping and rising in the wind.

There was joy on their faces, harmony in their steps, a fusion of their souls. A shiver went through the crowd. They knew that what they were witnessing was almost mystical, to be imprinted in their memories forever.

When the orchestra sounded its last note, there was silence. Robert and Sophia stood facing each other, holding hands. All the onlookers held their breaths, waiting. Then they wrapped their arms around one another and enjoyed a long, passionate kiss, disregarding the feeling of intimacy that it created. This was their wedding reception, after all.

The audience exploded in applause. The couple finally turned to face the crowd and bowed. The cheering continued.

Sophia whispered to Robert, "Enough." Robert signaled to the orchestra, and it began to play another tango. This time Dolores and Ricardo stepped onto the stage as planned.

On the way to their seats, Sophia whispered in Robert's ear, "When did you learn to tango?"

He whispered back, "This week on the dock. Dolores taught me."

Sophia stifled a cry.

Dolores addressed the crowd without a mic, her powerful voice carrying across the lawn and out into the streets.

"The tango is a dance about life, about love, and about marrying the music and dance so that they are inseparable. The colors we wear represent love and death, two extremes of emotion that all of us encounter in our travels through life. Watch and enjoy."

The orchestra began to play, and immediately the couple moved in lockstep, their artistry evident in the flow of their bodies, the reach of their arms, and the exaggerated stretch of their kicks.

Ricardo's body was that of an athlete, incorporating broad shoulders, a slim waist and strong thighs; his partner's silhouette showed off her full bosom and shapely calves. The men and women in the audience gazed wistfully at the dancers, either trying to discover some tiny flaw or imagining themselves in their shoes.

Dolores stomped her red heels on the floor, threw her body back at an impossible angle, and then lifted herself gracefully back to a standing position. Pivoting and swaying, her red dress flashing and spinning in a series of rapid, intoxicating moves, she strutted across the stage like a contessa in a palatial ballroom, performing for the nobility.

Ricardo lifted Dolores high up in the air and lowered her back down, spun her around on the floor, raised her, then twisted his legs around hers, all the while keeping time to the beat. Nobody's eyes left the stage, so hypnotic was their performance.

Many in the audience were recording the dance on their iPhones to prove to disbelievers what they were witnessing. The houses beyond the property, the downtown pedestrians and merchant;, indeed, almost all of Eastport had their ears cocked as the strains of tango music undulated far and wide through the summer night air, the residents sensing that there was an event of epic proportions happening on Ocean Drive.

At the finale, Ricardo stood, raised a hand in the air, and then pointed to Dolores, who was standing an arm's length away. The place erupted in applause. Their faces glistened with moisture and their chests heaved as they tried to catch their breath.

Then Ricardo turned to the applauding crowd and put his fingers to his lips, motioning for silence. When the audience had quieted down, he knelt down on one knee, took out a ring, and asked, "¿Quieres casarte conmigo?"

Dolores put her hands to her face; she blushed and trembled a bit. There was a long pause. Then she gasped, "Sí, sí, mi amor."

Everyone, even the Connecticut Yankees, understood those words. Ricardo rose and kissed her so fervently that it caused some of the more prudish to shift uneasily in their seats.

Sam looked around to see the audience's reaction, wondering if his lies about Dolores and Sophia were still believable. His eyes went to the back row, and he saw what looked like a row of faces half hidden in the darkness. Faces of his girlfriends. He blinked. It was true. *What are they all doing here?*

He looked for Sophia. She was in deep conversation with those around her, whispering about Ricardo's proposal.

When the dancers exited the stage, the orchestra struck up a waltz. Robert took Sophia in his arms, and they glided easily around the floor. Sophia smiled at her husband, whose worth and stature had increased exponentially in just one day.

Robert's mother and Andrew joined them on the stage. Then Sophia's father and mother, Joe and Grace, then Dolores and Ricardo. Finally, Cat and Joey and Cristina climbed up to the stage, stepping and turning, trying to mimic the others.

When the waltz ended, they all went back to their seats.

Sophia rose and, taking the mic, spoke directly to the lawyers and clients who had been invited.

"This next song is in honor of our special guests, our colleagues and clients, past and present, with whom we have had the honor to work or to represent over the past year. Please come up on the stage, everyone."

The orchestra struck up a popular Latin rhythm, and Marion and Phil moved onto the floor. Arthur Blake and his wife, then Eileen, Lara, as well as clients and their partners, joined them, swinging to the Latin tune.

All the lawyers were up there, except for Sam. He held Thea back, looking around for a way to escape without being noticed. He saw that the back row seats were now empty, and he breathed a sigh of relief. *Maybe I had just imagined it.*

Thea was pressing him forward. Friends around them were urging the couple on to the stage.

In slow motion, Sam followed Thea toward the dance floor.

Once on the stage, Sam held Thea close to him, as if they were dancing a waltz.

"What are you doing, Sam? We can't dance to the song this way."

"Okay. Okay," Sam said.

He moved close to the edge of the stage, feeling as if he might need to make a quick getaway. A light show began on the front of the Navarro house: flashes of faces that appeared and then just as quickly disappeared, mixed in with photos of the Navarros on their sailboat, hiking up trails, or at home with their children. Those were visible for much longer.

Sam stared at the pictures in disbelief. Every face he recognized immediately—women he had dated: Kitty. Judy. Honey. Jewel. Cathy.

His eyes flamed and his lips twisted. He tried to get Thea to move off stage, but she stood firm, expecting him to dance. He tried to pull her, but she slapped him. In desperation, he stepped away, hoping to get lost in the crowd. In his haste, he kicked his wife's ankle. Thea yowled in pain.

Those on stage had stopped dancing to watch and wonder why Sam looked so upset. Thea turned on Sam, complaining about his strange behavior. He stood still, fearing what might happen next.

Did Sophia invite my girlfriends here to torment me? Is there more to come?

He was unable to shake off a feeling of terror. Finally Thea gave up and stomped off the stage. Sam hurried after his fleeing wife.

Sophia felt avenged. *His secret affairs are no longer secret, and he is aware I could ruin him if I wanted to. I suspect he will not bother me and Robert anymore.*

EASTPORT, AUGUST 2

On the Navarro terrace the next morning, Sophia and Dolores relived the events of the previous evening.

"Dolores." Sophia sighed, sipping her morning cappuccino. "I noticed that the eyes of every single person there were on you while you were dancing. I have never seen the tango performed so beautifully."

"You and Robert did very well—for beginners," Dolores responded, her eyes a bit puffy from lack of sleep. The celebration of her engagement had kept everyone up very late.

"If I had only known ahead of time, I could have practiced," Sophia protested.

"It was better this way. You had so much on your mind, and you were suffering from *postpartum depression*. It was obvious to everyone. We did not want to make you more anxious than you already were. Besides, Robert was leading you, and he had practiced with me on the dock."

Yes, thought Sophia, *I get that now.*

"I did not have *postpartum depression*," Sophia said firmly. "That is a ridiculous notion."

"Yes, you did," Dolores insisted. "I recognized it immediately. You screamed at me and Robert one day for no reason. You stayed in Mateo's bedroom for hours. You were weepy. All those things are not like you."

"But I had reason to behave that way," insisted Sophia, glancing away so she did not reveal the shame in her eyes.

"What reason? There was no reason," Dolores pushed back. Sophia felt her friend's eyes scrutinizing her, wondering why she was looking embarrassed.

Sophia stared down at the dock and at the boat now anchored offshore. Cat had come out to join them, with milk and toast in hand.

"There were rumors going around." She turned back to see Cat looking at her, waiting to hear more.

"No, no, Sophia. That is not why you behaved as you did. You knew all those rumors were not true. Your hormones were going crazy, and you could not help yourself."

"I gave birth in April, and it's now August. It's been almost five months!" Sophia was not going to give in, even if she could not voice the reasons for her behavior. "So it was definitely not *depression*."

Robert came out to sit beside Sophia and held Mateo against his legs, enjoying his son's laughter as he tickled his belly. He knew nothing Dolores or he said was going to convince his wife that she had been depressed.

Dolores tried again. "It can last up to six months. I was with my sister after she gave birth and witnessed it firsthand." She stopped and waited for Sophia to say something, but she just laid her head back on the lounge chair and closed her eyes.

"I believe you are over it," Dolores continued. "You seem much calmer now."

Sophia gave a forced smile, but inside she was screaming, *I am calmer because I know why you and Robert were on the dock. If you had only told me, I would not have become suspicious.* There was nothing she could utter out loud, nothing to justify her belief at the time that Dolores and Robert were lovers.

She needed to change the subject. "Did you have any idea that Ricardo was going to propose?"

"Nada. Not even a hint." She looked down at her round diamond ring in its rose gold setting. "He was unusually quiet, though. I thought he was brooding over his brother, but afterward, he told me that he was thinking about when to do it. Your father told him, 'Do it on the stage, after you dance the tango.'"

"I liked dancing on the stage," said Cat. "Everyone had fun, except for that bad man."

"What bad man?" asked her mother.

"You know, the one who made Daddy mad when he came to our house."

"Cat, don't say he is a bad man," Sophia said, not wanting her daughter to think it was acceptable to speak that way about others.

"But he hit someone and he didn't apologize, like I had to."

"What are you talking about?" Sophia asked, wondering where Cat got that idea.

"That's what Marion said the night we had the party. Remember?"

Sophia thought back to that night when Sam criticized Robert and Cat. She remembered Marion saying the words, "*You were hitting on her.*"

"Cat, that was just an expression. He never hit anyone. He just needs to learn how to behave better."

"Didn't his mother and father teach him?"

"Apparently not."

Robert agreed, no longer defending his longtime friend or maybe *frenemy*. "Cat, that man got everything he wanted when he was a child, and he never learned to share. Let that be a lesson to you."

"I'll share my toys with Mateo."

"Even your Legos?"

Cat looked surprised. "Can't he have his own?"

Robert smiled. "He will want to grab what you built and topple it."

"Hmm. I'll put them up high where he can't reach them."

"That will work for a while, but I am sure he will figure out a way to get to them."

Cat was thoughtful. Robert saw the wheels in her head spinning. *She is so much like Sophia.*

"Are you still happy to have someone to play with?" Robert wondered.

"Yes," she insisted. "I'll teach him how to be a good brother."

Robert groaned. *She intends to have her way. Now I have two females who want to control everyone.*

Sophia smiled inwardly. *I like Cat's confidence. It will stand her in good stead in the future.*

"Dancing is fun, Cat. The music and the motion make you feel alive, joyous. Would you like to take dance lessons? It will teach you how to move gracefully, and it is good exercise."

"But if I dance with a boy, do I have to kiss him?" she asked.

"Why would you ask such a thing?" Sophia studied her, wondering where that notion came from.

"Because I saw you and Daddy dancing and kissing in the living room, and then on the stage, and Dolores and Ricardo kissed after they danced."

The two women burst out laughing.

Robert was not amused. "Cat, when I dance with your mother, I kiss her because I love her, but you, definitely, must not kiss a boy after you have danced with him."

"So when do I kiss a boy, Daddy?"

"When you are married to him," said Robert, very seriously.

"But you and Mom kissed before you were married. Remember? I saw you with my naked eye."

Robert smiled and sighed. "Okay, you can kiss him one month before you marry him, like when your mother and I first kissed."

Sophia and Dolores gave each other an eye roll.

"How easy you make it seem," Sophia said. "One day, her questions are going to be a lot harder to answer than that one. Robert, you are not going to be much help to me if I need some backup."

"In that case, I leave all her questions for you to answer. From now on, I will only answer questions that Mateo asks."

He tickled his son, thinking he was free from answering hard questions.

"You think his questions are going to be easier? Once, when my mother was giving Joe a bath, he asked, 'What are these for?' pointing to what was between his legs. My mother said, 'Ask your father.' I never learned how my father answered that one."

Robert rose from his chair, feeling the need to escape. "I am going to take Bruno for a walk." He gave Mateo to Sophia to hold and disappeared into the house.

Sophia waited until Robert was out of hearing range.

"Spoken like a father who suddenly sees what the future holds for him."

Sophia smiled at her son, who was pulling her hair. She tickled him, and as he let go, he laughed, a laugh that was so similar to Robert's. *How easy it is to make a baby happy.*

She looked over at her clever daughter, whose mind was as curious as her name implied. *She has all the necessary skills and cunning to get what she wants. It will be interesting to see what she does with her life.*

"To answer your question, Cat, you will know when you want to kiss a boy. Your heart will tell you."

Then she turned to Dolores and asked, "Why did you accept Ricardo's proposal? I thought you were a confirmed bachelorette."

"Simple. I saw how happy you were with Robert and he with you. Ricardo and I also have had different partners, but we found we are happiest when we are together. We make each other laugh. That's why I committed to marriage. It's as simple as that."

Sophia thought Dolores was wrong. *Committing to a marriage is never simple. Love of any kind is never simple. It takes work and maybe some luck. I picked the wrong partner the first time around. And I have had missteps with my second partner. I've had to make a course correction. I've changed my tune. Of course, Robert has changed too.*

She stopped. Her mind froze. *But has he?*

Nothing came to mind. Not one instance of any meaningful change. *He is still calm, considerate and caring, just as he was at National Services, just as he was when he stayed in my apartment, just as he has always been.*

I'm the one who has changed. I'm the one who reconsidered and put his name first on the shingle. I'm the one who admitted that my moral stance was too rigid. I'm the one who has stopped yelling at him. I'm the one who agreed to consult him before making any decisions regarding our law office.

The whole time we've been married, I thought I was turning him into a better man, but instead, he has turned me into a better woman.

A crazy thought made her laugh out loud. *There really is magic dust in this house.*

She thought she heard music playing, a beat pounding, and she felt herself in Robert's arms, dancing into eternity. She smiled with happiness. For the moment, she was utterly content.

A few seconds passed.

Hmm. Now if I can just get him to switch my back office with his front office.

EPILOGUE

Six Years Later, Eastport

LAW OFFICES OF NAVARRO AND BELLINI, AUGUST 29

"Hi, Dad. Guess what!" Caterina sounded excited.

Robert had answered his office phone while with a client, only because it was his daughter on the line and she knew she wasn't supposed to call him at the office unless it was important. *Oh, no,* he groaned. *This does not sound like an emergency.* As an eighth-grader beginning high school, she was probably going to tell him she had gotten the teachers she wanted or that her best friends were in her classes.

"Is this important, Caterina? I'm with a client."

"Yes, Dad. It's very important. I just got my period. I'm a woman!"

Robert shifted in his chair. He hoped his client had not heard.

"Dad? Isn't that wonderful?" More silence. "Dad, are you still there?"

"Caterina, call your mother," Robert managed to say. "Tell her. She'll know what to do."

"There is nothing left to do. The school nurse gave me some pads. I just wanted you to know."

"Have you told your mother yet?"

267

"No. I thought I'd call you first since you are always so cool about stuff. Mom is going to lecture me about what this means, and she won't stop talking until I tell her I'm going to miss my next class."

Robert smiled. Caterina understood Sophia so well. "Thank you for telling me. I'll talk to you later." He hung up and shook his head.

"Sorry. That was my teenage daughter. She likes to keep me informed of what's happening in her life."

"Good for you," offered his client. "Usually it's the opposite with teens. They want nothing to do with their parents, except when they need money."

A while later, after his client had left, Robert sat at his desk and reflected on how much had changed in his life during the past seven years. *Before I knew Sophia intimately, I was living day to day, hoping to tame Cat, who was becoming hostile, and wishing I could meet a woman who loved Cat as much as I did. Our marriage has had only one misstep, and that was Sam's doing. And now, on our wedding anniversary, my daughter calls to tell me about her period because she thinks I am cool.*

He walked down the hall to the front office, where Sophia was now located, and knocked on her door.

"Come in," she said.

He entered and saw that she was alone at her desk, staring at her computer. Her desktop was uncluttered, containing two neat piles of folders and, of course, the sign "*You are not the boss*" sitting prominently in full view. Having promised him to put it there as a reminder, she was true to her word. Not only had she discussed every office issue with him, but she also had no objection to him choosing a gorgeous-looking Latina as his secretary, without so much as a raised eyebrow.

He sat down heavily in a seat across from her. "Doing research?" he asked.

"Yes. I was reading the change in the state law regarding annuities and pensions. They are no longer considered taxable income. One of Cat's teachers asked me if she qualifies after she retires next year. I told her I'd check the new law. She does."

She finally turned to look at her husband and law partner, sitting with his shoulders slumped. "Why so glum?"

"I can't believe that Cat called me before calling you."

His bewildered expression made her laugh. "We now have a teenage daughter who is a 'woman.' And so the fun begins. I think we can expect the next five or six years to be"—she searched for the right word—"interesting?"

"How about unsettling?"

"That too." She leaned back in her chair and stared at him. He had started to turn a little gray around the temples, and his face had a few more lines, but those changes only made him appear more distinguished.

The night he came to my apartment was when I started to love him. We readily opened up our souls to each other, baring our faults and achievements, and believed that our feelings were understood and respected.

"You should take her calling you first as a compliment, Robert. It shows trust and love." She accepted Cat's actions, knowing that Robert and Cat had a special bond. "Together we will survive her teen years."

He raised his head, and his voice sounded hopeful. "Well, so far, she hasn't gotten into too much trouble. Besides forging my signature on a field trip permission slip for which she received a school detention and hanging out in the town square with her friends instead of coming straight home, for which she received a house detention, she's behaved."

Sophia pursed her lips. "Those are the things we know about. We can both assume she has found other ways to bend our rules. It's natural. We have to give her some space and try to be supportive and understanding when she goes too far."

"So when does the dating start?" he said, chewing his lip.

"Well, in my day, it was a lot older than thirteen, but today there are school dances in eighth grade. I think we can expect her to want to attend them. Her social skills are far better than mine were at her age. Actually, I pity the poor boy she gets to take her. She'll probably tower over him and monopolize the conversation."

"You said you've had the talk about…female matters, right?"

Sophia gave him a sympathetic look. "I have had multiple talks with her about getting her period, pregnancy and birth control, teenage motherhood, and—"

"Birth control!" he said, raising his voice.

"Robert, I want her to understand what having intercourse can lead to, that's all. The school nurse told me that she gives a talk to all eighth-graders about male and female anatomy, with both sexes present. She discusses menstruation, clitorises, penises, condoms—the works. She puts it out in the open so there is no mystery about how babies are born. Knowledge is power, right?"

"It's just all so sudden," he sulked.

Sophia shook her head. "Only to you. I have been answering all of Cat's questions for the last six years, ever since you decided that they were not in your area of expertise. Well, almost all her questions. I have never told her about how my daughter really died. Not yet."

"Do you have to?"

"Yes. I promised her that I would when she is mature enough to handle it."

She sighed, thinking back to those dark times, the years it took for her to regain her emotional strength and commit to marrying again. It was not easy, deciding to wed a man after only one day and night of companionship, and she was fearful at that time that she was acting rashly, but it had worked out with just a few bumpy patches.

Her eyes rested on her husband. "Have some faith in her, Robert. She is smart, and if she understands the consequences of her behaviors, she will be careful."

Robert stared out the window at the busy traffic on Eastport's Main Street. "I wonder how our neighbor, Dr. O'Malley, manages with his five daughters. They are mostly teenagers now."

"I had a long conversation with Mrs. O'Malley recently, when we happened to see each other on the street, walking our dogs. She told me that she preached to the oldest, Beth, and had her repeat the sermon to her younger sisters. A family grapevine. You should start preparing for what you are going to tell Mateo."

Robert raised his eyebrows. "He's only six!"

"Yes, but he has a sister who is thirteen. And he listens to her a lot, whether she is talking on the phone or hanging out with her friends at the house."

Her phone rang.

"I should take this. I'm expecting a call from Sam's attorney about his divorce."

He said, "Wait," and reached for her hand, which was on the receiver. Then he rose, leaned across her desk, and kissed her.

"Hmm. I love you, Ms. Bellini, in spite of the fact that you tricked me into switching offices."

"That was no trick, Mr. Navarro. Just a matter of first-class seduction, and you readily agreed to it. You have no case."

"Right," Robert said grudgingly. "But you caught me at a weak moment. Don't forget our luncheon date."

She nodded and picked up the phone as he went for the door.

"Give my regards to Sam." He grinned.

Putting her hand over the receiver, she shot back, "Like hell I will."

"Hello." Pause. "Yes, David. I have a list of demands and conditions that Thea gave me. It's rather lengthy. Let's start with visiting rights with the girls. Thea insists that visits with them must be supervised so that there is no repeat of Sam and his new girlfriend making out while the girls watched."

After an hour and a half of discussion, Sophia put down the phone and reviewed her notes. Most of Thea's demands were unreasonable, but Attorney David Smith raised few objections. She had her cheating husband dead to rights. Smith had to tell Sam the bad news, that his womanizing and public drunkenness were going to cost him plenty.

"Charge whatever you like for your services," Thea had told her. "It's Sam's money, not mine."

Sophia smiled. *My exorbitant fee must have sent him through the roof.*

It was almost lunchtime. She felt the need to stretch her legs. *A walk to one of the downtown restaurants will feel good.* Taking her notepad, she headed to the reception room.

It was quiet, except for the whir of a fax machine behind the screen.

"Hi, ladies," she said, looking at the three secretaries spread out around the room, each one busy at her desk. "Lara, I have a preliminary divorce agreement for you to type up. I believe my notes are legible."

"After working for you for so long," Lara replied with a self-assurance that she didn't possess six years ago, "I think I can translate all your scribblings into proper English."

Sophia gave her a wink. *I love her confidence and her professionalism. I was right to have hired her.* "You're the best."

Footsteps sounded in the hall, and Robert entered, carrying a sheet of paper.

"Am I allowed to interrupt this coffee klatch?" he said, even though no one was drinking coffee.

"Of course," the three secretaries answered in unison.

Sophia felt a pang of jealousy. *They stare at him like he's the second coming.*

"Inez, I need you to do research on the history of the land that my client wants to develop." He walked over to her desk. "Go back as far as you can in the surveyor's records and in the historical society records. Take your time. We need any information that may impact this proposal."

Inez, a dark-haired, flirtatious young woman with a paralegal background, took the paper he handed her.

"What about the county registry office and the county assessor's office?" she asked in an officious manner. "Do you want me to check there as well?"

"Right. They may have information also. Good thinking."

He turned to Sophia. "Ready?"

She nodded.

"We'll be gone most of the afternoon," he called back as they headed for the front door.

Something is up, Sophia thought. *Maybe he has remembered our anniversary!*

"Let's walk to wherever we're going for lunch," she suggested.

"Actually, we need to take the car. There is something I have to do at the house."

"Okay, if you have to." Sophia was disappointed. This was the only time during her day when she got to exercise, and it was sunny and warm.

*****

When Robert stopped the car in front of their home, he got out, while Sophia stayed in the car. He came around to her door, opened it, and said, "You need to come in with me." His grin betrayed his intentions. She obeyed and walked with him into the house.

"What have you planned? An afternoon tryst?" she said, thinking of the most outrageous thing possible.

"Perhaps. Take your clothes off."

Her eyes popped out. "What?" *He wants sex in the middle of a workday?*

"Strip! Get into something casual. We are going to celebrate our seventh wedding anniversary with a lunch on Long Island Sound, and we can't go sailing in business clothes."

"Really?" She started to undress before they got to their bedroom.

Within minutes, they were in the boat, casting off. Robert sat at the wheel with Sophia next to him.

She put an arm around his shoulder. "Now this is a treat. I wasn't sure if you even remembered."

"I have had it circled on my calendar for months, and it's in my iPhone." He turned to her and said, "You took a chance marrying me with only a few hours' notice. It will take me forever to make it up to you. And our wedding day wasn't very typical or pleasant, as I remember. It rained, you cried, and I wasn't able to kneel down in my car to propose."

"I didn't mind the rain that much or you not kneeling. The worst part of it," she said softly, "was telling you how I lost a child and that I was pregnant again, with ours." She closed her eyes and felt the sun's rays on her bare legs and arms. *Those memories are not going to ruin this day.* "So where are we going for lunch?"

"Here, in the boat. Everything is in the icebox in the cabin. Get ready for a lobster and champagne feast."

At three forty-five, Robert and Sophia returned to their law offices, a bit bedraggled.

Their tousled hair, tanned faces, and glazed eyes spoke volumes. They both nodded to the amazed staff and quickly disappeared into the sanctuary of their respective offices.

Eileen was the first to figure it out. "Today is their wedding anniversary," she whispered.

"That's right," said Lara. "We both attended a reception celebrating their first anniversary as a couple," and they took turns filling Inez in on the most memorable party ever seen in Eastport.

"But I want to know where they went for four hours today," Inez whispered.

"That's obvious. They were on their boat, sailing," Lara answered, sounding annoyed.

"But what were they doing on their boat?" Inez asked. Her eyes rolled around, hinting at some mischief.

"We sailed up the coast," said Sophia, appearing from nowhere. "Then we dropped anchor and feasted on lobster and shared a bottle of champagne, all of which is nobody's business but ours."

The look she gave Inez said, "*If you want to keep your job, you better shut up.*"

"Now let's pretend that this is a law office and you work for me. Any calls?"

*****

EASTPORT, NAVARRO RESIDENCE, EARLY SEPTEMBER

"Hi, Mummy," said Mateo, darting into the kitchen, as if he were being chased by Bruno, who lagged behind. "I'm hungry."

"You are always hungry. Just like your sister. We will be eating supper in a little while. Would you like a healthy snack? There are raisins in the cupboard and apples and string cheese in the fridge."

"How about a yummy snack, like potato chips or cookies?"

"Sorry, Mateo. We are all out of those. After you and Caterina gorged on them last week while Daddy and I were going over some bills, we have decided not to replace them."

"Cat says that we can sue you and Daddy for depriving us of nourishment."

Sophia raised her eyes to heaven. "*Dio mio!* She thinks she's already a lawyer."

"Nourishment means food," he added, thinking that his mother might not know.

"Thank you for explaining that term. You need to weigh very carefully what Caterina says. She can be a bad influence."

"Does that mean I don't have to obey her when she tells me to do something, like keep a secret?"

Sophia immediately became suspicious. "Give me an example of a secret she wants you to keep."

"Hmm. Like tell you she's in her bedroom when she's not."

"Oh. When did she ask you to do that?"

"Hmm. A few days ago," he answered nervously. "I heard her talking about it on her phone."

"Where was she, if not in bed?" Sophia's eyes showed fear.

"I promised her I wouldn't tell." His eyes filled up.

"Okay, Mateo. I will get to the bottom of this without you spilling the beans."

"I didn't spill any beans." The worried look on his face made his mother's heart melt. It reminded her so much of Robert.

"It's just an expression." Sophia stopped mixing the macaroni and cheese dinner that she was preparing for him. "Here, sit down and eat your supper early. It's ready."

She walked down the hall, muttering to herself. At Cat's bedroom door, she stopped. There was movement and a click. *She heard me coming.*

When she knocked, Cat said, "Come in."

275

Her daughter was on her bed, her five-foot-eight-inch body taking up almost the entire length. On one side of her was a computer, and on the other side, she held her iPhone.

"I want to talk to you," Sophia said in a quiet voice. "Did I interrupt anything important?"

"No. I was just reviewing my essay for English class," Cat answered casually. "It's due tomorrow."

"Will you read it out loud to me?"

Cat's eyes had a momentary flash of fear which did not escape Sophia's notice.

"It's nothing, really. Is supper ready?"

A diversionary tactic. "Not quite. We'll eat shortly. Now read me your essay." Sophia had moved over to the window and was staring at something on the screen.

"Why? It's just an essay," Cat pushed back.

"Cat…Caterina, you are avoiding my request. Is there something you wrote that you do not want to share with me?"

Cat knew she had lost her protest. "You can read it yourself," she grumbled, turning the computer to face Sophia.

"No, I want you to read it to me." Sophia knew her daughter. *There is something in her essay she'd rather not tell me.* "It's helpful when you read something out loud. You might notice you've used words that are repetitive or awkward."

Cat was silent.

"I'm listening."

Cat threw her head back on her pillow and said, "The assignment was to write a cause and effect essay, so I chose to discuss the rules that I am supposed to follow at home and their effects. It's all fiction. I made the whole thing up."

Right! Sophia tried to keep a straight face. "So read me what you wrote."

Life or Death

In my house, my parents make rules that
they say will keep me safe, but in reality, some of

> them are designed to keep me in bondage. Rules
> that keep me safe are things like don't run with
> scissors, look in the water before you leap, and
> keep your fingers tucked in when you use a knife.
> Those maxims are easy to accept because I know
> that the failure to obey them might cause pain
> or death.

Cat stopped to look up at her mother, whose face was a blank. She took a deep breath and continued.

> Rules that keep me in bondage are things
> like "Don't hang out with friends downtown after
> school," "No sleepovers unless all parents are on
> red alert," and "No posting of selfies on any social
> media." Those rules are either arbitrary, capri-
> cious, or just plain stupid. They harm my psyche
> because they limit my growth as a human being,
> thereby stunting my decision-making ability, and
> killing my soul.

Cat shifted her position, raising her legs up so that her face was partially hidden. "Do I have to read the rest of it?" she begged.

Sophia stared at her, as if she did not recognize her thirteen-year-old daughter. "No, you've made your point quite convincingly." Then she shook her head in disbelief. "I love it, Cat. You have a facility with language that is amazing for someone so young."

Cat dared to smile. "You're not angry with me?"

"What's there to be angry about? It's all fiction, right?"

"Yeah, mostly."

Sophia raised her eyebrows, as if to say, "*Really?*"

Cat sighed with relief. "What did you want to talk to me about?"

"Your escapade to visit Cathy."

"What?"

"Please tell me why you did it."

Her dark eyes widened. "Did Mateo tell you?"

"Mateo?" She sounded surprised. "No, when I was putting your clean clothes on your bureau the other day, I happened to notice that the window screen was pulled away at both of the bottom corners. The only reason someone would do that is so they can get back into the house after they climbed out of the window."

"But how did you know where I went?"

"By the process of elimination. You are too smart to walk down a street at night and be seen by passersby or policemen. You had to have gone somewhere close by, and the O'Malleys are the only nearby family with a thirteen-year-old daughter. Did you also disable the alarm on the window so it would not work?"

Cat grabbed a pillow and covered her face. "Yes," she cried. "I'm sorry."

"But why climb out the window? We would have given you permission to visit her."

"It was more fun to sneak out," Cat confessed.

She's acting like a typical teenager. Testing the boundaries.

Although Sophia understood psychologically why Cat broke the trust between parent and child, she felt the need to lecture.

"Caterina, don't hide what you want to do from us. Discuss it with me and Dad, and I promise you that we will listen. And we will still love you when you break our rules and are punished."

"Okay," she said meekly.

"Well, this talk has been revelatory. Let's have dinner and then discuss the matter with Dad."

"Does Dad have to know?" Cat begged.

"He is your father."

*****

As mother and daughter entered the kitchen, Sophia whispered to Cat, "Let me do the explaining."

Cat smiled, knowing full well that her mother intended to speak of her escapade in a most favorable light.

278

Robert stared at them as they moved to the table, wondering how his wife of seven years managed to keep such a tight bond with his teenage daughter, who looked pleased about something.

The ladies took their seats. Mateo had just finished setting the table, and Robert was now placing the main dish on a trivet.

"Hot out of the oven. Chicken breasts with vegetables. I'll get the salad and wine, and then we can eat."

"I already ate, so can I be excused?" Mateo asked.

"No, not tonight," said Sophia, sitting at one end of the table. "Please sit and eat some salad or try some of the roasted chicken and carrots."

"I hate carrots. And besides, they make my loose tooth wiggle."

Sophia shook her head in disapproval. "Mateo, I know you do not like raw carrots, but these are cooked in butter and have the flavors of the chicken juice on them. The taste and texture are very different."

"Okay, but then can I go?"

"'May I go' is the correct expression, and tonight you may not. After dinner, we are having a family discussion about rules."

Robert stared at his wife. *What's up?* he mouthed.

"Cat has an essay she is going to read to us, and she will make a small confession. Now will you pour me some wine? I need a depressant."

"That means she needs to relax," Cat whispered to Mateo.

"Oh, does Daddy need to relax too?"

"I guess so. It must be a parent thing. They are always so uptight about everything we do."

After dinner, Cat brought her computer to the table and read her complete essay entitled "Life or Death" to her family. When she had finished, she looked at her father.

"Mom loved it. What do you think?"

"Well," he said, clearing his throat while taking his napkin from his lap and placing it on the table, "technically, it is well-thought-out and supported with examples, but I feel the title is a bit, shall we say, dramatic?"

Cat gave her father a pathetic look. "Dad, don't you understand I did that for effect, to get the interest of the reader, my teacher?"

"Oh, she'll be riveted to the essay for sure, but how about substituting another title, like 'Freedom or Bondage' for 'Life or Death'?" Robert suggested.

Cat folded her arms across her purple sweatshirt and made a face.

"Fine. Let's have a vote," he suggested. "Whoever likes 'Life or Death,' raise your hand."

When Cat's hand went up, Mateo's did too.

"It seems like our children have each other's backs," Sophia said. "Let's move on to Caterina's confession. Tell Dad what you did."

Cat described in more detail her escape and how she had disabled the window alarm and pulled out the screening enough to get a finger through to slide the screen lock open and lift the screen.

"Wow, Cat, you're really smart," said Mateo, his eyes full of admiration.

Cat leaned over to ruffle his hair.

"Smart only if you don't get caught," said Robert sternly. "First Caterina is going to pay to have the damaged screen repaired out of her savings. And second she is going to research and present me ways to prevent such a thing from ever happening again. Short of putting bars on the windows, there must be a better security system out there, if my teenage daughter can bypass the one we now have."

"Is that it? That's my punishment?" Cat said hopefully.

"Unless your mother has something else in mind."

Sophia shook her head. "I'm good with that."

Cat got up and rushed over to Robert, throwing her arms around his neck. "Thanks, Dad. You and Mom rock."

Robert felt smug, but Sophia was not swayed. "Let's be clear. Dad and I have made rules, which we expect you both to follow, whether or not you like them. If you want to have a discussion with us and present your arguments to change them, fine. We will listen, but remember, we have the final say."

Cat put her hand to the side of her mouth and whispered to Mateo, "Like a dictatorship."

"No," said Sophia thoughtfully, "more like a diarchy with two rulers or an aristocracy with a king and queen, if you prefer. That would make you, Mateo, a prince, and you, Caterina, a princess."

"I'm a prince?" Mateo shouted. "What do I get to do?"

"Study hard and learn as much as you can about your kingdom so you will be ready to be king someday."

"Oh, is that all?"

Robert smiled at his son. "Let me enlighten you. Being a king is a powerful position. I could say 'Off with all your heads!'"

Mateo giggled, and Cat rolled her eyes.

"But instead I will be merciful. I command that the princess and prince be banished from this great hall of my castle and go to their chambers, but my fair queen will stay by my throne."

"That means we get to leave," Cat said excitedly. She danced out of the kitchen with Mateo hot on her heels.

"Well done, Your Majesty," Sophia said dryly, "but don't let all that power go to your head. You still have to take out the garbage."

*****

The next day after school let out, Mateo ran over to his mother's car as it pulled into the parking lot. He quickly jumped into the back seat, looking out the back window. When he turned around, Sophia noticed a prominent bruise on his chin.

"What happened to you?" she asked, looking at him through the rearview mirror.

"I got into a fight after school, but it wasn't my fault. I didn't start it."

Sophia's mind flashed back to Cat's first days of school and the fight that she had been in. *Is fighting a rite of passage in this family?* she wondered. "Tell me exactly what happened."

"After school, a kid was making fun of me because of my name."

"Your name? Matthew?"

"No. Navarro. He said it sounded funny."

"And for that, you hit him?"

"No, Mummy. He said we don't belong here. That we are filthy dagos. I don't know what dagos are, but I'm not filthy. Then I hit him, and he hit me back."

Sophia's heart sank. *Prejudice can take forever to go away.* "A dago is an insult said about people of Spanish ancestry, but you should not hit anyone just because they call you a name, even if they deserve it. Promise me that you won't do it again."

"I promise, but what should I do if he keeps saying that?"

"We will discuss the matter with Daddy later." *He is impulsive, like Cat. I need to have Robert impress upon him the need to think first before he acts.* "When we get home, I am going to clean your chin and put an ointment on your bruise and give you a big hug. Do you have homework?"

"Yes. Tomorrow everyone has to tell the class the thing they are most proud of."

"Really?" Sophia's mind started racing. "Maybe Daddy can help you with your homework and with the boy who is bullying you."

When Robert came home from the law office, Sophia pulled him into their bedroom and explained Mateo's fight and his homework.

"Who's the boy?" Robert wanted to know. "Maybe I should talk to his father."

"The boy's name is not important, and his father probably told him those things, so talking to him won't help. The best way to shut up a bully is to prove him wrong, to turn his words against him. This boy is making fun of your last name. Navarro is a pretty common Spanish surname. Maybe there were some famous people in Spain who had that name. See what you can find out about it."

Robert went on his computer and did some research. That night, after dinner, Robert talked about the history of his family name. Then he told Mateo, "When you use your fists to shut someone up, you do not change the person's mind. He will still think the same about you, and if you continue to use your fists, you will become known as a troublemaker. Use your mind instead, Mateo.

Think of what you can say to make this boy believe that our last name is honorable."

*****

The next day, Mateo stood in front of his class, holding up a picture of Spanish soldiers and said, "The thing that I am most proud of is my last name, Navarro. My daddy said it was a nickname for Spanish knights who fought on the fields in Spain to take back their land. The Navarros were brave soldiers. I am really proud of my name."

The bully never bothered Mateo again, and Mateo asked his friends not to call him Matthew anymore. "I like Mateo better. No one else has that name in school but me."

*****

A few weeks later, Cat came home from school in great excitement. The school principal had approved a dance for eighth-graders called *Black Cats Cotillion*, so named because it was close to Halloween and a way to showcase the young teens in a fun setting. To make the event more appealing to those who were shy or awkward, the organizers planned to award prizes for the best costumes, best makeup, best dancing, and a grand prize for a group (family and/or friends) whom the judges considered a showstopper.

Girls and boys were encouraged to dress as some kind of feline, anything from a pussycat to a leopard. No one needed to bring a date, but Cat had used her flirting techniques that Dolores had shown her and corralled a tall boy with dark brown eyes, a shy smile, and a pimply face to accompany her.

Two weeks before the dance, the school sent out an emergency email asking for parents to volunteer as chaperones; apparently, only a few teachers were available, and the number of students planning to attend was huge. Robert and Sophia decided that they both had to volunteer.

"Are you okay with that, Caterina? If you don't want us there, we won't go," Robert said.

Cat looked terror-stricken. "If there aren't enough chaperones, then the school will cancel the dance. I don't believe this is happening to me! Will you pretend that you don't know me? Put on costumes so that no one will recognize you, and don't use your real names. *Please* just sit in a dark corner the whole time and don't say hi to me or watch what I am doing!"

Sophia and Robert gave each other a hopeless look.

"So who do we say we are," asked Sophia, her hand on her hip, surprised at her daughter's demands, "Morticia and Gomez Addams from *The Addams Family* who just happened to be in the neighborhood?"

"Yes!" shouted Cat. "That's a great idea. Mom, you can easily look like Morticia, but Dad has to blacken his hair and wear a false mustache to pass as Gomez."

"I wasn't serious, Caterina. The chaperones do not have to dress in costumes for this dance, right?"

"Right, but it will make it so much more bearable. Nobody will recognize you. You'll blend in. Please, please, please!"

"Wait," said Robert, "didn't you tell us just recently that, as parents, we rock?"

Cat looked ready to explode. "Yes, but that's just at home. Not in public!"

Sophia was adamant. "No way, Caterina. I refuse to turn myself into a witch. After the rumors I've had to squash, I don't want to create more." She paused. "Too bad Dolores and Ricardo aren't your parents. They wouldn't have to change a thing."

Cat stared at her mother, wide-eyed.

*****

On the day of the dance, Cat seemed unusually nervous. She stared out the front window and paced around the living room as if she had ants in her pants.

About two in the afternoon, a strange car came up the driveway. Cat ran out to greet the new arrivals.

"Thank you so much for coming!" she cried, hugging them both.

"I see you have had your ears pierced—again," Dolores noted.

"Just last week," Cat said.

"You texted that you wanted to keep this a secret. You've told your mother by now, right?" asked Dolores.

Cat shook her head and gulped. "No. I was afraid she would convince you both not to come."

Ricardo said, "We would have come anyway, with or without her permission."

Dolores nodded. "Exactly. It'll be fine. We haven't been here for over a year, so it's about time for a visit. Let me do the talking."

The trio walked into the Navarro residence as Sophia was taking biscotti out of the oven to bring to the dance. Her shock at seeing them was overshadowed by her anger at Cat for not confiding her plans to her.

"You made them fly across the country to attend a dance?" Sophia scolded Cat after Dolores explained their appearance. "And you never told me about it?"

Having to be in control was one of her demons that she had managed to tame but not purge from her system. She was livid about not being informed.

Cat crossed her arms and stood her ground. "You are screaming at me, just like you used to do with Dad, and you promised that you wouldn't do that anymore."

Cat's mention of her former behavior embarrassed her, and she spat back, "Stop using my words against me. You know, you are too smart for your own good. Dolores and Ricardo have better things to do than to impersonate crazy characters at a high school dance!"

She tried to hide her hurt that Dolores was going to the dance as Cat's mother, and she deliberately turned her back on them and began to transfer the biscotti from the baking pan to a dish.

Dolores moved over to hold the dish while Sophia scooped the biscotti off the pan. She spoke in Cat's defense. "Don't be upset, my friend. First, Ricardo and I have no kids, so this is a chance to see Cat at her high school dance, and second, when she explained to me her idea, I, too, got excited. It will be fun, and you and Robert don't have to do *anytheeng*! Just sit in the back and watch." She picked a biscotti off the tray. "Mmmm, these chocolate pistachio biscotti are so good. You should sell them online. You'd make a fortune!"

Sophia acknowledged her friend's compliment by giving her a half smile.

"And I made an outfit for Mateo to wear."

"Mateo? What does he need an outfit for?" Sophia asked, still not fully grasping Cat's plan.

"Mom, Dolores and Ricardo and Mateo and I are going as the Addams Family, and Luis—that's my date—is going as Lurch, the butler. I asked Grandma to come as Grandmama, and she said she wouldn't miss it for the world! I bet we win the grand prize."

Sophia turned to Robert. "Your mother is a part of this too?"

Robert shrugged. "It's news to me."

A short while later, Caterina came into the living room dressed up like a cat girl in a black mesh bodysuit, long leather gloves that reached up to her elbows, tight leather leggings, and black boots that went up to her knees. On her head were cat ears made out of pipe cleaners. Her face was covered by a black cat mask.

"I had to dress up like a cat since that's the theme, but I will play the part of Wednesday Addams."

"You look twenty-five!" Sophia gasped. "And too sophisticated! Can't you go as a kitten instead of a cougar?" she pleaded.

"Mom, I am a woman now! Remember?" Cat smiled, thinking she had shot down her mother's concerns.

"So you're a two-month-old woman and this is how you have to dress?" Sophia rebutted.

Cat answered back, "Mom, Dolores and Ricardo will be with me during the dance. Nothing bad is going to happen."

Robert pressed his fingers against Sophia's shoulders, kneading the muscles where she carried her tension. He had found over the past seven years that this was the best way to calm her down. She let him, feeling her body decompress, knowing that she was overreacting. *He understands my need to control, and I have learned to trust his judgment when he thinks I am over the top.* Sophia sighed, totally deflated. *Cat can outmaneuver me.*

Cat saw the fight go out of her mother. "Mom, it's just a dance, very well-chaperoned, and my outfit was approved by the dance coordinators."

Sophia's face looked pained. "Well," her tone softened, "you should have asked for my stamp of approval first."

When Dolores and Ricardo appeared in black outfits with all the trimmings meticulously added, Sophia knew her judgment about them had been spot on. *They are not just dressed like their TV counterparts, Dolores and Ricardo are Morticia and Gomez.*

Mateo strutted around in his short black pants and striped jersey with *Pugsley* stitched on the front. Then Grandma hobbled in wearing a wig of long straight white hair parted down the middle, with a curious look on her face.

"Am I in the wrong house? I get confused a lot these days," she mumbled, keeping in character.

Cat jumped up and down. "You are all so cool," she said, looking at her "TV family." "I love you."

Her parents stood off to the side, feeling like discarded rags, no longer of any use.

Later that evening, Robert and Sophia, banished to a dark corner in the gym, watched as the teenagers and guests paraded past the judges. A boy dressed like a lion-tamer was leading his "cat" on a leash, chased by a girl who crawled by on all fours, hissing and meowing. Two kids in cat outfits sidled by dressed as Siamese twins, attached to each other at the waist. Along came Garfield, eating lasagna, followed by Puss 'n' Boots carrying a sword that reached from the floor to his feathered hat.

Near the end of the line, the Addams Family entourage emerged, arms linked in kinship. Morticia held up her hands with six-inch fingernails, trying to conjure up a spirit; Gomez, oozing flash and polish, gave the judges an evil grin. Wednesday and her brother, Pugsley, each wore a pained expression that said, *"Is this really my family?"* The butler, Lurch, had combed his hair forward to make bangs and kept his blackened eyelids half-opened, looking totally creepy. He carried a tray of mechanical spiders, some of which had crawled onto his hands and black suit and tie. Limping behind was Grandmama, holding onto Lurch's suit, muttering to herself while alternately scratching her head and wiping her lips with a hanky.

By the time the DJ announced the first song, the ice had broken, and everyone was ready to dance. The words to "*What's New, Pussycat?*" flashed across the wall while the cats sang to the music. Luis surprised everyone when he asked the DJ to play the Lurch dance and showed the crowd how to twist their legs and bend their arms in jerks and twitches. The kids swarmed onto the floor, copying him, looking like out-of-control robots.

Cat ran over to Dolores and whispered, "Isn't he great? I know how to choose a date."

Dolores gave her a smug reply, "I taught you *everytheeng* you know about boys, *mi amiga*. I started training you at age six."

From their hideaway in a dark corner of the gym, Sophia and Robert observed the proceedings. Seeing her daughter bond so happily with Dolores made Sophia's heart ache.

"I feel abandoned," she moaned, "like I've lost a child."

Robert whispered, "She is still ours. Dolores is not going to bundle her off to New Mexico," he joked.

Sophia's eyes showed fright.

"Relax." He squeezed her hand. "She has to stay with us until she leaves for college."

"Only five years away," she sighed. "I wonder where she will go. Hopefully not across the country to Stanford."

"She asked me recently what Yale was like."

"Really? That would be so perfect. She'd come home every weekend."

Robert smiled at her unrealistic expectation. "You think?"

Finally it was time to present the awards. After all the prizes had been handed out, except for the grand prize, the DJ began to play the theme song from *The Addams Family* TV series, and everyone knew who had won the showstopper award. There were laughs and cheers as Cat and her "family" accepted a metal plaque showing a black cat in silhouette.

Cat whispered to the DJ that it was time to play the music she had requested. Then she announced to her classmates that they were in for a special treat. "My friends are going to dance the tango for you."

Dolores and Ricardo moved to the middle of the gymnasium, took their positions, and waited for the music to start. Then they began to step, spin, and sway across the entire length of the floor, moving in even more dramatic fashion than they had done on the small stage in Robert's front lawn. At first, the teenagers were quiet, mesmerized by their style and flash. Then they clapped and roared every time Ricardo spun Dolores around or lifted her high in the air.

When the dance ended, the two Latin dancers were mobbed by the young people wanting to meet them. Cat, all on her own, had turned a simple school dance into a never-to-be-forgotten event. In spite of being annoyed by Cat's secret plans, Sophia felt proud of her daughter's cleverness.

When it was time for the last dance, a waltz in honor of the teachers and parents attending as chaperones, Robert took Sophia's hand and pulled her up.

"I think we are entitled to show our faces now."

They glided silently past Cat, who was pretending that they were strangers. Sophia radiated elegance in a long black dress with a bright orange shawl, her hair swept up in a bun at the back of her neck. She smiled at her husband, smartly attired in a charcoal gray suit accentuated with a soft orange tie. Their grace and beauty made them stand out. One by one, the other couples dropped out until only they were left, stepping smoothly across the floor, oblivious to the stares and whispers of others.

One of her classmates nudged Cat. "Where did they come from? Do you know them?"

Cat shrugged. "Sort of."

The girl persisted. "They look so perfect together. Who are they?"

Cat hesitated. She stared at her parents, so happy in each other's arms, and then at the onlookers, whose eyes were fixed on the dancing couple. "They're my parents," she said dismissively.

The girl's eyes showed surprise. "Don't you like them?"

Cat bent her head toward her friend and whispered, "They're okay, but raising parents is hard work. They don't listen and always think they know best. I don't know how many times I've had to repeat myself before they understand what I want them to do. Some days I'm so tired I just want to go in my bedroom and shut the door."

Her friend nodded vigorously in agreement.

*****

That night at home, Cat hung around with Dolores and Ricardo, swept up in their exuberance of life and their love of art. She peppered them with questions.

"What makes something art? How do you decide what colors or shapes or textures to use? Who decides if your works are good?"

Sophia kept her distance, not wanting to hover or intrude. *Cat is old enough to decide whose company she enjoys the most. I need to get used to not having her around all the time.*

When everyone had finally gone to bed, Sophia lay awake, thinking of how Cat had kept Dolores and Ricardo's visit a secret. *Why did she not tell me what she was planning? Is she pushing me out of her life, now that she no longer needs me as much? I know that teens are striving to be independent and may become rebellious. Somehow, I didn't think I would lose Cat's love during this adolescent phase.*

Her mind went back in time to her first meeting with Cat. *I remember as if it were yesterday when I saw her come around the corner of the hall and stare at me with her dark eyes. At that moment, I felt I knew her already, my own daughter, whole and well—and needing me. The hole in my heart began to mend that day, stitched with threads of iron, unable to be slashed at. Or destroyed.*

She closed her eyes and tried to go to sleep, but sleep wouldn't come. She tried deep breathing, then counting sheep, and then, giving up, simply stared into the darkness, feeling empty.

A light tap came from the bedroom door. *Who can that be?* she wondered.

"Come in."

The door opened slightly, and a thin shaft of light slipped in.

"Hi, Mom. Did I wake you?" asked Cat.

Sophia became alarmed. *She never comes into our bedroom at night.* "No. I was not asleep. What is it? Are you sick?"

Cat shook her head. "No." She lowered her voice to a whisper, noticing her father was fast asleep beside her mother, "But I want to ask you something."

Sophia sat up and glanced at the clock. It was 11:58. *It must be important.*

"Okay," she murmured. "Come sit on the bed." She moved her long legs over so there was room. Cat tiptoed to the bed, her dark eyes looking scared.

"Whatever you've done, I'll understand," Sophia assured her, assuming it was about some trouble Cat had gotten into.

"Mom, it's not about me. It's about your daughter."

Sophia stared at her, confused. An uneasiness began to grow in the pit of her stomach. "*You* are my daughter."

"Your first daughter, the one that you said died because she was sick. What really happened to her, Mom?"

"Oh, Cat!" Sophia fell back on her pillow and moaned. Her hands flew up to her face. "What makes you ask me that now?"

"I heard Dolores whispering to Ricardo about your first husband. Ricardo said, 'How could he do that to his own child?' Mom, what did he do?"

Sophia bit her lips, seeing once again Carlo bent over her with a bloody knife in his hand. Her eyes welled up, holding back tears.

"I had to lie to you because the truth was too terrible for a little girl to hear." Her next words were ragged, tripping over each other. "He killed her, Cat. He stuck a kitchen knife in my body as she was about to emerge from my womb, and it pierced the top of her soft skull and"—her voice trembled—"and later she died in my arms."

I've finally told her. I never want to utter those words again.

She looked at Cat's face, frozen in horror. Even in the meager light, she could see it drained of color.

"But I got her back"—she smiled, rising and reaching out for Cat with trembling hands—"the day I found you."

She hugged Cat, rocking her back and forth in a tight embrace.

"And I found you, Mom," Cat whispered, "and that was the best day of my life."

Sophia started to weep, realizing her fears were all for nothing, that Cat was still hers to love and to cherish forever.

Her sobbing woke up Robert. He looked drowsily at the two of them. "Has something happened?" he mumbled.

"No. It's nothing to worry about," Sophia sniffled. "I just had an epiphany."

"Oh," Robert sighed. "I had one once. It must be contagious." He turned to go back to sleep.

Cat stared at her parents, alarmed. "What's an epiphany?"

Her mother gave her a tired smile. "No more questions. I'll tell you in the morning. Good night, and Cat, I am so happy that by marrying your father, I got you for my daughter."

"But I was the one who first chose you to be my mother. Remember?"

Sophia shook her head. "That is not how it happened. I chose to marry Dad and you came with our marriage." But then she heard Robert say, "Cat is right. She chose you the afternoon of your visit. While you went to get a package, she told me she wanted you as her mother, so we hatched a plan to have you stay the night-and it worked."

"Then I didn't stand a chance against the two of you."

As Cat headed for the door, Sophia pressed her body against her husband's back, wrapped an arm around him and fell into a blissful sleep.

ACKNOWLEDGMENTS

My heartfelt thanks to my sister Linda Mendes, my daughter Rita, and my friends Dr. Louise M. Nolan, Marianne Roberts, and Sandra Hofmann for reading, editing, and commenting on my manuscript.

ABOUT THE AUTHOR

Joyce Gatta is a retired teacher and professor of English. In her first book, *In Hugger Mugger*, she describes the secret list of Lady Mary Sidney, a Renaissance woman who broke both church and state rules. Its sequel, *In the Shadows*, traces the journey of her daughter, Lady Anne, to the New World, where she and a learned midwife are judged harshly by the Puritans.

www.ingramcontent.com/pod-product-compliance
Lightning Source LLC
Chambersburg PA
CBHW031409030226
39154CB00009B/17